F

F

A

2

BLOOD MONEY

BLOOD MONEY

a mystery

ROCHELLE KRICH

AVON
TWILIGHT

AVON BOOKS, INC.
1350 Avenue of the Americas
New York, New York 10019

Copyright © 1999 by Rochelle Majer Krich
Visit our website at **www.AvonBooks.com/Twilight**
ISBN: 0-380-97379-0

Library of Congress Cataloging in Publication Data:
Krich, Rochelle Majer.
    Blood money : a mystery / Rochelle Krich. —1st ed.
      p.   cm.
    I. Title.
PS3561.R477B58   1999   98-42113
813'.54—dc21   CIP

First Avon Twilight Printing: February 1999

AVON TWILIGHT TRADEMARK REG. U.S. PAT. OFF. AND IN OTHER COUNTRIES, MARCA REGIS-
TRADA, HECHO EN U.S.A.

Printed in the U.S.A.

FIRST EDITION

QPM   10   9   8   7   6   5   4   3   2   1

For our grandson
Jacob Zachary Krich
Pure joy

ACKNOWLEDGMENTS

Boundless thanks to those who provided me with the information woven into the background of this book: LAPD Detective Paul Bishop, West L.A.; Henry and Regina Rechnitz; Paul Solomon; Jill Glasband; Nancy Saul, Reference and Information Services Specialist, Simon Wiesenthal Center/Museum of Tolerance; Adaire Klein, Director of Library/Archives, Simon Wiesenthal Center/Museum of Tolerance; Steven Wachtenheim; and my sons, Eli and David Krich.

My heartfelt gratitude to my editor, Carrie Feron, and my agent, Sandra Dijkstra, for their invaluable input and encouragement. And to my husband, Hershie, and our children—kudos for putting up with my single-minded, often frenetic dedication to meeting my deadline. I owe you, and will probably owe you again.

I'm especially indebted to my father, Abraham Majer, for having the courage to share with us the pain of his wartime tribulations and the miracle of his survival. His story is the essence and soul of this book.

"Then shall ye bring down my gray hairs
with sorrow to the grave."
GENESIS, 42:38

"Cast me not off in the time of old age;
forsake me not when my strength faileth."
PSALMS, 71:9

1

T**HE DEAD MAN** lay on a bed of twigs and leaves, half hidden by lazy, drooping branches that fanned him gently, nudged by a warm breeze. Early-morning July sunlight glinted off his thick brown hair, a startlingly youthful contrast to a weathered face whose crackled skin, mottled with reddish-brown stains, had been stretched paper-thin by decades of gravity into parallel, sagging furrows.

Only his head was visible. A dull brown, matted blanket, dampened by the sprinklers that hours ago had misted the park's rolling green golf course, covered the rest of his body.

He looked like a caterpillar emerging from a cocoon, Detective Jessica Drake thought as she rose from a kneeling position at the old man's side. She moved backward, careful to retrace her steps on the grass blades she'd flattened.

"I thought he was asleep," the golfer who had discovered the body said somberly. His forehead glistened. "I was looking for my ball, and there he was. It's not the first time I've come across some homeless person who decided to sleep in the park." A hint of "why-can't-the-police-clean-up-this-city?" peevishness had entered his voice.

She turned and looked at him, squinting because of the

bright sunlight. He was about five feet ten inches, in his late thirties or early forties. Probably worked out regularly, judging by the contoured biceps and flat abs behind the white Ralph Lauren Polo shirt that perspiration had plastered against his skin. A Movado watch cut a silver-and-gold-toned swath on the reddish-brown hairs of his tanned arm.

An attorney? Doctor? Investment counselor? Corporate executive? She'd read that golf was becoming increasingly popular, and not just among the retired; with a touch of elitism underscored by the panoramic expanse of the playing field, it spelled success and was an avenue for the important networking that led to it. O.J. Simpson had figured that out long ago.

"Did you touch him?" she asked, even though Steve Kolakowski, the West L.A. officer who had responded to the call, had told her the golfer hadn't touched anything.

"No." A grimace flashed across his square-jawed face, as if the very idea of touching the old man were repellent. "But his color didn't seem right. And flies were buzzing around . . ." Another grimace, followed by the exaggerated lurching of his Adam's apple. "So I used my cell phone and called 911." Removing his visored black cap, he wiped sweat off his forehead with the back of his hand, then repositioned the cap on his head. "You think it was a heart attack?"

Not a doctor, she decided. "Could be. Someone from the coroner's office is on the way." Or maybe he just died in his sleep. The autopsy would determine the cause of death.

"You look familiar, Detective." He had cocked his head and was studying her now, his tone more personal. "Have I seen your face in the papers or on TV?"

"It's possible." She couldn't tell whether this was a come-on or whether he recognized her from her media-covered press conferences a year ago. She'd been spokesperson for the Parker Center task force formed to hunt a serial killer—her reward for realizing there *was* a serial killer responsible for almost a dozen apparently isolated murders.

"I thought so." He nodded, pleased. "Of course, you looked different then."

The golfer—he was good-looking, no wedding band on his

finger—was eyeing her admiringly now, definitely flirting, and she couldn't decide whether she should be flattered or annoyed. The dilemma of being a female cop. She'd flashed her badge when she'd arrived on the scene, but she hadn't looked like a homicide detective in a scoop-necked, sleeveless baby-blue cotton knit dress and strappy white sandals that added two inches to her five feet six and revealed the blue polish on her toenails, still visible through the plastic police booties she'd slipped on before approaching the body.

No holster today—it didn't go with the dress. But her personal Airweight revolver was in her purse. *Don't leave home without it.*

She hadn't expected to be called in this Sunday morning. "Why can't your partner go?" her mother, Frances, had snapped when Jessie announced she had to leave the Martha-Stewart-perfect backyard brunch her sister had prepared. *Why don't you quit this distasteful, socially unacceptable job?* So Jessie had explained through gritted teeth that Phil, her partner of five years, whose name her mother always made a point of forgetting, had taken his wife and kids to San Diego for the weekend.

By that time Jessie hadn't really minded leaving, because her mother had been riding her from the minute she and Jessie's father had arrived from La Jolla. About her job, her hair (too long, too curly, why didn't Jessie have highlights put in to liven up the dark brown?), her toenails (she'd known the blue would get a rise from Frances—was that why she hadn't removed it?). About her ex-husband, Gary, the crime reporter.

"Why didn't you tell your father and me that you were seeing him again? Why did I have to hear this from Helen? Although I suppose I should be thankful that you've come to your senses and stopped dating that detective."

Helen is dead meat, Jessie thought, pursing her lips again at her sister's betrayal, feeling instantly abashed, because here she was, standing a few feet away from some old man who had come to this park to die alone.

Dead lay he. The line from a poem she'd studied in high school flashed through her mind. What was the rest—something about the "vigorous summer" and the "naked frailty of the dead"? The golfer was right—the deceased probably *was* one of L.A.'s homeless. That made his death all the more poignant, didn't it?

The sun was beating on her back. It was going to be another scorcher in a summer that had already proved "vigorous." She thanked the golfer and told him he could leave. He'd given Kolakowski his name and a Beverly Hills address and phone number; they'd call him if they needed more information. He seemed reluctant—torn, she supposed, between watching the drama that would continue to unfold and escaping the gritty reality that had aborted his game.

He was still lingering when the white medical-examiner's van arrived. Jessie signaled to Kolakowski, who shepherded the golfer to the partner waiting about thirty feet away near a golf cart and a handful of other spectators held back by the yellow tape of authority. Then she walked to meet the M.E.

Henry Futaki. Jessie had seen him frequently when she'd been on the task force, less often during the past year. She'd been an insider then. Once in a while she missed the perks and the status, the high-level tension and high-profile attention; most of the time she was happy where she was, with Phil and the others at West L.A. in relative anonymity. The mayor's framed commendation for apprehending the killer hung on the wall in her den. For Jessie, it was a chilling reminder that her sister had almost lost her life in the process.

The medical examiner was short and thin, with thick, bushy black brows above deceptively sleepy, onyx-black eyes that, from Jessie's experience, missed nothing. After exchanging hellos—warm on her part, a little curt on his—Jessie told him what she knew, which wasn't much.

She followed him back to the body, wondering what he thought of her ever since she'd ended a months'-long relationship with Detective Frank Pruitt, whom she'd met on the task force—Pruitt and Futaki were thick—and quickly decided the medical examiner wasn't thinking about her at all. He was thinking about the body, which was what she should be doing.

Futaki was a bit of a showman. She watched as he slipped on latex gloves, snapping them crisply onto his wrists before he peeled away the blanket with the flamboyance of a magician about to wow his audience.

The dead man was wearing navy wool slacks, a white-on-white striped shirt with French cuffs, a blue-and-gold paisley tie, and black loafers. Somewhat formal for the park, Jessie thought, frowning, and all in too-good condition—the creases in the slacks still crisp; the shirt starched, though soiled from contact with the moist earth. The dead man's fingernails were clean, recently trimmed. All out of character for one of the homeless.

Unless he'd joined their ranks last night? Jessie shook her head, dismissing the notion. More likely, he'd left his home intending to return. But why had he come *here*, to Rancho Park?

She looked to her left toward Pico, past the Hillcrest Country Club that abutted the park. Did the old man live in a nearby apartment or condo? In one of the smaller houses north of Pico? Did he live to the south in Cheviot Hills, near her sister Helen?

"When did the golfer find the body?" Futaki asked.

"A little after nine o'clock this morning."

The medical examiner nodded. "I'd say he's been dead since sometime last night, judging from the body temperature and lividity. Hard to tell, though, in this heat."

Had the old man decided to go for a walk last night? But that was dangerous—everyone knew that. What could have sent him out of his house? An angry fight with his wife? With his children? In either case, why had he taken a blanket with him, unless he'd planned to sleep in the park? Which didn't really make sense. . . .

"No knife or gunshot wounds, nothing that would suggest he was assaulted," Futaki said a few minutes later in his customary monotone. "No trauma to the head." He probed the dead man's neck and throat. "No bruising or swelling here that would indicate strangulation. Looks like natural causes."

The grass leading up to the body had been trampled by several pairs of feet—hers, Futaki's, the golfer's. The dead man's, of course, and maybe others'. Not that grass would yield much in the way of evidence. Squatting, Jessie examined the area immediately surrounding the body, exposed now that Futaki had removed the blanket. A single set of footprints was visible. She peered closely at the prints, then at the soles of the dead man's shoes.

She frowned. "These prints were made by patterned rubber soles, probably an athletic shoe. Our guy's soles are smooth, flat leather. I don't see any prints to match his shoes."

"You're thinking someone positioned him here?" Futaki was frowning, too, his bushy brows forming a single hedge.

She studied the area again and pointed to the ground near the dead man's feet. "He was dragged here. See those indentations leading in a curve from the grass? They could be heel marks." She would have SID make casts.

"Did you check for any ID?"

Was Futaki testing her? Some medical examiners were sticklers about being the first to touch the body. "Nope. I waited for you." Smiling at him.

No return smile. He slipped a gloved hand into one of the dead man's pants pockets and produced a small vial. "There's no label," he said, uncapping the vial and spilling its contents into his palm. He picked up one of the round, white tablets and examined it. "Lanoxin. That's the brand name for digoxin, or digitalis," he said, looking up at Jessie. "The code number is X3A, so I can verify how many milligrams. I believe this is point two five."

Futaki was showing off his knowledge. She nodded sagely, as if the dosage meant something to her. She knew digitalis was prescribed for cardiac patients to stimulate heart-muscle contractions and slow the rate of the heartbeat. So the dead man had been suffering from a heart condition. Arrhythmia?

Futaki checked the other pocket and shook his head. "No wallet."

No cuff links, either, in the French cuffs. A watch was missing, too—from the circle of lighter skin above his left wrist, Jessie assumed he'd worn one.

"Maybe the old man had a heart attack while being mugged," she said. "He couldn't reach for the Lanoxin, so he died. The mugger panicked, dragged him here, and hid him in the bushes." Which made this a homicide, even though there was no intent. "Either that, or he had a heart attack, wasn't able to take the Lanoxin in time, and someone came across his body and moved it after taking his stuff."

And covered him with a blanket? Maybe someone else had done that—a homeless person who'd found the old man before the golfer. Respect for the dead?

Futaki nodded. "There's no evidence of a struggle. Without a witness, you couldn't prove the old man died while being mugged."

Jessie thought that over. "Someone could have injected the old man with a substance that triggered the heart attack. This person waited until he died, then moved him and took his stuff."

"Why go to the trouble?" Futaki asked, but he rolled the dead man's sleeves up past the elbows. "No punctures," he said a little smugly.

"What's that?" Jessie pointed to a puckered two-inch strip on the inside of the old man's left forearm.

The M.E. glanced at the area. "Looks like he had a tattoo removed, but not recently. Not a great job, either."

"He doesn't strike me as someone who would have had a tattoo."

"No," Futaki agreed.

"Maybe he got the tattoo when he was young, regretted it later," she mused aloud. "But then, why on the *inside* of his arm, where no one would see it?" She leaned forward. "Can you tell what it was?"

A tattoo might help identify the deceased. Then again, identifying him might not be difficult at all. Frantic relatives might already have reported him missing. Unless the dead man had lived alone, and no one knew he *was* missing.

Taking a magnifying lens from his black satchel, Futaki peered closer at the dead man's arm. He moved his head back, then forward again. "Numbers. Maybe." He shook his head. "It's hard to make out."

Numbers.

2

"TEN-TO-ONE he's a Holocaust survivor," Jessie said, slicing mushrooms on a wood cutting board. "That's why the numbers—it's his concentration camp ID."

"You're probably right," Gary said. "So why are you so upset?"

She glanced at her ex-husband. "I'm not upset. It's just a comment."

"Okay." His dark blue eyes said otherwise. Reaching across the narrow room to the opposite counter, he opened a white drawer and frowned. "Where's the garlic press?"

She set her knife on the board and handed him a press from another, nearby drawer. "I rearranged some things," she said. *After you left.*

"Hey, it's your kitchen."

His tone was light and he was smiling his sexy, crooked smile, but she sensed hurt in his voice, a little wistfulness. Or maybe she was reading into things. She was glad he'd invited himself over for dinner, but she felt strange, too. Though they'd been dating for almost three months, it was the first time since he'd moved out two years ago that they were preparing a meal together in the house they'd fallen in love with and fixed up together. And made love in.

She studied him as he minced two garlic cloves and added them to the wine vinegar and olive oil in a glass measuring cup. He was tall and lanky in faded jeans and a gray UCLA BRUINS T-shirt that showed off his broad shoulders and muscular, but not look-at-how-developed-I-am arms. His curly, dark-blond hair was a little too long—the way she liked it. She had an urge to run her fingers along the nape of his neck.

Physical attraction had never been the problem. She'd been intensely drawn to him from the time they'd met almost eight years ago at a news conference. Even after the divorce (even when she'd been with Frank Pruitt) she'd felt her stomach tighten with a prickly, sexual tension whenever she'd seen her ex-husband. Although she hadn't admitted it to herself then.

She'd been up front with Gary about wanting to keep their renewed relationship nonintimate. She didn't want to confuse sex, and a longing for companionship, with love. She'd done that with Frank. "I want to take it slow," she'd cautioned, and Gary had agreed. "Absolutely—me, too." But "slow" had quickly escalated into nightly phone calls and several dates a week, and though Gary wasn't pressuring her about the sex, he'd been dropping not-so-subtle hints about remarrying.

She wasn't ready for that. Most days she thought she was in love with him, she was definitely happier than she'd been in years. But she'd been in love with him before, and there were issues they still had to resolve, and she was afraid she'd fail again and have to face her mother's renewed disapproval ("*You can't do anything right, can you, Jessica?*"). And her own.

"So what'd you find out about the dead guy?" Gary asked, and caught her looking at him. Another wry smile.

With the oven on, the kitchen was unbearably warm, even though she was wearing a white cotton sleeveless top and lightweight olive slacks. Bending her head to hide her blush, she picked a slice of red pepper from the beechwood salad bowl and wished for the hundredth time that she had the money for central air-conditioning, among other things. Or that she weren't too damn proud, as her sister Helen put it, to accept help from her parents. Independence had its price.

"We didn't find anything," she said. "No wallet, no ID. I went to West L.A. from the golf course—"

"Which one?"

"Rancho. Why? Are you planning to take up golf?" she teased.

He grinned. "Just the reporter in me. Go ahead."

"Anyway, no one called in a 'missing persons.' I checked with Hollywood, Wilshire, Culver City. Nothing. Same with Century City Hospital—it's near the park. None of their patients checked themselves out." She dipped the pepper into the liquid in the measuring bowl and took a bite. "Perfect."

"*Am* I? Oh, you mean the dressing." He smiled.

She smiled back. "You're not half bad, either."

"Gee, thanks." He tasted the liquid and added two twists from the pepper mill, then tasted it again. "So maybe the old man lived alone and no one knows he's missing."

"Possible." She nodded. "Or maybe he lived in a retirement home, and the manager doesn't realize he *is* missing. Or maybe he was staying in a hotel. We'll see what comes in tomorrow."

The broiled trout and dilled new potatoes were ready. She transferred the food to serving dishes, which she carried to the oak-trimmed Formica table in the breakfast nook, now covered with a peach cloth and set with the green Villeroy & Boch stoneware and Oneida flatware she and Gary had picked out seven years ago at Geary's. It was at least ten degrees cooler here, she thought, listening gratefully to the low, steady whirring of the ceiling fan she'd installed a while ago.

Gary came to the table with the salad, a corkscrew, and a bottle of red wine that he'd brought. "If I moved back in, we could eat in the dining room," he said, sitting down across from her. "More romantic."

She felt herself tensing. "You're tempting me," she said lightly. As part of the divorce settlement, Gary had taken the black lacquer oblong table and six chairs, along with the bedroom and living room furniture.

"Doing my best." Uncorking the bottle, he poured wine into the Orrefors goblets, a wedding gift from one of her parents' friends. "I remember these," he said, holding his up to the light. "Nice."

They were surrounded by memories. Maybe this was a bad idea, having him over for dinner. When he lifted his goblet toward her, she knew he was going to make a toast, and felt her stomach tighten.

"To good friends and happy days, Jess," he said.

"Good friends and happy days," she echoed, breathing easily.

The goblets clinked. She took a sip of wine, then, overcome with sudden melancholy, rolled her glass between her palms, studying the ruby liquid. For the nameless old man who had died in the park, alone, there would be no more happy days with good friends. . . .

Her thoughts drifted. She heard Gary say something and looked at him. "Sorry. What was that?" She put down her goblet.

"Nothing important." He cocked his head. "You're still thinking about the old man, aren't you? I can tell from your eyes. Whenever you're preoccupied, they're more gray than green."

"Are they?" She smiled self-consciously. "I can't get him out of my mind. I don't know why."

"Don't you?" he said gently. "You're wondering if he's a Holocaust survivor, and that probably made you think about your mom, and everything she went through."

"You're right," she admitted. She was pleased that he understood, surprised that he wasn't annoyed. Her work, and her preoccupation with it, had often been a thorn between them.

Three months ago, while investigating the homicide of a Jewish ACLU attorney representing the rights of neo-Nazis to parade in two L.A. neighborhoods populated by Holocaust survivors, Jessie had learned a stunning truth:

Her mother, Frances Claypool, née Freide Kochinsky, was Jewish. During the war the blond little girl had been hidden by a kind Catholic Polish man and his abusive wife. After the war Frances, then ten years old, had waited anxiously for her family to reclaim her. But everyone—parents, grandparents, brothers and sisters and their spouses, nieces, nephews—had perished.

Frances had eventually been adopted and brought to America by the Holtzes, a childless Orthodox Jewish couple, but her anger and bitterness at having been abandoned by her family and God had made her reject the Holtzes' religious lifestyle.

So Frances, burying her Jewish identity and name, had left their home and met and married Arthur Claypool. And she'd always led her daughters to believe that, like their father, she was Episcopalian.

But Frances was Jewish. And according to the Judaic law of matrilineal descent, Jessie had learned, she and her sister Helen, and Helen's son, Matthew, were Jewish, too. The revelation, though jolting, hadn't made Jessie unhappy or self-conscious. But she'd felt unsettled, confused about her spiritual and ethnic identity; so during the past three months she'd begun exploring her Jewish heritage, taking classes, learning Hebrew.

And today, when she'd seen the tattooed numbers on the dead man's arm, she'd been shaken more than she would have been three months ago.

"I couldn't help thinking my grandfather would probably have been the same age as the old man in the park," Jessie said now. "I don't know *anything* about my grandfather, aside from his name. Isn't that unbelievable?" She shook her head. "I wonder if he had numbers on his arm, too."

"I thought your mom said she'd tell you about her family."

"So did I." She smiled wryly. "Whenever I bring up the subject, she changes it." Frances had been reluctant to part with the truth, had been stingy with details. *There's nothing romantic about being Jewish, Jessie.*

"Maybe it's too painful."

Jessie nodded. "That's what I keep telling myself. But wouldn't it help her to talk about it, Gary?"

"Maybe, maybe not. My grandparents came to America before the war, but some of my parents' relatives and friends are survivors. Some of them talk about their experiences. Others can't." Gary shrugged.

"I guess you're right." She lifted a trout onto her plate.

He did the same. "This is really good," he told her after he tasted it. He took another bite and chewed thoughtfully. "She *did* send you that picture of her family," he said a moment later.

"True." Frances had surprised her with an enlargement of the sepia-toned photo Jessie had come across years ago, the formal photo of people Frances had initially dismissed as "some Jewish relatives I don't know much about." Jessie had hung the photo on her bedroom wall and studied it daily, filled with endless questions about the family she would never know.

"Ask her again," Gary said. "How long is she staying in town?"

"A few days. My dad has a medical conference at the Four Seasons tomorrow and Tuesday."

"Perfect. Take her out to dinner Monday night, just the two of you. Bond."

Jessie grimaced and crunched on a slice of pepper.

Gary sighed. "I take it brunch wasn't a wild success?"

"Not exactly. My mom was her typical, fault-finding self. And West L.A. paged me almost as soon as I got there. By the way, Helen told her you and I are seeing each other, so be prepared."

"I'm not worried. Frances and I get along great. She adores me, especially since I took you away from 'that detective.' " He was grinning now.

"Lizzie Borden would have adored you." Jessie smiled, too, then turned serious. "I *do* feel sorry for her, Gary. Every time I see her, I think about the hell she went through."

Learning that her mother had lost her entire family, that she'd been a hidden child and physically mistreated, hadn't erased the painful memories of Jessie's own traumatic childhood, but it had helped her understand the rage beneath the verbal and physical abuse Frances had inflicted on her own daughters. And it had helped Jessie begin to forgive.

"Doesn't that help you deal with her?"

"It should. But then she makes some dig, and I tell myself

not to react, but I do, anyway." She sighed. "So much for compassion."

"I guess behavior patterns are hard to break."

Was he faulting her? She bristled, then decided she was being overly sensitive. "You sound like Manny," she said, referring to a police psychologist she'd befriended. "You don't know what it's like, Gary. You're lucky—you get along well with your parents."

She liked her ex-in-laws. Harry Drake was an insurance salesman; Martha, a housewife. Nice people. *Uncomplicated* people. Whenever Jessie had seen them with Gary, either here or in their Phoenix home, she'd envied the easy closeness the three of them shared, the unforced affection, the laughter. This is what family is like, she'd thought.

"Hey, I'm their only kid—they have to treat me right," Gary said lightly. "Look, it's not like we haven't had issues, Jess. They're still hoping I'll give up being a crime reporter and go to law school. And you know my mom can be annoyingly overprotective. She still sends me health articles and vitamins and gets mad if I don't call home every other day." He paused. "But, yeah, I'm lucky." He sounded almost embarrassed.

"I *want* to have a good relationship with my mom, Gary."

"I know you do, Jess." He reached his hand across the table and took hers. "Keep trying."

3

PHIL OKUM WAS studying a "blue book" with photographs of a crime scene when Jessie entered the second-floor detective's room at the West L.A. station at seven-thirty on Monday morning.

"Hey," he said, looking up when he saw her.

She dropped her black Sac purse onto her scarred wood desk and sat down. "How was San Diego?"

"Hot, tiring, expensive. I *love* vacations." He grinned and swiveled toward her, folding his arms across his massive chest. "What'd I miss?"

"The crumbs in your mustache, for one. I thought you were on a diet." She exaggerated her frown, but she *was* worried about her partner's weight. He'd admitted that his cholesterol was high, over 260. "Coffee cake?"

"Cruller." His normally ruddy complexion had turned even redder. He sighed, brushing the evidence from his face. "Don't tell Maureen, okay? She'll kill me."

A mental image of petite, five-feet-one-inch-tall Maureen battling her six-foot-four-inch, burly husband made Jessie smile.

"What?" He narrowed his eyes.

"Nothing. No more donuts, okay?" she said sternly. She looked around. "Where are Simms and Boyd?"

"They left just before you got here. A shooting on La Cienega just before the on-ramp to the Ten. A ten-year-old kid's in critical condition 'cause his dad accidentally cut off some son of a bitch who had a handgun. They don't know if he's gonna make it."

"God damn it." Jessie sighed and shook her head.

"Yeah." He sighed, too. "Brian's ten, Chris is twelve. I'm thinking, that could've been my kid."

She thought about her nephew, who had just turned nine. She couldn't begin to imagine how parents dealt with that kind of pain. And if the child died? "Gary's doing a piece on road rage."

"Is he?" Phil nodded. "Lots of it going around. Driving is murder these days," he said with a lightness that belied the pained expression in his eyes.

She grimaced. She doubted she'd ever get used to the gallows humor that was so common among cops.

"So I hear you got a body yesterday," he said.

"Uh-huh." She told him about the old man the golfer had found. "I'm hoping someone will phone in a 'missing persons' today. Unless no one *knows* he's missing. Maybe he lived by himself in one of those apartment buildings near Rancho."

"In which case we'll have to go door to door and show his photo. What fun." Phil linked his arms behind his head and stretched.

Just thinking about the prospect tired her. "In the meantime, I think we should contact the retirement and convalescent homes near Rancho, see if he lived in one of them. And the local hotels."

"Good idea." He dropped his hands to his side. "What about hospitals? They wouldn't necessarily consider him missing. If he checked himself in, there's no law that says he couldn't check himself out."

"Or maybe they thought his family took him home." She nodded. "I thought of that. I called Century City. Nothing."

"Cedars?"

"Too far to walk. So is Midway."

"He could've taken a cab."

"To Rancho Park?"

"Why not?"

She thought for a moment, then nodded again. "You're right. I'll call those two and the other area hospitals. And I guess we'll have to contact a broader range of retirement and convalescent homes and hotels. He could've taken a cab from one of them."

Phil groaned. "There could be hundreds."

"It's your idea. Next time, don't be so damn smart."

He swiveled back and forth in his chair. "Maybe we can narrow down the list of homes. You think he's a Holocaust survivor. So wouldn't he choose a kosher retirement home?"

"Not necessarily. Not all survivors are observant. And I'm not sure he *is* a survivor." Her desk was a mess. She unearthed a Yellow Pages and pulled it toward her.

"Natural causes or homicide, huh?" Phil said. "Door number one or door number two. What does Futaki say?"

She shrugged. "Probably a cardiac arrest *before* he was mugged." She explained about the missing items. "Futaki said it would be impossible to prove the heart attack took place during the mugging. He found a vial with digitalis tablets in the old man's pocket," she added.

"There you go." He half swiveled toward his desk.

"The vial had no label, Phil."

"So? Could be it was a spare vial from some other medication. The old man used it to keep a few digitalis pills on him, just in case."

"You're probably right." Grudgingly.

"Autopsy?"

"Futaki said not until this afternoon, at the earliest. They're swamped."

"When aren't they?" Phil grunted and took a swig of coffee from the lopsided gray ceramic mug his younger son had made in day camp a few weeks ago. "And this guy isn't top priority, 'cause he probably isn't a homicide. Anything new on the hooker, or the baby?"

"No."

A twenty-year-old black prostitute had been stabbed to

death in her apartment around 2:00 A.M. last Thursday, not far from her beat on Santa Monica near Overland. The body had still been warm when the police had responded to a call made by an anonymous male. A week ago, a Caucasian male newborn—suffocated after being born alive, the M.E. had reported—had been found under a mound of tissue paper in a glossy orange shopping bag left in the underground parking lot adjacent to a department store in the Westside Pavilion mall.

No clues, no leads on either murder, but if Jessie had to place bets, she'd guess that they'd have a harder time trying to ID the baby killer.

SID had checked all the restrooms in the shopping complex—an enormous task, complicated by the fact that they hadn't been able to shut down the entire mall. But they'd found blood in one of the department store's bathroom stalls and, stuffed inside the trash can, other evidence of the birth. Jessie and Phil had spent hours questioning the department store managers and sales clerks and personnel in the other mall shops—"Did you see a pregnant woman in labor . . . ?" But no one had noticed, and there had been no video camera in the bathroom recording the grim event.

There were fingerprints on the glossy shopping bag. Some of them belonged to the shaken, sickly pale security guard who had discovered the bag and its gruesome contents. The other prints probably belonged to the woman who had killed her son, but ASIF, the computerized fingerprint databank, had found no match.

No surprise—what were the odds the mother had ever been arrested? So the prints were worthless, unless the police had a suspect. And the shopping bag belonged to a store that wasn't even in the mall. Which meant, Jessie had decided, that the mother had come to the mall with the bag intending to leave the baby in it.

But why had she killed the infant? Why hadn't she left it alive, to be cared for by someone else? Seeing the tiny, lifeless body had made Jessie physically ill and revived her own pain. (The fall hadn't necessarily caused her miscarriage, the doctor had reassured her two years ago, but Gary had believed otherwise. *You had to go chasing the bad guys, didn't you, Jess?*)

Phil said, "Espes probably won't let us spend a lot of time running down the old man's identity. Why don't we wait and see if any 'missing persons' comes in today? Save a lot of time and effort."

"I'd like to call some of the hospitals this morning, Phil."

"It's probably natural causes." He was studying her now.

"Futaki said so. I'm not so sure." Ignoring the question in his dark brown eyes, she opened the Yellow Pages.

"Trying to make me look lazy, huh?" Phil walked over to Boyd's desk and returned with another directory. "I'll do the hotels first, then start with the retirement and convalescent homes."

"Thanks, Phil."

"Self-protection. So you won't tell Maureen about the donut."

Jessie thumbed through the directory to HOSPITALS. Last week, working the infanticide, she'd looked through the same list and phoned all the L.A. emergency rooms and clinics, hoping to find that the mother had been admitted sometime after Monday with postpartum hemorrhaging. But there had been no such admission. The dead newborn was still unidentified. Maybe they'd have more luck with the old man.

An hour later she wasn't so sure. Phil had eliminated the hotels and was phoning retirement homes. She'd contacted eleven of the area hospitals and struck out with all of them. She was taking a break, talking with some detectives from JUVI at the watercooler at the far end of the long, partitioned room, when she saw Phil signaling to her.

She hurried back to her desk. "Find something?"

He shook his head. "One of Cassandra Jones's colleagues called with the name and address of a girlfriend. Delayed memory, I guess."

Cassandra Jones was the slain prostitute. Last Thursday night Phil and Jessie had canvassed Santa Monica Boulevard and tried to coax names from some of the other hookers who worked the area. We don't know anything, they'd all said.

Which was exactly what the girlfriend claimed a half hour later when Jessie and Phil sat in her stuffy, hot, one-room apartment on Bundy. No, Cassandra hadn't mentioned being afraid of any of her johns. And she never referred to any of them by their real names.

Cassandra's pimp, Henry Q., had said the same thing on Friday morning when Jessie and Phil had tracked him down to a bar near Beverly Glen. "Hey, man, I knew something, don't you think I'd tell you? I don't like the idea some jerk's offing my girls. It's not great for business, you know?"

Jessie had believed he was telling the truth. She wasn't so sure about the girlfriend, Lucinda Blake, and said so to Phil as they walked back to his green Buick Cutlass.

"Ditto," Phil said, removing a parking citation from his windshield. "Maybe she'll think it over, give us a call."

"Maybe. Did you see how scared she looked?"

"No shit. I thought she'd twist her fingers off her hands." He stuffed the citation into his pants pocket. "I hope you have better luck with the dead guy."

There had been no missing persons report for the old man. Jessie relayed the information glumly to Phil and wondered why she was taking this so hard. Because of your mom, Gary had said.

She wrote up the report on the interview with Lucinda Blake—Phil had offered to do it, but his handwriting was god-awful. When she was done, she hesitated, then picked up the receiver and dialed her sister's number.

Frances answered the phone. "Helen's not here, Jessica. She's playing tennis with some friends. It's a shame that you've given up playing, dear. You used to be so good at it."

"Actually, I called to talk to *you*, Mom. I thought you and I could have dinner tonight, while Dad's at the conference. It'll be fun," she added, thinking how sad it was that the concept of having fun with her mother was so foreign.

"What a *lovely* idea, Jessica. But why don't we *all* go out, my treat. Helen and Neil, you and I. That would make up for yesterday, when you had to leave so suddenly."

Translation: when you ruined the day. "Helen won't want to leave Matthew with the new housekeeper." Her nephew was shy around new people, and Helen was overprotective.

"Matthew likes Ismelda. He'll be fine. Maybe your father can get away for a while. And Gary is invited, too, of course."

She felt her stomach muscles contract. "That's so nice of you, Mom. I don't know if he can make it."

"Tell him I'm counting on seeing him, Jessica." Sweetly firm. "Seven o'clock, at the Ivy. Wear something appropriate."

Her mother hung up. Jessie did the same, wondering whether Frances had expanded on Jessie's "just the two of us" outing because she was reluctant to spend time alone with her daughter, or because she wanted to encourage Jessie's relationship with Gary, or ruin it.

With Frances, you never knew. She'd been opposed to Jessie's marrying a crime reporter ("that person," she'd called him), but had come to adore him. She'd said incredibly nasty things about him after the divorce, but at Matthew's birthday party in April—the first time that she'd seen her ex-son-in-law since he'd moved out of the house—she'd been sweet and charming. Which, Jessie knew from bitter experience, didn't mean anything.

She debated, then phoned the *L.A. Times* and left a message for Gary to call. Maybe he'd be busy tonight. If he was lucky.

Phil had gone to the cafeteria—"Just a salad," he'd promised. She was about to resume phoning the area hospitals, but someone had removed her Yellow Pages. Leaning over, she took Phil's directory, still open, and decided to make some calls to retirement homes. Not knowing where Phil had left off, she began from the back of the list.

No luck on the first four calls. On the fifth call, she introduced herself to the administrator of the Golden Palms and sensed from the hesitation in his voice that she might be onto something.

"As a matter of fact, I was debating whether I should call the police," he told Jessie in a pronounced South African accent. "My weekend manager saw Mr. Pomerantz on Friday, but on Sunday the housekeeper reported that his bed hadn't been slept in and that his things are all there. My manager assumed he'd spent the time with friends or family. Truth is, it wasn't our business."

"Why not?" She saw Phil approaching with a carton of

salad and a sandwich. Covering the phone mouthpiece, she whispered, "I may have a lead on the old man."

Phil nodded and sat down at his desk.

"Mr. Pomerantz wasn't a resident," the administrator said. "He was paying by the day, unlike our residents, who pay by the month. But one of our guest suites was available, so I agreed. Anyway, this morning he still wasn't back, and I heard on the news that they found an old man dead in the park. So I thought, what if?" He took a breath. "Of course, he could show up any minute, or tonight. Which is why I haven't called the police."

"What does Mr. Pomerantz look like?" Jessie asked, trying not to get her hopes up.

"Old. What should I tell you?"

She suppressed a smile, half annoyed, half amused. "Can you be a little more specific?"

The administrator sighed. "Quite honestly, I hardly saw him. This is a medium-size facility—a hundred twenty beds—and he's only been here about a week. He was from New York, by the way. He was thinking of moving here." He paused. "Good air, I think."

In Los Angeles, where Jessie could see the blanket of smog almost every day? She scowled. "He was moving here for the *air* quality?"

"*Hair*. You asked me to be specific about Mr. Pomerantz's appearance. I noticed that he had very thick brown hair. A little unusual for someone his age."

So did the dead man.

4

THE GOLDEN PALMS Retirement Home was a two-story, banana-colored stucco building on the corner of Croft and Willoughby. Tidy pockets of multicolored impatiens made a pleasing, if unspectacular, show in the small front and side yards, both of which were bordered by a tall, white wrought-iron fence.

The administrator, Gerald Mason, short and thin with graying dark blond, wavy hair, must have been watching for Jessie and Phil's arrival. He appeared almost instantly and whisked them away, giving Jessie only seconds to take in the air-conditioned lobby's furnishings: industrial tan carpeting; two groupings of solid navy sofas and navy-and-burgundy armchairs, in a flame-stitch pattern, centered around light-wood coffee tables; a thirty-two-inch-screen television on a wooden stand; several potted ficus benjamina. Still-life prints of flowers and fruits gave touches of color to the beige texture-papered walls.

Several elderly men and women were sitting on the sofas, watching what looked like a soap opera. Another man holding onto a walker was slowly making his way across the lobby. Jessie felt the residents' eyes on her as she and Phil followed

Mason to his office, which was considerably cooler than the lobby.

She showed the administrator a Polaroid photo of the dead man that she'd taken and cropped, and saw him blanch.

"That's him, Norman Pomerantz." His voice was subdued. "He seemed healthy enough when I saw him, but what does that mean, right?" He returned the photo to Jessie. "Did he have a heart attack?"

"It's possible. We're waiting for the autopsy results. Did Mr. Pomerantz have a heart condition?"

"Not that I know of." He sounded suddenly guarded.

Phil said, "We found an unlabeled vial with digitalis tablets in Mr. Pomerantz's pocket. Do you know anything about that?"

Mason shook his head. "This is an RCFE—retirement care for the elderly—and we *do* disburse meds. But that wasn't our arrangement with Mr. Pomerantz. As I told Detective Drake on the phone, he wanted a temporary place to stay. If he was taking meds, he was handling it on his own." He was defensive now, watching Jessie and Phil to see their reactions.

"When did he arrive?" Jessie asked.

"Eight days ago, on Sunday. I checked after I spoke with you. I assumed you'd want to know."

"Thanks." She smiled to show her appreciation and put him at ease. "Why was he staying here, instead of at a hotel?"

Mason relaxed against his chair back. "Less expensive. I charged Mr. Pomerantz forty a night for our guest suite— that included breakfast. Lunch and dinner were extra, but reasonable, too."

"A bargain," Phil drawled.

Jessie glanced at Phil—was he being sarcastic?—then at Mason, whose expression indicated he was wondering the same thing.

"Actually, it is," the administrator said. "Check out hotels, Detective. You'll see."

"Swimming pool?" Phil smiled. "Tennis court?"

A beat of silence. Then, "No pool, no tennis," the administrator responded coolly. "We *do* have a billiards room, a large-screen TV room, a chapel, a computer room. We have a physical therapist who comes regularly, and a beautician who does hairstyles and manicures. We're proud of the facilities and the services we offer our residents."

"Bet you are," Phil said. Definitely sarcastic now. "So how much do you charge your regulars for all these luxury accommodations?"

Jessie shot her partner a look—what the hell was bothering him? And what did this have to do with Pomerantz's death?

Mason's face had reddened. "If they don't need assisted care, we charge between eleven hundred to fifteen hundred a month for a private room and bath." His voice was clipped, his South African accent more pronounced. "That includes daily maid service, laundry service, nutritious meals, transportation to and from doctors' appointments, activities, crafts, exercise classes."

The administrator was practically glaring at Phil. Phil stared back, unflustered.

Enough of this, Jessie decided. "Mr. Mason, when Mr. Pomerantz registered, did he leave you a name of someone to contact in case of emergency?"

He turned toward her. "I'm sorry?"

She repeated the question.

He took a short, calming breath. "I'm sure he did. We always require that." His tone was friendly now. "Would you like me to check?"

"Please." She smiled politely.

"No problem." The administrator lifted his phone receiver, pressed a button, and spoke quietly. A moment later he was scribbling on a notepad. "Stanley Goldblum," he said, putting down the receiver. "He lives in Brooklyn, New York." He tore off the slip of paper on which he'd written the name and phone number and handed it to Jessie.

Jessie placed the paper inside her notepad. "A relative?"

"Friend." He played with his pen.

"Any local references?" Phil asked.

Still facing Jessie, Mason shook his head.

"So what did he do, pick your place out of a Yellow Pages?" Phil was frowning.

Mason turned toward Phil, his smile taut. "If I remember

correctly, Mr. Pomerantz told my manager that Mr. Gold-blum referred him." The edge was back in his voice.

"How would Goldblum know about your place?"

"I assume that one of our residents knows Mr. Goldblum. Otherwise, we wouldn't have accepted Mr. Pomerantz. We generally rent out the suites to friends or family of a resident, as a courtesy."

"Can you find out which resident knows Mr. Goldblum?" Phil was all business now.

"My manager would know, but she's not here right now." He put down his pen. "Why so many questions, Detective? I thought Mr. Pomerantz had a heart attack. What difference does it make how he came to be here?"

"Do residents sign out when they leave the premises?" Phil asked, leaving the administrator's question unanswered.

Mason opened his mouth to say something, then nodded instead. "We keep a log at the front window, and they write what time they leave, what time they return."

"What about where they're going?" Jessie asked.

"Sometimes they'll indicate that, but generally they don't." He shrugged. "I can't say we're terribly strict about enforcing the sign-out sheet, since all our residents are mentally competent. It's not like boarding school, is it?" His smile wobbled nervously before it disappeared.

Phil said, "Could you find out if Mr. Pomerantz signed out on Saturday, and if so, when. And where he was going."

Mason pursed his lips. "As I *explained,* Mr. Pomerantz wasn't a resident, so he wouldn't have been told about the sign-out sheet."

"Maybe he filled it out anyway," Phil said evenly. "Why don't you find out."

Mason sighed with exaggerated weariness and reached for the phone. "I'll have the receptionist check the log."

No "thank you" from Phil.

A minute later Mason faced him again. "Mr. Pomerantz didn't sign out on Saturday night." A tinge of I-told-you-so in his voice.

"So you have no idea where he went?" Phil said. "Did he mention having any friends in L.A.?"

"No, he didn't." He picked up a letter opener and tapped it against his fingers. "Detective Drake, is it true that Mr. Pomerantz's body was found in the park?"

"Yes."

Mason hesitated, then said, "Maybe he was taken there *after* he died. Maybe he was kidnapped."

Jessie stared at the administrator and exchanged a quick look with Phil. "What makes you think that?" she asked, watching Mason carefully.

"A few weeks ago, a new resident, Mrs. Braeburn, was going for a hearing aid when a woman got out of a car, approached her, and told her she was here to pick her up. Mrs. Braeburn was a little confused and disoriented, since she was new here, so she got into the car, thinking she was being taken to an appointment for a hearing aid. Instead the woman took Mrs. Braeburn to her bank and persuaded her to withdraw fifteen hundred dollars for the hearing aid, et cetera." Mason sighed.

Jessie felt stirrings of anger and sadness, but not surprise. The world was filled with cold-blooded people who preyed on the vulnerable. "What happened to your resident?"

"The woman drove Mrs. Braeburn back to our facility. Thank God she wasn't harmed, but she was extremely agitated when she realized what had happened. I tried to reassure her and her family that this had never happened before, but her family decided to make different arrangements." Mason sighed again.

Jessie wondered whether the administrator was more concerned about what had happened to the old woman, or about the vacancy created by her departure.

"The police detective I spoke to said this con isn't new," he said. "They accessed the bank's videotape, but this woman was smart—she had her back to the camera the entire time." He leaned forward. "Maybe a similar thing happened to Mr. Pomerantz. But he had a heart attack, so whoever did this had to dispose of the body."

"Banks aren't open on Saturday," Phil said.

"*Some* banks are—they have branches in local supermar-

kets." He sounded pleased to have corrected Phil. To Jessie
he said, "And what if he was kidnapped on Friday?"

Mason sounded eager to convince—no doubt he was trying
to distance himself and the Golden Palms from Pomerantz's
death and any resulting negative publicity. "It's possible,"
she said.

But unlikely. Futaki estimated that Pomerantz had died Saturday night. If he'd been kidnapped on Friday, in time to be
taken to a bank, and suffered a heart attack, even if it hadn't
been immediately fatal, what had the kidnappers done with
him until Saturday night?

"Can we look at Mr. Pomerantz's room?" she asked.

They took the elevator to the second floor and walked down
a long, low-ceilinged narrow hall permeated with a faint musty
odor. Mason stopped in front of room 205 and unlocked
the door.

"We have to have keys to all the rooms," he said, opening
the door. "Just in case."

The suite—a living room, bedroom, and bath—was surpris-
ingly spacious. It didn't have the ambiance of the Century
Plaza, but Mason was right—at $280 a week, breakfast in-
cluded, it was a definite bargain.

"I ought to sign up right now," Phil said to Jessie in an
undertone.

The living room had a gray tweed Herculon sofa and two
gray-and-navy plaid chairs facing each other across a walnut-
and-glass coffee table, a television, a desk, and a round walnut
table with four chairs. In the corner, next to a walnut-paneled
mini-refrigerator, was an occasional table on top of which sat
a coffeemaker and a basket with packets of flavored coffee.

In the bedroom were a full-size bed made up with a navy-
and-gray geometric print, an oak dresser, and two oak
nightstands. A smaller television sat on the dresser. Jessie had
noted emergency call buttons on the walls in both rooms.

"His luggage is still here," Mason said. "I looked this
morning, before you called. But I figured that didn't mean
anything was wrong, because he could have taken a small
overnight bag with him."

"I'll do the dresser," Phil said to Jessie.

She nodded and went into the living room. There was little to check besides a small guest closet, empty except for a black raincoat, and the desk, on which lay Saturday's *L.A. Times.* Pomerantz had looked at the business section and attempted the crossword puzzle. Which meant he *had* been here on Saturday. In another, larger closet in the bedroom, Jessie saw two suits, half a dozen shirts, and four pairs of slacks. She checked all the pockets and found nothing. On the floor of the closet, next to a pair of brown loafers, were a tan leather suitcase, a black nylon carryall, and a large opaque white plastic laundry bag filled with sleeveless ribbed T-shirts and boxer shorts, all folded. A neat man, the deceased.

She carried the black bag and suitcase to the bed. She wasn't surprised to find the suitcase empty; it had weighed very little. She reached inside the top and side flaps. Nothing there. She checked the many zippered compartments of the black bag and found a fine-toothed comb and several hotel-size bars of Camay soap, their wrappers yellowed with age.

The main section of the bag yielded an issue of *Art World,* a tour guide to L.A., and several copies of the *Forward*—an English-language Jewish newspaper, Jessie saw as she scanned the front page of one issue. Underneath the reading material was a navy velvet bag containing a white fringed prayer shawl, a prayer book, and a smaller navy velvet pouch with phylacteries. Embroidered in multicolored threads on the front of the outer navy bag were Hebrew letters.

"*Nachum ben Yehudah,*" Jessie said, still struggling after two months of Hebrew language class to imitate the clearing-of-the-throat, guttural "*ch*" her teacher produced so easily.

She repacked the black bag and returned it and the suitcase to the closet. If Pomerantz was Orthodox, she knew from her Judaism class, he wouldn't have traveled from the facility on Saturday until an hour after sundown. But she supposed that non-Orthodox Jews might also travel with religious articles.

She turned to Mason, who was standing in the doorway to the bedroom. "Are all your residents Orthodox?"

"Actually, I don't think any of them are. Our facility isn't kosher. We're kosher style," he added. "You know—tradi-

tional Jewish food. Lox and bagels, brisket, kugels, pickles."
He smiled.

She smiled back absentmindedly. Did that mean Pomerantz
wasn't Orthodox? Or was he Orthodox, and had he chosen to
stay here and eat elsewhere? Out of the corner of her eye,
she could see Phil rummaging through the dresser drawers.
"Find anything?"

He shut the bottom drawer. "Just clothing. No letters,
diary, anything like that. Nothing in the nightstands either.
You?"

Jessie shook her head. Odd, she thought, that they hadn't
found any personal papers.

"I'll check the bathroom," Phil said.

Jessie moved to the bed. She slipped her hand between the
mattress and bedspring, then searched under the bed, where
she found a pair of worn black leather slippers with frayed
lining. With a twinge of sadness for Pomerantz, she placed
them back under the bed.

On the round table against the wall lay another periodical
printed in the Hebrew alphabet. She picked it up and was
chagrined that she couldn't make out any of the words. Maybe
it was Yiddish, not Hebrew.

Phil returned from the bathroom, carrying a number of
small vials. "These are all Pomerantz's, from a Brooklyn pharmacy. Lotensin, Ditropan, Procardia, Zantac. Zantac's for the
stomach. I don't know about the others." He looked at
Mason.

"Lotensin and Procardia reduce high blood pressure," the
administrator said. "Ditropan controls urine."

"That's it?" Jessie asked Phil.

"No Lanoxin, if that's what you mean." He lifted his
shoulders.

"So where'd he get the tablets?" Jessie frowned.

Phil turned to Mason. "Maybe Pomerantz got the stuff
from another resident."

"Impossible." The administrator folded his arms across his
chest. "The medication supervisor is *extremely* careful about
ordering and disbursing the meds. We could be shut down if

she weren't. Mr. Pomerantz probably brought the Lanoxin from New York."

"In an unlabeled vial?" Jessie didn't buy it.

Phil shrugged. "We'll have to contact his New York physician, find out if he prescribed Lanoxin for Pomerantz."

"And if he didn't?" Stepping closer to Phil, she said in an undertone, "Someone could have planted the Lanoxin to make us think Pomerantz had a heart condition and died of a simple heart attack." But then they were looking at premeditated murder, not a mugging.

Phil's brow was furrowed in concentration. "I don't know."

She faced Mason. "Did Mr. Pomerantz receive any visitors while he was here?"

"Not that I know of. I rarely saw him in the lobby, and when I did, he was sitting by himself, reading."

"What about phone calls? I don't see a phone here or in the living room."

"Most residents bring their own phones and have service installed. The bills come to them, of course. But guests like Mr. Pomerantz would have to use one of the pay phones."

Along with all the other residents who didn't have private phone service. Which would make it much harder to trace any calls he'd made. "Did you provide him with transportation anywhere?" Jessie asked.

Mason shook his head. "One of our employees drives residents to and from their doctors' appointments, but as I explained, Mr. Pomerantz's arrangement was different." He sounded a touch impatient. "I assume he took a cab or bus if he wanted to go somewhere."

Jessie took out her notepad from the pocket of her navy blazer. "Do you recommend any particular cab company to the residents?"

"We generally refer to one or two. I have their names in my office." He looked behind him, then took a step closer. "There's something else you might want to consider," he said, his voice conspiratorially low. "I told you what happened to Mrs. Braeburn, how she was persuaded to give this woman fifteen hundred dollars? Well, there are people out there hijacking residents from board-and-care facilities and taking them to facilities run by other people, or to their own."

"*Jesus.*" Phil rolled his eyes. "Why the hell would they do that?"

"For the residents' social security checks, and their Medi-Cal and Medicare benefits. It's relatively easy to open up a board and care, especially a small one. It's tougher to fill the beds and keep them filled—the competition's fierce. Some facilities hire recruiters to bring in residents for a percentage of the government checks."

"Where do the recruiters recruit?" Jessie asked.

"Depends. Sometimes they take the homeless—there are so many now, that more and more people are going into the board-and-care business. Sometimes they get referrals from hospitals. And now they've started this hijacking business. But it's not only the recruiters. Six months ago, Detective, I caught one of our competitors—someone I *know,* for God's sake!—in a resident's room after midnight, trying to steal the poor lady right out from under us. Can you believe it?" Indignation flashed in his hazel eyes.

"So you think Pomerantz may have been kidnapped and taken to another home?" Jessie asked.

He cast another worried glance behind him, as if he were afraid a resident would overhear. "It's possible, isn't it? Whoever did it wouldn't have known that Pomerantz wasn't one of our residents, or that he had a bad heart. When he died, they couldn't very well return him here, could they?"

Phil threw a dubious look at Jessie. She raised her shoulders almost imperceptibly. Was this another attempt on Mason's part to distance himself from Pomerantz's death?

Mason must have noticed their silent communication, because his face had reddened. "Maybe that's not what happened to Mr. Pomerantz, Detective, but these people are *ruthless.* One manager I know was assaulted and held at *gun point* while two men kidnapped three of his people. They didn't take any of their belongings—just personal papers and some meds. The residents were upset and confused, but they were too weak to fight or run. One of them had diabetes and high blood pressure. Another was partially paralyzed from a stroke. *Monsters.*" Mason sighed.

"Was that an isolated incident?" Jessie asked.

"I wish." He grunted. "This manager told me he knows of other hijackings, but they're usually not reported." He ran a hand through his hair. "I love my work, Detective—I enjoy helping old people, trying to make them happy and comfortable. But to be honest, I'm getting nervous. I tell myself the facility that manager runs is near USC—a high-crime area, so it's more of a target for thugs. Our place is in a much safer neighborhood. But people are greedy, and this business is becoming more and more cutthroat. Who's to say when they'll target the Golden Palms?"

Maybe they already had, Jessie thought.

5

THEY HAD A name for the deceased, but little else.

Jessie and Phil wanted to question the residents at the Golden Palms—maybe Pomerantz had told someone where he was going that Saturday—but Mason resisted an immediate, room-to-room canvassing of his occupants.

"I'm concerned that a number of my residents may become agitated, even fearful," he explained when they were back in his office. "And I see no reason to upset them if they've had no contact with Mr. Pomerantz." His tone was polite but firm, and he'd avoided looking at Phil.

Jessie nodded. "I understand your concerns. But what if one of them *did* have contact and is afraid to admit it?"

"I'd pick up on that immediately, *believe* me. I know my people, Detective Drake. If I have even a *suspicion* of that, I'll let you know." He tented his hands. "Also, while all my residents are basically mentally competent—legally, we couldn't have them in our kind of facility if they weren't—some of them *do* get a little confused, so they might say something misleading." He shrugged and smiled lightly, inviting sympathy and understanding.

"We're kind of used to getting at the truth," Phil drawled.

Mason shook his head. "Trust me, it's better if I and my staff find out whether Mr. Pomerantz told anyone where he was going."

"Just find out whether Mr. Pomerantz talked to anyone at all," Phil said brusquely. "We'll take it from there."

He was scowling and sounded pissed off. Jessie didn't blame him. She wasn't thrilled with the administrator's take-charge position, either, but she could just picture the headlines if she and Phil insisted on questioning the Golden Palms's senior citizens. "How soon can you get us a list of the people Mr. Pomerantz talked to?"

"We'll talk to the residents immediately. But some of them are out—visiting with family or friends, going to doctors' appointments, shopping, to the bank. So it may take time. I promise to call you as soon as I know anything." The administrator stood and showed them to the door.

"That could be next week," Phil grumbled a moment later when he and Jessie were in the hallway.

"Optimist."

The lobby was occupied by the same people she'd seen earlier—at least they looked the same. As she stepped outside the air-conditioned building, the heat was so intense that she felt as if she'd stuck her head into an oven

"Why don't you like Mason?" she asked as they headed to Phil's car, parked around the corner.

"Mr. I'm-in-control-here?" Phil grunted and accelerated his pace. "What's to like? He's an oily, insincere, money-grubbing little twit."

She hurried to keep up. "You don't know that. He sounded genuinely concerned about his residents."

"They all sound sincere."

"You were rough on him."

He walked a few seconds in silence. "My Grandma Emily died in a place like this. Okay, maybe not as nice. But still, it had the same setup. Exercise class, crafts, a nutritionist on staff, yadda-yadda." He snorted. "Promised her the moon, gave her crap."

Stanley Goldblum, Norman Pomerantz's New York friend, wasn't at home when Jessie called. He didn't have an answering machine. William Cole, the doctor who had prescribed Pomerantz's blood-pressure medications, was in surgery. His receptionist promised Jessie she'd have the doctor contact West L.A. when he was done.

Jessie spoke to the dispatchers at both cab companies and asked them to check their records to see whether one of their drivers had picked up Pomerantz from the Golden Palms on Saturday. They told her they'd get back to her as soon as possible if they found anything.

So much of being a detective, Jessie had come to learn over the past fifteen years, was waiting. Knowing that, unfortunately, hadn't taught her how to be more patient.

Phil was taking a break. She hoped he hadn't cheated and bought another donut. She washed down a granola bar with a cup of Red Zinger tea and tried Goldblum again. This time the line was busy. That didn't mean he was home, she told herself—someone else could be trying his line at the same time. Still . . .

The phone rang. Maybe it was one of the cab companies, she thought as she reached for the receiver, or Pomerantz's doctor. "West L.A., Detective Drake."

"The Ivy, huh?" Gary whistled. "Tell your mom I'm delighted to accept her invitation, and not just because the place is so posh and expensive that I can't afford to take you there on my salary."

"Great." She could picture his crooked smile, and though she was still nervous about subjecting him to her mother—Frances's moods were so mercurial—she was glad he'd be coming, and told him so. "My mother asked me to wear something appropriate, as if I couldn't figure that out for myself."

"Sweats are out, you think?"

Jessie laughed. "Frances would die."

Gary laughed, too. "Speaking of which, what's with the old man in the park? Does he have a name?"

"Norman Pomerantz, from Brooklyn. I found out he was staying at a board-and-care facility."

"A survivor?"

"Could be. Definitely Jewish." She told Gary about the

prayer shawl and phylacteries. "How's the road rage piece going?"

"Scary as hell. Depressing, too. But thanks for asking. I like that you're showing interest in my work, Jess." His tone was arch.

"I learned that in *The Rules*—the first edition."

"Now *that's* a scary book." He intoned the refrain from the *Twilight Zone* theme song.

She laughed. "No kidding." She and some of the other female detectives at West L.A. had read the how-to-get-a-man-to-the-altar manual and laughed about its nonfeminist, subordinate-yourself-to-your-man strategies. She hesitated, then said, "The reason I asked is that we had another shooting this morning that could fit in with your piece."

"Sorry to hear that," he said quietly. A pause before he cleared his throat. Then, "Any details?"

Always the reporter, she thought, and decided she wasn't being fair. "I don't have any. If and when I do, I'll have to clear things with the detectives handling the case before I tell you anything." Which he already knew, but she had to say it.

"It's nice, isn't it, that we can share stuff. A year ago you wouldn't have trusted me to even mention this "

"A year ago you didn't deserve to be trusted," she said lightly.

He'd made front-page headline news from information he'd learned by eavesdropping on her conversation with another detective. Her supervisor had been furious. So had Jessie. The memory had rankled a long time.

There had always been a conflict between their careers: As a reporter, Gary believed that the people had a right to know. As a cop, Jessie knew the importance, often vital, of circumspection and confidentiality.

"I have to go, Gary. See you tonight." She was impatient to try Goldblum's number again.

"Pick you up at a quarter to seven. And Jess, try to wear something *appropriate*."

"I'll consider it." Still smiling, she pressed the phone's disconnect bar and punched in Goldblum's ten-digit number.

After five rings she was about to hang up when someone answered.

"Mr. Goldblum?"

"Yes."

"My name is Detective Jessica Drake, and I'm with the Los Angeles Police Department. I'm calling because—"

"Dis is for real? Not a prank?" He spoke with a heavy European accent, pronouncing the word "prenk."

"No, sir. Not a prank. Mr. Goldblum, I understand that you know Norman Pomerantz."

"You mean Nachum? Sure, I know him. He's mine best friend. Why? He's in trouble? I told him not to jaywalk in Los Angeles. In Los Angeles, I told him, they'll throw you in jail for that."

She could tell from his voice that he was nervous, that his humor was an attempt to postpone hearing what he feared was bad news. Gently she said, "Mr. Goldblum, I'm sorry to tell you that Mr. Pomerantz is dead." This was the part she hated.

There was silence on the line.

"Mr. Goldblum?"

"I heard you, Detective," he said softly. "I need a minute, all right?"

"Of course. I'm really sorry," she said again.

"You're sure it's Nachum?" he asked almost belligerently after another, shorter silence.

She felt a pang of pity for Goldblum. "The administrator at the Golden Palms Retirement Home identified him from a photo. We understand that you recommended the place to him."

"What happened? How did he . . . ?" Goldblum's voice broke.

"We don't know the cause of death yet, but he was found in a park. It may have been a heart attack." Or murder.

"He was feeling *terrific* when I saw him. I can't believe he's dead."

"When was that, sir?"

"Today's Monday? So two weeks ago, on Sunday. We had

dinner at my house. He was in a great mood, like always. Funny, like always."

"We found some digitalis tablets in his pocket. Were you aware that he was taking that medication?"

"No. I know he had high blood pressure, and his stomach bothered him sometimes. Too much schmaltz herring." He sighed. "Nachum, Nachum, what happened to you?" he whispered.

She could hear the pain in his voice, and then he was crying. She felt awkward and played idly with the phone cord while he composed himself. "Mr. Goldblum, do you know why Mr. Pomerantz came to Los Angeles?"

Goldblum cleared his throat. "He joked about it. 'Stanley, I'm going to be a star, a leading man,' he told me. He said he wanted to see the Pacific Ocean, Beverly Hills, Grauman's Chinese. Everything."

"So it was just a visit?"

"He said if things worked out, maybe he would move there. I know he didn't like the cold weather here, but I asked him why Los Angeles, with all that smog? Why not Miami? No offense, Detective," Goldblum added quickly. "Anyway, Nachum just smiled, like he had a big secret."

"What do you think he meant by 'if things worked out'? Did he have any investments he was pursuing here?"

"Investments?" Goldblum sighed. "Nachum made a living in the *shmate* business for forty years. With social security and what he was able to put away in a few bonds, he barely managed."

"What's the *shmate* business?" Jessie asked, writing down the word.

"Sorry." A half laugh. " '*Shmate*' is Yiddish for 'rag,' but we use it to describe the garment business. Dresses, blouses, skirts, suits—you know? Nachum had a retail store on the Lower East Side, on Ludlow Street. Mine was on Orchard. Sometimes after work we used to go to Ratner's and have a few pirogen with sour cream. You know Ratner's?"

She told him she didn't and heard him sigh again, though obviously not because she wasn't familiar with the restaurant. "Did Mr. Pomerantz have friends or family in L.A.?"

"No. At least, not that he told me. And Nachum told me *everything*. We go back a long way. I was at his wedding in Munich, in 1946, right after the war. My wife and I were there for him when his wife, Lola, died five years ago."

"Did they have any children?"

Goldblum clucked. "They wanted children so bad. But when Lola was in the camps, they did something to her and ruined her insides. You probably heard about things like that." His tone posed a question.

"Yes. It's horrifying, unbelievable," she said, knowing that the adjectives were almost banal to describe the inhuman "medical" experiments doctors like Mengele had performed in the name of science. Had someone performed an experiment on one of her mother's sisters or sisters-in-law? On her grandmother? The thought nauseated her. She swallowed hard.

"They thought about adopting when they came to this country in 1950," Goldblum said, "but people in our circle weren't so quick to do it then. Who knows why. Later, they changed their minds, but every agency they went to told them they were too old. But don't get me wrong, Detective. Nachum wasn't depressed. He and Lola had a beautiful life together, a full life. And they were godparents to my two sons."

"How old was he?"

"Eighty-four."

How old would her grandfather have been had he been spared? Should she ask her mother tonight, or would that put Frances in a foul mood and ruin the evening? "Mr. Goldblum, how is it that you recommended the Golden Palms to Mr. Pomerantz?"

"A friend told me about it. I mentioned it to Nachum when he told me he was going to L.A. He was so happy." Goldblum sighed.

"Because it was less expensive than a hotel?"

"That, and even better because he knew he'd be more comfortable. According to my friend, a lot of the people who live there are Jewish, probably *greeneh* like Nachum. Immigrants," he explained.

"Which friend is that?"

"Hilda Rheinhart. She's been there a couple of years. A nice lady. I knew her husband, he should rest in peace, from before the war."

Jessie wrote down the name, pleased that she finally had a possible lead. "So Mrs. Rheinhart is a survivor, too?"

"Sure," Goldblum said, in a surprised tone that asked, "Isn't everybody?"

"Did Mr. Pomerantz contact you from Los Angeles?"

"He called a few times last week, and he sent me a postcard from Universal Studios."

"What did he say when you spoke to him?"

"Mostly he asked about my sons and their families, about our friends. Who won at poker."

"Did he—"

"Now that I'm thinking, Detective, the last time we talked, he sounded excited. I asked him what was going on, and he said 'Nothing, why?' but I knew different. Nachum's not a good faker. When he had a straight flush, everybody at the table knew."

Her interest quickened. "What day was that? When you talked to him last, I mean."

"Wednesday or Thursday. I can't be sure."

She wrote that down. "And he was feeling well?"

"He didn't complain. Nachum walked a mile every morning, and he watched what he ate. He took his high blood pressure very seriously, this I can tell you."

"What about his mental health?"

"Excellent. Like I told you, he was always joking, always smiling. And sharp like a tack. You couldn't fool Nachum Pomerantz, no way."

Jessie asked Goldblum for the names and phone numbers of the dead man's other friends.

"Hold on. I'll get my book." Less than a minute later he was back on the line and dictated several names and numbers. "I'd be surprised if they told you something I didn't, Detective. Nachum and I were the closest. Like brothers."

"What about family?"

"All gone. Everyone was killed in the war—his parents, grandparents, a brother and two sisters, cousins. That's why he did that video, he said. So there would be a permanent record of his story."

What were the odds, she wondered, that she could get Frances to record *her* story? "He taped himself talking?"

"No, it was for a documentary. You know, like the one Spielberg is doing—interviewing Holocaust survivors? Nachum told me I should do it, too. I don't know. Maybe my wife and I will do it together."

"Do you know the name of the company that produced this documentary?" It was unlikely that Pomerantz had revealed on camera why he'd gone to L.A.—if in fact Goldblum was right, and there *had* been a mysterious motive. But Jessie was curious to see what the dead man had looked like alive, to hear him talk.

"He told me the name, but I'm not sure. . . . Let me think." Goldblum was silent a moment, then said, "I remember—Morton Productions. Like the salt."

Jessie thanked him and left her number. "If you think of anything else, Mr. Goldblum, please let me know. And again, I'm so sorry about your friend."

"Yah." He sighed again. "I guess I should start making the funeral arrangements, calling people. There's no one else to do it. I'll have to clean out his apartment, too, but what will I do with all his things?" he asked plaintively.

Jessie had no answer. "I wouldn't touch anything in the apartment just yet, Mr. Goldblum. The Brooklyn police may want to take a look around." She would call them as soon as she got off the phone with Goldblum.

"Look around? For what?" Goldblum sounded puzzled.

"Mr. Pomerantz may have jotted down something on a calendar or a memo pad, indicating where he planned to go while he was here in L.A."

"It's important where he went? Why?" A little suspicion had crept into his voice.

It's important if he was killed. "It's just routine," she lied. "We always like to have as detailed a picture as possible of the deceased's movements up until the time of his death."

"I see," Goldblum said in a voice that indicated he didn't.

He cleared his throat. "When will they send back Nachum's body?"

Jessie hesitated. "They have to do an autopsy first." Was Futaki performing it right now?

"It's terrible to cut him up like that, and for what?" His anger crackled through the phone. "You said it was probably a heart attack."

"We have to be sure." She thought again about the digitalis tablets in the unlabeled vial, about the cutthroat people who, according to Mason, were hijacking patients from board-and-care facilities. "I'll let you know when we're ready to release Mr. Pomerantz's body."

6

HILDA RHEINHART WASN'T in, Mason told Jessie when she phoned the retirement home. She was at a doctor's appointment and would be back in an hour or so.

"By then it'll be close to dinner, and right after that we're having a bridal shower for Clara. I know Hilda will want to be there. Tomorrow morning around ten will be better."

"Clara is one of your staff?"

"Clara's a resident. She's eighty-three, and she's marrying Simon, who's seventy-nine. Not the first couple who met here at the Golden Palms," Mason said with pride.

At least someone was happy. The thought of two old people finding love or companionship late in life made Jessie smile. "Have you located anyone who spoke with Mr. Pomerantz?"

"Not yet. We're working as quickly as we can, without getting people upset," he added, his tone conveying that he didn't need to be reminded.

She thanked Mason and hung up. She was on the phone with Directory Assistance, asking for the listing for Morton Productions—"As in salt," she told the operator, half smiling as she repeated Stanley Goldblum's reference, when she heard Karl Espes call, "Drake, in my office," from across the room.

Turning in his direction, she said, "Be right there, Lieutenant," and quickly wrote down the Manhattan number. She rose from her chair.

"Simms and Boyd are with me. Where's Okum? I want to talk to all of you."

She hadn't seen the other detectives since they returned from the field. "Phil is—"

"Right here, sir," Phil said, appearing at her elbow, wiping something powdery from his mouth with the back of his hand. He avoided Jessie's eyes.

Espes turned on his heel and disappeared into his office, shutting the door behind him.

Jessie hadn't made up her mind about her supervisor. He'd come to West L.A. from Foothill Division three months ago to replace Jack Kalish, who had taken an indefinite leave to nurse his wife after she'd suffered a stroke. Espes had given Jessie a hard time at first—partly, she believed, because he was close friends with Frank Pruitt's nemesis at Parker Center—but he'd soon turned more civil. And that was before she broke up with Frank.

She still missed Kalish. And she still thought Espes resembled a rodent with his beady brown eyes and sharp, pointed teeth. So who's perfect? Phil had said.

Certainly not Detective Marty Simms. He and Boyd were sitting on metal chairs in front of Espes's desk when Jessie and Phil entered the lieutenant's office. She chose the empty chair next to Boyd. Phil sat next to Simms.

She liked Ed Boyd—the young, six-foot-tall Arkansas native with the freckled, country-boy face and strawberry-blond hair was genuinely nice. She wasn't sure about Simms. At five feet eight with a slight build, he had thick, curly black hair, unfriendly brown eyes tented by bushy brows, a short, squat nose, and permanently chapped lips that he was always picking.

And major attitude. Which hadn't improved during the two years he'd transferred to West L.A. from Wilshire. Sometimes she wished he'd stayed there.

Espes dropped the folder he'd been examining and leaned back against his upholstered chair. Sitting behind the wood-tone Formica desk, he was all shoulders and looked shorter than his five feet ten inches. His light brown hair, always close-cropped, was newly shorn, like a badly mowed lawn.

"What's happening with the hooker?" he asked.

Phil told him about the woman they'd talked to this morning. "This Lucinda knows something, but she's too afraid to talk."

"Put me in a room alone with her, I could figure out a way to persuade her." Simms smirked.

"Come on," Boyd chided with his soft twang.

"So can Okum." Espes fixed his eyes on Simms. Back to Phil: "I'm getting flak from a women's group—they think we're not moving on this because we don't care when a hooker's killed."

"Which isn't true," Jessie said.

Simms grunted and shot her a look she couldn't interpret. Was he implying that she and Phil weren't putting their best effort into solving the hooker's murder? Or that they shouldn't be wasting their efforts? She knew Simms didn't like women— something about his mother having dumped the family for a career.

"Denying the accusations won't make them go away." Espes tapped a pencil on his desk and looked at Jessie. "What's with the baby? You struck out with the ERs and clinics. Anything new?"

Was that a criticism? She cleared her throat. "Going on the assumption that the mother may be a high school student, we contacted all the area schools. The problem is, a lot of the staff are off for the summer, and the people we *did* talk to won't identify which of their students were in late-term pregnancy when school ended in June. They claimed they'd be violating the student's constitutional rights."

The principals had even been reluctant to reveal how many pregnant students were attending their schools. Jessie had been shocked, and depressed, by the high numbers.

Espes snorted. "What about the rights of that baby?"

"What rights?" Simms raised his brows. "Do babies have rights?"

"We don't even know that the mother was in school at all,"

Jessie said. "She may have dropped out. Or she may be older." She could be from anywhere—a different city, a different state.

"Maybe the mom didn't check into an ER," Boyd offered. "Maybe she went to a private doctor."

Jessie shook her head. "If she went to her own OB or family physician with postpartum hemorrhaging, he'd know something was wrong because he didn't deliver the baby. If she went to a doctor she *didn't* know, he'd be suspicious. And the media have been giving this a lot of play." Gary was making sure it got decent daily coverage in the *Times*.

Simms said, "Maybe she found a doctor who isn't so bright. Or one who doesn't watch the tube." He shrugged.

"Good point. Or maybe her doctor knows but feels bad about turning her in." Espes was rolling the pencil between his fingers. "Find out."

Phil exchanged a quick look with Jessie. "I think it's a waste of time, Lieutenant. We don't even know that she *got* medical help. Basically, unless we get an anonymous call from someone close to the mother, I see this getting filed with the other unsolveds."

Jessie said, "I think the department should offer a reward."

"You do, do you?" Espes studied her.

"*Both* of us do," Phil said.

Espes snorted. "*Both* of you willing to donate toward it from your paychecks?"

"Don't look at me." Simms turned his pockets inside out. "What about you, Ed?"

"Cut it out." Espes dropped the pencil on his desk. "I'll bring up the reward, see what the brass says. In the meantime, it won't hurt to make some calls to gynecologists and OBs and family physicians." He paused. "So we're doing zero for two, huh?" He shook his head. "Any *good* news to tell me?"

"We *did* identify the old man found in the park." Jessie told him what they'd learned. "I'm waiting for a call from Pomerantz's New York physician, to find out whether he was taking digitalis. And we should be hearing from the cab companies today. If none of their drivers picked up Pomerantz, I'll call the other local companies. I also contacted the Brooklyn police. They're going to search Pomerantz's apartment for any pertinent information."

"Don't spend too much time on this, Drake. The old guy probably had a heart attack. You identified him. Good. Now concentrate on the hooker and the baby."

"Somebody moved the body."

"That doesn't mean he was murdered."

"What about the unlabeled vial of digitalis?"

Espes expelled a breath. "Drake—"

"The retirement home administrator thinks Pomerantz may have suffered a heart attack as a result of being hijacked to another facility. That would make it a homicide, wouldn't it?"

Espes grunted. "The administrator's probably a wanna-be screenwriter like everybody else in this city, trying his plot on you before he pitches it to his agent." But he looked thoughtful, and he was tapping the pencil again on his desk. "Drake, you keep with the old man since he was yours first. Okum, start making calls to doctors."

Phil threw Jessie a baleful look.

"And I want both of you to lean on the hooker's girlfriend until she talks." He faced Boyd. "What are you and Simms working?"

"We're still trying to ID the suspect who killed the shopkeeper on Robertson. And tomorrow Marty and I have to testify in Santa Monica about the Pillow Killer."

"Make sure you take along lots of Halls," Phil said. "Mentholated," he added.

Simms laughed. Espes and Boyd were smiling. Jessie rolled her eyes in mock despair but couldn't blame the others. The motive *was* bizarre—an elderly man smothering his wife of forty-eight years with a pillow because he was fed up with her late-night coughing. If it weren't so pathetic, it would have been perfect material for Leno. She felt sorry for the dead woman. For the old man, too. What would they do to him? Ship him off to prison?

"What's with the off ramp shooting this morning?" Espes asked. "Is that wrapped up nice and tidy for the D.A.?"

"The shooter's in custody, and we have witnesses. No motive, other than the fact that the other car cut him off." Boyd shook his head.

Simms said, "I'd like to cut the shooter's head off, plus a few other parts of his anatomy," and Jessie didn't disagree.

"How's the kid?" Phil asked quietly.

She held her breath.

"Hanging on by a thread," Boyd said softly. "Lots of internal bleeding. They don't know if they can stop it."

No one spoke for a moment. Then Espes cleared his throat and said, "That's it, then. Oh, yeah—one more thing." Walking around his desk, he picked up a stack of stapled papers and handed a set to each of the detectives.

"The chief wants a department-wide review of gender and race relations. So each of us has to fill out this evaluation. Have it completed and on my desk by the end of next week."

7

"THANK YOU, MARK Fuhrman," Phil muttered, slapping the questionnaire onto his desk.

"Not really his fault, is it?" Jessie said, but she could understand why Phil and the others were upset.

It was several years since the former West L.A. detective had brought the division under an intense and embarrassing international spotlight during the O.J. Simpson criminal trial, several years since the media had repeatedly explored accounts of MAW—Men Against Women—an underground group to which Fuhrman had allegedly belonged. Fuhrman was long gone, and MAW had supposedly disbanded. But the ugly echoes had lingered.

"What's he like?" her sister Helen had excitedly asked, phoning late at night from the Chicago suburb where she'd lived. She'd been disappointed when Jessie had told her she didn't really know Fuhrman; she'd been working Burglary at the time, and her interaction with Fuhrman and the other Homicide detectives had been minimal. Frances had phoned, too. "I can't understand why anyone would want to work in a disgustingly sexist, racist environment like that," she'd exclaimed. And Gary had wanted the inside scoop on Fuhrman, on O.J., on MAW.

Like her fellow female officers, Jessie had experienced harassment since joining the police force, and not just at West L.A. During her probationary period several male officers had tried to get her into trouble. One had instructed her to examine a body before the coroner arrived—"Lieutenant's orders," he'd said. Which, of course, was a lie. She'd tried to explain to the lieutenant what had happened, but the cop had scratched his head and stared at her, "dumbfounded" by her accusation, and his cop pals had backed him up. And all of them had grinned when the lieutenant dressed her down at roll call. The second time, she hadn't even bothered trying to explain.

Male officers had also usurped her authority in the field or left her to handle suspects alone. She'd been terrified one time when, struggling with a suspect in the backseat of a police car, she'd yelled in vain for her partner's help. Other incidents had made her furious. Always, she'd felt demeaned.

Some male detectives had refused to be partnered with her and had blatantly ignored her, sending her the message that women didn't belong in the LAPD. And when Phil had asked to be partnered with her, they'd tried to ostracize him, too. But they'd quickly backed off. Everybody liked Phil, and even though he was usually a teddy bear, you didn't want to cross him. She still wondered whether Marty Simms had been involved with all that. She'd asked Phil and he'd said, let it die. So she had.

And then there was the sexual stuff: leers and whistles; pats on the behind; tampons left on her desk; crude references during roll call to her anatomy and sex life. All of which had made her burn with humiliation and anger. And consider quitting, more than once. God knows Frances would have been thrilled. Which was probably why Jessie *hadn't* quit—that, and because she'd been determined not to give her oppressors the satisfaction.

Initially she'd ignored some of the minor incidents—"Don't be a baby," she'd told herself, unsure whether this was normal, juvenile locker-room behavior, whether she was entitled to be upset. Later, when she reported episodes of sexual harassment to her supervisor (this was before Kalish), he'd glossed over her complaints. Which had encouraged the harassers to continue, and discouraged Jessie and her female colleagues from reporting additional incidents.

Then O.J. went on trial. And Fuhrman testified. And a screenwriter produced tapes and transcripts of conversations she'd had with the detective in which he bragged about using excessive force on suspects, fabricating evidence, duping Internal Affairs. The tapes had instigated a seventeen-month LAPD investigation, and while most of Fuhrman's allegations had been found to be either exaggerations or lies, the report had concluded that his remarks about sexual harassment on the force, particularly at West L.A., were all too true.

So maybe she and all her female colleagues *should* thank Mark Fuhrman. Because of him, the department had taken a long, hard look at its practices. The LAPD report had strongly recommended changes, and Kalish had done his best to implement them, beginning with mandatory sensitivity training for everyone. Tense times all around as the division had tried to adjust to a new climate free of gender bias. Officially, MAW no longer existed, and those days were behind her, and behind West L.A.

Or were they? Women detectives were still a minority in the LAPD—about 20 percent at West L.A., she estimated—and she still heard stories from her female colleagues at other divisions, and occasionally from some at West L.A. So she had to wonder whether the bias was still there, though the behavior had been modified. And maybe it had been modified only for her, because Phil was her protector. She wasn't sure how she felt about that.

Now she and everybody else had to think about everything all over again. She wondered fleetingly what Marty Simms would be writing when he filled out his questionnaire.

She tossed the evaluation form onto her desk and punched the numbers for Morton Productions. After three rings, she heard a recording. She waited until the end and began her message.

"Sorry," a woman interrupted. "I stepped out of the office for a minute. Did you say you're with the *police*?" She sounded more curious than nervous.

"The Los Angeles Police Department. I'm Detective Drake. I understand that Morton Productions interviewed Norman Pomerantz for a documentary on Holocaust survivors. I'd like to talk to the person who conducted the interview."

"That would be me. Abigail Morton." Cautious now. "I

hope there's nothing wrong. Mr. Pomerantz *did* sign a consent form to be interviewed."

The woman sounded very young, Jessie thought, writing her name on a pad. Probably in her twenties. Quietly, she told her Pomerantz was dead.

"Jeez!" Abigail exclaimed softly. "What a sweet old man! That's so sad."

Jessie waited a moment, then asked, "When did he do the interview?"

"Three weeks ago? I'd have to check my calendar to tell you the exact date. What happened, do you know?"

"We're not certain at this point. He may have had a heart attack." She debated, then said, "We're not ruling out foul play."

"No kidding! But why would someone kill him? He was so *nice*."

"I was hoping you might be able to shed some light on that. Did Mr. Pomerantz say anything unusual when he was being interviewed? Did he say he was nervous about anything or anyone?"

"No, nothing. He was in great spirits, joking a lot. He had a great time doing the interview, which made me feel good. And he was excited about going to L.A."

"Did he say why he was going?"

"No. He told me about the trip before we started taping. I teased him and asked him if he was going to see a girlfriend. He just laughed. But he had this mysterious smile, you know? Like he was looking forward to something special."

"Do you think he might have talked to any of your staff that day?"

Abigail laughed. "There's not much staff. I'm doing this documentary for film school. NYU," she added. "I did get a business phone—I guess that's how you reached me. And I rent a studio for the interviews and use the studio's sound tech. I do the lighting myself, so I was with Mr. Pomerantz from the time he arrived till he left. I don't think he talked to anyone, but I can ask."

"I'd appreciate that," Jessie said. "Can I get a copy of the videotaped interview?"

"It's unedited. I've been conducting more interviews, and I haven't had time to edit the ones already done."

"Unedited is fine," Jessie told her. Maybe better, she thought. "Can you FedEx it to me overnight? I'll give you my credit card number."

"Sure. I'll make a copy and get it out before FedEx closes."

Jessie gave Abigail her Visa card number and the West L.A. station Butler address, thanked her, and hung up.

Maybe she'd ask Espes to reimburse her, depending on what was on the tape. Probably nothing that would help the investigation—not if Mason was right, and Pomerantz had been abducted by mercenary board-and-care recruiters, and had died in the process.

Every division handed out a daily occurrence sheet—a d.o.— listing the crimes committed the previous day in that division. Jessie went downstairs to Records and examined the last three weeks' reports. No hijackings of the elderly had taken place in West L.A. Good news for the elderly and West L.A.

Back upstairs, she walked over to CAPS (Crimes Against Persons) and checked the teletypes pinned to the bulletin board.

Two listings interested her, one from 77th Division, the other from Devonshire. Both involved abductions from board-and-care facilities.

At 77th she spoke to a detective with CAPS who told her the two men believed to be responsible for forcibly removing three elderly residents of a twelve-bed facility had been picked up and charged and were in the downtown jail, awaiting trial.

The detective at Devonshire, Andy O'Connor, hadn't been as lucky.

"Sons of bitches are still out there," he told Jessie. "It took us all day to locate four of the six old people they kidnapped. We still don't know where the other two are."

"How many suspects?"

"Four males. Ask the old people what they looked like, and you get four different descriptions. They can't even agree on the nationalities." He grunted. "So why are you interested?"

Jessie explained about Pomerantz and repeated what Mason had suggested.

"It wouldn't surprise me if that's what happened," O'Connor said. "Some of these old people look like they're about to keel over any minute. They get kidnapped, their tickers go. If I find anything, I'll let you know. And vice versa."

"I'll be in touch," Jessie promised.

Phil had been going through lists of OBs, grumbling loudly after each phone call. Jessie took pity and was about to offer her help when the phone rang.

It was William Cole, Pomerantz's doctor.

Finally. Her breath quickening in anticipation, she told him about Pomerantz's death.

"Norman's *dead?*" Cole exclaimed. "I examined him not too long ago, and he seemed fine. What happened?"

"We found a vial with Lanoxin tablets in his pocket, but the vial had no label. We're trying to ascertain—"

"I've *never* prescribed digitalis for Norman," Cole interrupted, clearly disturbed. "Are you saying he overdosed on digitalis?"

So someone *had* planted the digitalis on Pomerantz. "We won't know anything until we get the autopsy results."

"But you said he had a vial of the pills. Where did he *get* them? And why would he take them?"

Great questions. Jessie thanked Cole for his information and at his urging, promised she'd get back to him with the autopsy results. With all the negative press about money-grubbing physicians, it was reassuring to know that Pomerantz's doctor cared about his patients, even after they were dead.

Phil had been listening to the conversation. "So?" he asked after she hung up the phone.

"Soooo," she said, drawing out the word. "Cole never prescribed Lanoxin for Pomerantz." She allowed herself a self-satisfied, "I-told-you-so" smile.

"So Pomerantz got them from someone else."

"From who? You know I'm right. Someone planted the pills. Ergo, Pomerantz was killed."

Phil swiveled in his chair. "Mason says Pomerantz couldn't have gotten the stuff from one of the other residents, but maybe he's saying that 'cause he's scared."

"Come on, Phil. Why would Pomerantz have taken digitalis without a doctor's prescription?"

"Who knows?" Phil shrugged. "Maybe he didn't feel a hundred percent. So he's sitting in the lobby, shooting the breeze with some of the residents, and he's telling one of them about his problems. And one of them says, try this, you'll feel better."

"I don't know." Jessie frowned.

"My old man's always getting pills from his pals. For his constipation, for his anxiety, his swollen ankles, his backaches. His medicine cabinet is a goddamn pharmacy. My mom and I yell at him all the time that it's dangerous for him to take stuff without a doctor's okay. He says 'Fine, I won't do it anymore.' And the next time I see him, he's telling me about some new pill his friend gave him that's gonna make him feel ten years younger. It's like we never had the conversation before." Phil shook his head and sighed.

"So you think Pomerantz died of natural causes? What was he doing at Rancho Park late at night, Phil? Who moved his body? How do we know he wasn't hijacked, like those residents Detective O'Connor found?"

"How do we know he *was*? Maybe we'll find out he took a cab to Rancho Park."

"Why?"

"To meet a woman? All I'm saying, Jess, is that we don't jump to homicide."

Jessie thought about what he'd said. "Admit it—you just don't want to make all those calls to OBs yourself."

He nodded and grinned. "That, too."

GARY ARRIVED EARLY and Jessie was running late because she'd tried on half the clothes in her closet, searching for something her mother would deem *appropriate,* until she'd settled on a cream-colored, two-piece silk suit she'd bought at half price at Loehmann's in the Back Room.

When he rang the bell she had on only the short skirt. She slipped on the jacket, buttoning it as she hurried to the front door and opened it.

He was leaning against the door jamb, holding a long-stemmed yellow rose. He handed her the flower as he stepped inside and kissed her on the mouth. She relaxed against him and thought, damn, he looked good in a double-breasted navy suit. He smelled good, too.

He followed her through the empty living room into the kitchen, where she put the rose in a bud vase. "It's beautiful," she said, stroking the velvety smooth petals.

"Glad you like it."

His tone was casual, but he was smiling with a boyish shyness that she found immensely endearing. And sexy. She lingered a moment, then said, "Give me five minutes," and left the room.

Her bedroom was stifling. She removed the jacket, then rummaged through her jewelry box for the earrings and the short strand of pearls her parents had given her not long after she and Gary had split up. A divorce gift, she'd called it, laughing morosely to her detective friend, Brenda Royes. Take what you can get, girl, Brenda had said.

She glanced at herself in the mirror over the dresser. She'd blow-dried her hair stick-straight after she'd showered, hoping to please her mother, no big deal. But the humidity had done its work, and the waves had sprung back to life. She twisted her hair behind her into a knot—very Chanel, Frances would love it—but she felt too severe, too artificial, as if she were about to stride down a runway.

What the hell, she thought, yanking out the pins and shaking her head to free her hair. She was thirty-five. She had to stop worrying about what her mother would say or think. She heard Gary call, "Ready, Jess?" and the next minute he was in the room.

She grabbed the jacket and, turning her back to him, slipped it on. "You should have knocked," she said, feeling silly, because he'd seen her undressed countless times when they were married. But everything was different now that they were dating again.

"The door was open, and I thought you were done," he said with schoolboy contrition. "Want me to leave?"

"No, that's okay." She finished buttoning the jacket and faced him. "Thanks again for the rose."

"I'm glad you like it. You look beautiful, Jess. And very appropriate, now that you have the jacket on."

She blushed under the intensity of his gaze. "She's going to hate my hair."

"It's *your* hair."

Jessie nodded and slipped the pearl studs into her ears. She lifted the necklace and was fiddling with the clasp when he moved behind her.

"I'll do that." He fastened the strand of pearls, then grazed her neck with his lips.

Her stomach curled the way it always did when he touched her. "We'd better go," she said, turning around, and then he was kissing her, and she felt tingly and warm, and not because the room was like a sauna.

"My mom will kill us if we're late," she said, reluctant to pull away.

He sighed. "Remind me again why we're not sleeping together?"

She laughed and shoved him gently. "Because it's not a good idea."

"Says who?" His scowl was exaggerated.

"Dr. Renée." Renée Altman was a popular radio talk-show psychologist and one of Jessie's childhood friends. Jessie had caught her program several times—first out of loyalty and curiosity, then out of interest. She'd been fascinated hearing people reveal their most intimate secrets on air and knew she'd probably be addicted to the show if she had more time to listen.

"Dr. Renée's probably a frustrated, man-hating woman who wants to make everyone as miserable as she is," Gary said.

"She's happily married, as if you didn't know." Renée and her husband had attended Jessie and Gary's wedding, and the two couples had socialized once in a while before drifting apart. "She just doesn't believe in sex outside of marriage." Jessie picked up a black Chanel purse—another gift from her mother—and slipped a lipstick inside. "Speaking of which, the administrator of the retirement home where Pomerantz stayed told me two of his residents are getting married. Isn't that sweet?"

"Adorable. I'm jealous as hell. What's with Pomerantz, by the way? Case closed?"

"Not yet." She told him about her conversation with Stanley Goldblum and Abigail Morton. "Both of them got the feeling Pomerantz had a special reason for coming to L.A."

"He probably heard about all the action at the retirement home." Gary smiled. "So what if he had a special reason, Jess? That doesn't make his death suspicious. He was an old guy with a heart problem."

She reminded herself that her ex-husband was a crime reporter and said nothing about Mason's hijacking theory, or about the fact that the digitalis pills found in Pomerantz's pocket hadn't been prescribed for him. "You're probably right. That's what Phil thinks."

Outside the house, Gary waited while she locked the door. She brought two fingers to her lips, then touched them to the oblong hammered-silver cylinder Gary had helped her nail to the doorjamb. Her mezuzah. Three months ago her Judaic studies instructor, Ezra, had given her the case and the rolled parchment containing biblical verses, hand-written in Hebrew, that it housed. To protect you in your home, Ezra had told her.

She thought about her mother, and kissed the mezuzah case again, and hoped its aegis would extend to the Ivy.

A waitress led them to a center table where her parents were already seated. They stood when they saw Jessie and Gary. At five feet three inches, Frances looked elfin next to Arthur, who was six inches taller. For years she'd claimed to be six years younger than her husband, but she'd admitted her real age—she would turn sixty-one in October, a month before Arthur did—when she'd revealed her traumatic past.

Arthur shook his ex-son-in-law's hand, then turned to Jessie and hugged her and murmured, "Good to see you again, sweetheart," in her ear.

She'd seen him briefly yesterday, at Helen's brunch. He looked trim and fit and younger than his years, but now she noticed new fine lines around his hazel eyes, more gray in his dark brown hair. Probably because she'd been thinking about Pomerantz and the Golden Palms, and the elderly who lived there. She'd never really contemplated what would happen to her parents when they could no longer take care of each other, or if one of them died. . . .

"Gary," Frances said with simple majesty, extending her hand and leaning forward to accept his kiss on a cheek smoothed several years ago by plastic surgery. "I'm so glad you've joined us." She turned to Jessie. "You look beautiful, dear. The pearls are perfect, although you might want to try an updo next time with that suit. Dana Buchman?"

Jessie nodded, suppressing a laugh, and kissed her mother.

"You look terrific, Mom. Aren't Helen and Neil coming?" She was a little nervous for Gary—and okay, for herself, she admitted—and would have liked reinforcements.

"They should have been here by now," Frances said, her tone more disapproving than worried. "Why don't we have drinks while we're waiting?" She sat down and beckoned to the waitress, who came over and took their orders.

"So how's the medical convention?" Gary asked Arthur.

"Boring." He smiled, deepening the cleft in his chin. "They usually are. Your line of work is far more exciting, I should think. You're still happy at the *Times*?"

Small talk for the family of the divorced, Jessie thought, playing with her salad fork. It was especially awkward for Gary, who didn't know how to address her parents. They'd discussed it on the way here. "Mr. Claypool" and "Mrs. Claypool" was too formal; "Arthur" and "Frances" a little presumptuous. So far he'd avoided the problem.

"They're lucky to have someone of his caliber." Frances flashed a brilliant smile at Gary. "I *know* you have a *wonderful* career ahead of you."

For Frances, "wonderful career" meant a Pulitzer Prize piece that would propel Gary to literary fame. That's how she'd introduced her then future son-in-law to all her friends, after she'd given up trying to discourage Jessie from marrying him. Jessie glanced at Gary—he didn't seem to mind her mother's comment.

"Now if you could only talk some sense into Jessica, Gary." Frances shook her head, barely disturbing her carefully combed and lacquered blond hair.

"I'm proud of what Jessie does. Fighting the fight." He put his arm around Jessie's shoulder.

"*Really?*" Frances said, her smile freezing in place.

Jessie felt a surprising flash of sympathy for her mother— Gary had always been her ally in trying to convince Jessie to quit her job. She took a sip of water and wondered whether he was playing games with Frances, or hoping to score points with Jessie. He'd told her he'd come to terms with the fact that she loved her job; she didn't doubt his sincerity, but worried sometimes that he was deluding himself.

She was thinking about the possibilities when the waitress arrived with their drinks, followed by Helen and Neil, walking with their arms entwined, their faces glowing. So the therapy was continuing to work its magic, Jessie thought, pleased for her sister and brother-in-law, who'd survived a few rough years.

They made a striking couple. Helen's upswept halo-blond hair gave her a fairy-tale-princess quality. Neil, tall and good-looking with coal-gray eyes and almost black hair, would have done Cinderella proud. Still no gray in his hair, even though he was forty-four, fourteen years older than Helen.

"Sorry we're late," Helen said, walking over to Frances. "Matthew wanted me to read him a bedtime story before we left." She bent and kissed her cheek.

Her sister and mother looked so much alike, Jessie thought for the hundredth time as the waitress took their orders: straight, golden-blond hair, moss-green eyes, heart-shaped faces. Jessie's eyes were green, too, but a different green, with flecks of gray, and her face was oval, framed by hair a warm chestnut brown like her father's, before the invasion of gray.

Sometimes she felt oversized next to her mother and sister, who had petite, delicate frames; sometimes their physical sameness made her feel excluded. Their temperaments were the same, too, and their tendency to get migraines. Jessie didn't mind being excluded from either.

Frances was in an exceptionally pleasant mood—but then, she always enjoyed playing hostess. She described the Cézanne exhibit she'd seen this afternoon at the Los Angeles County Museum of Art, and Neil talked about his latest consulting project for a Seattle engineering firm. Gary entertained everyone with anecdotes about celebrities he'd met, and Arthur mostly listened, as usual. And Jessie tried to figure out when, if at all, she could ask her mother about her Jewish family. Maybe she should wait for another time, when the two of them were alone.

"Well, this is wonderful," Frances said when they were finished with the main course. "All of us together, just family. It's been too long, hasn't it, Gary?" She smiled at him.

"Too long. That's what I keep telling your daughter." He smiled, too, and winked at Jessie.

She kicked him under the table.

"Neil and I have an announcement to make," Helen said. "We were going to wait a while to tell you, but—" She glanced at her husband, who nodded and took her hand. "We're going to have a baby." She laughed shyly.

Neil drew her closer and kissed her. They were both laughing now, and Frances, in a voice that sounded just a little strained to Jessie, said, "Helen, how exciting!" and Arthur rose from his chair and embraced first Helen, then Neil.

"You look shell-shocked, Jess," Helen teased. "Aren't you happy for us?"

"Of course I am." She stood. "I was waiting my turn."

She kissed Neil and hugged Helen tightly, her eyes filled with tears. She was overcome with a confusing rush of emotions. She *was* happy for her sister and brother-in-law, who had been trying for some time to have another child, and for Matthew, who had confided to her his yearning for a sibling. She tried to dismiss the niggling worry that Helen wasn't ready to take on the stress of having another child, that she should have waited a while longer.

And she felt a pang of melancholy for her own child that had almost been. Hers and Gary's. She didn't look at him but knew he must be thinking the same thing.

"When is the baby due, Helen?" Frances asked.

"Mid-January. I finish my third month next week. I'm going to have an amnio, of course, but I'm sure everything's fine. We've decided we don't want to know the baby's sex," she added.

"*Helen* decided," Neil said, sounding not unhappy.

"And you agreed," she said sweetly. "Matthew is just thrilled, of course. We told him tonight, just before we came here." She exchanged another blissful glance with Neil.

"I would have waited a while to tell him—a pregnancy can seem to take forever. But you're his parents." Frances's smile was a mild reproof. "Have you thought about names?"

"We're not sure about a boy's name. If it's a girl, we're

thinking about Louise. If that's okay with you, Dad." Helen smiled at her father.

"More than okay." His eyes misted.

It was strange seeing her father near tears, Jessie thought—he generally kept his emotions in check. And it was lovely and fitting of Helen to name a girl after his mother. Louise had died almost ten years ago; her husband, William Matthew (Helen's Matthew was named for him), shortly after. Jessie and Helen had wonderful memories of Christmases at their home in Pittsburgh.

Frances said, "If it's a boy, what about Jacob, my father's name?"

Jessie stared at her mother, unsure at first whether she'd heard right. Frances had mentioned the Hebrew version of her father's name, Yaakov, only once, three months ago, and had done so reluctantly. Maybe she was overcome with sentimentality at the thought of having a second grandchild. Or maybe it was the three glasses of wine she'd drunk during the meal.

Helen and Neil exchanged quick looks. "I don't know, Mom," she said. "It's so . . ."

Jewish, Jessie thought. "*I'm Episcopalian, like Mom and Dad,*" Helen had insisted angrily when Jessie had told her about their mother's startling past. "*So is Matthew.*" Then she'd stormed out of the room.

"We'll think about it, Mom." Neil looked and sounded uncomfortable. "We have a long time to decide."

"Well, don't feel *obligated.*" Frances's nostrils flared. She picked up her menu.

"Mom," Helen began.

"Let's order dessert, shall we?" Frances's tone was cool, but her voice quivered with hurt.

"What was your father like, Mom?" Jessie asked, seizing the opportunity she'd longed for.

"It's not important. I think I'll indulge and have the white chocolate lemon cake. It's sinfully delicious, and they decorate it exquisitely, with fresh flowers. What about you, Arthur?"

"I really want to know, Mom." Out of the corner of her

eye she saw Helen's frown. Her father looked uneasy, too, but she felt Gary's reassuring hand on hers.

"I don't remember much. I was a little girl when the war broke out. I *told* you that." Snapping now, still hiding behind the menu.

"Tell me what you *do* remember."

Frances inhaled sharply. Helen blinked nervously. Jessie was nervous, too—maybe she'd pushed her mother too far—but she told herself that Frances wouldn't make a scene in public. Still, she tensed as her mother put down her menu.

"I remember my father's beard," Frances said in a low voice. "It was a thick, dark brown. He let me play with it whenever I sat on his lap, and with his long sideburns, too. I'd curl the hairs around my fingers, and he'd pretend to yelp. Then he'd tickle me." She smiled lightly, but her face was flushed. "That's my memory."

"What else, Mom?" Jessie prodded softly, not wanting to break the mood.

Frances was silent a moment, her green eyes focused somewhere above Jessie's head. When she spoke again, it was in a tender voice Jessie had never heard before. "He had a fur-trimmed hat and black silk coat that he wore on Saturdays and holidays—like a smoking jacket, but longer. I loved touching them, they were so soft, so plush." Unconsciously, she ran her fingers across the white tablecloth. "And they smelled of pipe tobacco. I loved that, too." Another smile, more wistful now.

"Once in a while he'd let me try them on. It always made my brothers and sisters jealous, and my mother disapproved. 'You're spoiling her,' she'd say. But he always let me do it." She glanced at Jessie and wiped tears from her eyes. "Now see what you've done," she said softly.

Her mother had used those words so many times in the past to chastise, to foreshadow punishment. But there was no anger now. "Tell me more, Mom. I want to know everything."

Frances cleared her throat and shook her head quickly. "Jessica, we can talk about this another time. This isn't dinner conversation."

"You're making Mom uncomfortable," Helen said.

Jessie shot her sister an irritated look, then turned to Frances. *"Please,* Mom. This is the perfect time. We're all here." Leaning her elbow on the table, she cupped her chin with her palm and waited.

"Jessica." Frances shook her head again, then glanced at Arthur. He squeezed her shoulder lightly and nodded.

"He was very kind," she said, facing Jessie. "All the servants adored him. And he was smart, and generous." She paused. "I have this memory of people always coming to the house, and my mother telling me that I couldn't bother Tatti—" She stopped. "That I couldn't bother my father because they'd come to ask him for advice or for loans. And my mother told me he never turned anybody away. Never."

"Your family must have been well-to-do," Neil said.

Frances nodded. "We had an enormous, two-story house with beautiful gardens. We had two carriages and several horses. My mother and sisters and I had beautiful clothes. And there were *always* presents." She smiled. "My father traveled on business once in a while, and he'd always come back with jewelry or toys or special fabrics. One time he brought me a cuckoo clock. Another time he brought me the most beautiful doll for my birthday. I used to spend hours combing her hair, styling it in different ways. It was long and blond, just like mine."

The way her mother's hair used to be, Jessie thought with a stab of pity. The Polish woman in whose care Yaakov Kochinsky had left his six-year-old daughter had taken cruel pleasure in lopping off Frances's long blond tresses one morning while she was asleep. Frances had awakened to find the woman at her bedside, brandishing tufts of golden hair. An iron hand had stifled her scream.

Jessie had a million questions. She was about to ask about Frances's mother, Yiska, for whom Jessie was named, but Helen asked, "What happened to the house, Mom? Do you think it's still there?" and Jessie could see from the slight stiffening of her mother's beautiful face that a door had closed.

Frances shrugged. "I don't know."

"You could try to get it back," Gary said. "My parents told

me there are lawyers who specialize in reclaiming property for survivors."

She shook her head. "I don't think so." Smiling politely, she lifted her water goblet and took a sip.

"Did your father ever travel to Switzerland, Mom?" Neil asked.

"I assume so. The clock was from Switzerland." She sounded suddenly uninterested, as if she were describing an object she'd seen in a catalog.

"If he was wealthy, maybe he deposited money in a Swiss bank before the war, like other European Jews."

"Do you think he did?" Helen asked Frances.

Jessie had been reading about the millions of dollars Holocaust victims had deposited in numbered Swiss bank accounts, about the millions more deposited by the Nazis during the war—money they'd obtained by confiscating and selling Jewish property and art and other belongings.

She knew about the gold bullion the Swiss had bought from the Germans—over four hundred million dollars' worth—some of it looted from other countries' treasuries, some of it melted down from concentration camp inmates' wedding bands and other jewelry. And gold teeth. She shuddered again at the image.

"He may have deposited money," Frances said. "I wouldn't know." All traces of the earlier tenderness in her voice had disappeared.

"It could be quite a lot, with all the interest that's accrued over half a century." Neil gazed intently at his mother-in-law. "I heard there are billions of dollars in those dormant accounts."

Frances picked up her menu.

"I saw something in the newspaper about the Swiss banks," Helen said. "But why haven't the victims' heirs claimed the money?"

"The banks made it almost impossible," Jessie said. "Until recently they denied that there *were* millions. They insisted on all kinds of documentation—like the death certificate of the account owner, which, of course, most heirs don't have, since concentration camps didn't give death certificates. But now the banks have agreed to cooperate, and they've relaxed their standards of proof. And they're setting up a reparations fund."

"Why now?"

Jessie wasn't surprised that Helen wasn't up to date on the Swiss banks—the topic wouldn't have interested her. Had Frances read the articles? Jessie wished she could see her mother's face, but it was hidden again behind the menu. She wondered what she was thinking.

Arthur sighed. "Apparently, Helen, aside from holding on to Holocaust survivors' assets, and allowing Nazis to deposit money and gold in Swiss banks, there's evidence that the Swiss laundered money for the Nazis."

"You're kidding!" Helen exclaimed softly.

"They probably helped prolong the war," Gary said. "So much for centuries of neutrality." His smile was grim. "The Swiss have been nervous as hell since all of this came to light. Bad PR for the banks—bad for the whole country, since its main industry is banking. So now they're trying to clean up their image."

"There's a list on the Internet of some of the names attached to the dormant accounts." Neil turned to Frances. "We could access it and check for your family, Mom."

Frances lowered the menu. "Thank you, Neil. That's very sweet." Her measured, cool voice indicated otherwise. "But this doesn't concern me."

Why not? Jessie wanted to ask. *For the same reason that you never want to talk about your family? So that you can pretend you were never Freide Kochinsky?*

"The Swiss Bankers Association released a list of dormant account holders," Gary said. "The *Times* ran it last Wednesday. Almost eight hundred accounts, and I heard it's a preliminary list. You didn't see it?" he asked Jessie.

"I saw the announcement. But I didn't check the list." She hadn't known then that it might concern her. She wondered what she would have felt if she'd seen her grandfather's name. Kochinsky, Yaakov. Or Jacob. Had Frances checked?

"I heard that quite a few of the accounts belonged to Nazis. Surprise, surprise." Gary grunted.

"Really?" Neil's brows rose. "Like who?"

"Hitler's tailor, for one. Eva Zimmer, aka Eva Braun, Hitler's mistress. Willy Bauer—that was an alias for an aide to Adolf Eichmann. Kurt Herrmann—apparently, he was involved in selling the jewelry stolen from the Rothschilds. Hitler himself had an account for his royalties from *Mein Kampf*. I read that every leading member of the governing groups in all the Axis countries had funds in Switzerland."

"Unbelievable." Arthur shook his head.

"Actually, *very* believable. Switzerland was the safest place in the world to keep your money, right?" Gary smiled wryly. "You want to hear irony? The banks used the secrecy laws to prevent heirs from accessing their parents' accounts, right? Well, they *implemented* those laws in '34 to encourage Jews to leave their money and valuables for safekeeping." He paused. "Anyway, you ought to check the list. Your family may have an account."

"I think we've had enough talk about lists, don't you?" Frances said with strained politeness. "Can we order dessert, please? It's getting late."

Neil said, "Mom, if your father deposited money—"

"I *told* you, I'm not interested in that blood money, if in fact there is any." Her face was flushed. "Thank goodness, I don't need it. Even if I did, I wouldn't touch it."

"Why not, if it's legally yours?" Helen asked. "Your father would want you to have it, wouldn't he?"

Points of red dotted Frances's cheeks.

"Leave it alone, Helen," Jessie said quietly. "It's Mom's decision." She wasn't sure how she would feel about claiming the money, if there was any.

"Of *course* it's her decision." Helen leaned toward her mother. "But why should the Swiss benefit from the money your father worked so hard to earn? The money they tried to steal?"

"All the money in the world won't change what happened," Frances said in a fierce whisper. "All it would do is remind me of everything I've tried to forget. I don't want it, not one dime!"

"Ten minutes ago you asked me if I'd name a boy after your father. Wouldn't that be a reminder, too?"

So cruel, Jessie thought, wincing.

Frances stared at Helen. "Ten minutes ago you weren't interested in being Jewish, were you?" She paused. "But you're right," she said softly. "It was a stupid suggestion. I can't imagine what came over me."

9

MASON KNOCKED ON the door of the second-floor room. "Hilda, I have someone with me who wants to visit with you. May we come in?"

Not exactly a visit, Jessie thought, annoyed by the administration's patronizingly false joviality.

"One second," came the muted reply.

It was almost a minute before the door was opened by a slender, elderly woman. She smiled shyly past Mason at Jessie, who was standing behind him.

"Come in, come in!" She stepped aside to let them enter, then walked across the room to a cherry wood rocking chair, where she settled herself and smiled again at Jessie while Mason shut the door.

The second-floor room was furnished like the bedroom of Pomerantz's suite, but was smaller and looked more lived in. A navy-and-beige, chevron-patterned afghan draped the edge of the bed. Centered on the dresser was a gilt-edged, mirrored vanity tray holding a mother-of-pearl handled brush and comb, tubes of lipsticks, and an assortment of perfume bottles, including some miniatures.

On the nightstand, next to a framed photo of a middle-aged man, a stack of well-read, dog-eared paperbacks leaned precariously to the right. On the cover of the top one Jessie could see the heroine, her ebony hair flung back, vibrant and seductive in embossed hot fuchsia and bright yellow. A romance novel. Cute, Jessie thought.

The musty odor Jessie had noticed in the hall yesterday and today was stronger here, maybe because the room, though air-conditioned, was warmer than the lobby. Not warm enough for the room's occupant—she'd draped an off-white, crocheted shawl around her shoulders, covering up the bodice of her rose-colored cotton dress. On her lap lay two knitting needles attached to an oblong length of mint-green knitted stuff that trailed into a ball of yarn at her feet.

"Hilda, this is the nice detective I told you about," the administrator said in the same overly genial tone. "Her name is Jessica Drake, and she wants to ask you a few questions."

The woman's smile had frozen, quickly replaced by disappointment, then anxiety. Mason had warned Jessie that Hilda Rheinhart would be nervous—that was one of the reasons she was handling this interview alone. Two cops would have been intimidating.

She smiled warmly at the woman. "Please call me Jessie." Stepping closer, she extended her hand and, leaning forward, caught a whiff of a powdery, floral scent. Roses, she decided. Her Grandmother Louise had smelled of lilacs.

Gingerly, Hilda accepted Jessie's hand with long, gnarled fingers. "That's a man's name," she said, a question in her voice. "Like Jesse James, the outlaw. I read about him." Her aquamarine-blue eyes blinked rapidly.

"It can be." Jessie smiled again and carefully released her hand. The old woman's skin felt like parchment and looked easily bruised, judging by the patches of mottled reddish brown and purple.

She must have been beautiful when she was younger. Her nose was short and straight with a defined tip, her ears small and dainty, her lined high forehead patrician. Her skin had sagged, softening the outline of her chin, and her sculpted cheekbones had been made more prominent by the shadowy hollows beneath them. Amid puffs of freshly combed, cloud-white hair, Jessie could see the pink of her scalp.

Hilda had brushed circles of pink blusher onto skin already purpled by the underlying crisscross of capillaries, and pink lipstick gleamed on her corrugated lips. Jessie wondered whether she always put on makeup, or whether she'd done so this morning for Jessie. Company. "She rarely has visitors," Mason had said, and Jessie had felt a pang of sadness.

"Well, I'll leave you two alone," Mason said, sounding eager to make his exit. He took a few steps toward the door then stopped. "Unless you'd like me to stay, Hilda?"

She shook her head slowly and kept her eyes on Mason until he left the room and shut the door behind him.

Jessie pulled over a chair and sat down near Hilda. "I like your shawl. Did you crochet it yourself?"

Hilda nodded. "The doctor says working with my hands is good for my arthritis. Also, it makes the time pass." She had an accent almost identical to Stanley Goldblum's.

"What are you making now?" Jessie asked, pointing to the green.

"A blanket for Tracy's baby niece. Tracy gives out medicines. I have a closet full of things—crocheted, knitted. You know how to knit?"

Jessie shook her head.

"I make things faster than I can give them away." She sighed. "I used to do needlepoint, too, but my eyes aren't so good anymore."

Jessie settled into the chair. "I just have a few questions to ask, Mrs. Rheinhart."

"You're really a detective? You have a badge?" There was a hint of nervousness in her voice. "You're such a pretty girl."

Jessie said "thank you" and smiled, hoping to ease the woman's anxiety, and because it had been a long time since anyone had called her a girl. She showed Hilda the badge and waited patiently until she'd examined it and returned it to Jessie.

Jessie pocketed her badge. "I understand that you knew Mr. Pomerantz."

The woman compressed her already thin lips into a line, then sighed. "Mr. Mason said he's dead. It's true?"

"Yes, I'm sorry," Jessie said gently. "We're trying to find out a little more about him, how he spent his last few days, whom he saw." No response from Hilda. "Stanley Goldblum told me he recommended the Golden Palms to Mr. Pomerantz because you live here."

Hilda cocked her head in a birdlike motion. "You spoke to Stanley? How is he?"

"He's fine." Jessie waited.

"That's good." She nodded. "Stanley was a friend of my late husband, Leon, he should rest in peace." Moving to the edge of the rocker, she pulled herself up and walked slowly but steadily to the nightstand. She brought back the photo and showed it to Jessie. "That's Leon."

"Very handsome." He *was*—silver-and-black hair, a square chin, twinkling blue eyes, a great smile.

Hilda looked pleased. "He was a catch, my Leon," she said tenderly. She stood lost in thought for a moment, then returned the photo to the nightstand and resumed her seat. "Stanley's a nice man. He calls once in a while."

She set the rocker in motion. The shawl had slipped off her shoulders, revealing her dress's elbow-length sleeves. Jessie stared with dreadful fascination at the two-inch ribbon of six faded blue numbers on her left forearm. Hilda adjusted the wrap, and the numbers were gone, but Jessie could still see snatches of blue in the spaces between the shell-shaped design of the stitches.

She wanted to ask Hilda why she'd kept the numbers, wondered why Norman Pomerantz hadn't. "Did you know Mr. Pomerantz before he came here?"

Hilda shook her head. "But I heard about him from Stanley so much, it was almost like I *did* know him. 'Nachum this' and 'Nachum that.' " She smiled lightly, deepening the creases at the sides of her mouth.

"Did you talk to Mr. Pomerantz?"

"Sure, I talked to him." She sounded indignant. "He was Stanley's friend. I introduced him around, told him what to eat, what not to eat. At our age you have to be careful, and some of the food they serve you here?" She rolled her eyes and shook her head.

Jessie couldn't help smiling. "What did you talk about?"

A guarded look came over Hilda's face. "Nothing special. People we knew from when I lived back East. The old times, the camps." Her hands had tightened on the arms of the rocker, pushing the veins upward into low mountain ridges.

No doubt she meant the concentration camps. "Did Mr. Pomerantz tell you why he came to Los Angeles?" Again Jessie stared at the woman's left forearm, at the numbers hidden beneath the shawl.

"Not really. Everybody likes to visit Los Angeles. Leon and I did, forty-seven years ago, and we fell in love with the Pacific Ocean. So we moved here, just like that." She picked up the knitting needles and wrapped yarn around the index finger of her left hand.

Hilda had visibly tensed, and she wasn't looking at Jessie. "Do your children live here, too?" Jessie asked, wanting to put her at ease, and was immediately sorry she'd asked, that she'd forgotten that the woman rarely received visitors.

"We don't have any children," Hilda said quietly. "Not that we didn't want." Her sigh sounded like air escaping from a balloon.

Jessie's face was flushed. "I'm sorry. I didn't mean to pry."

"That's all right. How could you know?" Hilda looked at her kindly, then reached over and patted her hand. "Sometimes I think, if I had children, I wouldn't be here, I'd be living with one of them. But many of the other residents have children, so it really makes no difference." She shrugged. "You know what my mother, of blessed memory, used to say?"

Jessie smiled. "What's that?"

" 'A parent can take care of eight children, but eight children can't take care of one parent.' I didn't believe her then, but now I see it's true." A touch of bitterness had entered her voice.

Jessie thought again about her own parents, about what would happen when one or both of them needed care. Would they move in with Helen and Neil? With Jessie? She didn't think she'd mind having her father live with her, but she couldn't picture sharing a house with her mother. She'd left home to escape Frances, and so had Helen, but that didn't rid them of the obligation to care for her. They could always send her to a retirement home like the Golden Palms. . . .

"This looks like a nice place," Jessie said. "Mr. Mason seems to care about the residents, and I understand there are lots of interesting activities." Was this how family members convinced themselves they were doing right by putting their parents into the care of strangers? *Promised her the moon, gave her crap.*

Hilda snorted. "Mr. Mason is worried he'll have empty beds." She paused. "In the end, you're still alone. But what else is there?" She inserted a needle into the length of green. Click, click.

Jessie felt a wave of sadness for Hilda, whom she hardly knew, for the other residents she'd never even met. "When was the last time you saw Mr. Pomerantz?"

The old woman rocked in silence for a few seconds. "Saturday or Sunday. I can't be sure."

By Sunday, Pomerantz had been dead. Maybe Hilda was confused about dates in general. "Do you know what day it is today?" Jessie asked gently.

"Of course I know. Tuesday. I'm old, but I'm not senile." She smiled, then dropped one needle and tapped her forehead. "It's all still here."

Jessie's face was tingling. "I'm sorry. I didn't mean to offend you." She shifted on her seat. "Do you know whether Mr. Pomerantz visited anyone in Los Angeles?"

"He didn't say, and I didn't ask." Hilda sounded suddenly edgy.

More disappointment. Both cab companies had phoned early this morning—neither had picked up Pomerantz from the Golden Palms on Saturday, or any day. She'd phoned the other L.A. cab companies and hoped to hear from them later in the day. She'd also contacted Pomerantz's other friends, whose numbers Stanley Goldblum had given her. All had been shocked and heartbroken by their friend's death, but didn't know where he'd planned to go, whom he'd planned to see.

Neither did the Brooklyn police. Detective Addison had phoned her early this morning—they'd found no clues in Pomerantz's apartment.

"Did he mention any friends?" Jessie asked.

"No." She was rocking a little faster, the metal-on-metal click, click, click of the needles keeping time with her finger, which dipped rhythmically, allowing the yarn to spin away and disappear into the sea of green.

"Did he seem to be in good health, Mrs. Rheinhart?"

"I'm a doctor?" She shrugged, still not looking at Jessie.

Jessie repressed a smile. "We found some digitalis pills in his pocket, but his doctor says he didn't prescribe them. Do you know where he could have gotten them?"

She shook her head.

"Did he mention that he had a heart condition?"

Hilda rocked and rocked. Suddenly, she stopped the rocker and dropped the length of knitted stuff onto her lap. She studied Jessie's face. "You think he died of a heart attack?"

The autopsy report still hadn't come in. "We don't know. That's why anything he said to you might be important. Do you know where he was going when he left here on Saturday?"

The woman eyed the door. She hesitated, then leaned forward. "They killed him," she whispered. Her eyes focused on the door again.

Jessie's heart thumped. "Who killed him?"

Hilda licked her lips. Her breathing was louder.

"Who killed Mr. Pomerantz, Mrs. Rheinhart?"

"He was afraid they were going to kill him, so he tried to run away. But they got him anyway. Evil never stops." She shook her head.

"Who is 'they'?" Jessie moved closer.

The old woman's blue eyes had taken on a haunted look. "You think I'm not afraid, too?" Still whispering, she cast another anxious look at the door. "I'm alone here, helpless. No family, no children to protect me."

"What are you afraid of, Hilda?"

"They're going to kill me, too, I know it! They're after my money! Just like they were after Anna Seligman's money."

Mason had mentioned a woman who'd been taken to the

bank and bilked of $1,500, but that wasn't the name Jessie remembered. Maybe the same thing had occurred to another resident. Or maybe Hilda was afraid she'd be hijacked to another facility that was after her government benefits. Was that what had happened to Pomerantz? Had he died in the process?

"Why are they after your money?" Jessie asked.

"Someone has to stop the evil, but who can do it? They're so clever." There was a feverish glint in the woman's eyes.

"Who is Anna Seligman, Hilda?"

Still no answer. Jessie bit her lips in frustration. "Mrs. Rheinhart, this could be very important. Did Mr. Pomerantz tell you that someone approached him?"

Hilda looked at Jessie for a long moment, indecision in her eyes. Jessie was sure the old woman was about to tell her something, but then she averted her head.

"He didn't tell me anything," she finally said. "I'm a little tired now." She picked up the knitting again and worked the row.

Click, click, click.

10

"HILDA IS A dear, but the truth is she's paranoid." Lilly Gorcheck smiled sadly at Jessie.

The Golden Palms manager was probably in her early forties, but her plump, matronly figure, tented in a beige, shapeless sacklike dress, aged her. She had a kind face, round and doughy and framed with black ringlets. Her eyes, an intense emerald green (contact lenses, Jessie decided), were fringed with impossibly long, spiked eyelashes, and she'd painted her Cupid's-bow mouth a bright vermilion. A voluptuous version of Betty Boop.

"Mrs. Rheinhart seems genuinely afraid that someone is after her money," Jessie said.

Another sad smile. "She doesn't have much money, I'm afraid. Just a small savings account, and what she received from her late husband's term life insurance. And of course, there's social security and Medicare benefits."

All of which, Jessie assumed, went toward paying for a private room and board at the Golden Palms. Mason had said the rates were $1,100 to $1,500 per month. "What happens when the insurance money runs out?"

"Well, she'd have to go to semiprivate," Lilly said a touch

mournfully. "That's eight hundred a month, or the state rate. Social security covers seven hundred and fourteen dollars a month rent, and ninety-two a month spending money."

Over $1,600 a month, then, for two residents. Jessie could see why facilities hired recruiters, and why no one wanted empty beds. Someone had figured out that the elderly were worth something, after all.

"Mr. Mason suggested that Mr. Pomerantz may have been hijacked by recruiters," Jessie said. "Do you think that's possible?"

"It's *possible*." The manager frowned. "We've certainly been unsettled since the hijackings started." She leaned forward. "But are you saying Mr. Pomerantz was definitely murdered?" Her lips parted slightly.

"It's a strong possibility," she said, and saw Lilly pale. "Hilda believes it. She thinks someone is going to kill her, too."

Lilly sighed. "You have to understand Hilda's background, Detective. She survived the Holocaust by a miracle. She saw her parents and siblings taken away to the crematoria." Lilly shuddered. "She's convinced that it could happen again, that she's in constant danger. When she heard what happened to Mrs. Braeburn, she was terrified—almost hysterical. Mr. Mason said he told you about that?"

Jessie nodded. *That* was the woman who'd been scammed.

"We tried to keep that quiet, but of course, all the residents found out." Lilly pinched her lips in exasperation. "And now she's heard about Mr. Pomerantz. Poor Hilda—I can understand why she's agitated, especially since she's always talking about dying."

Hilda had seemed somewhat frail, but not sickly. Then again, Jessie knew little about the infirmities of old age. "Does she have serious medical problems?"

The manager shook her head again, barely disturbing the black curls. "If she were, we couldn't keep her here. We're not a 'sniff.' "

"A sniff?"

"SNF—skilled nursing facility. They provide convalescent care. We contract with home health agencies if residents need physical or occupational therapy, oxygen, insulin shots, things like that. Medicare/MediCal pay. And we *are* licensed for non-ambulatory—people who need wheelchairs."

"I didn't see a wheelchair in Hilda's room." And she'd seen Hilda walk without assistance.

"Hilda is fully ambulatory, and proud of it." The manager smiled. "She's getting physical therapy for a fractured hip she suffered a while back, but she no longer has to use a walker. I'm not sure she still needs the therapy, either, but my guess is she likes the attention Gloria gives her. Gloria Pinkoff is the physical therapist. All our residents love her. She's a dear—so caring."

"So Hilda is in good health?" Jessie asked.

"She has elevated blood pressure, a touch of Parkinson's, some arthritis. She's going to need cataract surgery soon. But yes, I'd say she's in pretty good health, considering that she's eighty-six. But the body just doesn't work as well when you're that age. Neither does the mind." A sad smile flickered across Lilly's face. "Sometimes she imagines things. Between that, and her background . . ."

In her mind's eye Jessie could see the tattooed numbers on Hilda's arm. Pomerantz had probably removed them because he hadn't wanted a reminder of the trauma he'd survived. Had Hilda kept the numbers as a reminder to be careful?

"What about Anna Seligman?" she asked the manager.

"Who?" Her forehead creased in puzzlement.

Jessie repeated the name. "Mrs. Rheinhart said they were after Anna Seligman's money, too."

Lilly shook her head. "I don't recognize that name, and I've been here three years."

"Could she have been a resident here before that?"

"We keep records for about five years. I'll check for you." She walked to a gray metal filing cabinet against the right wall of the small office and, opening the top drawer, tabbed through the files. She faced Jessie. "Sorry. No one by that name." She shut the drawer and returned to her desk.

"Did Mr. Pomerantz talk with any of the other residents?" Mason had said no, but it always paid to double-check.

"Not as far as I've learned, and I've spoken to everyone on

staff—including the night attendants—and every resident, aside from those who are still away with family. Apparently, Mr. Pomerantz kept to himself. I didn't really spend any time with him myself, since he was just a guest." The manager said this with a note of apology, as if she'd been derelict in her duties.

"Thanks for your time. If you think of anything else, please let me know. And if Mrs. Rheinhart says anything, call me."

"I will." Lilly nodded. "But as I said, I don't think you should put too much weight into what she told you."

Mason had taken Jessie to Lilly's office, adjacent to his, and quickly left to meet with a prospective resident's family. The door to his office was shut, and he was nowhere to be seen. He was probably still busy with his prospective new resident, or hiding from Jessie.

She found her way to the kitchen and spoke to the staff and to the waitresses. No one remembered Pomerantz. Then again, he'd been here just one week, and if he kept kosher, he probably would have eaten only cereal or fruit. Even if he didn't keep kosher, he may have heard Hilda's disparaging comments about the Golden Palms's cuisine and decided to eat most of his meals out.

The activities director, a young, earnest-looking petite red-head named Lorna, didn't remember Pomerantz either. Neither did Mercedes, the head of housekeeping, or Tracy, the medication supervisor. Yes, Tracy told Jessie, three residents were on digitalis, but she'd personally given them their pills and none of the medications were missing.

Tracy was nervous. The kitchen staff and waitresses and head of housekeeping had been nervous. Rosa, the very pretty, twenty-something, pony-tailed Hispanic maid who had reported Pomerantz's possible absence to Mason, was clearly nervous, too, when Jessie approached her. She was fidgeting and licking her lips, but it was soon obvious to Jessie that the woman had no knowledge of what had happened to the dead man, or where he'd gone that Saturday.

Jessie doubted that Rosa or Tracy or any of the kitchen staff were involved with Pomerantz's death. Maybe some of them were illegals. More likely, they were all apprehensive because Jessie was a cop. As a rookie detective, having that effect on people had bothered her; now she welcomed it because most of the time it worked to her advantage. Nervous people—nervous *guilty* people—often made mistakes.

"What was Mr. Pomerantz like?" Jessie asked Rosa, and saw the young woman's shoulders relax.

"Mr. Pomerantz, he was always very friendly to me, always smiling," she said shyly in a lilting Hispanic accent. "An' he gave me a very nice tip on Friday."

She liked the fact that he'd treated her as a human being, she told Jessie, that he was neat and hadn't left his clothing and trash all over the place.

"You wouldn't *believe* what pigs some people can be," she said, but Jessie could. She'd investigated homicides where the scene of the crime—from a poor, run-down two-bedroom in South Central or Compton to a Holmby Hills mansion—had been so messy and filthy that she'd wondered how people could live like that. And her job and the criminologists' had been doubly difficult, because how did you determine whether anything was out of place at the scene of a crime when the entire residence was a sty and every room was carpeted with noncriminal litter, everything layered with dust and grime?

Mason had told Jessie that there were two personal care assistants, one for each shift, but that neither one had met Pomerantz. Neither had Gloria Pinkoff, the physical thera-pist—hardly surprising, since Pomerantz wasn't really a resident and had no apparent need for a therapist. Still, Jessie was determined to talk to everyone on staff at the facility. With Rosa's help she located the personal care assistant on duty—the woman had never met Pomerantz.

Ten minutes later Jessie caught the physical therapist as she was exiting one of the residents' rooms.

The large, muscular-armed woman, her face flushed, veri-fied that she'd never met the dead man. "I say this to Mr. Mason. I am sorry this man is dead, but why you are asking again?" She spoke laboriously in a heavy Russian accent and sounded aggrieved, running a hand through thick, mahogany-red hair.

It was nice to know that Mason hadn't lied, but it was frustrating that aside from Hilda Rheinhart, no one had one damn thing to say about Pomerantz.

Mason was still unavailable, and now Lilly was sequestered behind the closed door to *her* office. Jessie walked to Reception and waited impatiently for the man standing in front of the receptionist's window to finish. Not a resident, she decided when he turned his head and she could see his face—even with the gray hair, he looked too young, and he was wearing a suit. Probably a doctor or son of a resident. Nodding politely at Jessie, he walked past her in the direction of the residents' rooms.

She approached Reception and waited to introduce herself to the woman on the other side of the window, who had stepped away from her desk to a filing cabinet. Jessie had barely seen her before—Mason had been in the lobby when Jessie had arrived this morning, and like last time, he'd escorted her quickly to his office. She couldn't really blame him—obviously he was trying to limit her contact with his residents, who might understandably be upset knowing that a police detective was on the premises.

The receptionist returned, and Jessie couldn't help staring at her. Even without makeup she was model-beautiful—young and tall and slender and shapely, with a long, Modigliani column of a neck and pronounced cheekbones. Her brown hair, smoothed against her scalp and brushed back from her face, was fastened at her nape with a tortoise clip. Her skin was dark copper, her large eyes pools of velvet brown.

Her name was Yasmin. "I was real sorry to hear that Mr. Pomerantz died," she said in an incredibly soft voice. "I couldn't believe it when Mr. Mason told me." She sounded nervous, and her eyes were bright with curiosity and a little apprehension.

Out of the corner of her eye, Jessie could see that some of the residents in the lobby were staring at her, too. "We're trying to find out where Mr. Pomerantz went on Saturday, or whom he contacted here in Los Angeles."

"I have no idea. I didn't see him on Saturday at all, but he could have gone out without my noticing."

"Did he use the office phone to make any calls?"

"Long distance, you mean?" Yasmin nodded. "He had a prepaid calling card, and a few times when the pay phones were occupied, he asked if he could use the office phone. I didn't see why not, and he was so nice." She paused, absent-mindedly fingering the card Jessie had given her. "He brought me a rose on Friday, just like that. Wasn't that so sweet?" She smiled wistfully.

Jessie agreed that it was sweet. "Do you know whom he called?"

"A friend in Brooklyn. That's what he told me."

Stanley Goldblum, no doubt. No help there. "What about local calls?"

"I let him make a few of those. He offered to use his calling card, but I said don't be silly, even though technically this phone is just for business. I don't know who he called, and of course I couldn't tell you the number, but it was a 310 area code. I dialed it for him."

Beverly Hills or Culver City or Westwood or Santa Monica or any of a dozen other nearby areas. Long Beach, even. "Was it a person or a company?"

"Sorry, I don't know. I wish I could help you." She sounded sincere.

"Did Mr. Pomerantz receive any phone calls?"

"A few. One from the friend in New York. Another from a man who didn't give me his name. Oh, and another time someone—a man—called but didn't leave a name or a message. Mr. Pomerantz was disappointed about that."

"Was this the same man who spoke to Mr. Pomerantz but didn't give you his name?"

Yasmin frowned. "I don't know."

"Did Mr. Pomerantz mention that he planned to visit anyone?"

She shook her head. "I know he went to Universal Studios." She hesitated, then said, "He asked me if I wanted to come along. He was joking, of course. He was so cute." She smiled shyly, then sighed.

"Do you know if he received any visitors?"

"I never saw him sitting with anyone in the lobby—except for Mrs. Rheinhart, but she's a resident. And no one ever came to Reception asking for him. But I'm not here on Tuesdays. That's my day off. So if someone visited him on Tuesday, I wouldn't know."

"Who's at Reception on Tuesdays?"

"Lorna—she's the activities director—shares it with Mercedes. Mercedes is head of housekeeping. They take over for Mrs. Gorcheck, too, on the weekends."

Lilly Gorcheck hadn't seen Pomerantz with anyone. And the other two women hadn't even met him. "Did Mr. Pomerantz seem upset in the last few days? Did he complain of not feeling well?"

Yasmin seemed surprised by the question. "Oh, no. Not at all. He was in a terrific mood, always smiling, flirting—but not in a dirty-old-man way," she added quickly. "He just enjoyed life, you know? It gave me a lift, to tell you the truth, because a lot of the people here, they're kind of sad and quiet most of the time. I guess it's the loneliness."

"Don't the residents keep busy with all the activities?"

The receptionist blinked. "Oh, sure, there's lots to do here," she said brightly, but her voice and smile lacked conviction. She looked surprised when Jessie asked her for a Golden Palms information packet, but didn't ask why she wanted one.

"Mr. Mason told me someone on staff drives residents to and from appointments," Jessie said. "Is he here now?" Yesterday, when Jessie had been here with Phil, the driver had been out, chauffeuring residents.

"You mean Randy Taylor. Unfortunately, you just missed him. He left about ten minutes ago to take a resident to a doctor's appointment." Yasmin pulled over a printed sheet of paper and ran her finger down a column, then looked up. "He's not scheduled to take anyone else until three-fifteen this afternoon, so he may wait until therapy is done. I can page him if you want."

"I'd appreciate that." She thanked Yasmin and walked to the lobby.

The two men and one woman who'd been staring at her earlier were sitting on the sofas, watching a *Happy Days* episode. They glanced at her unabashedly—the privilege of old age, she thought, and young children. Smiling pleasantly, she sat on one of the upholstered chairs and opened the green-and-beige pocket folder Yasmin had given her. The old people, she saw, had returned their attention to the television.

Against the background of canned laughter and the rheumy cough of one of the sofa's occupants, she flipped through the folder's contents: a color brochure, a meal chart, an activities chart, a fee schedule. She scanned the schedule and learned that for $100 a month extra, a personal care assistant would bathe you; for $50, your laundry would be done. That was called "Independent Plus Living."

"Catered Living" offered more—and, of course, cost more: assistance with dressing was an additional $250 per month; escorting to meals and activities, monitoring food intake, orientation, incidental grooming care, $450. The fees for incontinent care ranged from $500 to $800 a month.

She had never thought about the expense of growing old, about the loneliness, the inevitable indignity. She felt heavy-hearted, depressed, and had an urge to leave the coolness of the air-conditioned lobby for the sweltering temperature outside its doors. She shut the folder.

"Are you thinking of bringing a family member here?" the woman asked Jessie in a quavering voice. She had thin, silvery hair, and her face was a jigsaw puzzle of wrinkles. A hearing aid was visible in her right ear.

Jessie shook her head. Obviously, these people didn't know she was a detective. Mason would be relieved.

"Were you visiting someone?"

"I can't watch if you're talking," one of the old men grumbled. He reached for the remote control and raised the volume.

The woman was looking at her expectantly. Jessie hesitated, then said, "Yes." If you could call questioning someone about a dead man a visit. "Mrs. Rheinhart," she added, even though she hadn't asked.

"That's nice." The woman bobbed her head. "I didn't

know Hilda had any family," she said, and Jessie didn't correct her. "My daughter's taking me to lunch today. It was supposed to be last week, but something came up. That happens sometimes. She gave me this for my birthday." She patted the black alligator purse on her lap.

"It's beautiful," Jessie said.

"Yes, it is. It's real leather, too."

She pulled up her sleeve, exposing a tiny, skeletal wrist, and peered closely at her watch. Pursing her lips, she leaned on her cane for support, pushed herself off the sofa, and walked to Reception.

Soon she was back. "She hasn't called, so she's probably coming," the woman said uncertainly. She sat down carefully and placed the cane at her feet. Cradling the purse on her lap, she stared at the lobby doors.

"Sometimes she's late," she said after a moment. "It doesn't mean she's not coming." She glanced at Jessie.

"Of course not." Jessie smiled reassuringly.

She was uncomfortable, seeing the hurt in the old woman's eyes, and felt burdened with the collective guilt of daughters who disappoint mothers. Excusing herself, she walked to Reception.

Yasmin shook her head. "Sorry. Randy isn't answering his page. Do you want to wait or come back later?"

It was a little past 1:30. "I'll come back later. By the way, do you know someone named Anna Seligman?"

"Anna Seligman." She frowned, then shook her head again. "No. But I'm pretty new here."

Jessie thanked her. She returned to the lobby and was headed for the exit when the old lady waved. It struck Jessie as a poignant gesture, though she wasn't sure why. She waved back and smiled. "It was nice talking with you. Have fun with your daughter."

"Oh, I will. I'm sure she's coming. It's just that she's very busy, you know. Are you planning to visit Hilda again soon?"

"Maybe." Not really a lie, she told herself. She probably *would* have to talk to Hilda again about Pomerantz.

"That's nice." The woman nodded approvingly. "Very, very nice."

11

"THE VIDEOTAPE ARRIVED," Phil told Jessie when she called the station from her Honda, using her cell phone. "I signed for it."

"Forging my name again, are you?" She was curious to see the tape. The station had a monitor, but she couldn't justify spending an hour or more of work time watching Pomerantz narrate his life story.

"Getting better at it all the time," he said dryly. "Wait till you see your next Visa bill."

"Any calls for me?"

"Stanley Goldblum from New York. He wants to know when Pomerantz's body is being released. I told him you'd call as soon as you had news. And Gary phoned. No message. So did you have any luck with Pomerantz's lady friend?"

Damn, it was hot. She'd turned the car air-conditioning on, even though she was still parked. Now she flipped the control to a higher setting. "They weren't exactly an item." She repeated her conversation with Hilda. "She told me they're trying to kill her for her money."

"No shit. The 'they' being the recruiter hijackers?"

She could picture Phil's raised brows. "Hilda didn't say.

And the Golden Palms manager, Lilly Gorcheck, says that Hilda's paranoid. And that she has no money to speak of." Jessie repeated what the manager had told her.

"You know what they say, Jess. Just because someone's paranoid doesn't mean no one's out to get him." He chuckled, then said, "So what do you think?" Serious now.

"I don't know. She seemed rational enough. I had the feeling she was keeping something from me—she may know who Pomerantz went to see. She was nervous when I asked her about him. Then again, he just turned up dead, and this Mrs. Braeburn was scammed. No wonder Hilda's spooked."

If Hilda knew something about Pomerantz's activities, the knowledge, and his death, might have frightened her. Or was she an elderly, Jewish incarnation of Madame Defarge, working her grievances and anxieties into her knitting?

"Do we have the autopsy results?" she asked.

"Futaki promised we'd have them by the end of the day. So are you coming in?"

"Can't handle things on your own, can you?" She smiled.

"Espes and I are lonely. And Simms and Royd aren't as pretty as you are."

"Sexual harassment, Phil."

"Note it in your questionnaire."

"Watch your cholesterol, or I will." She wondered suddenly how would she have reacted, if someone else—Simms, for instance—had made a similar comment about her looks. *Would* she have viewed it as sexual harassment? "Actually, I thought I'd take my lunch break now, then go back to the retirement home. I want to question the staff driver—he'll be back before two. Unless you need me?"

"No problem. Go ahead."

"What about the hooker's girlfriend?"

"Not in. I've been calling every half hour. I hope she didn't skip. And I've been in touch with just about every damn OB in the city, looking for the new mom. Some of the docs were real jerks. Some were nice. If Maureen and I decide to have another kid, I'll know who *not* to use."

Jessie's eyes widened in surprise. "You didn't tell me you were thinking of having another child."

"Maureen wants a girl. I'm okay with the two boys, but who knows? One of these nights I may let her have her way with me." Phil laughed.

"Helen's expecting," Jessie said casually. "She and Neil told us last night at dinner."

A fraction of a beat. Then, "That's great! Matthew must be excited as hell."

"He is. We *all* are."

"Well, sure," he said quickly. "I *know* you are. You're already a terrific aunt."

And someday, you'll be a terrific mother. She knew what Phil was thinking and was glad she'd told him the news over the phone. If he felt even an ounce of pity for her—and she was sure he did, she could hear it, mixed in with the awkwardness in his voice—she didn't want to see it.

"See you around four," she said.

She grabbed a salad at Souplantation in the Beverly Connection on La Cienega, intending to spend half an hour or so across the street shopping for a new dress in the taupe behemoth that was the Beverly Center. Instead, she drove to Ohr Torah, the storefront, one-story school on Pico near Livonia where she was taking classes in Hebrew language and basic Judaism.

The Pico-Robertson neighborhood, she'd learned, had a large population of Orthodox Jews. There were butchers and bakeries, a deli, several pizza shops, numerous restaurants—all kosher. Across the street from the school was a clothing store perpetually advertising BIG SHOE SALE! The kosher Dunkin' Donuts was gone.

Ezra Nathanson, her instructor, was in the small office, photocopying papers. Tall and rangy with dark brown, curly hair, he looked very much the teacher in brown slacks and a camel sport jacket with brown elbow patches. He must have a closet full of camel jackets and brown slacks—Jessie had never seen him wear anything else.

He raised his brows when he saw her. "Look who's here, Shulamit," he said to the pretty, chestnut-haired young secretary sitting at the wood-tone Formica desk. To Jessie: "I was about to phone the police and ask them to put out an APB."

She smiled. "I'm a little too old to be considered a truant. What's my offense?"

"Hurting his professorial ego." Shulamit looked amused. "Ezra takes it personally when someone misses his class. And I think he has a crush on you."

Ezra shook his head, but his face had turned pink. "Shulamit—"

"Just teasing." She grinned, then faced Jessie. "You *are* his star student, though. How about coming for Shabbos, by the way? My kids are dying to meet a real detective."

"Sorry, I can't this weekend. But thanks for asking."

This wasn't the first time Shulamit had invited her to spend the Sabbath weekend. Jessie had received similar invitations from some of the other instructors in the school, all of whom practiced Orthodox Judaism. She wanted to experience a Jewish Sabbath but at the same time felt hesitant, worried that Shulamit or Ezra or the others would misconstrue curiosity for commitment. Not that they were pressuring her . . .

"Anytime you want to come, just let me know. I don't need much notice." Holding a stack of papers, Shulamit stood and headed for the door. "Behave yourself, Ezra, or she'll have you arrested."

It felt good to belong, Jessie thought as the secretary left the room. Four months ago she hadn't known Shulamit or Ezra; now they were a part of her life. And they weren't her colleagues. She'd realized recently that over the past ten years she'd made no friends outside of work. Except for Gary, of course.

"Joking aside, I was going to call to make sure you were all right." Ezra stapled a set of papers and placed it on a chair.

"I missed only two classes." Jessie leaned against Shulamit's desk, careful not to topple a brass-framed photo of her two little girls.

"I thought maybe you'd dropped out."

"Not until I master the '*ch.*'" She'd forced her tongue against the back of her palate, but the sound still hadn't been quite right. She shook her head. "Damn it, if two-year-olds can do it, why can't I?"

Ezra laughed. "You're definitely improving. Tell you what—we can go out for coffee one evening after class and you can practice your 'ch' diphthong for me."

Was this professional interest, or personal? She knew he'd been widowed for over a year, and Shulamit had mentioned that she wished he'd start dating again. "That's very generous of you, Ezra."

"Actually, it's selfish. I'd like to get to know you better."

Her face felt uncomfortably warm. "I'm involved in a relationship, Ezra."

"I meant as a *friend*. Shulamit *was* joking, you know." Smiling, he stapled another sheaf of papers and placed them on the stapled sets. "So what brings you here in the afternoon?"

Obviously he had no intention of dating her. He was strictly Orthodox and no doubt was interested in dating strictly Orthodox women; she was just beginning to explore her religion. She felt embarrassed and silly, and sensed from the heightened color in his neck that she'd embarrassed him, too.

"I'm investigating the death of an old Jewish man, Norman Pomerantz," she said. "He's a survivor and was visiting L.A. We found him in Rancho Park. Could be a heart attack, could be murder."

Pain had pinched Ezra's face. "Why do you suspect murder?" he asked quietly. He leaned against the photocopier, his hands at his sides.

She told him about the unlabeled vial of digitalis that Pomerantz's physician hadn't prescribed; about the retirement-home hijackings; about Hilda Rheinhart's fears.

"When did all this happen?"

"The medical examiner estimated that Pomerantz died sometime Saturday night."

Ezra was frowning. "The coroner's office has the body? Have they done the autopsy yet? Can you check?" he asked urgently.

"As far as I know, they did it yesterday," she said, and heard his expelled breath. "We should have the results later today. Why are you so upset?"

Ezra folded his arms across his chest. "Doing an autopsy violates Orthodox *Halacha,* the law."

"The man is *dead,* Ezra."

"His *soul* isn't. And the dignity of his body, which houses the soul, has to be preserved. His body has to be buried intact."

"That's not always possible, is it? What if there are catastrophic circumstances? Explosions, fires?" She saw him blanch and remembered—too late—that his parents and his nine-months-pregnant wife had died in a fire started by neo-Nazis who had burned a cross on their lawn. "I'm sorry, Ezra," she said in a small voice. Her face tingled.

"It's okay." He was silent a moment, staring somewhere over her head. "In those circumstances, we do whatever we humanly can, Jessie," he finally said. He cleared his throat. "I'm sure you've seen television news videos of the terrorist suicide bombings in Tel Aviv and Jerusalem?"

She nodded. The videos and newspaper photos of the carnage had been gruesome—blood and body parts everywhere.

"When something like that happens, members of the Disaster Victim Identification Squad carefully check the area for anything belonging to the dead victims—limbs, organ parts, tissue, skin. Even the most minute fragment is collected for burial, and the blood is soaked up with cotton wool and water." He sighed. "It's heartbreaking work, but vital, Jessie."

"Autopsies are vital, too, Ezra. We need them to determine cause of death."

"Why?" he asked impatiently. "What's the difference how this old man died? Why does he need to be cut up?"

That's what Stanley Goldblum had asked. "It could help us learn how he was killed. And who killed him."

"*If* he was killed. You said it could have been a simple heart attack."

"I think he was murdered, Ezra," she said quietly. "Listen, I didn't come here to argue. I spoke to Pomerantz's Brooklyn friend, Stanley Goldblum. Goldblum said he'll arrange for the burial after the body is released, but I thought maybe something should be done here. Religiously, I mean. I don't know if Pomerantz was Orthodox, but he *did* have phylacteries with him and a prayer shawl."

Ezra pursed his lips. *"Religiously,* Norman Pomerantz shouldn't have had an autopsy."

Jessie sighed. "Ezra—"

"Okay. What's done is done. Number one, from the time of death until the burial, the body's not supposed to be alone. I'll contact the *chevra kaddisha* and arrange for someone to go down to the morgue, and we'll have to arrange for someone to travel with the body to New York. I'll get in touch with his friend. What's the name again?"

"Stanley Goldblum. Hold on a sec." She dug her notepad out of her purse and flipped through it until she found what she wanted. "Here you go," she said, and dictated Goldblum's number. "This *chevra kaddisha* is a group of rabbis?"

Ezra shook his head. "Most of them are lay people, volunteers. *Chevra kaddisha* means 'holy society.' They do the *tahara*—the purification of the body for burial. They bathe the body and prepare it and dress it in *tachrichim*—the white burial shrouds. Men attend to a male deceased, of course, and women to a female."

"Grim work," Jessie said softly. "I wonder why anyone would volunteer to do it."

"It's a big mitzvah. And it isn't really grim. Actually, I found it uplifting, and it left me with a sense of peace." He ignored the surprise in her eyes. "If you saw the tender, respectful way the body is handled, I think you'd be impressed."

She wanted to ask him whether he'd volunteered to do a *"tahara,"* as he'd called it, before or after his wife had died, but didn't want to pry.

Ezra cleared his throat. "Okay. We'll have to get the body released to the *chevra kaddisha.* It's Norman Pomerantz, right?" Pulling a pen from his shirt pocket, he leaned over the photocopier and wrote the man's name. "What's the name of the medical examiner I should talk to?"

"Henry Futaki." She spelled it. "Be diplomatic, okay?"

"The wrath of the Hebrews descends on the county morgue." Ezra smiled lightly. "Don't worry, I won't tell him you sent me." He wrote down Futaki's name, folded the paper into fourths, and slipped it inside his jacket pocket. "So you have no idea who killed Mr. Pomerantz?"

"None."

"He was found in Rancho Park, you said. And you have no idea where he was before that?"

"Not a clue. Why?" She looked at him curiously.

"Nothing, really. I'm just reminded of a law in the Torah. It doesn't *exactly* apply to these circumstances, but I've always found it fascinating. I think you will, too." He moved from the photocopier to a bookcase in the corner of the small room and took down a black-leather-bound Bible.

"This is in the portion called *Shoftim*—Judges—and it deals with all kinds of laws—martial, civil, sexual, domestic, criminal. You name it." He paged through the text, then stopped and looked up. "This deals with an unwitnessed, unsolved murder of a traveler whose corpse is found lying in an open field. A delegation of five members of the Great Sanhedrin—basically, the Supreme Court of that time—measures from the corpse to the cities near the field and determines which city was nearest the corpse."

"Why?" Jessie asked, intrigued.

"To determine moral responsibility. The elders of this city bring a heifer which has never done any work to what the Torah calls"—here Ezra read from the text—"a 'harsh valley, which cannot be worked and cannot be sown.' The elders decapitate the heifer and wash their hands over it. And they say: 'Our hands have not spilled this blood, and our eyes did not see.' "

Jessie pictured the desolate, forbidding valley that would never produce anything, the robed elders standing over the animal, slaughtering it before it could bear its young. Just like the victim, she thought, whose life had been cut short. In her mind's ear she heard the whistle of an eerie silence. She shivered.

"Why do the elders wash their hands?" she asked.

"To symbolize that they're free of any guilt in the man's death. Then they ask God to atone for his people and forgive the people for the innocent blood that was shed in their midst." Ezra shut the volume and glanced at Jessie. "Not exactly your case, especially since you're not sure there was a homicide, and here the dead person found in the field was clearly murdered—stabbed, according to some biblical commentators. But you can see the similarities, can't you?"

She nodded. Pomerantz was a traveler. His body had been found in an open area. "Why do the elders proclaim their innocence? They're not responsible for the man's death."

"Good question," he said in a proud teacher's voice. He smiled. "Some sages say the elders *do* have a measure of responsibility—if sinfulness hadn't been present in their town, something like this couldn't have happened."

"Imagine what they'd say about Los Angeles—Sin City." She thought about all the unsolved murders, about the bodies she and her fellow detectives had found in gullies and canyons, in uninhabited areas. "But no city was without sin, even then."

"Of course not. But murder was rare. At least, *then* it was. By the year twenty-eight of the Common Era, there were so many murders that this ritual was no longer practiced, and neither was capital punishment."

"Society advances," Jessie said wryly.

"Yeah." Ezra returned the text to the bookcase. "In essence, with this ritual the elders are saying that they didn't permit a known murderer to roam the land. And that they didn't know the traveler and had no part in allowing him to go on his way without food or escort. That's why when you have a visitor, you're supposed to escort him a certain distance from your home."

"I *am* my brother's keeper." Where had Pomerantz been heading that Saturday? No one had escorted him past the lobby doors of the Golden Palms. No one had known his destination. Had anyone, aside from Hilda Rheinhart, even cared?

"There was another reason for the ceremony," Ezra said. "Since the murder and the ritual were highly publicized, a large number of people would probably show up to watch. Maybe the elders would be able to obtain information that would help identify the murderer."

"Or maybe one of the watchers *was* the murderer." Which

was why cops generally attended the funeral of a murder victim.

Ezra moved back to the copier and readied a sheet of paper on the machine. "By the way, was Mr. Pomerantz's body out in the open?"

She shook her head. "Half-hidden among some shrubbery. Actually, the body was moved there—we're not sure by who. Why do you ask?"

"If the murder victim's body was moved or hidden, then the ritual ceremony with the heifer wasn't conducted."

"What's the difference?"

"Someone who kills and leaves the body out in the open, without any attempt to hide what he's done, shows his brazen contempt for life and for the society around him. Someone who tries to hide what he's done—well, he's still guilty of murder, but obviously he's troubled by what he's done."

"Most probably he's just afraid of being caught, Ezra."

"You're right. But that's something, too, isn't it? Fear, remorse, guilt—they tell you he's not a sociopath. That can help you narrow the field of suspects for Pomerantz's murder. So a lot would depend on who moved his body."

"I didn't know the Torah could profile killers," she said lightly, but she found this fascinating.

Who *had* moved the body—the killer, or someone not involved with the crime? A mugger wouldn't necessarily have tried to hide it. Hijacking recruiters would have made the death look like a mugging. . . .

"Does God forgive them?" she asked. "The people, I mean?"

Ezra nodded. "That's the purpose of the ceremony—the priests are there, to officiate. But the people are still responsible to execute the murderer." He paused. "If they ever catch him."

12

A BEIGE SUBURBAN van with GOLDEN PALMS and a large dark green palm painted on both sides was parking at the curb in front of the retirement home just as Jessie arrived. She found a spot half a block away and through her rearview mirror, she watched a blond young man in navy Dockers and a white knit shirt come around from the driver's side and help the passenger out of the vehicle and into the lobby. When he returned she locked the Honda and approached him.

He was wiping bird crap off the hood of the Suburban. The sun was unbearably bright, and the hood sizzled and steamed from contact with the wet gray rag.

"Randy Taylor?"

He looked up, flashing a mega-watt smile. "That's me."

He was in his twenties, medium height, wiry and muscular. Damn good-looking. Electric-blue eyes, strong chin, thick blond hair that had obviously been styled professionally. Probably a wanna-be actor, driving a van until he got his break.

"I'm Detective Drake, LAPD. I'd like to ask you a few questions."

The smile dimmed a little, and she could see that he was adjusting to the information, shifting gears. He swiped the hood, then dropped the rag onto it and somehow worked his hands into the pockets of his incredibly tight-fitting pants. She was surprised he hadn't broken a finger or two in the process.

"What kind of detective?" he asked. Curious, but not nervous.

"Homicide."

He nodded somberly. "This is about the old guy who died in the park, huh? They told me he stayed here for a week." Cocking his head. "I thought they said he had a heart attack."

"We're not certain what caused his death. We're trying to trace his activities while he was in L.A., and I thought you might be able to help."

Randy shook his head. "Gee, I wish I could. But I never even met the guy. I only drive the residents."

That's what Mason had told Jessie. She studied the driver, unsure why she didn't believe him. Just a prickly feeling. More often than not, she'd learned, you had to trust your instincts.

She frowned. "That's very strange, Randy, because one of the residents told me you *did* drive Mr. Pomerantz somewhere."

He scowled. The fingers emerged from the pockets. "Who told you that?"

She smiled.

"Well, whoever did was lying. I'm not allowed to drive non-residents. That's the policy, so why would I risk losing my job?"

"For some quick cash?"

Pomerantz wasn't a skinflint—he'd tipped the housekeeper. He'd bought Yasmin a rose. He'd probably offered to pay Randy for his chauffeuring services. It was more convenient than calling a cab—and probably less expensive.

Randy shook his head again and folded his arms across his chest. Stared right at her. "Didn't happen."

Sweat had formed on his forehead, but that could have been the heat, not anxiety. The back of her olive-green cotton blouse was beginning to stick to her skin, and she'd been standing here only a minute.

"I think it did, Randy." She smiled again, patiently. "I know you don't want to get in trouble with Mr. Mason, but that's not the worst thing that could happen to you." She leaned closer. "You could be charged with obstructing the police in their investigation."

He shifted his weight to his other foot. "Like I said, I never drove him anywhere."

She tapped a finger against her lips. "Unless, of course, you're scared because you killed him. Is *that* why you're lying?"

Randy's electric-blue eyes had widened, and he was gaping at her. "You're nuts! Why the hell would I hurt a nice old guy like that?"

She let the words hang in the silence between them for a moment. Then she asked softly, "How do you know he was nice, Randy, if you never met him?" She could see by the way he froze that he realized his mistake. "I'm going to have to take you to the station," she said, her voice conveying regret.

Randy licked his lips. "I didn't hurt him. I didn't do anything! I'm telling you the truth."

"Where did you drive him?"

No answer. Then, "Does Mr. Mason have to know?"

"I won't tell him. But I can't promise that he won't find out. Where did you drive Mr. Pomerantz?" she repeated.

His sagging shoulders signaled defeat. "No place special. I drove him to Santa Monica—he wanted to see the ocean. I dropped him off at the Beverly Center so he could buy gifts for some friends back in New York. And he liked museums. I took him to the big one on Wilshire, and to a Jewish one off the 405. I don't remember the name—something with 'ball' in it. That's the first place he wanted to go."

The Skirball? That was in West L.A., on Sepulveda off the freeway. Pomerantz's interest in visiting museums wasn't surprising—Jessie recalled seeing an art magazine among his few personal belongings. "Where else?"

"Farmer's Market. He was going to pick up a tour bus there for Universal Studios. For an old guy, he had a lot of spunk, lemme tell you."

"What about this past Saturday?" she asked, trying not to sound impatient. "Where did you take him?"

"Nowhere. That's the God honest *truth*," he added quickly

in response to Jessie's frown. "I'm off every other Saturday."
He was looking at her closely to see if she believed him. "I
did take him somewhere else, earlier in the week—I don't
remember which day. Tuesday or Wednesday, I think."

"Where?"

"It was on Beverly Drive, south of Wilshire. But I don't
remember which block."

"Think hard, Randy. It's important." She watched as he
puckered his brow in concentration and hoped he was a fast
thinker. Sweat was trickling down her back. The pavement
was baking the soles of her shoes.

Finally, he said, "It was one or two blocks before Olympic.
On the west side of the street."

At least he'd narrowed it down somewhat. "Was it a shop
or an office building?"

"An office building. But I don't know the number. Why
would I?" he asked with a hint of defiance.

Because it would make my life just a little bit easier. "I'd
like you to come with me to identify the building."

"No way I can do it now." He shook his head emphatically.
"In five minutes I have to take a resident to a doctor's
appointment."

A reasonable excuse, she had to admit. "Where's the
doctor?"

"On Third Street, in the medical towers."

That was only minutes away by car. "We'll take my car.
We'll drop off the resident, go to Beverly Hills, and I'll have
you back in time to pick the resident up."

"I don't know if I'll recognize the building. I was only there
that one time." He was practically whining now.

She gritted her teeth. "You're a bright guy, Randy. I have
faith in you."

Randy was sullen and uncommunicative in the car, more
so after he escorted the resident, a heavily jowled, overweight
woman, to the east medical tower. Jessie had a fleeting moment of anxiety when he didn't reappear right away—Randy's
flown, she thought, he killed Pomerantz, and how would she

explain this to Espes? But then she saw him, ambling back to her Honda.

They drove in total silence. She took Third Street to Doheny, Doheny south to Wilshire, then turned right and continued on the wide boulevard until she reached Beverly Drive. She turned left and drove up Beverly past the first intersection, then slowed to ten miles an hour, ignoring the honking of the cars behind her. One eye on the road, one eye on Randy.

When they neared Olympic, he shrugged. "These buildings all look alike. Can you go back up the other block?"

She drove around to Wilshire and came up Beverly Drive again. They were several hundred feet past Gregory when he said, "I think that's it."

She stopped abruptly, eliciting an angry round of honks, and looked past Randy's pointed finger to a three-story building with a brick facade.

"Or maybe it's *that* one." He gestured toward another brick-faced building less than a hundred feet up the block.

She tried not to glare at him. "Which one is it, Randy?"

"Honest, I don't know. But it's definitely one of the two. Can we go back now? Mr. Mason will have a fit if I'm late picking up Mrs. Lubner."

Jessie looked at her watch—3:45. It would take her at least half an hour to drive Randy back to the Golden Palms and return here. Longer, probably, with the customary late afternoon traffic. She'd have to come back tomorrow morning and try to discover whom Pomerantz had visited last week.

Randy was visibly more relaxed on the way back, tapping his fingers on the Honda's cushion in time to the song on the radio. But he made an eager exit when Jessie parked in front of the retirement home, and headed for the Suburban without looking behind him. She watched him drive off and was about to do the same, but changed her mind.

Yasmin was at reception. She smiled anxiously when she saw Jessie. "If you're looking for Randy, I'm afraid you missed him again. But he should be back soon."

"Actually, I already spoke to him. He said he wasn't here this past Saturday, so he had no idea where Mr. Pomerantz might have gone. Too bad."

"Too bad," the receptionist echoed. "Last Saturday was Randy's day off. You'll want to talk to Joseph, the maintenance man. He drives the residents on alternate weekends."

So Randy had been telling the truth. "Where can I find him?"

"He's not here right now. He had to get a part for something that broke. Sorry." She flashed a smile. "He should be back in an hour or so. Or you can reach him first thing in the morning."

Jessie handed Yasmin her card. "I forgot to give you this earlier. If you think of anything concerning Mr. Pomerantz, please call." She took several steps away from the window, then turned back.

"There was a woman sitting in the lobby earlier when I was here. She was waiting for her daughter to come and take her out to lunch."

Yasmin looked blank.

"She was wearing a hearing aid." Still no recognition. "She had a black alligator handbag that her daughter gave her for her birthday?"

Yasmin smiled. "Mrs. Korda. She's very sweet, isn't she?"

"Yes. I was just wondering whether the daughter showed up." Jessie felt silly asking—it wasn't any concern of hers— and saw the question in Yasmin's deep brown eyes.

"No. She called and said something came up. A problem with the plumber, I think."

Jessie nodded. She thanked Yasmin and left the facility.

13

"**FUTAKI CALLED WITH** the results," Phil told Jessie when she arrived at the station. "Pomerantz's heart gave out, like we thought."

She tensed. "And?"

"Enough digitalis to jump-start a Mustang. That plus some wine which he drank sometime Saturday evening."

She smiled in satisfaction. "I knew it."

"Don't celebrate yet. The coroner hasn't decided yet whether to go with homicide or accidental death."

She threw her purse onto her desk. "Dammit, Phil. He *knows* Pomerantz's body was moved. He *knows* Pomerantz's wallet and watch are missing." She slumped into her chair.

Phil nodded. "Pomerantz's body was definitely moved—*after* he died, but Futaki says that doesn't add up to murder. And he says Pomerantz was probably mugged after he was dead."

"Why would a mugger put an unlabeled vial of digitalis in Pomerantz's pocket? Did you tell Futaki Pomerantz's doctor didn't prescribe Lanoxin?"

Phil nodded. "He says Pomerantz may have gotten the pills from a friend, or may have had them prescribed by another doctor. Pomerantz's fingerprints were on the vial."

"So the murderer placed the vial in Pomerantz's hand before he slipped it inside his pocket." She clenched her fists. "This is ridiculous! Why is Futaki hedging?"

"My guess? The guys downtown don't think this case will be easy to prove. Pomerantz will look better as an accidental death than a homicide we can't pin on anyone. The D.A. doesn't want to rack up any more unsolveds. Neither does the chief." Phil swiveled in his chair.

Politics, Jessie thought angrily. "Did you tell Futaki about the retirement-home hijackings?"

"Yeah. From his tone, I don't think he was overly impressed. But he said to let him know if and when we find out anything concrete."

"What does he want? A signed confession?"

"Don't we all?" He played with his mustache. "So what's with the chauffeur? Did you learn anything?"

"Pomerantz did a lot of tourist stuff, and he bought gifts for his friends."

"I'll call Futaki with the news." Phil pretended to reach for the phone.

"Plus he visited someone in a building on Beverly Drive, just south of Wilshire." She told Phil about her drive with Randy Taylor. "I'll check out both buildings in the morning." She stood and slung her purse strap over her shoulder.

"Aren't you forgetting something?" He reached across his desk and handed her a FedEx package.

The tape. That was why she'd stopped at the station instead of driving home from the Golden Palms. "Thanks, Phil. See you in the morning." She took the package.

He smiled. "Make popcorn, and I'll come watch it with you."

Abigail Morton had included her business card and a handwritten note with the tape: "As I said, this is unedited and has preinterview footage. I hope this helps. I'm genuinely sorry about Mr. P's death."

The house was stifling. Jessie usually changed into shorts the minute she came home, but she was too eager to see the tape. She slipped the videotape into her VCR and, kicking off her shoes, sat cross-legged on the black leather den couch. Switching on the television and the video player with the remote, she nibbled on the first of two semiwarm slices of pizza she'd picked up on her way home.

Black-and-white fuzz appeared on the screen, followed by bands of color. Then a far shot of a sparse studio set—a high-backed chair upholstered in gray; a small round table, covered with a solid green floor-length cloth; a vase with flowers; a potted plant in the background.

Sitting on the chair was a slight, elderly man with a shock of medium brown hair and ruddy cheeks. Norman Pomerantz. He shifted his position—not a spectacular action, but after examining his still body and studying his pale face in the postmortem photo, Jessie was momentarily startled to see him animated, his pallor replaced with color.

"In the beginning, God said let there be light," Norman Pomerantz *said in a high, heavily accented voice, "but who knew it was so hot?" He blotted his face with a snow-white handkerchief.*

"Sorry about that. These do give off a lot of heat. Would you like something cold to drink? Water? Soda?"

The speaker—she was out of camera range—sounded concerned. Jessie wondered who she was, then remembered that Abigail had told Jessie she'd done the lighting herself.

Pomerantz shook his head. "You're thinking, 'What if the old man faints?' right?" He smiled. "Don't worry, Miss Morton, I'm used to the lights. I did another documentary a few months ago. Now if you were offering champagne . . . ?" His gray-blue eyes twinkled mischievously.

"I wish I could. This is a low-budget film."

"Maybe when you're big, like Spielberg. He started small, too." The old man chuckled. *"What's your first name, if you don't mind I'm asking?"*

"Abigail."

"Abigail." He pronounced the A like "ah." "A lovely name for a lovely young lady." He cocked his head. "It's okay I said that? Nowadays you have to be careful."

"It's fine."

Jessie could see why Yasmin, the receptionist, had been

taken with Pomerantz. He was charming and cute, and a benign flirt. A moment later she saw a tall, angular young woman with a mass of long, curly red hair approach him.

"My wife had a beautiful name. Lola." His eyes glistened. He bent his head and unbuttoned his navy wool jacket.

The woman clipped a tiny black microphone to his lapel.

"They're going to check how I sound now, yes?" he asked. *"I know from last time."*

"Just speak naturally." Abigail adjusted the mike. *"It must be hard for you to talk about what happened to you during the war. I appreciate your doing this interview."*

"It's hard, and it's good, you know?" He shrugged and buttoned his jacket, hiding the microphone's lead. *"And it's important. Without these tapes—"* he gestured in the direction of the camera trained on him—*"when I'm gone, and the others are gone, who will be here to say it really happened? Maybe I'll do another interview when I'm in Los Angeles. What do you think? I have star quality?"* He moved his shoulders back and struck a pose.

"Definitely." The woman sounded amused. *"The next Sean Connery."*

"I was thinking more Mel Gibson. But Connery is okay." He chuckled again. *"You're a nice girl. You have a boyfriend, Abigail?"*

"Yes."

"He's wonderful?"

She laughed. *"I guess."*

"You shouldn't have to guess." He wagged his finger at her. *"And don't settle for less than wonderful, Abigail. I didn't."* His smile was wistful. *"How old are you? If you don't mind I'm asking."*

"Twenty-seven."

"Ach, so young!" He sighed and shook his head.

"How about you?"

"Me? I'm a thirteen." He said this with pride.

"A what?" Abigail had moved back out of camera range.

"A thirteen. I was born in nineteen thirteen. My friend Stanley, he's a fifteen. Max, a twenty-one. A baby." Pomerantz smiled.

Jessie smiled, too.

"So you're going to Los Angeles," Abigail said. "Will this be your first visit there?"

He nodded. "My first time out of New York since I came to America, can you believe it? Maybe I'll move there. It all depends."

"Depends on what? Do you have a girlfriend there?" she asked archly.

"A girlfriend? No." He smiled and shook his head.

"Then what?"

"Aha!" He raised his brows. "That I can't tell even you, the lovely Abigail."

"A secret?" the young woman said coyly, playing the game.

His response was an enigmatic smile. "A very, very big secret. It could change my life."

"I hope you won't be disappointed."

"I've been disappointed before, Abigail. You get used to it. But this time—this time I have a good feeling."

Ironic last words, Jessie thought sadly.

She watched the entire tape—over two hours of unedited footage. Pomerantz was everything his friend Goldblum had promised—alert, bright, whimsical, warm. Seeing the varying emotions play across his wizened face, listening to his animated and sometimes droll retelling of his life, Jessie was moved to tears for Nachum Pomerantz, who had miraculously survived the concentration camps only to be killed and subjected to an autopsy, to be stripped once again of his identity, of his dignity.

She told herself not to personalize Pomerantz's death, but she knew she was crying, too, for Yaakov Kochinsky, the grandfather she'd never met, the one Frances had refused to talk about until last night. How had he died? What had happened to his body? Chances were, she would never know.

Jessie had learned all about Pomerantz's childhood and adolescence; about his family, all gone; about the brutal years in a number of concentration camps; about his miraculous survival. She'd discovered nothing about the secret that had brought him to Los Angeles a little over a week ago.

If, in fact, there *was* a secret. Maybe he'd been joking

around with Abigail Morton, trying to make himself sound like a more interesting subject for her interview.

But Stanley Goldblum had said his friend Nachum had sounded mysterious about what he was doing in L.A.

"A very big secret," Pomerantz had said. "It could change my life."

Had ruthless recruiters prevented Pomerantz from pursuing his secret quest?

Or had the quest itself led to his death?

14

"YES, WE WERE a close family." *Pomerantz nodded at the camera. "My father, my mother. A younger brother and two younger sisters. A dog, too." He smiled. "I'm lucky—I managed to save quite a few pictures. Some of my friends have only memories.*

"I remember how cold the winters were—no central heating, you know." He laughed. "But we had fun. Snowball fights, sleds, picnics. In the summers we had campfires in the mountains. A normal life. . . ." He sighed. "Hard to believe, no?

"My brother, Moshe, was very handsome. Thick black hair, eyes blue like the sea. The girls were crazy about him." Pomerantz smiled wistfully. "He was strong, too, but he died of typhus in Auschwitz, right before the liberation. That's what the Americans told me. I wasn't so strong, and here I am." He shrugged.

"My sister Liebe—she was the older of the two—died in Treblinka. The younger one, Chava, was blond. She looked just like a Polish shiksa. She used to sneak out to get us eggs, milk, flour, soap— whatever was available. 'Don't worry,' she always told my parents. 'They won't catch me.'

"But one time they did. . . ."

Between the two brick-faced buildings on Beverly Drive, Jessie learned on Wednesday morning, there were more than fifty tenants. They included an import-export company, a wholesale wig distributor, a photography studio, several law firms, investment counselors, CPAs, a public-relations firm, a real estate company, and a masseuse. No doctors—most Beverly Hills physicians' and dentists' offices were concentrated on Bedford or Roxbury Drive, between Wilshire and Santa Monica. There was two-hour free parking on Bedford and Camden, compliments of the city of Beverly Hills.

L.A. could take a lesson.

Two hours later she was tempted to return to the masseuse—her feet were aching and her temper was frayed, and though she'd flashed Pomerantz's photo to more receptionists than she cared to meet in a year (some had been perky and bright-eyed, others nasal and terminally bored), not one had recognized the old man or remembered his name.

Five more offices, and she'd be done. Maybe Randy had been wrong about the building. Or maybe he'd lied, just to get her off his back.

She stepped into a travel agency and gazed longingly at the huge, inviting posters. Australia. France. The Alps. The Yucatan. Alaska. Her last vacation, aside from an occasional day off which she'd spent driving up to Santa Barbara, had been her five-day honeymoon in Maui. And as she recalled, she and Gary hadn't done much touring. . . .

The receptionist glanced at Pomerantz's photo and shook her head. "He may have been here last week, but I wouldn't remember the face. You can't believe how busy we were. We've been swamped all summer." She ran a hand through overpermed long blond hair, then looked at Jessie with interest. "What about you, Detective? Can I tempt you with a weekend getaway to Mazatlan? We have some terrific packages." She smiled.

"Wish I could," Jessie said, meaning it. The heat had broken a little, but the temperature was still too high for her liking. Phil and the kids had gone to San Diego. Helen and Neil were taking Matthew to Epcot Center in Florida in August. Last night on the phone Gary had mentioned getting away for a long weekend to Tahoe. Separate rooms, of course, he'd said. Maybe she should tell him yes. Or would that give him too much hope?

Across the hall from the travel agency were Hollister Graphics and the Steele Foundation. Door number one or door number two, as Phil would say. The Steele Foundation first, she decided. It sounded familiar—and there was an ornate silver mezuzah on the door post.

The woman behind the beautiful inlaid mahogany desk was on the phone when Jessie entered. She was in her fifties, Jessie guessed, judging by the delicately lined face and silver-and-dark gray hair swept into a sleek chignon. She was wearing a tailored, ivory-colored suit with Chanel-like navy braiding on the jacket pockets. Mabe pearls in her ears. Frances would approve.

The reception area was spacious and decorated like a foyer of a private home: Two plush sofas upholstered in chintz. A sage-green Chinese fishbowl, filled with fresh flowers, on a dark wood butler's table with brass fittings. Jessie glanced at the artwork on the ecru silk-moiré-covered walls. No clues as to the Steele Foundation's purpose (fund-raising of some sort?), but even to her untrained eye, the Chagall and Matisse looked like originals.

"They're exquisite, aren't they?" The receptionist put the receiver in its cradle and smiled at Jessie. "I'm Barbara Louin. How can I help you?" she asked in a soothing, elegant voice, perfect for hosting a classical music station.

"Detective Jessie Drake, LAPD." She handed her a card.

Not what the woman had expected. Jessie saw a flicker of distaste in her gray eyes that was intensified when Jessie explained why she'd come and presented Pomerantz's photo, its sheen long ago obliterated by tens of fingerprints.

The receptionist had slipped on half-glasses and was studying the photo intently. "What did you say his name is?" she asked when she finally looked up at Jessie.

Jessie felt a thrill of anticipation. "Norman Pomerantz. He was visiting from New York."

The woman nodded. "A large number of elderly people come to us, so it's difficult to distinguish. But I *do* remember this gentleman. He was here one day last week." She tapped a French-manicured fingernail against her pale coral lips. "Tuesday, I think. Yes, that's right—because it was *before* Mr. Steele took ill, and that was on Wednesday. Mr. Pomerantz was terribly disappointed when I told him none of the Steeles were available." She returned the photo to Jessie. "What happened? Did he . . . ?" Her voice trailed off.

Finally, a lead. Don't get excited, Jessie told herself. "We're not sure about the cause of death. We're trying to reconstruct Mr. Pomerantz's last few days in L.A. Which Mr. Steele did he want to see?" She slid the photo into an envelope, which she put in her purse.

"Mr. *Maurice* Steele. He hadn't been coming to the office regularly for quite some time, even before his heart condition became so serious. Then Mr. Pomerantz asked if he could talk to Mr. Maurice's sons—Charles and Henry. He said it was important, but they were in meetings. I couldn't *possibly* disturb them." She sounded troubled, her voice filled with regret.

Death didn't allow for retakes. "You couldn't know," Jessie said kindly, granting the woman the absolution she clearly wanted. "Did Mr. Pomerantz indicate why he wanted to talk to Mr. Steele?"

The woman tapped her finger against her lips again. "There *was* something. . . ." She frowned in concentration, then shook her head. "Sorry. We see *so* many people," she added with a rueful smile. "I offered to have one of our staff help him, but Mr. Pomerantz refused. He *insisted* on talking to one of the Steeles. He said he'd come all the way from New York and wasn't going home until he did. Very adamant, in a cute way." Another, more amused smile. "I felt sorry for him, but what could I do?"

"He never returned?"

"Not as far as I know. He may have come during my lunch break. I *did* take his name and a phone number where he could be reached. I passed that on to both Mr. Charles and Mr. Henry, but I don't know whether either one of them ever contacted Mr. Pomerantz. The foundation's been *extremely* busy," she added, "and the Steeles have been preoccupied with their father's illness."

Yasmin, the Golden Palms receptionist, had told Jessie a male caller had phoned for Pomerantz but hadn't left a message. And either the same caller, or another one, had spoken to the old man. Maybe the caller was one of the junior Steeles. But if so, why hadn't he left a message?

The door to the hallway opened. Jessie turned as a handsome man entered the office. He was medium height, well built, probably in his forties. Great double-breasted navy suit; great salt-and-pepper hair. The charcoal alligator attaché case he was carrying looked expensive.

"Do you have those files, Barbara?" he asked the receptionist in a voice that conveyed that his time was valuable. He didn't even acknowledge Jessie's existence.

"Here they are." The receptionist handed him a stack of folders held together with a rubber band. "Mr. Henry would like you to phone him at his father's house when you're done. I wrote the phone number down for you." She pointed to a green Post-it attached to the top folder. "And there's one letter he'd like you to read before you leave." She handed him a folded sheet of paper.

He frowned. "I didn't plan on staying. I'm parked at a meter."

"This shouldn't take long. You can use the conference room, if you like."

"All right, then." Mr. Attaché Case smiled. It was a tight smile, with a hint of a Michael Douglas-type sneer. He left the folders on the desk and, taking the letter, disappeared around the corner.

"Is he a lawyer?" Jessie asked the receptionist and was rewarded with a quizzical expression.

"Yes. How did you know?"

"Just a lucky guess."

Barbara looked uncertain a moment, then allowed herself a half smile. "Mr. Reynolds can be a little abrupt. But he's been doing a wonderful job, advising the people who contact the foundation."

"What exactly is the Steele Foundation?" Jessie asked.

The woman's raised brows indicated she was surprised Jessie didn't know. "The Steeles established the foundation to help Holocaust survivors retrieve the assets that are rightfully theirs. Mr. Maurice is a survivor himself." She said this gently, with pride.

"The Swiss accounts, you mean?" *That* was why the foundation name was familiar—Jessie had seen it in an article in the *Times*.

Barbara nodded. "We're also trying to help survivors establish that they're the legal beneficiaries of life insurance policies taken out and paid for by their murdered family members. You wouldn't *believe* how many policies haven't been honored—policies issued by companies that encouraged Jews, before the war, to insure themselves to protect their families and their property." She shook her head with indignation.

"I think I read that some people are suing several of the European insurance companies."

Barbara nodded. "That's correct. We're hoping that will get things moving. And of course, there are the personal belongings. Paintings, sculptures, jewelry, tapestries, works of art." She sighed. "All confiscated from Jews in Poland, France, Germany, Austria, Hungary. . . . They're worth a fortune."

"Can you trace the pieces?"

"Mr. Steele certainly hopes to—that's Mr. *Charles* Steele. He's committed to recovering the art and personal effects and returning them to their rightful owners. And like his father, he's passionate about art." She smiled warmly. "Mr. Maurice has a renowned collection. He's loaned out pieces to various museums around the world. The works you were admiring are part of his collection."

"Isn't he concerned about theft?"

"The pieces are wired from the back to an alarm system. And of course they're heavily insured."

Jessie cast a sideways glance at the paintings on the wall. How much did it cost to insure the artwork in this office? Or were the pieces covered under Steele's personal policy? "And the Swiss banks and the insurance companies?" she asked. "All the lost funds?"

"That's Mr. Henry's domain. He's the businessman in the family. Mr. Maurice was a keen businessman, too." Her smile had returned, but now it was wistful. "Mr. Henry is also producing a documentary of survivors' interviews."

Pomerantz had told Abigail Morton that he might give another interview when he was in Los Angeles. Maybe that was why he'd come to the Steele Foundation. But if so, why hadn't he been willing to see one of the foundation's staff members? Why had he insisted on talking to one of the Steeles?

Vanity, maybe? Pomerantz had already done two interviews—in his own mind, he was a pro. A star. Maybe he'd viewed himself as above being assigned to an assistant. But nothing in the videotape Jessie had watched last night had shown Pomerantz to be arrogant.

"Did Mr. Pomerantz mention wanting to be inter—" Jessie began.

"*Now* I remember!" the receptionist exclaimed softly. Her eyes sparkled with satisfaction. "When Mr. Pomerantz gave me the phone number where he could be reached, he said something like, 'Tell the Steeles I want to talk to them about a lost and found.' There was something else, but I can't remember his words exactly."

So Pomerantz probably hadn't come about the documentary. And if he'd wanted to obtain help in filing a claim against the Swiss banks, he could have easily done so from his Brooklyn apartment—Jessie had seen an 800 number the Swiss Bankers Association had listed in their newspaper announcement, along with an E-mail address. Was this about an insurance policy? Missing art or valuables?

"He didn't explain what he meant?" Jessie asked.

Barbara shook her head. "I had the feeling he was enjoying being a little mysterious."

Lost and found. Maybe Pomerantz had been interested in finding something that had been taken from his family, or in helping the foundation restore lost items to others. Maybe he'd spoken to one of the Steeles and explained it to him.

"I'd like to speak to Charles and Henry Steele," Jessie said.

Barbara leaned forward and clasped her hands. "I'm *so* sorry. Neither one is in. I believe I mentioned that Mr. Maurice has taken ill? Well, Mr. Charles and Mr. Henry have been conducting their work at their father's home so that they can spend time with him and monitor his condition. They're devoted to him, and to their mother."

"Where do they live?" If Pomerantz had talked to Charles or Henry, Jessie wanted to know.

The woman's face and posture stiffened. "I couldn't tell you that."

Jessie suppressed her irritation. "I can get the information by making a few phone calls, Ms. Loura, but you can save me valuable time by telling me."

"They don't need to be bothered with this, not now. They're trying to deal with Mr. Maurice's illness, and continue all their projects." The receptionist seemed on the verge of tears.

"Homicide investigations aren't known for being conveniently timed," Jessie said gently. "The Steeles may unwittingly have vital information about Mr. Pomerantz that could help us catch his killer." Not necessarily true, but you never knew.

Barbara looked at Jessie, hesitation in her eyes. Then she shook her head. "I'm sorry about Mr. Pomerantz. Really I am. And I hope you find his killer. But I'd prefer that you get the Steeles' home address from another source."

"What about the home phone number, then? If I get the information I need over the phone, I won't have to disturb the Steeles." And if she had a phone number, she could obtain the street address from a reverse directory.

Barbara Loura pursed her lips and looked away.

Jessie could have intimidated the receptionist with talk about "obstruction of justice" and "interference with an official police investigation" but she didn't. She was only mildly annoyed. She knew she'd get Steele's home address somehow.

And she admired the woman's loyalty.

Espes wouldn't have admired it, Jessie thought as she left the foundation office. She was glad he hadn't been here, watching.

She found a parking citation on the Honda windshield, even though she'd prominently displayed her official pass. She entered the car, kicked off her shoes, and massaged the balls of her feet. God, they ached. She put her shoes back on and drank water from the plastic bottle she always carried with her. Warm, but wet. Then she checked in with the station and spoke to Boyd, who told her Phil was out chasing a lead on the hooker's girlfriend.

Go, Phil. "Any news on the little boy?" Jessie asked, surprised to find that she was holding her breath again.

"Still hangin' in there. It don't look good, but like my momma says, there's always hope."

"How'd court go this morning?"

Boyd sighed. "Postponed. The Pillow Killer took sick, lucky son of a gun."

Jessie would hardly call the old man "lucky."

There was no directory listing for Maurice Steele in the Greater Los Angeles area or Beverly Hills, she found out. No big surprise. She considered requesting Steele's address from one of the Jewish community organization leaders she'd recently met while investigating neo-Nazis and skinheads, but decided to use them as a last resort. Like Barbara Loura, they'd probably balk. Not out of loyalty to Steele, she guessed, but out of the fear that the millionaire philanthropist would cut off whatever funds he directed their way if he found out.

Gary might know. Jessie tried reaching him, but he was somewhere out in the field. Another incidence of road rage? The thought depressed her—everything, she admitted, was depressing her lately. She really *did* need a vacation, and soon. She would probably tell Gary yes about Tahoe. She left a message for him to call her, then phoned Ohr Torah.

"You just missed him," Shulamit told her.

Phil, Gary, now Ezra. Strike three. "Do you know when he'll be back?" Out of the corner of her eye, she saw a parking enforcement vehicle pull into an angled slot several hundred feet up ahead. The same one who'd left the citation on Jessie's windshield?

"He has an hour between classes. I'm pretty sure he went to the pizza place down the block. You could look for him there."

Not a bad idea. Ezra might have the information she

needed, and Jessie could grab a quick lunch. She'd eaten nothing all day except the half grapefruit and a bowl of apple-cinnamon instant oatmeal she'd had for breakfast, and her stomach was rumbling.

A short, big-rumped woman exited the parking enforcement vehicle and waddled toward a meter in front of a Lexus. Looked around, first to the right, then to the left.

Then jiggled the meter!

Jessie stared for a second, open-mouthed, then got out of the Honda just as one of the double doors to the building she'd left a few minutes ago swung open and Mr. Attaché Case hurried out to his car. Where the meter reader was punching data on her computerized citation pad.

Talk about moral dilemmas, Jessie thought wryly. What was worse, letting the meter reader get away with what she'd done, or defending a lawyer? A tough call. She debated a moment, then walked toward them.

The man was looking at his wristwatch. "I'm *certain* I had a few more minutes."

"Sorry," from the meter reader, who didn't sound sorry at all.

"The meter must have skipped ahead. Can't you let it go?" He smiled his tight smile.

"Once I start writing up the citation, that's it." Smug, now.

Jessie said, "You jiggled the meter."

They both turned and stared at her.

"This isn't your concern, ma'am." Meter Woman was scowling, her little pinball eyes disappearing into the folds of her beefy face.

The attorney looked puzzled. It was obvious to Jessie that he was trying to figure out where he'd seen her. She decided not to tell him.

"You actually saw her do it?" he asked Jessie.

She nodded. "You should contest this." She wished Phil were here—he really hated Parking Enforcement. So did Gary. For that matter, so did just about everyone she knew. Not that they liked attorneys. . . .

"I fully intend to." Turning, he fixed the meter reader with an icy stare.

Meter Woman bristled. "This citation is totally warranted. The meter expired just as I arrived." Still entering data.

Jessie shook her head. "You encouraged it to expire a little ahead of schedule."

The woman was clutching the computer pad with both hands as if she were Moses, about to smash the Ten Commandments. "If you don't stop interfering, I'm going to call the police." Glaring at Jessie, she handed the man a copy of the citation.

"I *am* a police detective," Jessie said coolly. The attorney, she noted, looked startled.

The woman placed her hands on her hips. "And I'm Demi Moore."

Jessie took out her badge. . . .

It was an insignificant, petty little victory, she thought a few minutes later as she walked back to her car. Not exactly what the city was paying her to do.

But she felt damn good. She couldn't decide which had given her more satisfaction—seeing the lawyer's grateful smile (no sneer now), or watching the power-pumped arrogance seep out of Meter Woman's face, like air from a punctured tire.

Jessie Drake, the people's hero.

15

EZRA WAS SEATED at a booth at the end of the long, narrow pizza shop. His back was toward Jessie, but she recognized his camel-colored jacket. He was nibbling on a slice of pizza while reading a book and didn't notice her until she was standing in front of him and called his name.

He looked up, his brows raised in surprise. "You really *are* a good detective, Detective."

She smiled. "Shulamit said I'd probably find you here. Okay if I join you?"

"Sure." He shut the text and placed it on top of a stack of books, moving them over to make room. "What would you like? My treat—don't even try to argue."

"Thanks." She sat across from him and eyed the vegetable-smothered slice of pizza. Peppers, mushrooms, eggplant. The sautéed onions smelled heavenly. But she'd had pizza yesterday. Too much cheese in two days. "Do they serve pasta?"

"The angel hair with tomato and basil is great."

"Perfect." She gave herself mental points for willpower as he slid out of the booth and walked to the front of the shop. She picked up the book he'd been reading—a philosophical text, she saw, paging through it—and put it down when he returned with a paper plate, napkin, a Styrofoam cup, plastic utensils, and a can of caffeine-free Diet Coke.

"It'll be a few minutes," he said, setting everything in front of her. "I hope you like Coke."

"My favorite. Don't you ever relax?" She pointed to the book.

"For me, reading *is* relaxing." He slid back into the booth. "I have other hobbies. Hiking, bike riding, tennis. Why do you look so surprised? Did you think I was permanently attached to a desk?"

She laughed. "Not exactly. I suppose it's because you're a teacher." She hesitated. "And you've always struck me as very serious."

" 'Serious' is definitely a part of me." He nodded. "But not all of me. And you really mean 'religious,' right?"

"Not really." Bending her head, she snapped off the Coke can tab and hid the blush that belied her words.

"A lot of Orthodox Jews lead normal lives, Jessie. I have friends who are stockbrokers, doctors, plumbers, physicists, electricians, engineers. They play Little League and basketball, go skiing and boating."

"I don't know many Orthodox Jews," she admitted, "Except for Manny Frieberg. He's a police psychologist. We've become friends over the years." She poured soda into her cup and took a sip.

"I don't know if I'd call a police psychologist 'normal.' " Ezra chuckled. "Anyway, what brings you here? You decided to practice your 'ch' after all?"

She smiled. "Actually, this is related to Mr. Pomerantz, the old man I told you about yesterday."

Ezra tensed. "I spoke with Mr. Goldblum, but I haven't been able to reach Futaki." He looked at her questioningly.

"They did the autopsy, Ezra."

He stared at his plate. "I was hoping you were going to tell me they hadn't done it after all." His voice was quiet, but angry.

"Sorry," she said gently. She waited a moment, then asked, "Do you know Maurice Steele, of the Steele Foundation?"

"They do say hope springs eternal, right?" Ezra sighed. "*Everybody* in the Jewish community knows about the Steeles.

They're major philanthropists. Next to Edgar Bronfman, their foundation is putting the most pressure on the Swiss banks to do right for the Holocaust victims' heirs."

"Number six!" a male voice called from the front of the shop.

"That's me." Ezra left the booth.

Bronfman's name was familiar. Jessie drank more soda and wondered where she'd heard it.

Ezra returned with the pasta and a plate of cheese-smothered nachos surrounding a mound of guacamole. "You have to try the nachos," he said, sitting down. "They're the best."

Jessie sighed. So much for willpower. "Just one, or there goes my diet for the week." She took a triangular chip, dipped it into the guacamole, and moaned with pleasure.

He smiled. "Good, huh?"

"Sinful." She tasted the pasta. "You're right—this is good, too," she told Ezra, then asked him about Bronfman.

"He's chairman of Seagram and president of the World Jewish Congress—the WJC. He's Canadian, by the way."

She took another chip. "So the Steeles work with Bronfman?"

Ezra shook his head. "The Steele *sons,* not the father, decided to go after the Swiss bank accounts, et cetera. Maurice was more into philanthropic work. They wanted to join forces with the WJC, but Maurice said no. So I guess it was a compromise."

Father knows best. Or thinks he does. Jessie wondered why Maurice had balked at joining the WJC. Maybe he liked running the show, or getting the credit. "I see I came to the right source. How do you know all this, Ezra? Do you have a mole in the Steele home?"

He finished chewing a mouthful of pizza and hesitated before he spoke. "I study Bible with Henry Steele once a week. Not lately, though, because his father's ill."

"Pretty sneaky, Ezra." She laughed. "When were you planning to tell me?"

"When you asked. Nothing that I've told you is confidential, by the way." He sounded anxious.

"Or you wouldn't have told me." She smiled. "I know."

She was struck by the contrast between Ezra, who scrupulously avoided spreading gossip (the Hebrew was *"rechilus"*—another word with that impossible phoneme), and Gary, whose profession thrived on it. So did her own. In investigations she'd often relied on informants and family members and friends of suspects and victims eager to tell all.

"Are the Steeles Orthodox?" Eyeing the nachos, she twirled pasta around her fork and lifted the food to her mouth.

"No. But Henry's interested in learning more about his tradition. The Steeles support all Jewish institutions—Orthodox, Conservative, Reform. And they contribute to non-Jewish causes as well. They're major patrons of the arts, by the way."

"I know. They've got a great Chagall in the foundation's reception area."

Ezra leaned forward. "You should see the rest of the collection, Jessie. Henry once took me on a tour of his parents' home. I thought I was in the Louvre. He told me curators all over the world are hoping Maurice will bequeath one or two important pieces to their museum collections."

"They must be drooling in anticipation. The foundation receptionist said Charles is an art lover. He'll probably want to keep all the best ones for himself."

"Maybe he's not that greedy. They're philanthropists, remember." He moved back. "Why are you interested in the Steele family? How is this connected with Mr. Pomerantz?"

She told him about Pomerantz's fruitless visit to the foundation. "Maybe one of the Steele sons contacted him. If so, I want to know what he told them."

"You think he wanted to be interviewed for the documentary?" Ezra frowned. "Why would that be significant to your investigation?"

"It wouldn't. But maybe Pomerantz said something in passing that *is* significant. I saw a videotape of another interview he did for a documentary being produced in New York. He talked about coming to L.A., said he had a big secret that could change his life."

Ezra munched thoughtfully on a chip. "Maybe he was just playing to the camera."

"Possible. By the way, where did old man Maurice make his money?"

Ezra shrugged, visibly uncomfortable again.

"It's not gossip, Ezra. I can look him up in a dozen resources and get the info." She waited.

"New construction," he finally said. "Half the tract homes in Orange County were built by Steele. Most of Marina del Rey is his, and many of the homes in the San Fernando Valley. This was years ago, when construction was good business."

Jessie's father had lost a considerable sum of money investing with some builders in Orange County. Frances still needled him about it. "But where did Steele senior get the start-up money to do all that, Ezra? His receptionist said he was a Holocaust survivor."

"Henry told me his father came to New York from Germany with some money right after the war, parlayed it into a small fortune on the stock market, then moved west." He shrugged again.

She ate another forkful of pasta. "Funny that I've never seen his face in the papers, considering that he's such a bigwig."

"Not funny at all. Maurice Steele is a *very* private person. He doesn't grant interviews. He doesn't allow his photo to be taken. He's never allowed himself to be honored by any of the organizations he supports—and believe me, they've all tried. His sons aren't as camera shy."

"That's good, because as I said, I want to talk to them. Where does the dad live?"

Ezra shook his head.

"Come on, Ezra. This could be important."

"I went there as a guest, Jessie. I don't feel right betraying their hospitality."

She'd been impressed with Barbara Loura's loyalty. Now she was irritated. "Look, I understand how you feel, but I need that information."

"Can't you get it some other way?"

"Probably. But it'll take time I don't want to waste."

He was silent a moment. "And you think this is important to the case?"

"I don't know," she said truthfully. "It could be pointless.

But I have no other lead." She still had no idea where Pomerantz had gone Saturday night—Joseph, the Golden Palms maintenance man/driver, had never spoken to him. She was still waiting to hear from the other L.A. cab companies. "Help me out, Ezra."

He sighed, then nodded and gave her an address on Carmelita in Beverly Hills. "It's near Robinsons-May."

"Now you're getting in the spirit. I'm just *joking*, Ezra," she said when she saw his consternation. "Thank you."

He grunted in answer. They ate a while in silence. She finished the pasta, then found herself reaching for another chip.

"I wasn't completely honest the other day," Ezra said.

She looked up at him, startled. "About what?"

He cleared his throat. "When I said I wanted to get to know you, I didn't mean just as a friend. I'm attracted to you, Jessie. I . . . like you very much." His face and neck had colored.

Hers, too. Her face felt hot. "I'm flattered, Ezra. But I *am* involved with someone. That wasn't an excuse."

He tried a smile. "I was hoping it was. I thought you might have been uncomfortable about the idea of going out with me because I'm your teacher. Or because we're different—religiously, I mean. And if that *was* the case, I didn't want it to stop us from getting to know each other."

"But we *are* different. You're practically a rabbi. I just found out I'm Jewish. I don't keep kosher or anything. I don't know that I ever will."

"I'm not a rabbi, Jessie. And my brother and sister will tell you I'm no saint." He smiled. " 'Ever' is a long time. You're taking classes, learning Hebrew. I sense that you have a real interest in Judaism, a yearning. Who knows where you'll be six months or a year from now?"

She shook her head. "I'm not unhappy the way I am, Ezra. I don't know that I want to change."

He looked at her thoughtfully. "You ask the most questions of all my students. You want to know all the details of the laws, all the nuances, the explanations. I sense that it's more than intellectual curiosity."

She considered before she spoke. "I've felt more settled since I found out I was Jewish. I can't explain why, except that I never had a clear idea of who I was, what was important. Being Jewish has given me a new direction, one I like. It just feels . . . right, somehow. And I *do* want to keep learning about my heritage and my religion. And no, it's not just intellectual."

He waited.

She played with her fork. "Right now I feel as if I'm in the gourmet section of a supermarket. Everything is new, exotic, fascinating. I may want to sample everything, but I may not want to make a steady diet of it."

"But you haven't really allowed yourself to sample anything, have you? Shulamit keeps inviting you for Shabbos. My sister Dafna told me she invited you. So have some of the others at the school. You turn everyone down. What are you afraid of?" His brown eyes were intent.

She thought for a moment. "Maybe that I'll really like it. Orthodoxy is a major commitment, Ezra. It would change my entire lifestyle. I don't know that I want to do that." She set the fork down. "Even if I did, it would complicate my already complex relationship with my family." She could just imagine Frances's reaction if she told her she was planning to keep kosher or observe the Sabbath. And what would Gary say?

"You can take little steps, if you want to. I can help you."

She smiled. "You'd be Henry Higgins to my Eliza?"

He laughed. "I don't see myself as your superior, Jessie. In fact, I think you could teach me a few things." He paused. "Anyway, you're involved with someone. He's a lucky guy. How long have you known him?"

"Eight years. He's my ex-husband." She saw the lift of Ezra's brows. "We both made mistakes. We're trying not to repeat them. He's Jewish," she added, not knowing why she felt the need to tell Ezra.

"I hope it works out." He checked his watch, then rose. "I have to get back. Jessie, what I said won't make you uncomfortable around me, will it? You won't drop my class?"

She smiled. "No chance."

"Because I mean it when I say that 'friends' is fine."

"It's a great show," she said, trying to lighten the moment, wondering suddenly if he understood her allusion to the sitcom.

"Six singles living in Manhattan, right?" He caught her look and smiled. "Yes, I *do* watch TV, though not often. I don't find much worth watching." He picked up his books and tucked them under his arm. "Good luck with Maurice Steele, Jessie. And think about spending a Shabbos with Shulamit or Dafna. I think you'll enjoy it."

She watched him leave the pizza shop. There were a few remaining nachos, their tips soggy now from contact with the guacamole. She ate them anyway.

She sat in the car, thinking about what Ezra had said. Thought some more about the Steeles and their foundation, and Norman Pomerantz and his secret, and the possibility that he'd shared it with someone.

Like Hilda Rheinhart.

The elderly woman had been nervous talking to Jessie; Jessie had felt she'd been keeping something back. Maybe she knew that Pomerantz had visited the foundation, and why. Maybe she knew what "lost and found" meant.

A different woman—an older one, judging by her voice—answered Jessie's call. Jessie asked to speak to Hilda.

There was a long silence. Then the woman said, "May I ask who's calling, please?" She sounded cautious.

"Detective Jessie Drake. Is she available?"

Another silence. Then, "Let me get the manager."

Jessie had a prickling feeling. "Is something wrong?" she asked, but the woman had put her on hold.

"Detective Drake?" a familiar voice said a minute later. "This is Lilly Gorcheck. How can I help you?"

"I wanted to speak to Mrs. Rheinhart. I wondered whether I could stop by now."

"I'm sorry, Detective." The manager sighed. "I'm afraid that Hilda's gone."

16

JESSIE'S HEART THUMPED. "Gone" as in "disappeared"? Had Hilda been kidnapped by recruiters? Or had something worse happened to her? She cleared her throat, surprised by how shaken she was. "What happened? Was she . . ?"

"We had to transfer her to an SNF—a skilled nursing facility."

"So she's all right?" Jessie asked, tingling with relief. *Don't identify,* she told herself. But she *wasn't* identifying with Hilda—she was feeling justified concern about a frightened, lonely old woman who had no family, no one to care for her.

"Hilda was becoming more and more agitated, poor dear, and her blood pressure was elevated. Mr. Mason and I reluctantly decided we had to move her."

"Agitated in what way?"

"Insisting that someone was going to kill her. Demanding round-the-clock protection. When we explained that we couldn't provide that, she became irrational."

Poor Hilda. Jessie sighed.

"I felt terrible for her, Detective Drake," Lilly said, as if she were echoing Jessie's thoughts. "So did Mr. Mason. We're sure this was triggered by Mr. Pomerantz's death." The manager paused. "Mr. Mason feels that her anxiety may have been exacerbated by the police questioning."

Translation: by you. Jessie felt herself becoming defensive. "Mrs. Gorcheck, I *had* to talk to Hilda. She's the only person who knew Mr. Pomerantz."

"I *totally* understand, Detective. You were doing your job. As I told you, I'm sure her paranoia has to do with her Holocaust background more than anything else. In any case, we were afraid she might hurt herself."

"Couldn't you give her something to calm her?"

"We don't prescribe medication. We only disburse it. We felt it was best for Hilda to place her in a facility where she would have nursing supervision and medical care." Lilly lowered her voice. "And quite honestly, her outbursts were making some of the other residents nervous."

Not great for business, Jessie thought. "Exactly where is Hilda now?"

The convalescent home was five blocks away from the Golden Palms—and five blocks closer to Cedars Sinai Medical Center. Very convenient, Jessie thought as she parked her Honda. And good for business.

The lobby, decorated in varying shades of rust, was smaller than the one in the Golden Palms, and empty except for a middle-aged woman who was probably visiting one of the residents. The facility seemed to have a more hospital-like odor— or maybe that was a product of Jessie's imagination.

Arnold Samber, the manager, was tall and gangly with impossibly long arms that reminded Jessie of a pretzel.

"Mrs. Rheinhart is resting," he told her somberly after she introduced herself and explained why she'd come.

"Is she all right?"

"That depends on what you mean by 'all right.'" He frowned. "Physically, she's okay, but she was highly agitated when they brought her here, and we had to sedate her."

He said this pointedly, and she decided he'd probably talked to Mason. "Is she awake? I'd like to speak with her, if I can."

His glance was disapproving. "She's probably awake, but I

suggest that you come back tomorrow. She's had a rough morning."

"I'd rather speak to her now, if possible," Jessie said. "I won't stay long." Politeness first. If that didn't work . . .

Another frown, some tightening of the lips. Then, "All right."

Hilda was in a hospital bed in a small room on the third floor. The manager seemed reluctant to leave Jessie alone with his charge, but Jessie said, "I need to speak with Hilda privately," and Samber finally nodded and exited the room.

"You're the detective," the old woman said in a half-whisper. "Jessie James, right?"

"That's right." Approaching the bed, Jessie was startled to see how pale the old woman looked without blusher and lipstick. She forced herself to smile at Hilda, whose watery eyes were riveted on Jessie's face. "How are you feeling, Hilda?"

"How should I be?" she said, her voice faint. "They doped me up."

Jessie took Hilda's hand. Thin bones covered with a transparent sheath of skin. "You were upset, Hilda. They wanted to make you feel better."

Hilda attempted a grunt. "They don't believe me. I told them someone is going to try to kill me, just like they killed Anna Seligman and the others. Nobody believes me."

"What others?"

"People like me." She licked her lips. "Survivors," she whispered.

Jessie frowned. "Why would someone be killing survivors?" No answer from Hilda. "Who's trying to kill you, Hilda?"

"I don't know *who*," the old woman said petulantly. "I don't know how many there are, but they're all over." Her eyes darted around the room.

Jessie suppressed a sigh—Lilly Gorcheck was probably right. Hilda was paranoid because of her Holocaust experience. Who wouldn't be? "Mr. Pomerantz visited the Steele Foundation last week, Hilda. Did he tell you why?"

"I know the foundation." The old woman nodded. "They do good work."

"Did he tell you why he went there?" Jessie repeated patiently.

"No." She shut her eyes briefly and sighed.

"Hilda, Mr. Pomerantz said something to the foundation receptionist about a lost and found. Do you have any idea what that could mean?"

"Something's lost, that's where you look for it. Or if you find something, you give it in. They have a lost and found at the Golden Palms."

The old woman was obviously being evasive. Jessie was frustrated, but couldn't muster up anger. "Hilda, we're trying to find out who killed your friend. I know you're scared. If you tell me what you know about Mr. Pomerantz, that will help *me* help *you*."

Hilda's faded blue eyes assessed Jessie for a moment. "You asked me when was the last time I saw him," she finally said. "It was Saturday, not Sunday. I remembered." She sounded pleased. "He told me he was going to the Century Plaza that night to meet someone. He was excited."

Jessie felt her stomach muscles curl. "Did he say whom he was meeting?" she asked, holding her breath.

Hilda shook her head.

Naturally—that would have been too easy. "Did he say why he was excited?"

Another shake of the head.

She doesn't trust me, Jessie realized. "I hope you feel better, Hilda. I'm sure they'll take good care of you here, and then you can go back to the Golden Palms and your friends."

"They don't miss me. Mr. Mason will find someone else to put in my room." She looked suddenly anxious. "Will you ask them to tell Gloria that I'm here? Gloria's my physical therapist. She'll want to know. She cares about me."

"I'll tell them," Jessie promised. "Is there anything I can do for you before I go?"

"You don't have to feel sorry for me. Poor Hilda. She's all alone." She pursed her lips. "I'll be okay. I'm tough, you know." She thrust her chin forward defiantly.

"I'll bet you are." Jessie smiled. "I don't feel sorry for you, Hilda."

"Sure." Hilda grunted. A moment later, she asked, "You like romance novels?"

"I used to read them under the covers when I was in high school. My mother didn't approve." She and Helen used to sneak them into the house and back to the library. Frances had caught them once—she'd shredded the books, made Jessie and Helen pay the library. Still, it had been worth it. . . .

"My mother didn't like when I read Polish novels, too." Hilda smiled. "I love to read—that's how I learned English, you know. Books. But my eyes aren't so good—cataracts, the doctor said, but not big enough to operate on yet. You want to read to me, Jessie James? Unless maybe you don't have time. You're a busy detective."

"I can read to you for a few minutes. I'd like to very much." Reaching over, she took the romance novel from the nightstand—the same one she'd seen the other day. The heroine looked even more fetching. "Where should I start?" she asked, flipping open the dog-eared paperback.

"Chapter Four." Hilda settled herself against her pillow. "Don't skip the sexy parts. I like those the best, next to the parts that make you cry. You, too?"

Jessie smiled. "Me, too."

"I used to read the sexy parts to my Leon. And then we would . . . you know." She smiled impishly, then glanced at Jessie's left hand. "You're not married, a pretty girl like you?"

"Divorced. But my ex and I are dating again," she said, wondering why she was volunteering personal information to an old woman she barely knew.

"So maybe this time it'll work out."

"Maybe." She thumbed to Chapter Four and cleared her throat. " 'Conrad ravished her with his smoldering eyes,' " she began. " 'Eleanor felt weak-kneed, dizzy. . . .' "

Jessie was familiar with the Century Plaza—her parents used to stay there when they'd come up from La Jolla, before Helen and Neil moved to L.A. and bought a home complete with guest house. Frances had enjoyed the proximity to the nearby open-air shopping mall, and the Shubert Theater was just across the street. Jessie had spent several pleasant evenings there with her parents.

She and Gary had stayed there one night, too—a first-anniversary celebration. When they'd checked in, they were told that the room he'd reserved wasn't available—a terrible mistake, we're so sorry, and would they mind taking the penthouse suite instead?

They minded terribly, they'd told each other, laughing, after Gary opened the door and carried her over the threshold and they excitedly took a tour through the magnificent rooms. She savored now the taste of the champagne that had been waiting for them, delicious, ice-cold, and was lost for a moment in a flood of memories.

Back to business. Pulling the Honda into the semicircular driveway, she waited for a uniformed parking attendant to open her door. She showed her badge and gave him points for maintaining his polite demeanor, even though he probably figured there'd be no tip.

"Will you be long, ma'am?" he asked.

If she had any luck, she might be. "I don't know," she said, and entered the refrigerated lobby.

The reception clerk didn't recognize Pomerantz from his photo. Neither did the manager or any of the doormen Jessie approached, or the bellmen or valet parking staff. She even showed his photo to the handsome pianist playing *Phantom of the Opera*—she loved that music—at the baby grand in the enormous step-down lobby.

She hadn't really been hopeful—she didn't know for a fact that Pomerantz had ever arrived at the hotel.

Still, it was a lead. She showed his photo to the staff at the hotel's restaurant. More negatives, but the manager told her the waitress who handled the weekend evening shifts was off Wednesdays and Thursdays.

"Maybe she saw him," the woman said. "If you come Friday night, you can ask her."

"What's her name?"

"Patsy Williams."

Jessie wrote that down and left her card. "In case someone remembers something," she said.

She tipped the parking attendant. Just because she was having a bad day didn't mean he had to.

17

"**WE LEFT OUR** hometown on a Friday and headed to Cracow with two wagons—one to ride on, the other to carry our goods," Pomerantz said. "My father had bought another horse because he knew the war was going to break out, and that we would have to move. We packed the wagons with all our best textiles and other bags of goods for shipment to Europe.

"Everywhere we went, we heard that Germans were blocking the way with tanks and armored cars and were killing Jews. We turned the horses around and headed toward Cracow by another direction. In Kreszowice we left textiles with friends, because we were being slowed down by the load. Then one of our horses got sick. We had to unload the wagon and buy another horse.

"With the new horse we continued. Soldiers came to stop us— we bribed them with goods and money. We gave away so much that eventually we had no more goods to give." Pomerantz smiled wryly. "We heard that there was shooting up ahead, so we had to stay in Melitz.

"It was almost Shabbos. A Jew there let us stay with him. We had a box with various silver goods and precious things which we couldn't leave anywhere. My mother buried them in the basement where no one would find them.

"We were awakened by the sound of shooting, and decided to leave. We harnessed the horses to the wagon and were on the way to Cracow when the Germans caught us. They took us men to a nearby house and forced us to strip naked in a pool. They would have killed us, for sure, but one soldier said, 'Ask them for money.' So the captain threatened that unless my father gave him a check for ten thousand zlotys, they would kill us all. My father wrote the check but told them it was unlikely the bank would honor it. They took the check and let us go, still naked, back to the wagon. So I guess the soldier saved our lives."

"Until this day, those goods my mother buried are probably still in Melitz, hidden in a basement." Pomerantz smiled. *"Who knows? If I went back there and found those things, I could be a rich man. . . ."*

Maurice Steele lived on a deep corner lot in a light mocha stucco mansion that was as graceful as it was grand. Jessie had been prepared for large—this was Beverly Hills—but in spite of the heat she stood on the sidewalk for a moment, taking in the stately architecture and impeccably kept grounds. And the windows. She was passionate about windows. There were two enormous bays on the ground floor, and the mullioned second-floor windows had balconies, painted cream, like frosting on a cake.

The property was gated with scrolled black wrought iron, broken up every fifteen feet by tall mocha pillars that stood like sentries. Two of the wrought-iron sections on either boundary corresponded with the ends of the flagstoned driveway that swooped in a semicircle around the massive lawn. Jessie recognized a white Rolls-Royce, a navy Cadillac, a black Porsche, and a camel Volvo.

Thankful for the shade of two towering jacaranda trees, she rang the bell at the front section of the gate. From the metal oblong slotted panel on the wall to her right, she heard static, then a crackled, "Yes?"

"I'm Detective Drake with the LAPD. I'd like to speak with Mr. Charles or Mr. Henry Steele."

"Do you have an appointment?" the woman asked.

"No."

"Please wait." Half a minute later more static, and a new voice on the line. "May I ask what this is in reference to?"

"I'd prefer to discuss that with the Steeles."

"One minute, please." Another wait, longer this time. Then, "I'm letting you in."

The gate clicked open, then swung automatically forward to the left. Jessie passed through and crossed the lawn to a cobbled walkway that led her to the massive double doors. Before she had a chance to use one of the large lion-head brass knockers, the door was opened by a petite blond uniformed maid. She stepped aside to let Jessie enter.

In the center of an airy, octagonal, two-story entry, a tall, angular, brown-haired woman in a gray silk suit stood, as if posing, next to a round stone table bearing a magnificent floral arrangement. Still life with human, Jessie thought.

The woman smiled politely and approached Jessie. "I'm Sarah Miller, the Steeles' assistant. Both Mr. Charles and Mr. Henry Steele are tied up right now, and they asked if you could come back another time or allow me to help you."

Voice number two. She probably belonged to the Volvo. Smiling in return, Jessie said, "I don't mind waiting. And I need to speak with them personally."

"It might be some time."

"Not a problem," Jessie said cheerily.

The woman hesitated, then said, "All right, then. Follow me, please." More resigned than gracious.

Jessie heard footsteps and, turning her head to her right, recognized the lawyer. What was his name—Reynolds? She wasn't surprised to see him here, but he looked startled to see her.

"You're the *detective!*" He clutched his chest. "Don't tell me you've been following me."

He sounded nervous, and Jessie didn't blame him. Sarah Miller, she saw, looked confused. "I'm here to see the Steeles. As a matter of fact, you and I almost met earlier today." She enjoyed seeing his puzzled frown. "I was in the foundation office when you arrived. You were in a hurry, so you probably didn't notice me."

Recognition dawned. "I *thought* you looked familiar. I'm

generally in a hurry, but I definitely should have paid attention." He smiled, then cocked his head, studying her. "But you didn't say anything later."

"It didn't seem relevant to the situation. And I didn't want the meter reader to think we were colluding."

"Good point." Reynolds turned to Sarah, who had been standing patiently, listening. "This lovely person saved me from an unfair parking ticket. The meter reader jiggled my meter. Can you imagine?" He faced Jessie again. "I didn't thank you properly for coming to my rescue."

"It wasn't a big deal. Actually, it was the highlight of my day."

"Mine, too." He chuckled. "So you're here to see the Steeles? I know they donate generously to community causes."

She heard the curiosity in his voice and knew he was fishing. "So I've heard."

"Well, once again, thank you. See you tomorrow, Sarah," he said, saluting the assistant, then walked toward the front door.

"Do you think either of the Steeles are available now?" Jessie asked Sarah as Reynolds opened the door and left.

"I'll check. You can wait in the living room."

Her heels clacking on the beige marble tiles, she led the way out of the entry and down three bleached-wood steps into a hotel-lobby living room that was larger than Jessie's entire house. The furniture—couches and chairs upholstered in tapioca raw silks, marble-based glass coffee tables and end tables, Aubusson rugs in muted shades—was beautiful and elegantly understated, but the art stole the show.

Ezra was right. It was like entering a museum. "What a stunning collection," Jessie said, unable to stop staring. Frances would love this, she thought.

"It is, isn't it?" Sarah smiled with pleasure. "This is only part of it. The entire house is filled with pieces that Mr. Steele has spent his life acquiring. Aside from the paintings, there are exquisite objets d'art around the room. Quite valuable, as you can imagine, so I *do* have to ask you not to touch any— Oh, Mr. Larkins, you startled me. I didn't know you were still here."

This *was* a busy household, Jessie thought as she turned to her right and saw a thin, dapper, medium-height man with pumpkin-colored hair and a trim mustache. He was holding a pad of paper.

"Miss Miller." He actually bowed. "I was just taking some notes." He looked curiously in Jessie's direction.

"This is Ms. Drake." The assistant turned to Jessie. "Donald Larkins is with a private Pasadena museum that will be showcasing a significant representation of Mr. Steele's collection in their fall exhibit. Paintings, sculptures, a number of ceremonial items. We're all extremely excited about it."

"How do you do, Ms. Drake. A pleasure." Another bow.

One of the drooling curators. Jessie was tempted to curtsy. Interesting that Sarah had introduced her minus the "detective," but not surprising.

"Nice seeing you again, Mr. Larkins," Sarah said. "If you need anything, do let me know." To Jessie: "I'll tell the Steeles you're waiting." She left the room.

Jessie wanted to study the paintings, but decided it would be rude to walk away from the curator, who was looking at her. "You must be very busy preparing the exhibit," she said after a few seconds.

"Oh, quite." He bobbed his head. "Aside from putting together this show—a *monumental* undertaking, I can tell you—there's the catalog. I've retained an outstanding art photographer, of course, and a gifted copywriter. But my dear, the *details*!" He pressed his free hand against the side of his head. "So much to do, and July is gone."

"I'm sure it'll be wonderful. It's very generous of Mr. Steele to loan his collection."

"*Very* generous, indeed. We feel quite fortunate, and proud, that he chose us. But then, if I may say so, our museum, though small, is developing an important reputation. And Mr. Steele and I have a special relationship. Are you involved with the art world, Ms. Drake?"

Was Larkins hoping that this "special relationship" would inspire Steele to bequeath part of his collection to Larkins's museum? She smiled. "No. But I do appreciate art. My parents always took my sister and me to museums and galleries."

He nodded approvingly. "I'm acquainted with quite a number of serious collectors, but I can tell you that Mr. Steele has the *keenest* eye for composition and color that I've ever seen. He knows quality and talent."

"It's unfortunate that he's ill. It would be a shame if he weren't able to attend the exhibit."

Larkins sighed expansively. "Yes. One can only hope that he'll recover his strength in time. His heart condition is rather serious, and he's no youngster. But he's a fighter. You know his background?"

"You mean the Holocaust?"

"Exactly." More head bobbing. "He survived against incredible odds. We're praying that he does so again."

Larkins sounded genuinely fond of Steele. But if the collector didn't survive, and Larkins was the recipient of his largesse, would he really be devastated? Jessie had read recently that the Los Angeles County Museum of Art had just received a twenty-five million dollar donation of Mexican art. How much was the Steele collection worth?

"What line of work are *you* in, Ms. Drake?"

"I'm a detective." Sarah Miller, she guessed, would probably have preferred that Jessie tell Larkins she was involved in "community service."

He pressed his hand against his chest. "Ms. Miller didn't say anything about a theft. Has there been—"

"Actually, I'm a homicide detective."

Larkins had visibly paled. "How very unusual. I would never have guessed."

He couldn't have looked more shocked if she'd told him she was a hooker. He was staring at her, his discomfiture so complete that she felt sorry for him. "I'm just here to ask the Steeles about someone who stopped by their foundation," she volunteered.

"I see. Well," he added after a moment, and cleared his throat. "I'd better be going. It's been a pleasure meeting you, Ms. Drake. I hope you'll come to the exhibit when it opens." No bow this time, no extended hand.

She smiled. "Thanks. I'll certainly try."

After Larkins made a quick exit—more of an escape,

really—Jessie walked around the room, studying the paintings, wondering which ones the curator had selected for the show. They all looked fabulous to her.

She was admiring a small oil when Sarah Miller called her name.

"I don't know how you get anything done, working here," Jessie said, taking a last look before she walked toward the woman. "I'd be staring at these all day."

"That's all I did, at first. I used to sneak in on the hour." The assistant smiled. "Mr. Steele can see you now."

"Charles or Henry?"

"Actually, they're both available."

Both Steeles. Talk about luck.

18

CHARLES WAS ABOUT five feet eight and had thinning walnut-brown hair and brooding, dark brown eyes. Henry, several inches taller, had hair and eyes the color of ginger. The brothers—Jessie guessed they were in their late forties or early fifties—looked trim in similar, but not identical, navy suits that fit so well they must have been custom-made. Henry wore a conservative burgundy tie with a thin diagonal gray stripe. Charles's had a geometric yellow-on-gray design. The Porsche was probably his; the Cadillac, Henry's. And the Rolls, no doubt, belonged to Papa Bear.

Both men had purplish bags under their eyes behind their bifocals, and from the shadowy growth on Charles's face, she assumed he hadn't shaved this morning.

"Why don't we sit down?" Henry said after Sarah had performed the introductions and left the room. He gestured toward a round mahogany table in the corner of the library. "Something to drink? Mineral water?" He sounded weary.

"Diet Coke, if you have it." Déclassé, but she loved it.

Charles remained standing with his hands in his pockets while Henry walked over to a center cabinet, behind which was a glass-shelved bar. Jessie headed for the table and stopped in front of a large family portrait—Papa, Momma, and the two boys looking serious in dark, somber oils. Henry resembled his mother, a petite, strawberry blonde who was a little chubby in a too-tight black velvet dress. Maurice looked like Charles—same thinning brown hair, same brooding eyes. Not a handsome face or a distinguished face or one you'd remember—certainly not a face that said, "I am a millionaire."

"What a nice portrait," Jessie said to fill the silence.

"Yes," Charles said.

End of conversation. Jessie sat on a dark green chenille armchair, inhaling the scent of the orange-edged yellow roses on the table. Henry brought an ice-filled tumbler and a can of Coke. He placed both on white paper doilies and sat down. So did Charles.

"Thanks." She snapped the tab off the can and, filling the glass, watched with alarm as the soda erupted into a volcano of foam that threatened to spill past the doily onto the brightly polished wood. Bending her head, she took a quick sip to avoid disaster. The brothers, she sensed, were staring.

"I know that your father is ill, and that this is a difficult time," she said. "I appreciate your seeing me."

"You didn't give us much of a choice." Charles's voice— cool, a little arrogant—conveyed his annoyance. "What's so secretive and urgent that you couldn't discuss with Miss Miller?"

Jessie was surprised that Barbara Loura hadn't told them about her visit. "We're investigating the death of a Holocaust survivor, Norman Pomerantz, who was found in Rancho Park early Sunday morning." She had their attention now—they were staring at her and had sucked in their breaths. "Your foundation receptionist confirmed that he visited the office last Tuesday and was disappointed when he couldn't meet with your father or with one of you."

"You're a *homicide* detective." Henry sounded mildly shocked.

"I would say that's pretty obvious, Henry," his brother said dryly. "Barbara phoned earlier and left one of her 'urgent' messages—no doubt this is why." Charles turned to Jessie. "Since our father took ill, we've been spending most of our time here at the house. I'm sorry about Mr. Pomerantz, but since we've never met him, I don't understand why you're here."

"I thought he might have returned another time, when Ms. Loura was on her lunch break. We're trying to reconstruct Mr. Pomerantz's last few days. Anything he might have said to you might help us in our investigation." She took a sip of soda and watched the brothers over the rim of her glass.

"Pomerantz, Pomerantz," Henry repeated, his brow furrowed in concentration as he drummed his fingers on the table. "Why is that name familiar?" He glanced at his brother.

Charles shrugged. "Doesn't ring a bell."

Jessie took out the photo and handed it to Henry. He looked at it without commenting, shook his head, and passed it to Charles. Another silent examination, another shake of the head, and the photo made its way back to Jessie, like a peace pipe passing hands.

Henry said, "Detective, I don't know if you're aware that our foundation has been helping Holocaust survivors gain access to funds they or their families deposited in Swiss bank accounts before the war."

Jessie nodded.

"Well, as you can imagine, we've been inundated with elderly people coming to us for assistance. Quite a number resemble the man in this photo."

"Ms. Loura told me she took Mr. Pomerantz's name and the phone number where he could be reached and passed the information on to both of you." She took another sip of soda.

Charles snorted. "If Barbara left a memo on my desk, it's probably still there, buried under others. I've barely been at the foundation all week, and I dread seeing the pile of calls I have to return."

"I've returned dozens of messages in the past few days," Henry said. "Did Barbara indicate why Mr. Pomerantz came to the foundation?"

"He mentioned something about 'lost and found.' He wouldn't explain. But he told someone else that he had a secret that could change his entire life. He was very excited about it." Blank looks from both Steeles. "He was visiting from New York, by the way, and was staying at the Golden Palms Re—"

"A retirement home." Henry nodded. "I *did* get Barbara's memo. I phoned him, but he wasn't in, and I'm sorry to say that with everything going on lately, I didn't try again. And I didn't leave a message, or my home number." A quick, apologetic smile. "Unfortunately, we've had to become careful about giving out our home numbers."

So there had been *another* male caller—the one who *had* spoken to Pomerantz but hadn't identified himself to Yasmin. "Do you still have the memo? Ms. Loura told me Mr. Pomerantz said something else, but she can't remember what. She might have been more specific when she wrote the note."

Henry shook his head. "Sorry. I'm pretty sure I tossed it out."

"What do you think Mr. Pomerantz meant by 'lost and found'?" Jessie asked. "And why would he be so interested in talking to someone in your family?"

"No idea," from Charles. He sounded uninterested.

Henry rubbed his chin. " 'Lost and found' could mean anything. The Swiss bank accounts, perhaps? Or the insurance companies? It's well known that the foundation is helping survivors with claims in both those areas."

"He didn't need to travel from New York to file a claim," Charles said impatiently. "And he didn't need to talk to one of us, if that was his goal."

"You're right, of course. *Thank you* for pointing that out."

Some sibling hostility there, Jessie sensed. Or maybe their father's illness had put them on edge.

"Your father might know," she suggested. "Mr. Pomerantz specifically wanted to talk to him. I understand that like Mr. Pomerantz, your father is a Holocaust survivor. Maybe the phrase 'lost and found' would have some special significance to him."

Charles shook his head. "We can't trouble our father with any questions right now. Even if we wanted to, his doctor would never allow it."

"Charles is right," Henry said. "But to be honest, I don't think he'd be able to tell you anything more."

Which was basically nothing. "Maybe Mr. Pomerantz was hoping to find some lost valuables that belonged to his family," Jessie said. "That might explain this secret he mentioned, and why he was so excited about it." Charles, she saw, looked skeptical. "If the item or items he recovered were worth a lot of money, that would certainly have changed his life." According to Goldblum, Pomerantz had set aside only a little money for his old age.

"That's a long shot, I'm afraid," Charles said.

"Are most of the stolen valuables worth a lot?" she asked him—he was the art aficionado, she remembered.

"That varies. And it's hard to evaluate worth with the passage of so much time." He sighed. "It's really heartbreaking, you know. Survivors come to us, hoping we'll be able to restore what was theirs—artwork, porcelain figurines, jewelry. Not for the money, usually, but for the sentimental value, and for justice. But it's a long, difficult task, and establishing provenance is sometimes next to impossible."

"I read that a great many pieces of art owned by Jewish victims found their way to France," Jessie said.

"*Quelle* surprise." Charles's smile was closer to a sneer.

Henry said, "France is finally confronting its pro-Nazi Vichy past, and the fact that seventy-five thousand Jews were rounded up by its citizens and sent to the death camps. Under the Vichy regime two thousand precious artworks—paintings, sculptures, rare books, jewels—were confiscated from French Jews."

"The Rothschilds, the Bernheim-Jeune families, Alphonse Kann, to name a few." Charles leaned back in his chair. "Paul Rosenberg was a Jewish dealer—he had extensive art holdings. Kann owned more than twelve hundred works, including twenty Picassos. Can you imagine?"

She couldn't. She shook her head, astounded by the numbers. "What happened to the art?"

"If you want to know details, read *The Lost Museum* by Hector Feliciano," Henry said. "Some of the confiscated works were sent to Germany for storage—Hitler planned to build the world's greatest museum in Linz, Austria, and fill it with the precious art he was looting from every country he vanquished. Some of it was warehoused in the Musée de Jeu de Paume, which was also used to sell the modern art Hitler so disliked."

"He called it 'degenerate.'" Charles snickered. "How's that for irony?"

"Where is the art now?" Jessie asked.

"The Louvre supposedly has at least five hundred of the paintings," Charles said. "The Pompidou Center, the Musée D'Orsay, the Rodin Museum—I heard they all have some of these works of 'unknown ownership.'" Another sarcastic smile. "They say some pieces are hanging in French government ministries. Picassos, Légers, Matisses, Van Goghs, Renoirs—collectively they're worth millions of dollars."

Jessie had never been to the Louvre—had never been out of the country, for that matter. If she did go there someday, would she look at every painting and wonder? "The French kept everything?"

Henry shook his head. "After the war the government returned over forty-five thousand confiscated objects. And they passed a law requiring authorities to find the owners and return the works. But I understand that French authorities either ignored claims or worked around them."

"France isn't the only country holding on to stolen art," Charles said. "They say the Swiss museums and public collections are filled with looted art Swiss dealers and collectors bought at the Jeu de Paume during the war. One-stop shopping—better bargains than at Kmart." Another smile. "And I wouldn't be shocked to learn there are stolen pieces in this country."

The thought was appalling. "I hope you're wrong," she said and saw Charles shrug.

"It isn't just a question of a museum or a country or a private party reluctant to relinquish items of great value," Henry said earnestly. "It's also the tacit admission that the acquisition of these valuable objects was made possible by the persecution and looting and annihilation of its original owners. And in some cases, by direct complicity with the Nazis."

Jessie ran her finger around the rim of her glass. "Even if there was no complicity, and no knowledge of the origin of the items, I imagine it would be hard to part with them. I understand that your father has a renowned collection. I'm sure he'd be devastated to learn that even one of his acquisitions had a shady origin." She saw immediately that she'd said the wrong thing. Both men had stiffened.

"My father and I," Charles said with studied coldness, "take great pains to ensure that the provenance of each item in our collection is above reproach."

"I didn't mean to suggest otherwise," Jessie said sincerely. "I apologize if I've offended you."

"Well, you *have* offended me. As a survivor, my father is the last person in the world who would want to benefit from the terrible plight of our people."

"I don't think Detective Drake implied anything, Charles," Henry said quietly.

Charles looked at his brother, then nodded perfunctorily at Jessie.

There was an awkward silence. Jessie thought for a moment, then said, "What if Mr. Pomerantz wasn't hoping to recover something? He said, 'lost and found.' I know he appreciated art and enjoyed going to museums. What if he saw something in one and recognized it as having belonged to a Jewish family—his own, or someone else's? What if he tried to contact you to tell you about his discovery?"

The brothers, she'd noticed, had exchanged a brief look, and were staring at her again, frowning.

"It would have to belong to his own family," Jessie continued, thinking aloud. "Otherwise, why would the discovery change his life?"

"Maybe he thought he'd get a reward," Henry said. "Or maybe he meant that restoring the item to its rightful owner would change his life by giving him tremendous satisfaction."

"Maybe," Jessie said, trying to be polite.

The door opened, and a frail-looking, elderly woman with dyed gray-blond hair entered the room. "I'm sorry," she said quickly in a high, accented voice. "I didn't know you had someone here."

Henry and Charles jumped to their feet. Henry crossed the room. "Is Dad—"

"He's all right." She looked curiously at Jessie.

"This is Detective Drake," Henry said, clearly unhappy to make the introduction.

Jessie didn't blame him. She pushed the armchair back and stood. "Thank you both for your time. If you think of anything else, please call me." She took a business card from her purse and left it on the table. To Mrs. Steele, she said, "I hope your husband makes a speedy recovery."

"Thank you," she said softly. She blinked back tears.

Henry walked Jessie to the entry. "I'm sorry we weren't of much help," he said, opening the heavy door. "If I think of anything, I'll definitely call."

"Thanks. I may have some more questions for you or your brother. Where can I reach you if you're not at the foundation?"

"Probably here." He took a card from his jacket pocket and scribbled down the phone number.

A moment later the door shut behind her. Making her way down the stone walkway, she contemplated Pomerantz's 'lost and found' phrase. The more she thought about it, the more sense it made that Pomerantz had found something that had been lost.

If he *had* recognized stolen art that had belonged to his family, he would logically have kept his discovery secret to protect his interests until he obtained the help he needed in establishing his ownership.

Maybe he'd divulged his discovery to someone in whom he'd believed he could safely confide. Maybe that someone had told someone else, who had told someone else . . .

Had the discovery ultimately been divulged to the wrong person?

Had Pomerantz been killed because of it?

19

"BELIEVE IT OR not, I was in the bakery when I met the woman who would be my first wife," Pomerantz said. "It was her parents' bakery, and she worked behind the counter. Her name was Esther—Estusha, I called her. She was beautiful and smart, and she always had a smile for the customers, even for the ones who were demanding. So it was love at first sight—at least for me." He placed his open palm on his chest and smiled. "Estusha didn't even know I existed, but she thought I had some sweet tooth—I was showing up four, five times a week, pretending my mother had sent me. My sisters were thrilled—all that pastry!" He chuckled.

"I was nineteen, she was eighteen. I couldn't ask her out—that was unheard of in my day. Marriages were arranged, you know. So I had a cousin suggest the match to my father, and my father, who knew about Estusha's family, called a shadchen—a matchmaker. And the next thing I knew, Estusha and I were formally introduced. . . ."

"We had two daughters, Malka and Baila. Malka was almost two and Baila was eight months when the Germans came and made the first 'selection'—who would go to a labor camp, who to Auschwitz. They knocked on every door, ordering all the Jews to go into the street.

"During the first round-up, we were lucky—we were able to buy off the German doctor. During the second one, Estusha wasn't home. They took our daughters and her whole family to a collection point. When Estusha found out, she went to the collection point with a bucket of water and told a policeman she wanted to bathe the children. A miracle—he helped her." Pomerantz shook his head. "He led her to the factory where the Jews were being held, and she washed several children while looking for our daughters. She found them, and was able to get them out to a friend. Also, with the policeman's help, her sister-in-law and grandparents.

"Then came the third round-up." Pomerantz sighed and was silent for a moment. "Before this I wanted to leave the girls with a Polish woman who offered to take care of them until the war was over, but Estusha was afraid. 'What if she won't give them back?' she insisted. So we kept them with us. And then one night they rounded up the women. The Germans gave my wife a choice—she could give up her children and go to work in a labor camp. Or she could go to Auschwitz." Pomerantz paused. "She wouldn't give up the girls.

"The Germans didn't delay. They took my wife immediately with our two children and my mother. I went to the train station, and through one of the windows I saw Estusha. She was looking for me, too. She held up Baila, and my mother held up Malka. And they helped my little girls wave to me as the train pulled out of the station.

"Bye-bye, bye-bye," Pomerantz whispered, his eyes bright with tears. Lifting his right hand, he bent his fingers and waved. "Bye-bye."

"This is for the baby," Jessie said, taking a wrapped box out of the Bloomingdale's bag she was carrying and handing it to Helen. "I know it's early, but I couldn't resist."

"This is so sweet of you, Jessie!" Helen hugged her, then placed the box on the round glass table in her breakfast room.

Jessie smiled, taking pleasure in the little-girl glee that lit her sister's face. She'd been tired after leaving the station, but was glad now that she'd stopped at the Century City shopping mall before coming to Helen's to say goodbye to her parents, who were returning to La Jolla in the morning.

Helen undid the yellow-and-white glossy wrapping, careful

not to tear it, and removed the lid from the box. Like Frances, she saved wrapping paper, ribbons, bows, and stored everything neatly in a spare closet off the hall.

"This is *adorable!*" she exclaimed, holding up a mobile with black and white sheep.

"The sales person told me the first colors babies see are black and white. Funny, I always thought it was red."

"Me, too." Helen placed the mobile on the table. "Thanks, Jess. I can't wait to hang this in the baby's crib." Stepping on tiptoe, she kissed her sister. "I wish you'd let me know earlier that you were coming. You could have joined us for dinner."

"That's okay. I grabbed a bite." Pizza again. If they took a blood test, they'd probably find cheese and tomato sauce in her veins. "Where's Neil?"

"He went to Borders—the new Clancy is out." Helen rolled her eyes. "He should be back soon."

"Mommy, can I—oh, hi, Aunt Jessie!"

Jessie turned toward the doorway and smiled at her nine-year-old nephew. He looked cute in blue shorts and a black T-shirt decorated with some action figure she didn't recognize. "Where's my hug?" she asked.

Grinning, he ran and pressed himself against her.

She pretended to stagger backward. "Whoa, you're getting to be a bruiser! Move over, Rambo!"

He giggled. Folding her arms around him, she kissed his cheek and tousled his coal-black hair, identical to his father's, and felt, once again, an almost aching gratefulness that Helen and Neil had moved to L.A. from Winnetka, Illinois, a year ago and brought Matthew into her life.

"Matthew, honey, look at what Aunt Jessie bought for the baby. Isn't it adorable?"

He stayed in Jessie's embrace a few seconds longer, then picked up the mobile. "Does it play music?" he asked, spinning it.

"Uh-huh." Leaning closer, Jessie turned a knob several times, and softly tinkling nursery-rhyme tunes filled the room. "I have something for you, too." From the shopping bag she pulled out a white Power Ranger.

He took it in both hands. "*Tommy!* This is the *best!*" He turned toward Helen. "A kid in my class has the whole collection!" Tearing open the box, he removed the five-inch action figure. He pressed the figure's belt—the chest and back separated, and the "human" head flipped into the helmeted head of a Power Ranger.

"Say thank you to Aunt Jessie," Helen prompted, placing her hand on his shoulder.

"Thanks, Aunt Jessie." His wide smile revealed several missing teeth. "Can I play with this now, Mom? Please?"

"Is your room cleaned up?"

"Almost." He looked sheepish.

"Finish that first."

Killjoy, Jessie thought.

" 'Kay. See you later, Aunt Jessie." He slipped out from under his mother's hand, kissed Jessie again, and bounded out of the room.

Helen watched him leave. "He's growing up so fast, isn't he?" Sighing, she turned to Jessie. "He really loves the toy. And it's obvious that he adores you."

Was that jealousy in Helen's voice? Jessie walked into the spacious, newly remodeled, all-white kitchen—it was spotless, as usual, the dinner dishes cleared away—and opened the fridge. "It's mutual. He's a terrific kid."

"He is. The *best*. It was smart of you to get him something, Jessie. But then, you *always* do the right thing."

Jessie turned and glanced at Helen, surprised by the edge she heard. Where was this coming from? "No, I don't."

"Anyway," Helen said, indicating she didn't want to argue the point. "I'm going to have to remember to pay a lot of attention to Matthew when the baby comes. I don't want him to feel jealous." She pulled over the wrapping paper and started picking carefully at the Scotch tape.

"I suppose a little jealousy is inevitable." Jessie rummaged through the fruit bin, chose a Gala apple, and shut the fridge. "But you'll be fine, Helen. You're a good mother. You'll know what to do."

"And what *not* to do," she said, looking up. "That's what

you're thinking, isn't it? You're probably worried about my having another child." Her smile was brittle.

"No, I'm not," Jessie said calmly, hoping she sounded convincing. She returned to the table. "You've been in therapy for over a year, Helen. You're not the person you were." She took a bite of the apple. "What does Dr. Rossman say?"

"You've had therapy—you know shrinks don't say much." She smiled wryly. "He asked me to think about why I wanted a baby—aside from the obvious reasons, like a sibling for Matthew. You know what I figured out?"

Jessie shook her head.

"I wanted to have another chance to do it right. I wanted to have the closeness I never had with Matthew." Her eyes filled with tears. She wiped them with her hand. "God, these pregnancy hormones are the pits." She laughed lightly.

Jessie's eyes teared, too. "You'll do it right," she said softly, patting Helen's arm.

"I'm glad you think so." Helen returned her attention to the paper. A moment later, with an abrupt movement, she crumpled it into a ball. "Mom doesn't."

Jessie narrowed her eyes. "Did she tell you that?"

Helen grimaced. "She's barely been talking to me since the other night in the restaurant. But she's dropped hints." She sat down and stroked a white sheep. "You're lucky you don't have a guest house."

"Not much fun," Jessie agreed, sitting down. She knew all too well what it was like to be the victim of one of Frances's stony silences. She hesitated, then said, "She's hurt about the name thing, Helen."

Helen pursed her lips. "It's *my* child, Jessie! Mine and Neil's! Don't we have a right to choose its name?"

"Of course you do. But telling her that giving her father's name would be as much of a reminder as reclaiming Swiss bank money was a low blow. And it isn't even true."

"I know. That was mean." Helen's face was flushed. "Sometimes I *feel* mean around her—I want to pay her back for everything she did to me when I was a kid. Maybe that's why I don't want to name the baby for her father, if it's a boy." She shrugged.

Jessie didn't answer.

Helen turned the music knob on the mobile. "You think I don't like the name Jacob because it's too biblical, too Jewish. Don't deny it, Jess—I can see it in your face. I'm not stupid."

"I never thought you were." Jessie listened to the mobile play its lullaby. *Twinkle, twinkle, little star.*

"You think I should name a boy Jacob, don't you?" she challenged. "*You'd* do it."

"Like you said, Helen, it's your baby."

"She can't expect me to become someone else just because she finally admitted she was Jewish. She doesn't consider herself Jewish. She told me so herself."

When had Frances discussed this with Helen? "People change."

"Madeleine Albright found out her parents were Jewish, but she's still Episcopalian. She hasn't changed her life around."

"No, but she's researching her family history, and she visited her ancestor's birthplace." *How I wonder where you are. . . .* "No one's forcing you to change your life around, Helen."

"You made me look bad, asking all those questions about Mom's father, not backing me up about the Swiss bank account. I thought you'd be on my side," she said, petulant now.

"For God's sake, Helen, this isn't about *sides*! I want to know about our grandfather—is that so unreasonable?" she demanded, annoyed by her sister's self-absorption. "I want to know about *all* of Mom's family. I can't help it that you don't." She bit angrily into the apple. Juice dripped down her chin. Very nice, she thought, wiping it with her hand.

"Don't start this again, Jess. Mom's not interested, so why should I be?"

"She *is* interested. She just won't admit it. She was practically in tears when she was talking about her father. You saw her."

"Exactly." Helen leaned closer. "What's the point in dwelling on the horrible things that happened? Nothing will change that, Jess. Nothing will bring back the family Mom lost."

"So you pretend they didn't exist?" Jessie shook her head impatiently. "I can't do that. I don't *want* to do that."

"That's your choice." Helen lifted the mobile, still playing its music, and put it in the box.

"What about Matthew? Doesn't he have a right to know about his Jewish roots?"

Helen paled. She darted a look behind her. "You haven't said anything to him, have you?"

"I promised I wouldn't. But that doesn't mean Mom won't say something at some point."

Helen sniffed dismissively. "Mom's the *last* person in the world who'd do that."

"She asked you to name a son after her father. Did you ever think Mom would do *that?*"

"Did you ever think I'd do *what?*"

Both sisters turned toward the doorway to the dining room, where Frances was standing, looking impeccable in white slacks and a short-sleeved, red cotton knit sweater.

Jessie felt as she had hundreds of times during her childhood and adolescence—a fist was twisting the inside of her stomach; her heart was beating faster; her hands were clammy. She licked her lips and glanced at Helen, who had frozen and was gazing imploringly at her older sister. *Help me.*

"Helen and I were just talking about the fact that you had the chocolate cake last night," Jessie said, uttering the first words that came to her mind. "You're always so strict about what you eat. We were just surprised."

"But *proud* of you," Helen added.

Frances smiled at Helen, then at Jessie. "Well, if you don't want to tell me, don't. I know you two criticize me behind my back." She spoke in the clipped voice of long-time suffering.

Jessie sighed. "Mom, we weren't criticizing you."

"I have to check on Matthew and see how he's coming along with his room," Helen said. "Be right back."

Liar. Jessie almost laughed aloud as she watched Helen practically run from the kitchen—this was pathetically ridiculous, two grown women afraid to talk openly with their mother.

Frances said, "I was in the guest house, finishing packing, when I saw your car parked in front of the house."

She faced her mother. "I came to say goodbye. I know you're leaving in the morning. Where's Dad?"

"Watching CNN. Did you have dinner?"

"Uh-huh. Not as good as the Ivy, though." She smiled. "Thanks again for the evening. Gary had a good time, too. He asked me to tell you." They were planning to go to a late movie tonight, depending on how his piece was coming along. She was looking forward to a relaxing evening.

"Are you sleeping with him?"

The bluntness of the question made her laugh. "No. I don't want to rush into anything."

Frances nodded approvingly. "He's a fine young man, Jessie. Bright, handsome. Clearly, you like him, or you wouldn't be seeing him again. And he's obviously crazy about you. If he's willing to remarry into a family as dysfunctional as ours, you should grab him before someone else snatches him away."

"You didn't want me to marry him the first time, remember?"

Frances flinched. "What's your point, Jessica? That I was wrong? Fine. I admit it. I was *wrong*." Her voice had taken on a shrill note. She took a breath, and in a calmer tone said, "Why is it that you find it necessary to constantly remind me of my shortcomings as a mother?"

Was that what she did? The thought shamed Jessie. "I'm sorry."

Frances turned away. "I'll tell your father you're here," she said, taking a few steps toward the dining room.

Jessie reached out and touched her mother's arm. "I'm *really* sorry, Mom. Please don't go." Her mother didn't respond, but she hadn't stomped off or jerked her hand away. A positive sign. "Look what I bought for the baby," Jessie said, going to the table. She picked up the mobile and out of the corner of her eye, saw that her mother was walking toward her.

"This is precious," Frances said a moment later, holding the toy. She smiled. "I remember the one I bought when you were born. It had little gingham-clothed clowns—blue, pink, and yellow. You used to stare at it for hours." She handed the mobile back to Jessie. "Do you think Helen's ready to have this baby?"

"Matthew's nine years old." Not really the question her mother was asking.

"Is she . . . doing better with Matthew?"

"Do you mean, is she still hitting him?" Jessie asked softly. "I don't know. Neil hasn't said, and I don't feel I can ask. Matthew *seems* happy." Far happier than he'd been a year ago. Less fragile, less jumpy.

"A baby creates so many pressures," Frances said. "Months and months of sleepless nights, feedings every two to three hours, colic, teething. And when the baby's older, there's so much else. . . ." She sighed. "Helen doesn't cope well with stress."

Neither do you. "Helen can afford to get a nanny, if she feels the need. More importantly, Neil isn't traveling as much as he used to, and she's getting therapy."

"For *my* problem, you mean." Frances smiled tightly. "I'm sure the therapist tells her that this is all my fault."

What should Jessie say? *You beat us, Mom. You punched us. You terrorized us with your anger.* She would gain nothing by doing that. Certainly, not the beginnings of the close mother-daughter relationship she wanted.

"I tried my best to be a loving mother," Frances said. "I did the best I could."

"You did." Knowing what she now did about her mother's past, Jessie believed that Frances *had* done her best. "Helen is upset because you're not talking to her."

Frances drew herself up, prepared for battle. "She was rude and insensitive. And I don't mean because she refuses to name the baby Jacob if it's a boy."

"She's sorry for what she said. And she hasn't refused—she wants to think about it." Jessie hesitated, then said, "You told me and Helen that you're not interested in being Jewish. So why should *she* be interested?"

"This has *nothing* to do with being Jewish," Frances

snapped. "This has to do with perpetuating a name, with respect for those who died."

"You're sending mixed messages, Mom," Jessie ventured.

Frances narrowed her eyes. "That's *your* opinion."

"True. What if I'm right?"

"*Then,* Jessica—" Frances stopped. In a less strident voice, she said, "Then I might just have to think about it." She gazed at her daughter. "You think I should pursue the Swiss money, if there is any, don't you?"

"I don't know." It was Frances's money. It was Helen and Neil's baby. Why were her sister and mother asking her to make choices for them?

"How is your work?"

Jessie tried not to stare stupidly—Frances *never* asked about her job. Was she trying to reach out, or change the subject? "Hectic. We're investigating the death of a Holocaust survivor, as a matter of fact." She told her briefly about Pomerantz, saw her mother's green eyes darken.

"How terribly sad," Frances said softly.

"Isn't it? I have a videotape of an interview he did. He sounds like such a sweet man. He was eighty-four. Probably around the same age your father would have been if he'd lived."

"I don't know exactly how old my father was. Or my mother, for that matter. You think I'm lying, don't you? I can see it in your face."

"I don't think you're lying. I'm just terribly disappointed."

Frances touched Jessie's arm. "I'm not trying to keep anything from you. I could make something up, but that's not what you want, is it?"

"No. No, of course not." She couldn't be angry at her mother for not remembering—that wasn't fair or reasonable. But she felt disconsolate, bereft—illogically—of something she'd never even owned.

"I've been talking to a friend of Mr. Pomerantz," Jessie said. "She's in a nursing home. She's a survivor, too. A widow, no children." She hesitated, then said, "I can't help wondering whether any of your family survived." And if they had survived, had they rebuilt new families? Or were they living lonely lives in a residential facility, waiting for relatives who rarely visited?

"They didn't," Frances said a little sharply. In a gentler tone she added, "The Red Cross checked, Jessica. I would have heard."

"There are stories about survivors who discovered that a sibling or relative was still alive. . . ."

Frances shook her head. "I hope you aren't becoming personally involved with this case, Jessica."

"I'm not."

Her mother looked at her with interest. "This Mr. Pomerantz isn't your grandfather," she said kindly. "This old woman isn't your grandmother."

Jessie flushed. "I know that."

Frances nodded. "As long as you know."

20

THE TEN-YEAR-OLD BOY shot on the La Cienega off-ramp died during the night.

That was the first thing Phil told her when she arrived at the station on Thursday morning. It explained his solemn expression. Boyd was swiveling back and forth in his chair, looking glumly into space. Simms looked glum, too, and he didn't make one of his typical wise-ass comments. She felt sick to her stomach thinking about the dead boy, about his grieving parents.

They talked a while about the increase in road rage. Last night Gary had told her a guy driving the wrong way on the 101 Freeway had rammed his Jeep into five cars for no apparent reason. No one had been hurt. "A goddamn miracle," Gary had said, and how many times could you count on miracles?

They talked about what they'd like to see happen to the shooter.

"Just give me five minutes with him," Boyd said.

"Two is enough." Simms slammed his fist into his palm.

A few minutes of silence. Then Boyd asked, "You finish that department evaluation yet?" Addressing no one in particular.

Phil grunted. "Don't we have better things to do?"

"I'm not doing it." Simms chewed on his bottom lip.

"Espes said we had to," Boyd said earnestly.

Simms snorted. "You think they're really going to read thousands of these?" He mimed taking a paper and throwing it into the trash. "Of course, Jessie probably filled hers out already. Just like she probably handed all her term papers in on time."

"Jealous, Marty?" Phil asked.

Simms looked at her. "Am I right?"

She smiled enigmatically. She'd intended to work on the evaluation form last night, but Gary had stayed late, and then she'd been too tired, and hadn't wanted to spoil what had been a wonderful evening with tedious paperwork. She still had plenty of time—Espes had said by the end of next week.

"That's a joke, by the way." Simms winked at her. "Don't go writing me up. I don't need the hassle."

She wondered whether he was serious about not filling out the questionnaire. Probably not—he was often more bluster than bite, and he wouldn't risk making Espes or his department look bad.

Simms and Boyd left for the downtown courthouse to testify at the "pillow murder" trial, which was resuming this morning. Maybe. If the defense attorney didn't ask for a continuance.

Jessie checked her messages—nothing from any of the cab companies re Pomerantz. Big surprise. She walked to the hot water dispenser, wondering whom Pomerantz had planned to meet at the Century Plaza, and filled her mug.

Back at her desk, she dunked a strawberry-kiwi herbal tea bag into the hot water, inhaled the fruity fragrance. Phil was scribbling on a notepad.

"Find out anything about the hooker?" she asked.

He looked up at her. "*Nada.* Dragged my sorry butt all the way out to South Central to talk to a former colleague of Cassandra Jones. She says Cassandra was nervous lately—told her some regular john had been acting weird. But the friend didn't know his name. Naturally."

She tasted the tea—too hot. It singed her tongue. "What about the baby?" She blew on the tea.

He stabbed the open Yellow Pages in front of him. "Espes wants me to continue calling doctors. I know you're dying to help, so jump right in." He grinned at her. "What about you? Any luck with Pomerantz?"

"I found out where he went on Beverly Drive." She told Phil about the Steele Foundation receptionist and her visit to the Steele home. "It's like living in a private museum, Phil. You wouldn't believe it."

"Maureen's into art. Me, I'm a dunce when it comes to *cultshuh,*" he said, pronouncing the word with an exaggerated Brooklyn accent. "So Pomerantz didn't talk to either of the Steele sons?"

Jessie shook her head. "Some other man phoned him at the Golden Palms but didn't leave a message or a name. Maybe that's the guy he went to see Saturday night at the Century Plaza. I checked with the hotel—nobody recognized Pomerantz, but the waitress who's on weekends is off today. I'll talk to her Friday."

Phil cocked his head. "Who told you he went to the Century?"

"Hilda Rheinhart, his friend at the retirement home. She's not at the Palms anymore, by the way—she was too agitated, so they moved her to a convalescent home." The old woman had fallen asleep while Jessie was reading. Jessie hoped she was feeling better.

"So you found out Pomerantz phoned the foundation, but you don't know why. You think he may have discovered a piece of stolen art, but you don't know for sure that he did. And *if* he did, what it was. And he planned to go to the Century P, but we don't know why, either, or whether he ever got there." He paused. "Lots of unanswered whys." He linked his fingers behind his head. "You still think he was hijacked?"

"Not really. It's too much of a coincidence that he had this big secret and was killed. But who knows?" She shrugged. "Coincidences *do* happen." She took another sip of tea. Better now. She rummaged in her purse for a granola bar. She'd overslept and had only a glass of milk for breakfast after doing a compressed version of her twenty-minute daily workout.

"Futaki still hasn't ruled the death homicide."

She nodded. "I'm going to call him, tell him Pomerantz told a few people he had a secret." Not that the M.E. would be impressed with that information, but it might give him pause. She took a bite of the granola bar, downed it with a sip of tea.

"Good luck. What now?"

"I'm sure Hilda knows more than she's telling. I'll talk to her again. And I want to go back to the foundation. Maybe the receptionist can remember a little more about this 'lost and found' thing." She bit off another chunk of the granola bar.

Her phone rang. She picked up the receiver, chewing quickly, and said, "Drake," her mouth half full.

"Do you have access to the Internet?" Helen asked excitedly.

"Why?"

"Neil saw the complete listing from the Swiss banks. He found Mom's father's name—Jacob Kochinsky! Can you believe it?"

Jessie didn't know what to say. She chewed thoughtfully.

"I don't know if Mom's going to check the list," Helen said. "I think we should tell her, don't you?"

"She's not interested in the money. She made that clear." Phil, she saw, was looking at her with interest.

"I don't think she means it. And even if she feels that way now, she may change her mind down the road. And then it may be too late." Helen paused. "I think *you* should call her, Jessie. She'll listen to you."

"A, she won't. B, I'm not going to try to persuade her to do something she doesn't want to do."

"But—"

"Call her yourself, if you're so interested in this."

"At least think about it."

"Helen—"

"*Please,* Jess?"

Please, can you tell Mom you broke the vase. Please, can you do this paper for me. Please, Jess. Please, please, please.

Jessie sighed. "I'll think about it."

Barbara Loura didn't look thrilled to see Jessie.

"How can I help you, Detective?" she asked in a voice as frosty as a 7-Eleven slurpy.

She'd probably gotten flack for speaking to Jessie. Or maybe Steele and Steele thought she'd given out their dad's home address. "I was hoping you could remember exactly what Mr. Pomerantz said about 'lost and found.' Did he say anything about having found a piece of art?"

The receptionist shook her head. "Nothing like that. As I told you, I think he was intentionally vague."

"Did he seem anxious in any way?"

"Not at all. Just disappointed that Mr. Steele wasn't in. If that's all?" she said, half turning to her computer.

"You mentioned that you left notes for Charles and Henry Steele. Maybe you wrote more specific information on the notes."

"I don't think so."

"Maybe you could check," Jessie said. Pleasant but firm.

"All right," Barbara sighed resignedly. She stood and moved away from her desk, then turned a corner and disappeared down a carpeted hall.

Jessie walked to the Chagall. What would happen, she wondered, if a visitor to the foundation removed it from the wall and walked right out? Alarm bells, for one. She was admiring the painting when she heard a door open, then a male voice.

". . . call me again."

Turning around, she saw Henry Steele and a distinguished-looking man with graying hair and metal-framed glasses. He looked familiar, and she wondered where she'd seen him.

"Detective Drake." Henry's eyes had widened with surprise. "I didn't know you were here. How can I help you?"

His politeness sounded forced. "Actually, I had a few more questions for your receptionist. She's checking on something for me." Smiling pleasantly, Jessie addressed the gray-haired man. "I'm sorry if I've interrupted something. I'm Detective Jessie Drake, L.A.P.D." And *you* are . . . ?

He bowed and extended his hand. "Ernst Zimmer. A pleasure to make your acquaintance." He spoke in a cultured, European-accented voice.

Jessie shook his hand firmly. Out of the corner of her eye, she could see that Henry looked annoyed. Invasion of the working class? Or maybe he was annoyed with Barbara for leaving her post, and with Jessie, for causing her to do it.

"I hope nothing's wrong, Henry," Zimmer said with unfeigned curiosity.

"Not at all," Henry said quickly. "Detective Drake is investigating the death of a Holocaust survivor. By sheer coincidence, the poor man happened to visit the foundation office last week."

"Tsk," Zimmer exclaimed softly. "He came here to file a claim?"

"I don't really know." Henry faced Jessie. "Mr. Zimmer is our liaison with some of the Swiss banks. He hopes to expedite claims for survivors who come to the foundation for help."

That was why he looked familiar. She'd probably seen his photo in the newspapers, connected with an article about the Swiss banks or the foundation.

Another bow from Zimmer, accompanied by a warm smile. "I trust your faith in me won't be unwarranted, Henry. My accomplishments thus far have been less than stellar."

"But not through lack of effort," Henry told Jessie. "I'm afraid Ernst must be neglecting his own business interests with all the hours he's spending, trying to move along the claims process. And he's receiving no compensation for this."

"Neither are you, Henry. This is the least I can do to redress the wrongs my country has done." Zimmer sounded uncomfortable.

Modesty or remorse? "You're affiliated with the Swiss Bankers Association?" Jessie asked.

Zimmer shook his head. "A few of us have formed an independent group—low profile, I might add. While I know many Swiss who are eager to acknowledge our country's blemished past, we wouldn't be terribly popular with those who don't think Switzerland should have set up a fund to reimburse Holocaust survivors. They don't think Switzerland has done anything wrong. They don't want to hear that we turned away thirty-two thousand Jewish refugees and handed them over to the Germans, that we stamped Jews' passports with a J to make them easily identifiable." Another shake of the head. "Denial."

"A number of Swiss Jews aren't happy about the fund, either," Henry said. "Or about the pressure being put on the banks to open dormant accounts. They're worried about a resurgence of Swiss anti-Semitism."

"I wish I could tell you their fears were ungrounded." Zimmer sighed deeply. "Well, I should be going, Henry. I'll speak with you tomorrow." A half turn to Jessie: "Good luck with your investigation, Detective Drake."

"Thanks. Good luck with your work."

"I'll need it." Zimmer smiled wryly. He nodded politely at Henry and Jessie, then walked to the door and left the office.

"He sounds like an unusual man," Jessie said.

"Yes, yes he is. Quite remarkable." Henry's eyes were still on the door.

"It's wonderful that he can devote all this time without worrying that his own business interests will suffer. What line of work is he in?"

Henry turned toward her. "He raises capital for various projects. Real estate, telecommunications. Things like that. Have you made any progress with your investigation?"

She had the feeling Henry was changing the subject. "We're pursuing several leads," she said, wishing that were true. "How's your father?"

"A little better. Thank you for asking." He nodded crisply.

The receptionist appeared and stopped short when she saw Henry. "Oh, Mr. Steele. I was just looking for something for Detective Drake."

"Yes, I know. She told me." His tone was a little cool.

Barbara flushed. She smiled uncertainly at Henry, then addressed Jessie. "I'm sorry, Detective Drake. I couldn't find the memo I left. Mr. Charles must have picked it up." She frowned. "Which is strange, because I didn't see him yesterday or today."

Henry cleared his throat. "As a matter of fact, Detective, I cleared off my brother's desk late yesterday—he asked me to bring home the messages that required his immediate attention. I *did* see the one regarding Mr. Pomerantz, but there was nothing other than what you already know, so I threw it away."

Jessie found it difficult to restrain her annoyance. "Would it still be in your wastebasket?"

He shook his head. "The janitorial service cleans up every evening—unfortunately for you, they do a thorough job." He smiled.

She wasn't amused. "What was the wording, exactly?"

"From what I recall, just, 'Said something re lost and found.'" Henry turned to Barbara. "Does that sound right?"

The woman hesitated. "I *think* so."

Jessie said, "You told me there might have been something else."

"I guess not." The receptionist smiled nervously and sat at her desk.

"Barbara, when you have a minute, there are some letters I need to dictate." Henry turned to Jessie. "If I remember anything else, Detective Drake, I'll call you immediately." He turned and walked into his office, shutting the door behind him.

Jessie looked at his door thoughtfully for a moment, then turned to the receptionist. "Mr. Steele seemed a little annoyed that you weren't at your desk. I hope I didn't get you in trouble."

Barbara sighed. "He's tense because of his father's illness. So is Mr. Charles. I'm not surprised that they haven't been themselves lately." She frowned. "Did someone come into the office while I was away from my desk?" She sounded suddenly anxious.

"No. Just Mr. Henry, and Mr. Zimmer."

"You met him?" Barbara relaxed against her chair back. "He's a very nice man, a real gentleman. He's working hard to help the survivors who come to the foundation get their claims processed more quickly. And he's shown tremendous interest in Mr. Henry's documentary."

"He seems very nice." Jessie should have asked for his card, in case Frances decided to file a claim. "Would you please check your files to see whether Mr. Pomerantz mailed in a request for help in accessing a Swiss bank account or getting payment from an insurance policy? I forgot to ask you last time."

Barbara wrinkled her forehead. "Why would he do that, if he lived in New York?"

A good question. "He probably didn't. I just want to be thorough. My boss doesn't appreciate loose ends." She smiled—worker to worker—and was pleased to see a sympathetic smile in response from Barbara.

"What's the first name?"

"Norman. Or you might try Nachum. I'm not sure which name he would have used."

Barbara turned on the computer, accessed a program, then typed in the name on her keyboard. A moment later, she typed another name. "Sorry," she said, swiveling toward Jessie. "I tried both names and came up with nothing."

Jessie wasn't really surprised. "I assume that you have the lists the Swiss bank association posted on the Internet—of the names belonging to dormant accounts. Could you please check to see if there's a Pomerantz on it? I don't have a first name."

The receptionist accessed another document, then scrolled downward. "Sorry. No Pomerantz at all."

"Well, thanks for trying." Jessie started to leave, then turned back. "One more thing—this has nothing to do with Mr. Pomerantz. Could you check another name on the Internet list? Jacob Kochinsky. Or Yaakov."

"Do you know for a fact that this person had a numbered Swiss account?" She was looking curiously at Jessie.

"My brother-in-law saw my grandfather's name on the Internet this morning. I just wanted to verify it." She took a sort of pleasure in the surprise that flashed across the woman's face. "I'm not sure how you spell the last name."

"Let me check for you." Barbara returned to the top of the

document. She scrolled down slowly, then stopped. "Jacob Kochinsky, Poland." She pointed to the middle of the screen, then looked up at Jessie.

Jessie leaned forward and caught her breath. "That would be it," she said softly.

She didn't know why she was surprised. She hadn't doubted Neil—why would he make this up?—but there was something shocking about seeing *Kochinsky, Jacob. Poland.* Just like that. Proof that her grandfather, whom she'd never known, had really existed.

Barbara Loura said something. Jessie asked her to repeat it.

"I asked whether you'd like an application and some explanatory information."

She had no intention of filing a claim. She just wanted to go through the motions, to see what it would be like to write her grandfather's name on the lines.

She stood undecided for a moment, then said, "Yes."

Hilda was half-sitting in her bed when Jessie entered the room. Her eyes were closed, and she'd dropped her knitting on top of her gray blanket.

Approaching as quietly as she could, Jessie reached over and was about to place a small bag on Hilda's nightstand when the woman's eyes fluttered open.

Fear bleached her face of color, and her body stiffened. She made a short, little gasping sound and clutched the blanket protectively to her neck.

Suddenly she sank back against her pillow. "It's you," she wheezed, her voice shaking with relief. She took a deep breath and placed her hand on her chest. "You shouldn't sneak up on an old lady like me." She tried a smile.

Jessie's face was red. "I'm so sorry. I wasn't thinking." About the fact that Hilda had high blood pressure. About the fact that she was certain someone was trying to kill her and would naturally be petrified to find someone standing at her bed—it didn't matter whether she was paranoid or not. *Way to go, Jessie.*

"It's okay. You gave me a scare, is all." She lifted her arm to adjust the pillow behind her head, and revealed the tattooed numbers.

Again Jessie found herself staring at them. "You're sure you're okay?" The woman's color was better, but she still looked pale, and the artery in her sagging neck, visible now that she'd dropped the blanket, was throbbing.

"Why do you want to know—so you can ask more questions?" She narrowed her eyes. "I already told you everything I know."

"Actually, I brought you something."

"What, a subpoena?"

Jessie laughed. "No." She handed Hilda the bag.

"Borders. You brought me a book?" Hilda darted a shy smile at Jessie, then pulled out a paperback. "Nora Roberts. I like her."

"I hope you haven't read that one yet. The salesclerk said it's pretty new." She'd been amazed by the proliferation of romance titles, fascinated when the clerk told her that romance readers were exceptionally avid fans, often returning several times a week to buy more books.

Hilda looked up. "To tell you the truth, I don't get the new ones so often. They're too expensive. But I like reading the ones I have over and over." With an abrupt movement, she shook her head. "Just listen to me! I didn't even say thank you."

"You're welcome." Jessie smiled with pleasure.

"Such a surprise." Sighing happily, Hilda ran her hand over the embossed cover, then read the copy on the back of the book. After a minute she turned the book over and placed it carefully on her nightstand. "This is a very nice thing you did, Jessie James. I don't even know why."

She knew without looking in a mirror that her cheeks had reddened. "I just thought you'd enjoy it." It had been a spur-of-the-moment purchase. After spending a frustrating afternoon helping Phil make calls to OB-GYNs and family physicians, she'd decided to relax by browsing in a bookstore when she'd seen the stacks of romance novels.

The old woman's eyes were suddenly wary. She cocked her

head. "You bring me a present, so you think I'm going to tell you things I didn't tell you before?" she asked quietly.

Obviously she'd misinterpreted Jessie's blush. "That's not it at all." She wet her lips and chose her words. "I just thought that it must be hard for you, being here without anyone you know."

Hilda hadn't moved. She was just staring at Jessie.

"I don't have any grandparents, but if they were living somewhere away from family, I'd hope that someone would be trying to make their days a little less lonely. That's all," she added, knowing that she wasn't telling the complete truth, that on some level she *was* trying to win the old woman's confidence. She hoped Hilda couldn't read her mind.

Hilda kept her eyes locked on Jessie a while longer. "It's hard to trust," she finally said.

Jessie nodded.

"You can stay a while?" Hilda asked. "If you're busy . . ."

"I'm not too busy." She sat down on the chair at the side of the bed and picked up the top paperback. "Should I continue in Chapter Four?"

"Sure. So you have no grandparents?" she asked while Jessie found the place.

"My father's parents died quite a few years ago. They lived in Pittsburgh. My mother's parents were killed in the Holocaust."

Hilda glanced at her with interest, then nodded. "Hitler killed a lot of Catholics. Gypsies, too."

"My grandparents were Jewish," Jessie said, and saw interest turn to surprise.

"So you're Jewish, too?" A half smile. "You're pulling my foot, yes?"

"Your *leg*," Jessie corrected, smiling, too. "No, I really *am*." She hesitated, wondering again why she would reveal personal information to a woman she hardly knew, then said, "I only found out recently." She told Hilda briefly what she'd learned from her mother.

"So," Hilda said when Jessie had finished. "It's like from a novel, no? But not a romance," she added quietly. "You're angry your mother didn't tell you sooner?"

Jessie considered. "No. I understand her reasons."

Hilda patted Jessie's hand approvingly. "A friend of mine left her daughter with a Polish family. Very nice people. After the war, she went to get her daughter back—the Polish family didn't want to let the child go, the child didn't want to leave. She cried, she screamed, she wouldn't let my friend touch her. She called her a dirty Jew." Hilda sighed. "Such pain."

"What happened?"

"In the end, my friend hired someone to kidnap her daughter. She got her out of Poland and to America, but it was never good between them. The daughter ran off with some boy, and my friend hears from her maybe once, twice a year." Hilda shrugged. "Family is everything, no? You're lucky you have both your parents. You have brothers and sisters?"

"One sister. She's married and has a nine-year-old boy. Matthew."

"Your parents live close?"

"They live in La Jolla, near San Diego, but they visit us pretty often." Too often, Jessie had thought until now.

Hilda nodded. "Very lucky."

She supposed she was.

21

"I WONDER SO many times what my brother would be like if he had lived, what my sisters would be like. Chava, the younger one? She would have been a famous designer. She could make anything from nothing. Liebe, the older one, I don't know. And my brother Moshe—he had the head for business. Me?" Pomerantz smiled. "My head was somewhere in the clouds, my father would say. 'Always dreaming.' And I loved art." He sighed. "Music and art. You, too?

"I wasn't so religious like my brother, even before the war. Not to say I didn't keep everything—I did. I was just a little soft. But not my wife Estucha. She was a hundred percent, like her brother. When he was in the camps, he ate kosher or nothing, can you believe it? He even figured out a way to bake matzoh for Passover. Me, I wasn't so good. I ate whatever they gave me, which to tell you the truth, wasn't much.

"After the war?" Pomerantz shrugged. "I won't lie—I kept nothing. I was bitter. God let them kill my family, my wife, and my daughters, all of them saints. And me he kept alive? Why? I asked Him, but He didn't answer.

"Do I believe in God now? The million-dollar question, right?" Pomerantz smiled. "I'll tell you an interesting story. One time—

*this was in the beginning of the war—my grandfather sent me to the Reb Eliezer Kaminke, a famous rebbe in Oświecim, for a bra-*chah, *a blessing. This rebbe put his hands on me and prayed I should be saved from the Germans and survive. Later, when I was working in a labor camp called Füenfteichen, I had a terrible accident. The Germans made us break up flooring in order to make basements. I was using a sledgehammer, when suddenly the flooring gave way and I was thrown down into the basement. My face hit a post, which broke the whole front of my face and tore away my nose. There was so much blood, they couldn't see my face.*

"When my face hit the post, I saw an image of the Reb Eliezer. It was as if he was standing by me, holding up his hands. And when he held up his hands, I felt better." Pomerantz paused. "So maybe his blessing kept me alive, because they took me to the hospital and I survived.

"Do I believe in God? I believe, but I don't keep kosher or the Sabbath. But I stay in touch with Him. I go to the synagogue on Rosh Hashanah and Yom Kippur. I go to a seder on Passover. And I always take my tallis and tefillin wherever I go. Because you never know, right?"

Someone had left a large padded mailer on her doorstep. Ezra, she saw, picking up the mailer and glancing at the return address. No postage, so he must have dropped it off himself. She hadn't given him her home address, but the school had it.

He'd probably sent her notes on the classes she'd missed, she thought as she unlocked her side door. Dumping her purse on the kitchen counter, she ripped open the mailer and found a gift-wrapped box. She eyed the box, wondering what was inside, trying to decide how she felt about getting a gift from Ezra. Uneasy more than flattered. She undid the wrapping—not meticulously, like Helen, just tore it right off—and saw from the label on the box that it was from his sister Dafna's Judaica store.

He'd bought her a pair of ceramic candlesticks—to light Sabbath candles, she knew. They were beautiful, a smoky blue swirled pattern on a glazed white background. He'd included two glass inserts and a box of short, squat candles that fit into them.

She read the note he'd enclosed: "To help you take that first step, whenever you're ready. Ezra. P.S. Exchange them if you like. . . ."

Ezra the spiritual advisor? Ezra the friend? She thought for a moment, then placed the candlesticks on the ledge of the narrow cabinet attached to one wall of her breakfast room.

She checked the mail—mostly bills, an advertising flyer from a roofer advising her that El Niño was coming and she didn't want to be caught unprepared, another from a stucco company with the same dire warning.

Helen had left a message on Jessie's machine—had Jessie thought more about calling Frances? Helen, she decided as she changed into a pale yellow, cropped cotton T-shirt and shorts, needed to learn the art of the subtle pitch. She was thinking about Helen and the application she'd picked up at the foundation when the doorbell rang.

"I brought supper," Gary said when she opened the door. He was holding a large brown shopping bag. Stepping inside the entry, he shifted the bag to one arm and kissed her. His free hand slipped around her bare waist. "Nice," he murmured.

She wondered if he could tell how much she loved his touch. "Please, please tell me it's not pizza," she said, her lips still on his.

"Chinese—lots of it. Speaking of which, my arm's going dead."

She laughed and pulled away. He followed her into the kitchen and deposited the bag on the counter. While she took down dinner plates and serving bowls from an upper cabinet, he removed the steaming containers from the bag.

His eyes went to the torn wrapping paper. "Did I miss a birthday?"

She took forks and knives from a drawer. "Ezra Nathanson sent me candlesticks for the Sabbath. He's my Judaism teacher, remember?"

Gary nodded. "He gave you the mezuzah, too, right?"

"Uh-huh." She walked into the breakfast nook and placed two woven green mats and napkins on the table just as Gary brought the plates and cutlery.

He looked at the candlesticks. "Pretty," he said, picking one up. He set it back on the ledge. "Ezra's a widower, right? So is this usual, a teacher giving gifts?"

"Only to police detectives. Maybe he's hoping I'll get rid of some of his traffic tickets." She smiled. "He's just trying to be encouraging, Gary." She arranged the cutlery and plates, debating how much to reveal.

"I don't know, Jess. Maybe he's interested in you."

Honesty was best, she decided. "Actually, he asked me out. But I told him I was seeing someone seriously."

She returned to the kitchen, where she emptied one of the containers into a bowl and inhaled the spicy aroma. Her stomach rumbled. "God, this smells good!"

"*How* seriously?" Gary asked, joining her. "Seriously enough to have this someone move in with you?"

"Seriously enough so that I'm not interested in seeing anyone else," she said lightly and pecked his cheek. "Help me with these." She pointed to the other containers, hoping to change the subject.

He'd brought pepper beef, Mongolian chicken, fried rice, egg rolls. She ate too much of everything, savoring the pungent sauces, and then finished what was on Gary's plate. Afterwards, they did the dishes—she washed, he dried.

They went into the den. She put on a Vivaldi CD and, sitting next to Gary on the sofa, encircled by his arm, told him about her latest visit to Hilda.

"Sounds like you're fond of her," he remarked. "Business or pleasure?"

"Obviously, I'm hoping she'll open up once she trusts me. But I feel sorry for her, Gary. She's lonely, she has no family. And I enjoy talking to her."

"Why do you sound so defensive?"

"Do I?" She sighed. "My mom thinks I'm identifying with Hilda, substituting her for the grandmother I never knew."

He stroked her arm. "Are you?"

She thought about that. "I don't know," she finally said. "And if I am? What's so terrible? Who am I hurting?"

"She's not a well woman, Jess. What happens if you get real close to her, and she dies?"

"No pain, no gain," she said quietly.

"What if she starts identifying with *you*, Jess? What if she sees you as the granddaughter she never had? And when the case is solved, and you no longer visit her all the time? What then, Jess? Where does that leave Hilda?"

"Don't worry—this case isn't going to get solved all that soon." Not really an answer. Gary was right to be concerned about Hilda. She'd have to give serious thought to what he'd said.

"It's not going well?"

She grunted. "No suspects, no motive, no leads, except for a message Pomerantz left with—" She saw the flash of curiosity in Gary's eyes and wished she could take back her words.

"What message?" he asked.

"Gary—"

"This is off the record, Jess. Hell, I'm not interested in your case. I'm up to my ears in road rage crap."

She hesitated.

"You have to learn to trust me, Jess."

What had Hilda said? *It's hard to trust.* "Off the record?"

"Off the record."

She searched his eyes. "I'm not going to read about this in tomorrow's paper?" she asked quietly.

"Nope."

She told him about the Steele Foundation and the two brothers, about the "lost and found" message Pomerantz had left for them. "I replayed Pomerantz's documentary interview—he didn't make any reference to 'lost and found.' I think he recognized a piece of art as stolen Jewish property and wanted to share his discovery with the Steeles. That's why 'lost and found.' "

Gary nodded. "Maybe. And that's why he was killed? Because he recognized this artwork, whatever it is?"

"Maybe the person who owned the art—or stole it—wasn't thrilled to learn that Pomerantz was on to him. Art can be very valuable, Gary. You know that. A single painting can go for millions."

"So you have motive."

"Maybe." She chewed her upper lip. "I'm not sure good

ol' Henry was telling the truth when he said he threw out the memo the receptionist left on his brother's desk."

"Why would he lie?"

"Maybe brother Charlie *did* get the message, but didn't fess up. So Henry covered for him and said he trashed it."

"Why would Charles lie about getting the message?" Gary frowned. "You think he's involved?"

"Not necessarily. According to Yasmin, the retirement-home receptionist, two men, neither of whom would give Yasmin his name, phoned for Pomerantz. One spoke with Pomerantz. The other didn't. The second one is Henry. He says Pomerantz wasn't in when he returned his call. I think Charles is the other caller but is reluctant to admit it."

"Why?"

She threw him a "get-real" look. "This is a well-known, wealthy family, Gary. Major philanthropists. People like that don't want to be involved in a murder investigation. It's not the kind of publicity they're used to. And Ezra told me Papa Steele doesn't like *any* publicity. Can you imagine how he'd react if he read in the papers that his sons were being questioned by the police? Especially now that he's ill?"

"Ezra again, huh?" Gary smiled knowingly.

"Don't start." Jessie playfully punched his shoulder.

"So who do you think killed the old man?"

"I have no idea, and it's making me crazy. I should probably read the *National Enquirer*—they'll know before I will."

He laughed. "Probably. What about—"

"No more shop talk," she said, settling against him. "This case is giving me a headache—or maybe it's all that MSG."

Closing her eyes, she let the Vivaldi float over her. She felt Gary's breath, warm on her cheek, and then he was kissing her. She sighed and turned into his embrace.

"I miss you like crazy when we're not together," he whispered a moment later. "I want to be with you, Jess. I want to wake up next to you."

She tensed. "I miss you, too, Gary." She dreamed about him sometimes and woke up disappointed to find the space next to her empty.

"Let me move in."

"I have to be sure."

"How can anyone ever be sure? We're smarter than we were, Jess. We're more open with each other. We've talked through a lot of the stuff that was wrong. True?"

"True," she admitted. All of it was true.

"We could be happy. We could start a family—"

"Like Helen and Neil, you mean?" She pulled away. "I don't want to get married just to have a baby, Gary." *To replace the one I lost,* she added silently.

He stared at her. "Neither do I. That's not what I meant." He sounded hurt, angry.

The silence lay heavily between them. She pretended to listen to the music and wondered what he was thinking.

He blew out a deep breath. "Look, I'm sorry I pressured you. I don't want to ruin what we have."

She turned toward him. "I don't want to, either. Be patient with me?"

He smiled lightly and took her hand. "Like I have a choice?"

The CD had ended. She picked up the remote control and clicked on the TV. A *Seinfeld* rerun was on. She nestled against Gary and tried to become engrossed in the story line, which was bizarre, but engagingly funny.

"You think you're going to use the candlesticks?" Gary asked suddenly.

"I don't know. Maybe." She'd been thinking about that off and on since she'd unpacked them. Could you light one week, and not the next? Could you do it whenever you were in the mood?

He stroked her hair. "You're pretty interested in all this, aren't you? The Judaism classes, I mean."

She nodded. "But I don't know where it's going to take me. How do you feel about that?"

" 'Whither thou goest . . .' " He smiled. "My mom lit candles every Friday night, even though she and my dad were never observant. I remember liking it as a kid."

"There's much more to it than lighting candles, Gary. I don't know if or when I'll ever be ready to make a commitment. I don't know if this is right for me."

He looked at her thoughtfully. "Sometimes, Jess, you have to take a leap of faith."

She knew he wasn't referring only to religion.

She had a hard time falling asleep. Her bedroom was stifling, and though she'd opened all the windows, the air was still. She lay in bed, hoping for a breeze, and thought about Gary. She'd been tempted to have him stay the night, but at the last minute had decided not to. She wondered how long he would be patient living apart.

She padded into the kitchen and, filling a glass with cold water, went into the den. Pomerantz's interview tape was on top of the VCR. She inserted it into the video player and listened again to the pretape conversation.

"Don't worry, Miss Morton, I'm used to the lights. I did another documentary a few months ago. . . ."

Maybe he'd been more revealing in the other interview.

22

ABIGAIL MORTON DIDN'T remember the name of the other production company that had interviewed Pomerantz.

"He mentioned it to me when he first made an appointment to be interviewed," she told Jessie Friday morning. "But I didn't write it down or anything. Sorry."

Jessie drew a line through Abigail's name. "If you do remember, please call."

"I will. Detective, do you still think he was killed?"

"It's a strong possibility. By the way, did Mr. Pomerantz say anything to you about artwork?"

"Art? No, nothing like that. Sorry."

Everybody was sorry. Jessie thanked her and hung up, then dialed Goldblum's number. Busy. She called nine doctors—two OBs, two general practitioners, five internists. None of them had treated a woman who had just given birth.

She tried Goldblum again. This time he answered.

"When are they sending the body?" he asked Jessie in an aggrieved tone the minute she identified herself. "The rabbi's asking me. Nachum's friends are asking me. Everybody wants to know, when is the funeral, and I tell them we can't have a funeral without we have the body."

"I'm terribly sorry, Mr. Goldblum. I spoke with the medical examiner this morning—he's releasing the body today to Ezra Nathanson. I understand that Ezra has been in touch with you?"

"He's with the *chevra kaddisha*, yes? A nice man. So, good. That's taken care of. Thank you for calling, Detective. I appreciate it."

"Mr. Goldblum, that's not the only reason I called. I know that Mr. Pomerantz was interviewed for several documentaries. I have the videotape of the one he did for Morton Productions. Do you know who produced the other one?"

"This has to do with his murder? You didn't tell me you think Nachum was killed," he said accusingly. "I heard it from Ezra Nathanson. Him you told."

She felt thoroughly chastised. "I didn't want to upset you more, Mr. Goldblum. Especially since I wasn't sure."

"Who would *do* such a thing, I ask you? Nachum wouldn't hurt a fly. He did only good. Such a friend you don't find." Goldblum was crying softly.

Jessie felt inadequate as she often did in dealing with others' grief. Phil was a softy, too. Marty Simms was probably better at this, she guessed.

"So what is it you want to know?" Goldblum asked after a moment. He sounded more composed. "Who produced the other documentary?"

"Yes."

"Give me a minute, I'll look for the card Nachum gave me."

She heard the clank of the receiver against a hard surface. A minute passed, then two. He probably couldn't find it, she decided, but then he was on the line.

"Robert Hahn Productions. Also in Manhattan, like the other one I told you." Goldblum read aloud the phone number and address. "You want the fax number, too? It's here."

"No, thanks. You've been very helpful, Mr. Goldblum. One more thing: Did Mr. Pomerantz mention anything about finding a piece of stolen art?"

"Stolen art? No. He never said anything about it. He loved rt, though. And music. He loved going to museums, to art auctions. He could never afford to buy anything, but he liked watching, trying to guess how much a piece would go for."

Had Pomerantz spotted a piece of looted art at an auction? Had the person who sold the piece—or the one who'd bought it—learned of Pomerantz's discovery and panicked? "What about the term, 'lost and found'? Did Mr. Pomerantz ever use that?"

"Not that I can remember. It's important?"

"Maybe." Or it could be nothing.

"I'll try to think."

She thanked Goldblum and hung up, then punched the numbers for Hahn Productions. A young woman with a nasally Brooklyn accent answered. Jessie introduced herself and explained that she wanted a copy of the video of Pomerantz's interview.

"Spell the name, please?"

Jessie spelled the name. Was it her imagination, or was the woman chewing gum?

"Hold on, please." A moment later she was back on the line. "Mr. Pomerantz did do an interview for us, but you'd have to get his written permission before we can release the video."

"That would be difficult. Mr. Pomerantz is dead."

"No kidding!" She was silent a moment. "And you need the video because . . . ?"

"Official business."

"Oh. So, like, was he *murdered* or somethin', huh?" she said in an awed whisper. "I have to check with Mr. Hahn. Just a sec." Another, longer wait. Then, "Mr. Hahn asked could you send in a request on official stationery."

It was just a video, for God's sake. "Please explain to Mr. Hahn that we need the video immediately. If he wants to verify who I am, he can call me here at the station." Jessie gave her the number.

"I'll tell him. Hold on, please."

"Jess," Phil called.

She swiveled toward him, the receiver pressed to her ear. "I'm on a call."

He waved his receiver at her. "You have another one. They put her through to my line. Lilly Gorcheck?"

The Golden Palms manager. Had she found another resident who had talked to Pomerantz? "Ask her to hold a minute," she said, and heard again the nasally voice.

"Detective Drake? Mr. Hahn said he can FedEx a copy of the video right away if you give him a Visa card number. Do you want it to arrive on Monday, or Saturday?"

"Saturday." It was more expensive, but Jessie didn't want to wait. She gave the woman her card number and the station address, thanked her, and hung up. This time she would bill the department, she decided as she reached over and took Phil's receiver.

"Mrs. Gorcheck?"

"Detective Drake, I've been trying to reach you." The manager sounded breathless. "I called the convalescent home to see how Hilda's doing, and they told me she had a heart attack."

"Oh, my God!" Jessie's heart was pounding. She bit her lip. "Is she—"

"She's okay, thank goodness. Weak, but okay. I spoke to the doctor, and he was reassuring."

Phil was looking at her anxiously. She covered the receiver's mouthpiece and whispered, "Hilda Rheinhart had a heart attack," then removed her hand. "Where is she now?" she asked Lilly.

"Cedars. I thought you'd want to know."

Hilda looked tiny and shriveled in the ICU bed. Maybe it was all the tubing attached to her, Jessie thought as she stepped farther into the small room. Tubes up her thin nose. Tubes running from circular patches on her chest to a blinking monitor on the wall behind her bed. An IV tube attached to her arm. The tattooed blue numbers were all too visible.

Jessie had talked to the resident on duty—a mild heart episode, he'd called it. Hilda could probably return to the convalescent home tomorrow if all her vitals continued to be stable. So why did Jessie feel weepy?

Hilda's eyes were open, but she was staring up at the ceiling.

"Hilda," Jessie said softly, afraid to startle her. "It's Jessie James."

The woman turned her head slowly toward Jessie. "You don't have work to do, you're here all the time?" she asked weakly.

Jessie smiled. "I told them I had to question an important witness." She moved closer and took Hilda's hand. "I spoke to the doctor. He said you're going to be fine."

Her lips quivered. "I'm going to die, just like Anna Seligman," she whimpered. Her eyes welled with tears.

"You're not going to die," Jessie said firmly.

"*Anna* was fine. All of a sudden she died. Just like that."

"You're not Anna, Hilda."

Her fingers tightened around Jessie's. "They killed her, don't you see? And now they're going to kill me."

"*Who*, Hilda? Who killed Anna?"

"I don't know," she whispered. She drew her hand away. "They're everywhere. They're watching me."

"*Who* is everywhere? Hilda, if you don't give me information, I can't help you." She could see from the tortured look in Hilda's eyes that she was thinking that over.

Finally Hilda sighed. "I told Nachum about Anna, that they killed her. He said he would try to find out what happened. And then he was killed, so he must have scared them. And now they know that *I* know. So they have to kill me, too!"

Jessie frowned. If what Hilda was saying was true, Pomerantz's death had nothing to do with the 'lost and found' business and the stolen art. But was it true? Or was this a product of Hilda's paranoia?

"How long ago did Anna die?"

"Two months ago. She was in a convalescent home. Before that she was in an old age home, like I was, but then she wasn't feeling so good, so she couldn't stay."

"What's the name of the convalescent home?"

"I don't know."

"What about the retirement home?"

"This I don't know, either, but it's on Gardner near Melrose, not far from me. We used to visit each other all the time." Fresh tears sprang into her eyes. "You'll check into it for me?"

"I'll check into it." Jessie patted her hand. "You have to try to relax, Hilda. This isn't good for your heart."

"I can help it I'm scared?"

"Nothing's going to happen to you. I promise."

"From your mouth to God's ears," she whispered.

23

THERE WAS A retirement home on Gardner, just north of Melrose. Hilda had been right about that. And Anna Seligman *had* been a resident there for several years, Jessie learned from Sheila Henkins, a frazzled-looking woman with blond hair bleached too blond and styled too long.

"Do you know where she was transferred from here?" Jessie asked.

"I don't remember off-hand, but I'd be happy to check for you," the administrator said in a tightly polite voice that implied she wasn't all that happy that Jessie had added one more task to her already overly full agenda.

Jessie waited in the lobby. There was little difference between this one and the one at the Golden Palms, aside from the color scheme—green instead of navy. There was little difference, too, between the residents she saw sitting here and those she'd seen at the other facility. They all looked lonely, she thought. Or maybe her anxiety over Hilda was coloring her perception.

Sheila Henkins reappeared. "Mrs. Seligman went to Lindenhurst Gardens. It's a nice place—we refer many of our residents there. It's on Fairfax, south of Fourth Street. You know where that is?"

Jessie told her that she knew and thanked her.

Another lobby, another administrator. This one—his name was Vance Lemar—told Jessie that of course he'd known Anna Seligman.

"A very nice woman." He sighed. "We were so sorry when she died."

"What happened to her?"

"Complications from diabetes, I think. That's why they transferred her here from the board and care."

"Was there anything unusual about her death?"

He shook his head. "Not at all." He sounded suddenly wary.

"How long was she here?"

Another sigh. "Not long, I don't think. A month, month and a half? Not more than that. Poor dear, she kept hoping she'd get better and be able to return to her friends at the board and care."

"Could you give me the name of her physician? And her closest family member, please."

"Mrs. Seligman *had* no family. She was a Holocaust survivor— she lost all her family in the war, poor woman. That made her passing away even sadder. No one to mourn her. Except for friends, of course." He smiled sadly.

"Who handled the funeral arrangements?"

"Luckily, she'd taken care of all that a long time ago. Very simple arrangements—she didn't have much means, just social security and a small pension from her husband. Let me get the doctor's name and phone number for you." He was gone briefly, and when he returned, he handed Jessie a slip of paper on which he'd written the information.

DR. ELLIOTT WALGREN, she read. An address on Wilshire Boulevard.

"Basically, her kidneys gave out," Elliott Walgren told Jessie over the phone. "Anna had been diabetic for years. She'd been getting insulin at the board and care—Medicare pays to have a nurse from a home health agency administer the shots daily. But when her condition deteriorated to the point that she needed nursing, we switched her to a convalescent home."

"There was nothing unusual about her death?"

"Unusual?" He sounded puzzled. "Not at all. Why do you ask?"

"A friend of hers has suggested that Mrs. Seligman met with foul play."

"What are you saying? That Anna was *murdered*?" Walgren snorted. "That's ridiculous!"

"You signed the death certificate, Dr. Walgren?"

"Yes, I did, and I had no question at all as to the cause of death," he said, his tone a little testy. "The woman was eighty-six years old, Detective. She died of renal failure. She was lucky she had the years she did. The only thing that might have saved her was a transplant, and at her age she wasn't eligible for a kidney."

It looked as if Lilly Gorcheck *was* right about Hilda's paranoia. Hilda claimed that "they" had killed Anna and other survivors, but Anna Seligman had apparently died of natural causes. The only similarity between her and Hilda was that both women were Holocaust survivors, bereft of family.

Anna was eight-six when she died. Undoubtedly, other Holocaust survivors had died recently, and would die in the near future. Hardly a sinister development—merely nature taking its inevitable course.

Still . . .

Jessie phoned the Department of Health Services, and after waiting an interminably long time, was connected with a clerk she knew.

"How's my favorite homicide detective?" Corinne Ayers asked.

"Just fine. And you?"

"Can't complain. Even if I did, who'd listen? What can I do for you, honey?"

"Corinne, I need to find out about any elderly people—men or women—who died within the past two to three months of natural causes." She'd chosen three months arbitrarily. "All of them would have been born in Eastern Europe—Germany, Austria, Czechoslovakia, Romania, Poland, Russia. Think you can help me out?"

"Talk about needle in a haystack. You have any idea how

many old people die every day of natural causes?" the woman grumbled. "How old is 'old'?"

Jessie considered. Frances was sixty-one, and she'd been three when the war had started. Most Jewish children that young had perished. "No one under sixty," she decided. "And they'd be Caucasian. Did I mention that?"

"No, you didn't. That helps some, but not much. Next you'll be tellin' me you need this today, right?"

Jessie smiled. "That's right."

"Well, honey, it ain't happenin'. We have death certificates that haven't even been filed yet. And we don't have the staff to go lookin' through hundreds of pieces of paper."

"The ones that *have* been filed are on computer, right, Corinne? Let's start with those."

"That's still a hell of a lot of names. Anything else you can tell me that would narrow down the list?"

All of them would be Holocaust survivors, but that information wouldn't be recorded on a death certificate. Neither would the fact that they were Jewish. "That's it."

"Well, I'll try to find somethin' for you as soon as possible, Jessie. But it's gonna take some time."

"Thanks, Corinne."

She hung up and sat at her desk, doodling on a notepad. The thought occurred to her that many of the survivors might have wanted a Jewish burial, and might have made arrangements with Jewish mortuaries.

It was worth checking. She reached for the Yellow Pages— her best friend, lately—looked up MORTUARIES, and jotted down the names of seven whose ads or listings indicated that they provided Jewish burials. Several were in Downey, she saw. One near the City of Industry. Another near Universal Studios—she'd been there several months ago with Phil, on another case. That was where Ezra's wife and parents were buried.

She phoned the first name on her list, Lieberman Mortuaries, and after identifying herself, was connected to the director, a man with a gravelly voice.

"What can I do for you, Detective?" He sounded guarded.

"I need information relevant to a case we're investigating," she said in what she hoped was a nonthreatening tone. "As part of your record keeping, do you indicate the age of the deceased and the country of birth?"

"I can assure you that we keep very accurate records." Definitely cautious now. "In answer to your question, yes, we do indicate that data."

"I'm interested in men and women who died within the past two to three months, were in their sixties or older, and were born in Eastern Europe."

"May I ask why?"

"I'm afraid I'm not at liberty to say."

"I see."

Clearly he didn't. But that wasn't Jessie's problem. "Do your records also indicate where the deceased was living at the time of his or her death?"

"Yes, of course. We have all the information that's noted on the death certificate."

Including cause of death, then. "I'd like that information as well. How soon can you have a list of names for me?"

"Without a court order, Detective, I'm afraid I can't give out any information regarding any of our clients. It's privileged," he said in a "you-should-know-better" tone.

"I can get a court order, but that takes time, and this information could be vital." She was lying like a rug, as Phil would say. She had no indication that the information could be vital, or even significant. And no judge would grant her a court order based on the nonspecific fears of a paranoid old woman who was afraid of dying.

"Sorry. Bring the court order, and maybe I can help you." He hung up the phone.

The directors of the next two mortuaries she called were unavailable. Jessie left her phone number but no message. At the fourth mortuary she spoke to Thelma Gradon, who repeated the same thing about privacy laws as director number one, but did so much more pleasantly and sounded genuinely sorry that she couldn't help.

"Basically, we can't violate the confidentiality of our clients, even though they're dead. I know that sounds strange, but often there *are* sensitive issues involved. Cause of death, for instance. If the deceased had AIDS, he might not have wanted that information to get out, even to his family. That's just one example."

"So if I'm not interested in cause of death, you'd be able to help me?"

"Well . . ." Thelma paused. "I suppose that would change things *some*what. But to be honest, we can't afford to have someone on staff spend the necessary hours to call up all the files of the past three months and separate the ones that fit your criteria."

"Your files aren't computerized?"

"Not the death certificates—those we file manually. We *do* enter data in our computer system, but we use a basic program designed for mortuaries, and it doesn't sort by age or country of birth. Basically, it's alphabetical, by last name, and by date of death. Other mortuaries may have fine-tuned their programs, but we haven't." She sounded apologetic.

"What if I come down and go through the files myself?"

"As I said, I couldn't let you look through the files without a court order." Another pause. "We don't enter 'cause of death' in our computer records, so it wouldn't show up on the screen, but I'd still be uncomfortable giving you access to our files without some legal authorization. Even if I knew for certain that you were really a detective." Thelma laughed.

"You can call me here at the station if you need to verify my identity. I won't be insulted."

"Oh, you sound legitimate. But you'd be surprised how many con artists call mortuaries, pretending to be police so that they can get information—like social security numbers. They're noted on the death certificate, you know. Can you tell me what you're looking for?"

Director number one had asked her the same thing and she'd blown him off. Maybe that had been a mistake. "An elderly woman I know believes that her friend, who apparently died of natural causes, was really killed. She thinks it's happened to other Holocaust survivors."

"My goodness!" Thelma exclaimed softly. "Does this woman have any proof?"

"No. And it may amount to nothing. But I promised her I'd

look into it—she's fearful for herself. I didn't realize it would be so complicated. I tried Health Services first, then thought about Jewish mortuaries to narrow the field. I figured most survivors would choose to be buried in a Jewish cemetery."

"You're absolutely right. Even those who aren't religiously observant—and they're the majority, by the way—want a Jewish burial. And so many of them make prior arrangements. Especially those who are in convalescent homes—the facilities generally require the name of the mortuary that will be handling the arrangements."

When the unhappy time comes. Creepy information to have to write down when you were checking into a nursing home, but obviously necessary and practical. Jessie wondered whether her parents had made any burial arrangements. Her father was very methodical, well organized, but thinking about death made many people squeamish. Like me, she admitted, and grimaced.

"Look," Thelma said. "Why don't you leave me your number, and I'll see what I can find in the next day or so."

"That would be great." Jessie gave her the station number and thanked her. She'd hoped for quicker information, but at least this woman was cooperating.

She phoned Corinne and told her about the mortuaries. "So you don't have to bother checking that out," Jessie said. "Thanks anyway."

"And here I was, getting all excited about doing this research for you, honey. I am *so* disappointed." She chuckled. "You take care now. And good luck."

Jessie phoned the four other mortuaries—all four directors were busy with funerals. The business of dying was obviously booming. She was about to call the convalescent home to check on Hilda when the phone rang.

It was Thelma Gradon. "After we hung up, I looked through our calendar, Detective. Actually, we had a burial just recently that might interest you."

"Oh?" She pulled over a sheet of paper.

"Yes. Mendel Blumenkrantz." Thelma spelled the name. "He was seventy-eight when he died. A sweet man—I met him when he made arrangements with us, and that was quite

some time ago, right after his wife died. No children, unfortunately, so he was very much on his own. We handled her
funeral, too. They have adjoining plots."

"And Mr. Blumenkrantz was born in Europe?"

"Poland. Anyway, according to our files, he died a few
weeks ago at a convalescent home."

"Can you tell me the name of the home?"

A short hesitation. "I don't see why not. It's the Crestview
Arms, in Burbank." She gave Jessie the address. "And while I
can't tell you the cause of death, I *can* say it was natural causes."

"Do you know where Mr. Blumenkrantz lived before he
entered the nursing home?"

"Let me check. Here it is—his residence was the Belleview
Manor, also in Burbank. Actually, I know the place. It's a
board-and-care facility. Anyway, I thought this might interest
you. I'll call you if I find anything else."

It *did* interest Jessie. Very much.

Mendel Blumenkrantz had lost his spouse and had no
children.

Like Anna Seligman. She'd resided in a board and care
until she'd been transferred to a nursing home. And she'd
died soon after.

Hilda was a widow, too. No children, she'd told Jessie.
She'd been transferred from a board and care to a nursing
home and had suffered a "heart episode" twenty-four hours
later.

So maybe Blumenkrantz and Seligman had been very ill.
That's what happened to people as they aged. And Hilda had
high blood pressure, Parkinson's, imminent cataract surgery, and
God knew what else. She was tense, anxious about Pomerantz
and her friend Anna. That alone could have triggered her attack.

Jessie frowned. Unless someone else had triggered it, and
aggravated Seligman's diabetes, and Blumenkrantz's medical
problems, whatever they were.

But why? She wished Phil were here—she always thought
better when she bounced ideas off him—but he was off chasing another lead on Cassandra Jones's murder. Jessie drew a
series of boxes on her notepad and swiveled in her chair,
thinking.

Hilda claimed that someone was killing Holocaust survivors. Was this "someone," if he or she existed, doing so to eliminate survivors as voices of testimony? But that didn't make sense. There were numerous documentaries now—Pomerantz himself had done two that Jessie knew about. The testimony had been permanently recorded, preserved for future generations when the victims would be long gone.

Neo-Nazis targeting survivors to finish what Hitler hadn't? But why now? And why go to the trouble to kill lonely old people who were going to die soon anyway?

She stopped the chair abruptly. Maybe this wasn't about malice. Maybe someone, in an act of twisted mercy, was killing survivors not to punish them, but to spare these men and women who had suffered unspeakable atrocities from an empty, bleak life certain to be filled with pain and the indignities of old age.

Mercy killings?

It was possible, Jessie thought. And whoever was responsible was smart: He or she had minimized the risk of exposure by engineering the victims' removal to skilled nursing facilities. Deaths by natural causes that take place at those facilities, Jessie knew, don't have to be verified by a call to 911.

Maybe Pomerantz had stumbled onto what was going on. He'd promised Hilda he would investigate Anna Seligman's death. Had he asked one too many questions of the right person?

And who was that person? It had to be someone who had a natural reason for visiting numerous board-and-care facilities, someone who came in close contact with the elderly residents, someone who could come and go without arousing interest or suspicion.

A nurse from a home health agency? A doctor? A therapist? A social worker?

Someone who was killing with kindness. . . .

"They're going to kill me, just like they killed Anna Seligman."

Or maybe there was no killer. Maybe Blumenkrantz and Seligman *had* died natural deaths. Maybe, Jessie thought, she was becoming infected with an old woman's paranoia.

24

"*MY BROTHER MOSHE and I were together at first, in a labor camp. Then they sent him to Auschwitz and me to Blechhammer, a concentration camp that was part of Auschwitz. That was in '44. The camps weren't so far apart, so we were able to sneak messages to each other. In April of that year they tattooed the numbers on our arms.*

"*Not every camp gave numbers. You didn't know?" Pomerantz nodded. "None of the labor camps did. Treblinka didn't, so far as I know. Dachau, also not. You know who did mine? A Jew I knew from my hometown. Life is funny, no?" He smiled and shook his head. "Why did he do it, you're asking?" Pomerantz raised his brows. "The Germans told you do something—you did it. You didn't ask questions.*

"*After the war, when I came to this country, I had a doctor get rid of the numbers. He didn't do such a good job. And later I was sorry. I thought if I didn't see them all the time, maybe it would be easier to forget. Like you could forget something like that." He grunted. "My friend Stanley, he wanted his boys to see his camp number. He wanted they should ask questions. Now he shows it to his grandchildren." Pomerantz's eyes took on a distant look. "Moshe wouldn't have gotten rid of the numbers," he said quietly. "Not Moshe. . . .*

"In the camps there were stacks of beds, three high, one on top of the other. You know something? Stanley's children bought bunk beds for their kids. I was at their house one time, and they showed me the beds. 'So practical, Uncle Nachum,' they said. 'Look how much room it saves. Aren't they great?' All I could think about was sleeping on the top bunk in the camp. . . .

"How did I manage in the camps? I was luckier than most. Before the round-up, I had put my wife's diamond ring in my vest pocket to be fixed at the jeweler's. Had I known we were going to be taken, I would have hidden it somewhere else. But as it turned out, it was better I didn't know. The diamond was worth a lot of money. I found someone who dealt in buying and selling jewelry with a sales force of people who went out to Catowice, Sosnowice, and other places. Germans also worked for him. Anyway, this man sold the diamond for me, and with the money I got for it—three thousand deutsche marks, a lot of money at the time—Moshe and I were able to survive.

"What did we use it for? An extra piece of bread. A potato. An egg, a tiny piece of meat. A warm shirt. A pair of gloves to use when you had to dig in the snow." Pomerantz smiled wryly. *"Luxuries."*

Hilda was fine, the nurse reassured Jessie when she phoned—her condition was stable, her vitals had improved. She'd been moved from ICU to a regular room, and would probably be released in the morning.

"Has she been receiving a lot of visitors?" Jessie asked.

"I couldn't say. It's not like ICU, where visitors are restricted. People come and go all the time. But you could ask main floor Reception—visitors are supposed to check in and get visitors' passes."

Jessie checked with Reception and learned that Hilda hadn't had any visitors so far.

"You're positive?" Jessie asked.

"At least not according to the log," the woman told Jessie. "I'm not saying it's impossible for someone to slip by us—sometimes we're so busy, and there are so many people in the lobby. And it's also possible that a person who told us they were going to visit one patient decided to visit another one, too."

And of course medical professionals—doctors, nurses, therapists—who looked the part and were familiar to the Reception staff could whiz on by, no questions asked.

Jessie wanted to instruct the hospital not to allow Hilda to have any visitors, but without a guard watching her door, the hospital couldn't ensure that no one would get into the old woman's room.

Espes was in his office—she'd seen him go in a while earlier. She crossed the room, knocked on his door, entered when he said "Come in" in his usual gruff tone.

"I hope you're bringing me good news," he said when he saw her. No smile.

She told him about Hilda Rheinhart, about Anna Seligman and Mendel Blumenkrantz, about her suspicions. "Hilda asked Norman Pomerantz to check into Mrs. Seligman's death. If someone killed Mrs. Seligman and Pomerantz, he may know about Hilda, too. I'd like to station a guard at her hospital room."

Espes was frowning and tapping his pen on his desk. "Sounds far-fetched," he finally said. "Old people die, Drake. Tell me something new."

"A few days after Mrs. Rheinhart asked Pomerantz to look into Mrs. Seligman's death, he turns up dead in Rancho Park. You think that's coincidence?"

"We don't know that Pomerantz checked into the Seligman woman's death." More tapping of the pen. "I thought you were gung ho on this stolen art stuff."

She'd told Espes about her meeting with the Steele men and what she'd learned. "I'm not sure about that anymore."

"You said Pomerantz told people he had a secret—what would that have to do with this Seligman woman's death? The *secret* is what brought him to L.A., Drake, not this Mrs. Seligman."

"I think Hilda needs protection," Jessie said stubbornly.

"Based on what you've told me, I can't justify allocating department funds to pay for a guard for this woman. Give me a more convincing motive, or some evidence, and I'll see what I can do."

She turned to leave.

"Speaking of funds," Espes said. "You'll be glad to hear that Downtown okayed offering a ten-thousand-dollar reward for information about the mom who killed her infant son. It'll be on tonight's news."

She *was* glad—without the reward offer, they'd probably reached a dead end with that case. She hoped they wouldn't reach another one with Norman Pomerantz.

She phoned Health Services and asked for Corinne.

"You again," Corinne said when she got on the line.

The woman always made her smile. "Check something for me? Mendel Blumenkrantz." She spelled the name. "He died a few weeks ago. I'm interested in the cause of death and the name of the physician who signed the death certificate."

"The things I do for you," Corinne grumbled. A few minutes later she was back on the line. "The doc's name is Sheldon Abel. Cause of death, congestive heart failure. Does that do anything for you, honey?"

"I don't know." How easy was it to induce congestive heart failure, or its symptoms? Would digitalis pills do the trick?

She phoned Abel and learned that he'd gone for the day.

"He's away for the weekend. I can page the doctor on call," the receptionist told her.

She needed Abel. "Please tell him it's important," she said, and left her home number as well as the station number.

She sat at her desk, drumming her fingers on the scarred wood, thinking. Then she picked up the phone again and punched the numbers for the Lindenhurst Gardens, the convalescent home where Anna Seligman had stayed until her death.

Vince Lemar, the manager Jessie had met earlier, came on the line quickly. "How can I help you, Detective?" he asked in the same funereal voice.

"I need a list of all the medical professionals who provide care for your residents. Doctors, nurses, physical therapists, social workers, shrinks. But not people contracted to work only for you."

"You're *not* interested in staff personnel?" He sounded puzzled.

"Only those who work for your facility and others." Those who had natural, easy access to residents at various facilities—board and care, convalescent.

"We deal with nurses and therapists from a home health agency. Residents have their own doctors, of course. I know many of the physicians by name, but to give you a complete list, I'd have to check our files."

"I'd appreciate that."

"It'll take some time. I could have it for you by Monday."

"I need it sooner than that," she said firmly. "Why don't I stop by tomorrow afternoon and pick it up."

A short hesitation. Then, "All right. I'll do my best."

She phoned the board and care where Anna Seligman had stayed and requested the same information. She did the same with the facilities where Mendel Blumenkrantz had stayed, then with the convalescent home where Hilda had been transferred. Finally, she spoke to Lilly Gorcheck at the Golden Palms and explained what she wanted.

"I'll have it for you as soon as I can," Lilly said. "I checked with Cedars. They said Hilda is going to be all right. I hope so."

Jessie hoped so, too.

It was four-fifty. Simms and Boyd were downtown—they'd spent all day at the courthouse yesterday and still hadn't testified. Phil was still out—he probably wouldn't come back to the station. She made a half-hearted attempt at straightening up her desk, then slung her purse over her shoulder and left.

She stopped at a supermarket and bought milk, detergent, cereal, fruits and vegetables. Gary was taking her out to dinner and a movie, so she didn't have to bother about supper.

At home she put away the perishables, changed into shorts and a tank top, and threw a load of laundry into the machine. She listened to her messages. Helen had phoned—"Just to say hi," she'd said, but Jessie knew otherwise. Her cop friend Brenda Royes had phoned and wanted to get together.

She filled a glass with refrigerated bottled water and took it into the breakfast nook, where she glanced at the mail. Nothing of interest—just more bills, and a reminder from her gynecologist that she was due for her annual checkup. Thrills.

She really ought to pay some bills—they were piling up. She turned on the radio, then brought the stack of bills from her bedroom desk and fanned them out on the dinette table. So many bills, so little money. And it was so damn hot. Sighing, she drank half a glass of ice-cold water and wondered whether she should swallow her pride and borrow money from her parents for central air-conditioning, as Helen had suggested.

Not that Helen's ideas were always sound. Jessie thought about her sister, and her parents. She wondered how they were. Picking up the receiver, she dialed the La Jolla number.

Her mother answered. "How nice of you to call, Jessica," she said when she heard Jessie's voice. "Is everything all right?"

"Everything's fine. I just wanted to say hi." *You talk to Mom.* Jessie shook her head to dismiss the thought—she wouldn't mention the Swiss accounts, she decided. "I miss you," she said awkwardly, not because it wasn't true—strangely enough, it was—but because she wasn't used to saying it, or feeling it.

"That's very sweet, Jessica," her mother said softly. "I miss you, too. Your father and I were just saying how much we enjoyed visiting with you. How's Gary?" No trace of coyness.

"Great. We're going to dinner and a movie. I was thinking about you the other day, Mom. I told you about the case I'm investigating—the Holocaust survivor? Well, I was talking to some people who have an amazing art collection in their home. Actually, it's their father's home. Maurice Steele?"

"The name sounds familiar."

"He's a collector. You may have seen some of his art—apparently, he lends out works from his collection to various museums. Anyway, I was looking at these fabulous paintings, and I thought of you. You would have loved seeing them."

"That's so nice of you to think of me, Jessica. Maybe next time your father and I drive up, you and I can spend some time at the museums."

"There's going to be an exhibit in Pasadena in the fall. I can let you know when." This was going well—a normal, nonconfrontational conversation. Gary would be proud.

"That would be lovely. To tell you the truth, Jessica, I thought at first that you were calling because of the Swiss bank accounts." She laughed lightly. "I figured Helen had put you up to it—she's obsessed with this whole thing, but she's probably afraid I'll bite her head off if she calls herself. Frances the Terrible," she said wryly with only a trace of self-pity.

Instant tension. Jessie felt her stomach muscles knotting and was glad her mother couldn't see her face. "Helen knows this is your decision, Mom," she said, choosing her words carefully.

"Yes, but she thinks I'm being stupid and selfish. The whole thing is ridiculous, Jessica. I don't even know for a fact that my father *had* a Swiss account."

Jessie hesitated—to tell or not to tell? "I saw the list on the Internet yesterday—it had to do with the case I'm investigating. Your father's name was on it."

Dead silence.

"Well," Frances finally said. "It doesn't change how I feel. I don't want the money."

"Okay." She didn't know what else to say.

"You're sure it was my father?"

"The listing I saw was for a Jacob Kochinsky from Poland." She thought about the application she'd brought home yesterday from the Steele Foundation. It was lying on her nightstand.

"It could be someone else with the same name," Frances said.

"It could be," Jessie agreed.

Another silence. Then, "So you *did* call about the banks." Her voice was soft with hurt. "Helen asked you to call, didn't she? Did she want you to convince me to file a claim?"

"No." Her face flushed at the lie.

"You're always protecting her," Frances said, more sad than angry.

"I called to say hello, Mom. I wanted to tell you about the art I saw. I thought . . . I thought it would give us something in common." A start, maybe. "I'm sorry if I've upset you. Say goodnight to Dad for me."

"I will. Jessica—"

She braced herself. "What?"

"Let me know about the exhibit. I'll make plans to join you."

Just when you were sure you had a person figured out.

25

JESSIE DECIDED TO light the candles. She'd showered and put on a short black linen skirt with a teal silk blouse that Gary loved and had gone into the breakfast room to wait for him when she noticed them on the ledge.

Ezra had included a small calendar that listed the candle-lighting times for the entire Jewish year, along with a small, laminated card printed with the Hebrew blessing for the lighting of the candles and beneath it, the transliterated English.

Candle lighting for this Friday was 7:37, she read. It was almost 7:30 now. She inserted a squat white candle into each of the candlesticks, struck a match, and watched the flames leap to life.

The doorbell rang.

She went to the front door and let Gary in. "I'll be just a minute," she told him, and returned to the breakfast room.

He followed her. "You lit the candles," he said in a non-committal voice as he entered the room.

"I have to do the blessing." She showed him the laminated card and began reciting the transliterated words. *"Baruch atah—"*

"You're supposed to circle your hands around the candles

before you say the prayer," Gary said. "Three times, I think. That's what my mom does."

She nodded. "You're right. Ezra said you do it to welcome the Sabbath into your home." She lifted her hands and encircled the candles three times, as if she were embracing them, then brought her hands to her eyes. She stopped. "If I cover my eyes, how will I say the blessing? I don't know it by heart."

"I'll say it with you, if you want."

He recited the prayer, pausing after each word so that she could repeat it. When she was done, she stood for a moment with her hands covering her eyes, enjoying the serenity of the enveloping silence. Frances's mother had lit Sabbath candles like these every Friday night, Jessie suddenly realized; she'd recited this same blessing, and Frances had probably watched her. Frances's grandmother had lit the Sabbath candles, too, and *her* mother before her, and her grandmother. A long link of tradition going all the way back to the matriarch Sarah, Abraham's wife, who had been so spiritually elevated and her tent filled with so much harmony that her Sabbath candles had lasted from Friday to Friday.

A link, Jessie thought with a pang of sorrow, severed by unspeakable violence that had forever undermined a little girl's faith in God and man. She wondered whether her mother had ever lit Sabbath candles. Someday she would ask her.

She dropped her hands to her sides. "Thanks," she said, and kissed Gary lightly on the mouth.

"Any time." He took her hand and linked his fingers through hers. "Ready to go?"

"Uh-huh. Two stops first, though, okay?"

"Where?"

She smiled enigmatically.

Patsy Williams stared at Pomerantz's photo.

"That's definitely him," she told Jessie. The waitress pointed a sharp, burgundy-lacquered fingernail at Pomerantz's head. "He was here around nine o'clock on Saturday night. I remember his hair—I thought it was neat, especially since he was obviously kind of old. And he was a real gentleman—called me 'young lady.' " She smiled.

Jessie felt a tiny thrill of satisfaction. At least they knew that Pomerantz had actually arrived at the Century Plaza. "Was he alone?"

"At first he was. He said he was waiting for someone. I asked if he'd like to order a drink in the meantime. He asked for some wine—said he was too young for hard liquor. He was kind of cute." Another smile. "The other guy showed a few minutes later."

Jessie's heart skipped a beat. "Can you describe him?" she asked with forced calm.

The waitress narrowed her eyes. "Gee, sorry. He didn't make an impression, you know?" She shrugged.

Jessie tried not to show her disappointment. "Was he tall or short? Heavy or thin?" she asked, forcing herself not to sound impatient.

"Well, he was sitting, so I couldn't tell his height. But not real tall or real short, or I would've noticed. And he wasn't heavy. I would've noticed that, too."

Jessie wasn't so sure. "Do you remember how old he was?"

"Mmnn, in his forties or fifties? Definitely younger than the other man."

"Was he wearing glasses?"

"I don't remember."

"What about his hair color?"

More narrowing of the eyes. "Maybe brown? I'm sorry. Like I said, I didn't pay much attention. Oh, then this *other* guy showed up."

Jessie frowned. "A *third* man?"

The waitress nodded. "The first two looked surprised to see him. The old guy didn't look all that happy at first, but then he seemed okay with it."

Patsy couldn't describe this man, either. "Sorry. But I'm not good with stuff like that." She had the grace to blush. "Anyway, the third guy ordered coffee and pie. A little later the second guy left, but the old guy stayed and had another coffee."

Terrific. They didn't have *one* mystery man—they had two.

"Do you happen to remember who paid?" If Pomerantz's companion had paid with a charge card, maybe they could trace him.

"The third man. He paid in cash."

So there went *that* possibility. "Was he—"

"Not a big tipper," Patsy interrupted. "He left exactly ten percent. But that's not going to help you identify him, huh?"

"Not exactly." Jessie smiled, hoping her frustration didn't show. She supposed it was funny, what people *did* remember and didn't. "Did they leave together?"

"Uh-huh. I saw them walking out." The waitress frowned. "Actually, now that I think about it, I remember that the old guy was kind of leaning on the other one."

Jessie frowned. "You think he didn't feel well?"

Patsy thought for a moment, then nodded. "Maybe."

Had mystery man number two slipped digitalis into Pomerantz's drink, then taken him to Rancho Park and left him there to die? "If you remember anything else, Patsy, please call me. It's very important." She handed the waitress a business card and left the restaurant.

Gary was sitting in the lobby, where she'd left him.

"Any luck?" he asked, rising when he saw her.

She repeated what she'd learned. "The waitress can't remember anything about either guy. Except that the third one was a bad tipper."

Gary held his palms up high. "Don't look at me—I have an alibi for Saturday night. I was with a cop."

She smiled.

"You said two stops. Where to next?"

Hilda was sleeping. Her chest rose lightly with every breath that whistled through her nose in a fluttery snore.

"She looks so frail," Gary whispered to Jessie.

"Actually, her color's better than it was this morning. I guess we should go." She turned to leave.

"Her eyes just opened, Jess."

She turned back. Hilda was looking at them. Jessie approached the bed and lifted the woman's hand. "I just wanted to see how you're doing. The doctor says you're going home tomorrow." She squeezed her hand.

"Home? Where is home?" Hilda sighed. "That's your boyfriend?" She gestured with her chin toward the doorway, where Gary was standing.

"Uh-huh. Cute, isn't he?"

"Why is he standing so far away? He thinks I'm going to bite him?"

"I told him to wait there. I'm worried he'll take one look at you and dump me."

Hilda chuckled. Jessie beckoned to Gary. A moment later he was standing at the old woman's bedside.

"So you're the ex?" Hilda looked at him appraisingly. To Jessie, she said, "A handsome young man."

"Thank you." Gary smiled. "Jessie's told me a lot about you."

"You're treating her good?"

"Very good," he said seriously.

Hilda nodded. "She told you somebody's trying to kill me?" she asked, suddenly somber.

Gary glanced quickly at Jessie. "She told me you're worried."

"But does she *believe* me?" Hilda asked urgently.

Jessie squeezed her hand again. "I've been checking into Anna Seligman's death, like I promised. I wanted to ask you some questions."

"So ask."

"Did Anna mention having a special relationship with her doctor or her nurse?"

Hilda shook her head. "She didn't like her doctor—too busy, she always told me. Never had time for her. She didn't say anything about the nurse." Her eyes narrowed. "You think a *doctor* killed her?" She looked suddenly frightened and seemed to shrink beneath her hospital blanket.

"I'm just checking into some possibilities. I'm not sure anyone killed her, Hilda." She patted her hand. "Did you know a man named Mendel Blumenkrantz?"

"Blumenkrantz?" Hilda squinted. "No, I don't think so. Why?"

"I just wondered."

Hilda paled. She licked her lips. "He's dead, too?"

"No," Jessie lied. What was the point of increasing the old woman's anxiety? "Hilda, last time you told me that someone was trying to kill survivors. What did you mean by that?"

"What did I mean?" She tried to shrug her shoulders, but the effort was too much. She sighed. "To finish what that *rotzeach*, Hitler, tried to do. That murderer."

No help there. Jessie thought for a moment. "The first time we talked, you said they killed Anna for her money. But I understand that she didn't have much money."

"So why did they kill her?" Hilda challenged.

"Do you know whether Anna had a life insurance policy?" If she'd had a policy, a health practitioner may have ingratiated himself or herself with her and persuaded her to sign over the death benefits.

"I don't know. We didn't talk about it."

But that didn't mean Anna Seligman hadn't had a policy. Mendel Blumenkrantz may have taken out a life insurance policy, too. It was possible that the killings—if in fact there *were* any—were about greed, not mercy.

"Maybe you should talk to Bernice," Hilda said. "That was Anna's best friend at the retirement home. Maybe Anna told her something."

Jessie wished fervently that Hilda had mentioned this woman Bernice before. "What's her last name?"

"I don't know. But you can find her, no?"

"I'm sure I can."

Hilda sighed again. "You're a nice girl, Jessie James. You kept your promise. You won't let me die, right?"

26

"**WHEN I WAS** in Markstadt, an all-Jewish labor camp, an aunt of mine put me in touch with a neighbor's daughter, Pola, whose fiancé worked in the Aryan kitchen. There the food was better. Real meat instead of horsemeat." Pomerantz smiled. "Pola told me she wanted to help me, so once I went over with a large plate, which she filled with stew and a friend of mine warmed up in the bathhouse where he worked. Another acquaintance of mine was angry with Pola, so he told the Germans I was stealing extra food from the kitchen.

"Three Jewish bullies came after me, looking for the stew. I told them where it was, and they demanded to know where I got it." Pomerantz tightened his lips. "I wouldn't give them Pola's name. One of the bullies hit me hard, twice, with his hand that had a large ring on it. My glasses flew off, and again he ordered me to tell the name of the girl. Again I wouldn't. Then he told his friends to lay me down over a bench so they could hit me with a rubber hose. Usually, they would do about forty, fifty lashes, enough to kill a person.

"They put me down, and still I wouldn't tell. Then one of the bullies, named Weiss, said he knew me, and that if at this point I still didn't tell, then I really didn't know. So they let me off with a warning.

"Later, I ate the stew with my friend. Delicious." Pomerantz paused, then smiled wryly. "And all it cost me was two hits."

Sheila Henkins looked even more harried on Saturday morning than she had the first time Jessie had seen her, when she'd come to ask about Anna Seligman.

"I spent most of yesterday and all of this morning compiling the list of medical professionals you asked for," the administrator said, her tone just short of accusation. "It isn't quite done yet."

"I really appreciate this." Jessie smiled warmly. "I'm sure you didn't need this extra work. I know how busy you must be, running this facility."

The woman exhaled deeply and rolled her eyes. "You can't even imagine." She sounded mollified. "One of our MIs— mentally incompetents— just attacked a female resident— apparently, they were having a thing, and he got jealous. The woman wasn't hurt, but her family is furious—I can't blame them. So now I have to transfer the MI to another facility— if I can find one that'll take him."

"Not a great day, huh?"

"The truth? Not much worse than most." She smiled weakly. "Look, give me a half hour, and the list'll be ready. You can wait, or I can fax it to you."

"I'll wait. And thanks again. By the way, have you ever seen this man?" Jessie took the photo of Pomerantz from her purse and showed it to the manager. "He may have come to ask about Mrs. Seligman."

Sheila gazed at the photo, then shook her head. "I don't think so. But I don't see all the guests who come to visit our residents. You might ask the receptionist."

"I did. She can't say one way or the other." Jessie returned the photo to her purse. "Do you know whether Mrs. Seligman had a life insurance policy?"

The administrator looked at Jessie with curiosity. "I wouldn't know. We never discussed it."

"I understand she was friendly with another resident who lives here, a woman named Bernice. I don't know her last name." *Please, let there not be fifty residents named Bernice.*

"You probably mean Bernice Kotowitz." Sheila nodded. "She and Anna *were* friendly. She was very upset to hear that she died."

"I'd like to talk to her. Is she in?"

The woman frowned. "To tell you the truth, she might be anxious about talking to a detective."

Exactly what Mason, the Golden Palms administrator, had said. "I understand your concern, but I *do* need to talk to her."

Sheila leaned forward. "What exactly is going on, Detective?" She sounded suddenly anxious, and the hardness was back in her voice. "What's the purpose of these lists? I spoke to Mrs. Seligman's doctor yesterday—he assured me she died of natural causes. Are you saying she didn't?"

"I'm afraid I can't comment, other than to say that this is part of an ongoing investigation," Jessie said with practiced smoothness. "Can you please check to see if Mrs. Kotowitz is available?"

The administrator hesitated, then picked up the phone.

"That's Bernice." Sheila pointed to a stout woman with a huge bosom and red, Little-Orphan-Annie tightly curled hair who was standing in front of a Ping-Pong table in the recreation room, talking to an elderly, hunched man.

Sheila approached Bernice. Jessie followed her, but stayed a few feet behind her.

"Bernice, there's someone here who would like to talk to you," the administrator said cheerily. She addressed the man. "Would you excuse us, please, Mr. Orrins?"

"What?"

She leaned closer to him and spoke loudly and slowly into his ear. "Would you excuse us, please?"

The old man blinked. "We were about to start a new game."

Bernice was looking curiously at Jessie. Jessie smiled at her.

"This won't take long," Sheila said.

"Sure," he grumbled. He placed his paddle and ball on the table. "Two out of three games," he told Bernice. "And it's my serve. Don't forget." He waited for her nod, then shuffled off across the room, casting several over-the-shoulder glances behind him.

"This is Detective Drake," Sheila told Bernice. "She'd like to talk to you about Anna Seligman."

Bernice's eyes widened. "About *Anna*?"

"Just a few questions," Jessie said reassuringly. "Thanks for your help," she told the administrator, hoping she'd take the hint and leave.

"Do you want me to stay, Bernice?"

"No, it's okay."

Sheila looked uncertain. "If you need me, I'll be in my office."

Jessie waited until the administrator had left. "Would you like to go to the lobby, or to your room?" she asked. "Wherever you'll feel more comfortable."

"Can we stay here? I had to wait an hour to get the table, and I don't want to lose my turn."

The room was filled with elderly men and women. Some were watching TV. Some were playing cards. Some, like Mr. Orrins, who was sitting on one of the sofas, were reading. Jessie doubted that anyone could overhear her conversation with Bernice.

"Okay," she said.

"You like Ping-Pong?" Bernice asked.

"I like it." She and Helen used to play it on weekends with their father in the playroom that had once been a garage. They'd never been able to coax Frances into playing.

"I play it all the time. It relaxes me, and I can think better when I'm playing. Strange, no?" She tried a smile.

Another man came to the table. "You're finished here?"

Bernice shook her head. "I'm just starting a game."

"I don't see no partner." He put his hands on his hips.

"*She's* my partner." Bernice gestured toward Jessie. "We were just going to start."

What I do in the line of duty, Jessie thought. She dropped her purse at the side of the table and picked up the paddle. The man sidled away.

"What a hog," Bernice whispered angrily. "Always trying

to take someone's turn. Don't turn around! He's looking at us, I know it. Hit the ball," she ordered. "Volley for serve?"

Jessie repressed a smile. "Volley for serve." She bounced the ball, hit it, and sent it diagonally across the short net and over the table. She laughed ruefully. "Sorry. It's been a while."

Bernice bent to retrieve the ball. "So what do you want to know about Anna?"

How much should she tell? "Do you know Hilda Rheinhart?"

"Sure. Anna's friend." She narrowed her eyes. "Why? Something happened to her?"

"She had a heart attack, but the doctor says she's going to be fine." She heard Bernice's sigh of relief. "Hilda thinks something happened to Anna."

Bernice frowned in puzzlement. "What do you mean, 'happened'? She died." She looked at Jessie questioningly.

"Hilda thinks someone killed her," Jessie said quietly.

"That's crazy. Anna had a bad heart." Bernice was gaping now. "She told me Hilda's always scared, always looking over her shoulder, expecting the worst. Anyway, why would someone kill Anna?" She snorted.

"Hilda says it was for the money, but from what I understand, Anna didn't have any money." Was it Jessie's imagination, or had something flickered across the old woman's face? She waited.

Bernice picked up the ball and served it. Jessie returned the serve. They volleyed for several seconds until Jessie hit the ball into the net.

"Was Anna particularly friendly with her doctor or any of the nurses?" Jessie asked.

"She didn't love her doctor, she didn't hate him." Bernice shrugged. "He was always busy, always running. And Anna didn't have any children."

Jessie looked at her, puzzled. "What difference does that make?"

Bernice's smile was sad. "You're young, you don't know what happens." She held the ball in her hand. "Let me tell you something, darling—it's different if you have children, family. If you have family, the doctors spend more time with you. They explain things better. They call to check how you're doing. That's just the way it is." Bernice's serve sliced the ball. It bounced on Jessie's side and careened off the table.

"What about the nurses? I assume that someone gave Anna insulin shots for her diabetes."

Bernice nodded. "The nurse was okay. Anna really liked the physical therapist—a Russian woman. Hands like a sculptor and a heart of gold, Anna said."

Had the therapist had taken pity on Anna and hurried her death? Or had she ingratiated herself with Anna for monetary gain? "What was her name?"

"I don't remember the last name. The first name started with a G. Gladys, maybe."

"Gladys" didn't sound familiar. Then again, Jessie had heard so many names in the past few days. She'd have to check her notes. "Did Anna have a life insurance policy?" she asked casually.

A grunt. "For what? She didn't have any children or close family, so why did she need life insurance?"

A good point. Which meant there was no motive for monetary gain. . . . Back to square one.

This was probably a waste of time, investigating Anna Seligman's death. Jessie had drawn sinister connections between the deaths of Mendel Blumenkrantz and Anna Seligman only because of what Hilda had said. Maybe Pomerantz, like Lilly Gorcheck, had recognized Hilda's fears as paranoia. Maybe he'd only been humoring her when he'd promised to check into Anna's death.

"Do you know a Norman Pomerantz? Or Nachum Pomerantz?" Jessie asked.

Bernice thought for a moment. "Doesn't ring a bell." She lobbed the ball to Jessie.

"Did anybody call you recently and ask about Anna?"

The woman shook her head. "Your serve."

Another volley, another point for Bernice. And zero information for Jessie. She decided to play the rest of the game—what the hell, Bernice would finish her off in a few minutes. Let the old lady have fun.

They played for a while without speaking, the silence filled by the rhythmic click-clacking of the ball against the table top. Jessie couldn't tell from the tense expression on Bernice's face whether she was concentrating on the game or thinking about Anna. The score was nineteen to three, Bernice in the lead, when Bernice suddenly walked around the table to Jessie.

"Anna *did* have money," she whispered. "She made me promise not to say anything to anyone. She didn't want anyone here to know—she was afraid they'd raise her rates. But now she's dead, and you're asking all these questions. . . ."

Jessie's heart thumped. Don't get excited, she warned herself. "Where did she get this money?" And how had she hidden it from the retirement home administrator?

"Her parents had insurance," Bernice said, still whispering. "From Europe. The company was going to pay off the policy." She looked around anxiously, then back at Jessie. "Anna said that with the interest, it was worth millions of dollars." Bernice's eyes gleamed. "She said her parents also put money in a Swiss bank before the war."

Jessie tried not to show her disappointment. "But she died before she got any of the money."

Bernice shook her head vigorously. "She got the money *before* she died. From the insurance *and* from the Swiss bank."

"Mrs. Kotowitz," Jessie said patiently, "as far as I know, the banks and insurance companies have just started settling claims."

Bernice leaned closer, until her mouth was only inches from Jessie's ear. "Yes, but Anna had a smart lawyer. He arranged for her to get the money *now*. Of course, she would have gotten more if she'd waited to settle the claims, but this way she had a sure thing, and she got the money right away. She wasn't supposed to tell anyone—he made her promise, because he said if too many people knew about this, something could go wrong. But of course she told me." A hint of pride in her voice.

Jessie frowned. "What happened to the rest of the money?"

"I guess the bank and the insurance company kept it. Anna signed over her rights to the lawyer. She asked me what I thought—if she should wait and get everything, or take less money now. 'Life's too short,' I told her. 'Take the money.' Who knew, right?" Bernice sighed.

Jessie's chest tightened. Maybe the bank and insurance company *hadn't* kept the money. Maybe the attorney had. "Do you know the attorney's name?"

"She never told me. He came here a few times to see her, but I never met him. Anna said he was nice—a real gentleman. She didn't plan to spend the money on herself, you know. For Anna, it wasn't about getting rich. It was about what was right. She was going to give most of it to charity."

That's what Frances could do, Jessie thought, if she didn't want to keep the money. If she ever processed a claim. "If you remember anything about the attorney, or anything else, please let me know," she told Bernice and handed her a card.

The woman nodded. She studied the card, then glanced up at Jessie. "Do you think Hilda could be right? That someone killed Anna?" Her voice quivered, and she looked suddenly frail and vulnerable in spite of her robust size.

"You're playing or talking?" asked the old man who'd coveted the Ping-Pong table. He came nearer.

Bernice dropped the paddle on the table. "You want to play, play," she said quietly.

27

THE BELLEVIEW MANOR, the Burbank board-and-care facility where Mendel Blumenkrantz had lived, was smaller than the Golden Palms but had the same general ambiance.

Jessie introduced herself to the manager, a portly man in his fifties who wore suspenders and a bow tie.

"You called about the list," he said. "I have it ready for you." He lifted a stapled set of papers from under a folder on his desk and handed it to Jessie.

"This is terrific. Thanks." She folded the papers lengthwise and put them in her purse, next to the list she'd picked up from Sheila Henkins. "Actually, I wanted to ask a few questions about Mr. Mendel Blumenkrantz. I understand that he lived here for quite a few years."

The manager nodded. "A very, very nice man. A *gentle* man. Everybody loved him." He sighed. "We were sorry to hear that he died."

Jessie nodded in sympathy. "Was he ill for a long time?"

"He wasn't exactly a poster boy for good health." The manager smiled lightly. "He had crippling arthritis, a touch of emphysema, high blood pressure. He wasn't well, but he managed. A lot of spirit, Mr. Blumenkrantz."

"Why was he transferred to the convalescent home?"

"He was having heart palpitations, and his emphysema worsened. We were concerned that he needed full-time nursing. Obviously, we were right. Not long after he left, he got worse and died. Congestive heart failure, I think they said."

Jessie nodded again. "I'd like to speak to some of the people Mr. Blumenkrantz was close to when he lived here. Who would they be?"

The manager looked instantly uncomfortable. "I'd really hate to disturb them. Old people can become anxious very quickly, you know."

"I understand. But it's important that I speak to them." She said this pleasantly but firmly and wondered how many more times she'd have this kind of exchange with a manager of a board and care. "Who was his best friend?"

A short hesitation. Then, "That would be Joe Lifshutz. But he's not here right now. He went to his son's for the day."

Jessie wrote down the man's name. "When will he be back?"

"I don't know. I'd guess around five or six."

Too long to wait—it was just past noon now. "Did Mr. Blumenkrantz have any other close friends?"

"He had a *lot* of friends, but Joe was the closest. They shared a room." The manager leaned forward. "Mendel and I talked quite a bit, you know. Maybe there's something I can help you with?"

Maybe. "So he had a semiprivate room?" No money, then.

"That's all he could afford. But the semi's are very nice," the manager said defensively.

"I'm sure they are. Do you know whether he had a life insurance policy?"

"I don't think so. He *did* have a policy that covered funeral arrangements—he told me that when he first arrived. Mendel liked having everything taken care of in advance."

"Did he indicate that his financial situation was going to improve anytime soon?"

The manager shook his head. "I don't see how. He was completely retired. He had only social security and MediCal/Medicare. No other investments or property."

No Swiss bank accounts or European insurance policy? She'd have to come back later and talk to Joe Lifshutz. Maybe he knew more about Blumenkrantz than the manager did.

Or maybe there was nothing to know.

An hour later she had four lists of medical professionals: One from Blumenkrantz's board and care; one from his convalescent home; one from Anna Seligman's board and care; one from the Golden Palms. Arnold Samber, the manager of the convalescent home where Hilda was staying, hadn't finished compiling his list yet. Ditto for the manager of the convalescent home where Anna Seligman had died. The two lists would be ready tomorrow.

Jessie drove to the station and picked up the videotape of the earlier documentary interview Pomerantz had done. At home she changed into a pair of shorts and a white T-shirt. She thought about attacking the weeds that had invaded the small flower bed in her backyard, but it was too damn hot.

Gary was at his apartment, working on his road rage piece. She was tempted to call and invite him over, but that wasn't fair. His deadline was looming.

So was hers. The questionnaire was due by the end of the week. She prepared a tuna sandwich and, sitting at the breakfast room table, started answering the questions. An hour and a half later she was only half done. She treated herself to a glass of iced tea and went into the den.

The lists were on the coffee table, next to the newly arrived video.

She was curious to watch the video, but Sheila Henkins and the others had worked hard to accommodate Jessie's request so quickly. Not that they'd know what she was doing. Still . . .

She sat cross-legged on the couch and picked up the top list. Mendel Blumenkrantz's board and care. She scanned three pages of names, then put down the list and picked up the next one. Blumenkrantz's convalescent home.

There were repeat names of doctors, nurses, therapists. Hardly a surprise—both facilities were in the Valley; and since board and care referred residents to convalescent homes, there was a natural transference of the medical people who attended them.

She looked at the list Sheila Henkins had given her. She didn't recognize the names of any medical professionals—which could mean that there were so many names on the lists, that she'd have to figure out a way not to miss any repetitions.

She *did* recognize one name: Gloria Pinkoff, physical therapist. That was the name of Hilda's therapist—Jessie was almost positive, but she checked her notes to make sure.

There it was: Gloria Pinkoff. Jessie had spoken to the woman at the Golden Palms. Hilda, she remembered, loved her. She'd worried that no one had told Gloria about her having been transferred to a convalescent home.

Bernice Kotowitz had mentioned that Anna had adored her physical therapist, too. Gladys something. Jessie scanned Anna's board and care list again but didn't find any "Gladys."

Maybe Bernice had been wrong about the first name. She'd told Jessie she wasn't sure. Maybe Anna's therapist had been Gloria Pinkoff.

Jessie reexamined the first two lists—no "Pinkoff" on Blumenkrantz's convalescent home list, but there she was, in all caps, on his board and care list. GLORIA PINKOFF.

Which didn't mean anything yet, Jessie told herself. Healthcare professionals probably freelanced at numerous facilities.

Gloria was a large woman, Jessie recalled. Muscular, with strong arms. Not that you needed physical strength to administer lethal medications.

Hilda adored her. So had Anna. A heart of gold, Anna had told her good friend Bernice. Had that been real? Or an act? Had Gloria ingratiated herself with Anna and Mendel so that they would make her their legal beneficiary? Was she doing the same now with Hilda?

Anna had received a large financial settlement. But according to Lilly Gorcheck, Hilda didn't have *any* money. And Mendel Blumenkrantz probably hadn't had any, either. If he had, why had he been living in a semiprivate room?

Maybe Gloria's motive hadn't been money after all. Maybe she *did* have a heart of gold.

Maybe she'd been consumed with pity for Anna and Mendel and felt driven to end their suffering.

And what about Hilda?

28

POMERANTZ LOOKED THE the same on this video—in fact, Jessie was pretty certain that he was wearing the same suit he'd worn during the other interview. There was no pretape chitchat, and he seemed a little stiffer here initially, less comfortable with his surroundings. But he quickly loosened up.

He talked about his childhood, about his family, about the war. Midway through the tape there were one or two incidents that Jessie found unfamiliar, but nothing about them caught her attention or seemed significant. And she heard no reference to stolen art or anything that would explain the secret he'd mentioned to Abigail Morton and his friend Stanley.

She doubted she'd learn anything, but she continued watching. Five minutes later her interest quickened. Pomerantz was talking about his family again, about their lives before the war. . . .

"My father, Yerachmiel Shtuelberg, was a sharp businessman. My brother, too. What's that? Why do I have a different last name?" He smiled. "My parents were married by a rabbi but didn't have a Polish marriage certificate when I was born. So officially I was given my mother's maiden name, Pomerantz. When my brother was born, my parents were already married by

Polish civil law. So he was called Shtuelberg, like my father. End of mystery." Another smile.

"My father relied on my brother and trusted his advice, even though Moshe was just in his twenties. A year before the war broke out, he convinced my father to open a bank account in Switzerland. 'Just in case,' he said." Pomerantz pursed his lips. "They traveled to Switzerland together. Moshe knew the number to the account, and my father knew, of course. I knew just the name of the bank. 'After this crazy war is over,' my brother told me just before we were separated, 'I'll find you and our sisters and parents. We'll start over.' But Moshe died, and my mother and sisters died, and my father died, and the number to the account died with them." Pomerantz sighed.

"I went to the bank in Zurich after I was liberated. Very polite, very formal. They wanted a death certificate. They wanted numbers. I told them I didn't have a death certificate, I didn't have numbers. All I had was a name—Yerachmiel Shtuelberg. I told them, 'My father deposited money in your bank. This I know.' 'Sorry,' they said. 'So very sorry, but we can't help you. We have rules, there are laws.' They acted like the world was a normal place, like people had their lives in order." He shrugged. "Now, finally, they're starting to cooperate, so maybe I'll file a claim. I don't know. . . ."

Had Pomerantz filed a claim after all? Jessie had asked Barbara Loura to check the list of dormant accounts, but she'd given her Pomerantz's last name. She hadn't known that his father had gone under the name Shtuelberg.

But even if Pomerantz *had* filed a claim, and was expecting large sums of money that would change his life, that was hardly a "secret."

And what was "lost and found"? Had he found the numbers for the Swiss bank account? But he didn't really need them now—the banks were cooperating. They weren't insisting on papers and numbers.

She continued watching. Pomerantz was describing his home and the art his father had acquired over the years. Pomerantz had obviously inherited his love of the arts, Jessie thought.

"We had magnificent paintings—oils, watercolors, charcoal drawings. My father collected Jewish ritual objects, too. Menorahs,

kiddush cups, megillah scrolls, mezuzah cases—all very intricately crafted, very unusual. We had a beautiful chalice—the cup of Elijah the prophet, we called it. Gorgeous, really. I can still see it." Shutting his eyes, Pomerantz traced an imaginary cup with both hands. *"My father told us an Italian artist made only five like it. I would recognize it anywhere, even if it didn't have my father's initials etched inside the base. It was gold, and set with emeralds, sapphires, diamonds, rubies. My father and Moshe took it and a number of other priceless items with them to Switzerland. So many beautiful things, all lost."*

Lost—and then found? Jessie frowned. Was that what Pomerantz had meant? Had he recognized an item that had belonged to his family? The chalice, maybe? Had he gone to the Steele Foundation to ask their help in retrieving it?

Maybe he'd confided in Hilda. But then what about Anna Seligman, and Mendel Blumenkrantz? What was the connection?

She watched the rest of the tape, and wondered.

Joe Lifshutz seemed fascinated rather than anxious when the manager explained that Jessie was a police detective and had come to talk about Mendel Blumenkrantz.

"A real detective?" he said, gawking at her after the manager left them in the lobby. "I would never have guessed."

She smiled and sat down on one of the two brown Naugahyde sofas in the room. He was a short, thin, bony man, and she tried not to stare at his head. Apparently he'd grown his few remaining hairs so that he could comb them from above his right ear and up across the top of his head, to camouflage his balding pate.

"How many years you're doing this?"

"Fifteen." Sometimes it seemed like a century. Sometimes she felt as though she'd just graduated from the academy. "Mr. Lifshutz—"

He leaned closer. "You're scared sometimes, or not?" he asked in a conspiratorial voice.

"Sometimes," she admitted. "To tell you the truth, though, patrol officers face more danger than detectives. We just get to ask a lot of questions."

He nodded. "My son's a science teacher. He and his wife live in Woodland Hills. A nice house—three bedrooms, and they just added a room. He wants I should move in with him, but I told him I'm fine here. I keep busy, I have friends. Who needs to be a burden?"

Jessie smiled. "I'm sure you wouldn't be a burden."

"Today, no. But who knows what's going to be in two, three years?" He shrugged. "It's better like this. To tell you the truth, I like being with people my own age. We kvetch, we laugh. We compare gas pains." Lifshutz chuckled. "But he's a good boy, my son. My daughter-in-law, too. Wait, I'll show you a picture."

He showed Jessie wallet-size photos of his son and daughter-in-law and two granddaughters and beamed when she told him how adorable they were.

"Mr. Lifshutz," she said after he'd returned his wallet to his pants pocket. "I understand that you and Mr. Blumen-krantz were close friends."

"We were like this." Sighing, Lifshutz crossed his index and third fingers. "I miss him terribly. But what can you do? That's life. We're all getting older. Every year is a bonus, right?"

Jessie nodded. "Was he especially friendly with his doctor or nurse, or anyone else like that?" She held her breath.

Lifshutz considered, then shook his head.

"Did he have a physical therapist?" Maybe she had to ask a more specific question.

"Sure. He had bad circulation in his legs."

Jessie's pulse raced. "Who was his therapist, do you know?" G-L-O-R-I-A, she sang silently.

"A thin guy."

Jessie blinked. "A man?"

Lifshutz shrugged. "I told him, 'Mendel, get a woman. Have a little fun.'" He laughed. "But he liked this guy, and that was it. Go figure."

"Did he ever have a woman therapist?" Give it up, Jessie told herself.

"Nope. Not since I know him. And I know him a long time."

So that was that. Just coincidence, fueled by Jessie's overactive imagination. She thought a moment. "Do you know if Mr. Blumenkrantz had life insurance?"

Lifshutz nodded. "He took it out a long time ago to protect his wife, but she died first, a few years ago. He told me he changed the policy so the money would go to a Jewish organization after he died."

So no individual benefited from his death. Ergo no motive and no murder. And coming here had been a waste of time. She picked up her purse.

"He and his wife had no children," Lifshutz said, "so this organization is having someone say kaddish for Mendel the whole year, and then after, on his yahrzeit."

"Yahrzeit?"

"The anniversary of the day he died," Lifshutz explained. "I don't know what he did with the other money."

Jessie tensed. "What other money is that?"

"Mendel was a survivor, like me. He knew his father had money in a Swiss numbered bank account, but Mendel didn't have the numbers. Then, all of a sudden, the Swiss banks are saying you don't need the numbers. So he decided to file a claim. And then—" Lifshutz stopped. Indecision flickered in his eyes. "He made me promise not to tell, but I guess he's dead, so it doesn't matter," he said, as if he were thinking aloud.

Jessie's fingers started to tingle. It was hard not to prompt Lifshutz, but she didn't want to risk intimidating him.

"A lawyer contacted him," Lifshutz finally said. "He offered to help Mendel get the money faster. Mendel wasn't supposed to tell anyone."

Jessie nodded. "And in exchange for getting the money sooner, Mr. Blumenkrantz would take a smaller amount?" she asked quietly.

Lifshutz looked surprised. "How did you know? I told him to check out this lawyer, but Mendel trusted him. To tell you the truth, I was a little worried, because when it came to business matters, Mendel wasn't so sharp lately. Anyway, he signed some papers and gave the lawyer power of attorney, and sure enough, the lawyer got Mendel his money."

Jessie felt a familiar mixture of excitement and alarm. This was too much of a coincidence: Two elderly survivors, hoping to reclaim assets from Swiss banks, had retained someone who had promised them a quicker, though smaller, settlement. Both survivors were childless, without family. Both had recently died, of "natural causes."

This wasn't about neo-Nazis targeting survivors, or about mercy killings, Jessie decided. This was about greed. Anna Seligman and Mendel Blumenkrantz had been easy prey for someone who ingratiated himself with lonely, isolated elderly people, someone who gained their confidence and manipulated them into giving him power of attorney and access to their long-hidden wealth.

Easy prey, especially since there were no children or family members to interfere or object, or to wonder why their loved ones had died soon after signing away their rights to considerable sums of money. Before they could change their minds and nullify the power of attorney.

Jessie was filled with outrage at what she suspected had happened. And fear. Hilda was childless, vulnerable, lonely. Had her parents, or her late husband's parents, hidden money or valuables in a Swiss bank? Had Hilda legally empowered someone to process her claim?

She'd suffered one "heart episode" and was back in the convalescent home.

Would her next heart attack be fatal?

"You mentioned that the lawyer contacted Mr. Blumenkrantz," Jessie said. "How did that come about?"

"A friend of a friend, I think?" Lifshutz shrugged. "I don't remember exactly. But Mendel told me the lawyer knew a lot about him—it's not like he just got his name from a list."

"Do you know the lawyer's name?" she asked and held her breath.

Lifshutz shook his head. "He told me once, but I don't remember. Sorry."

Jessie swallowed her disappointment.

"So maybe Mendel was right after all," said Lifshutz. "All he had was social security and Medicare—he worried about every dollar. If he'd filed the claim and waited, he would have died without seeing a penny. Like this, he was rich for a few months. That's something, isn't it?"

29

"I SAW HORRIBLE things in the labor camps," Pomerantz said. "People fighting over a piece of bread. Jews turning against Jews, hoping to win the favor of the guards." He sighed. "We were building a road into the forest where the Germans stored ammunition. We had a work gang, and every gang had a Jewish leader. Ours—a Chrzanower who everyone from Chrzanow hated—often beat us," Pomerantz said in an offhand manner, as if he were describing the weather. "One Sunday it was raining and muddy, and I had placed two sacks of cement on my shoulders, when suddenly one of the sacks fell and split open. The German leader said nothing. The Jewish leader hit me twice, very hard. I saw stars, and for days I was dizzy. . . .

"Sometimes I saw beautiful things. Acts of loving kindness." Tears sprang to Pomerantz's eyes. "They say what goes around, comes around. I wouldn't be alive today if not for the acts of kindness my father did for others. No, it's true." Pomerantz nodded vigorously. "One time—this was in Markstadt—I was seriously injured—a trailer ran over me and broke my shoulder and arm. In the infirmary the doctor told me I was unable to work. He was a Jew, but he became a Christian so the Germans would treat him better. This doctor refused to help me. I knew what that *meant—I would be sent to Auschwitz to be 'taken care of.' My friends all cried—I told them that sooner or later, we all come to this.*

"One of my best friends, Chaim Lubliner, persuaded the doctor to fix my shoulder. 'I promised his father I would bring him home alive!' Chaim insisted. My father, you see, had saved Chaim's father's life and refused compensation. Chaim had connections to a German businessman, and he managed to get all the supplies and medications the doctor needed. A few days later, while I was recuperating in the infirmary, the doctor came running in and told me to quickly go and hide under the bed in his room. The SS were coming to get those who couldn't or wouldn't work. I hid for four, five hours, until the doctor returned." He paused. "Of the sixty or so people in the infirmary, only two were left. The rest had been sent to Auschwitz. . . .

"The Jew who hit me? Later, he tried to apologize, but I wouldn't listen. After the war, he came to me often to buy textiles, and I tried to forget what he had done to me in the camp." Pomerantz shrugged. "How long can you hate?"

Driving home from Burbank, Jessie kept her eye on the traffic and wondered about the "attorney" who'd worked with Anna Seligman and Mendel Blumenkrantz—she was certain it was the same person.

A con artist hoping to reap millions by cleverly taking advantage of the Swiss banks' recent decision to open long-dormant accounts opened by Holocaust victims and return the moneys to their heirs.

Not a young man, she decided. Someone middle-aged—who would inspire confidence. *I know the horrors you've suffered. I want to help you reclaim what is rightfully yours.*

He'd have to have some background in law or contracts. He'd have to know how to negotiate with the Swiss banks, handle all that paperwork. Maybe he *was* an attorney—one who specialized in international law. Maybe—

Her thoughts suddenly shifted to Reynolds, the attorney she'd met at the Steele Foundation. He was supposedly helping the survivors who filed claims. But what if he was taking advantage of them instead? He had access to the foundation

records. He knew which survivors had reasonable chances of
settling their claims. He knew where they lived. . . .

Steering with her left hand, she rummaged through her
purse with her right hand and found her notepad. She flipped
through it to the page where she'd written the phone number
for the retirement home where Joe Lifshutz was living. Then
she dialed the number on her cell phone.

Lifshutz was in, the receptionist told Jessie. A moment later,
he was on the line.

Jessie identified herself. "Mr. Lifshutz, the attorney who
helped Mr. Blumenkrantz. Was his name Reynolds?" Unconsciously, she tightened her hand on the steering wheel.

"Reynolds? No. That wasn't it."

"Well, thanks anyway." She tried to sound sincerely appre-
ciative—this wasn't Lifshutz's fault. And she should be used
to disappointment. Every time she thought she was making
progress in this damn case, she faced a dead end.

"You're welcome. I told you he was Swiss, the lawyer,
right? I said to Mendel, 'How can you trust him—it's his
country that stole your money?' But Mendel said this man
was very upset by what happened, all the accounts. That's
why he was helping Mendel and the others. But it's ironic,
no?"

Jessie agreed that it was ironic. She thanked Lifshutz again
and hung up and thought about Zimmer, the Swiss man who
was the liaison between the foundation and some of the
Swiss banks.

She shook her head. "Not Zimmer," she said aloud. Zimmer was trying to expedite matters for the foundation's claimants. A remarkable man, Henry had called him. He'd set aside
his own business interests to devote himself to helping settle
these claims.

What if settling claims *was* Zimmer's business? What if he
was expediting claims by persuading survivors to settle for less
money now rather than risk dying before they received anything? He could be doing it for profit. He could be a right-
wing patriot, doing it to minimize what could potentially be
a crippling loss to the Swiss economy.

Barbara had told Jessie that Zimmer was interested in the

survivor documentary Henry Steele was producing. Had he shown interest in the documentary to camouflage his real purpose—canvassing the survivors who'd been interviewed so that he could select those who were in retirement homes, those who were childless? Those who were easy targets?

Jessie phoned Lifshutz again. "Sorry to bother you," she said, and asked him if he recognized Zimmer's name.

Lifshutz was silent for a moment. "Maybe yes, maybe no. I don't remember."

Not a *definite* no—she supposed that was progress. She thought again about the documentary. Had Anna Seligman and Mendel Blumenkrantz been interviewed for it? Had Hilda?

Was Zimmer the mystery man who had left the Century Plaza with Pomerantz? If so, who was the *first* companion?

And how the hell did all this connect with Pomerantz's murder?

Hilda was sound asleep.

"I'll phone you if she wakes up," the manager promised Jessie. "But my guess is, she's out for the night. She's had an exhausting day, poor dear, what with being transferred from the hospital and all." He shook his head.

"What room is she in?"

"Two-oh-six. But I don't think you should disturb her."

"I won't. I'd just like to look in on her," Jessie said, and walked quickly down the hall before the pretzel-shaped manager could object.

Maybe Hilda would wake up, she thought a minute later as she opened the door to her room and stepped quietly inside. Approaching the bed, she saw the gentle rising and falling of the old woman's chest. She stood for a few minutes, watching. Open your eyes, she willed silently. *Come on, Hilda.*

She waited a while longer. Then she leaned closer, kissed Hilda's papery forehead, and left the room.

It was seven-thirty by the time she got home. She phoned the Steele Foundation and learned from the answering-machine message that the foundation was open Monday through Thursday, ten to five; Fridays, ten to one. No number where someone could be reached in case of emergency, Jessie thought with a flash of irritation, though to be fair, she couldn't imagine what emergency would necessitate getting in touch with one of the Steeles.

Rummaging through her purse, she found the card Henry Steele had given her and dialed the phone number he'd written down.

Two rings, three rings. A maid finally answered and informed Jessie that neither Mr. Henry nor Mr. Charles was in.

"Is Ms. Miller in?" Maybe the assistant knew something about Ernst.

"Sorry, no."

"How is Mr. Maurice feeling?" Jessie thought to ask.

"A little better, thank you. You call back tomorrow, yes?"

"Yes." Good news for his sons—that was probably why they'd taken the night off.

She prepared a salad and warmed a pita in the microwave. Gary had wanted to come over tonight, but she'd said she'd let him know—she wasn't sure whether it was a good idea, going out almost every night.

In the den she turned on the TV and clicked it off a few minutes later. Nothing of interest was on. She phoned Helen. A baby-sitter answered and informed Jessie that Helen and Neil were out for the evening. On an impulse, she looked up Ezra's home phone number in her Rolodex—she really should thank him for the candlesticks. She punched the numbers but hung up before the first ring. Ezra might misinterpret her call. She would thank him in person the next time she went to class.

She hesitated, then picked up the phone and called Gary's apartment.

He wasn't in. Serves you right, she told herself as she left a message on his machine. She wondered where he was.

She turned on the VCR and slipped in Pomerantz's video, the one Abigail Morton had produced. Jessie had watched it so many times that she could anticipate every one of Pomerantz's smiles and shrugs, every inflection.

She knew it by heart and was teary anyway.

*   *   *

Sarah Miller was clearly surprised to see Jessie on Sunday morning, but she covered her reaction quickly with a smile.

"Detective Drake. How can I help you?" she asked, stepping forward into the entry hall.

"I need to speak with either of the Steeles." She assumed both brothers were in—the driveway was occupied with the same cars she'd seen here last week.

"This isn't a good time. They're with their father."

"I hate to intrude, but it's important. Otherwise, I wouldn't be here on a Sunday morning, believe me." She smiled pleasantly.

A beat of hesitation. Then, "Let me see if one of them can talk to you. Excuse me, please."

Jessie waited in the entry hall, next to the large center accent table. Several minutes later Henry Steele appeared. He looked unhappy.

"Detective Drake," he said in a weary tone that asked, What now?

"I'm sorry to intrude, especially on a Sunday." She smiled her best apologetic smile. "I have a few questions, and I need some information from your foundation files."

"And I take it this can't wait until Monday?" A little sarcasm in his voice. He played with an orchid in the fresh-flower arrangement on the table.

She ignored it. "I need to find out whether certain individuals were interviewed for your documentary on Holocaust survivors."

He stared at her for a long moment. "Are you suggesting that my documentary is connected in some way with your murder investigation?" he finally asked. He sounded appalled.

"Not necessarily. But there's a possibility that someone used your documentary to victimize these people." Henry's hand, she saw, had tightened around one of the flowers. "Their names are Mendel Blumenkrantz, Anna Seligman, Hilda Rheinhart."

Henry shook his head. "I don't conduct the interviews, Detective, or review the applications. My staff does all that. I've reviewed some of the unedited footage, of course, but I don't remember the names of any of the interviewees."

"I'm sure you have a database of all the interviewees. I'd appreciate your checking these names against it."

He sighed. "Can this wait until Monday morning, Detective? I don't want to go into the office today unless I absolutely have to."

"I understand, but I need that information today. Tell you what—I'll follow you to your office now. That way, you won't have to bother phoning me, and I won't have to disturb you anymore." She could tell from his pursed lips that he was annoyed. He was probably accustomed to giving orders, not receiving them, especially from a woman. Too bad.

He didn't respond immediately, and she wondered whether he was going to assert his authority and refuse to go, or humor the cop.

"I'll tell my brother I'm leaving," he finally said in a terse voice. He turned on his heel in an almost theatrical manner and left the hall.

While she waited, she stepped closer to the floral arrangement. The flowers were beautiful. There were several types of white orchids, yellow and lavender roses, yellow tulips, and some exotic flowers whose names she didn't know. She wondered how much the arrangement cost, how often it had to be replaced with fresh flowers.

She heard approaching footsteps, and slung her purse higher on her shoulder, prepared to leave, but it wasn't Henry returning to the hall. It was an elderly man supporting himself on a cane. Maurice Steele?

He didn't see her at first. He tapped along the marble floor, and only when he was halfway into the hall did he look up. He stared at her.

He looked much older than he had in the portrait that she'd seen in the library. Thin, bony arms protruded past the elbow-length sleeves of his light blue cotton robe. His face had shrunk inside folds of skin, and the sparse remnants of his hair had turned almost completely white. Only his dark brown eyes were the same—intense, brooding.

"Hello," she said, not knowing what else to do. She smiled.

"All right, we can go," Henry said, coming into view. He

looked startled to see his father. "Dad, aren't you supposed to be in bed?" he asked sternly.

"I'm tired of staying in bed," the old man whined. He cast a questioning glance at Jessie.

"This is Miss Drake," Henry said. "She's helping me with something related to the foundation." To Jessie, he said, "This is my father, Maurice Steele."

The old man nodded. "A pleasure to meet you." He extended a trembling hand.

"Thank you." Jessie stepped forward and shook his frail hand.

"Dad, Miss Drake and I are going to the foundation office. I'd feel more comfortable if I knew you were back in your room."

"The doctor said I should walk a little, if I feel like it." He sounded petulant, defensive.

"But not on your own. Where's Mom?"

"She had to make some phone calls."

"The nurse will be here soon. She can even take you outside."

"It's too hot outside."

"You can sit on the verandah for a few minutes," he said, with clearly strained patience. Excusing himself to Jessie, he took his father's arm and escorted him out of the hall.

She watched the old man shuffle out. Even if you had a lot of money, she decided, it wasn't always easy dealing with old people.

She couldn't help but compare Maurice Steele with Hilda. They were both old and unwell. But while Hilda was all alone, dependent on the kindness of strangers and social security, he was surrounded by devoted family and could afford round-the-clock nursing and top medical care.

And no one was trying to kill him.

30

T**HEY ENTERED THE** building and took the elevator to the third-floor foundation offices. Henry deactivated the alarm, unlocked the outer door, and ushered Jessie in.

He walked around the desk and switched on the computer. Sitting down on Barbara's chair, he swiveled impatiently until the system booted, then punched several keys.

He hadn't said a word since they'd left his parents' house. Jessie wasn't sure whether he was deliberately not talking to her, to show his pique at having been dragged down here, or whether he was preoccupied with worry about his documentary. Maybe both, she decided.

"What was the first name?" he asked.

"Anna Seligman." Leaning over the desk, she watched the screen, tensing with anticipation as he typed the name.

The cursor blinked. A few seconds later, a document appeared on the screen. At the top Jessie saw the heading: SELIG-MAN, ANNA. Her chest tightened. The rest of the screen was filled with biographical data. She scanned it quickly.

"I'd like a printout," she told Henry.

He frowned. "I don't feel comfortable doing that. It would be a violation of this woman's privacy."

"She's dead," Jessie told him, and saw his eyes widen in surprise. "I don't think she'd mind."

Henry hesitated. "All right," he said. He sounded unsure, but he activated the printer, and a minute later handed her two sheets of paper.

She was grateful that he was less cautious, or less knowledgeable, than the funeral director who'd balked at letting her look at mortuary records. And she hadn't even had to threaten to get a court order. "The next name is Mendel Blumenkrantz."

Henry typed in the letters. Jessie fully expected to see Blumenkrantz's file pop up on the screen. Still, when it did, she inhaled sharply.

"I'd like a copy of this file, too," she said calmly though her mind was racing.

No argument from Henry this time. He printed the file and stood. "I take it Mr. Blumenkrantz is dead, too?" he asked in an unnaturally quiet voice. His hand shook a little as he handed Jessie the printed pages.

"Yes, he is."

He nodded solemnly for a few seconds, mulling over the information. "And you think they were *murdered?*" He whispered the word.

"Mr. Steele—"

"I know. You can't discuss the details," he snapped. He ran his fingers through his hair. "If there's some connection between the deaths of these two people and the foundation, I have to know about it." He sounded agitated.

She couldn't blame him. She debated, then said, "Mrs. Seligman and Mr. Blumenkrantz were planning to file claims to access Swiss accounts opened before the war." No reaction from Henry. "Apparently, someone who claimed to be an attorney offered to help them receive their money sooner if they were willing to accept a reduced settlement."

He raised his brows in surprise. "Really? Who?"

"I'm trying to find out."

Silence. Then, "You suspect that this person tried to cheat them, is that it?"

"I think he persuaded them to give him power of attorney so that he, or whoever he's working for, would keep the larger portion of the assets when the official claim was eventually settled. Neither of these people had heirs—they lived in board-and-care facilities."

Henry shook his head. "Despicable," he said with quiet loathing. He was silent a moment. "But the fact that they were interviewed by the foundation is obviously a coincidence. *All* of the people we interview for the documentary are survivors, Detective. And we've been *deluged* with calls from survivors asking for help in processing their claims."

"These two people are *dead*, Mr. Steele."

"Old people die," he said not unkindly. "That's the purpose of the documentary—to record survivors' experiences for posterity." Suddenly he frowned. "Are you saying they died under suspicious circumstances?" The anxiety was back in his voice.

Natural causes, Anna Seligman's doctor had told Jessie. Ditto for Blumenkrantz. Jessie didn't answer. Let Henry assume what he wanted. "There's another name I'd like you to check."

Henry opened his mouth to say something, then shut it and pursed his lips. He sat down heavily and, placing his hands on the keyboard, typed Hilda's first and last names as Jessie spelled them for him.

A moment later her bio was on the screen. Jessie clenched her fists.

Henry stared at the screen. "She's dead, too?" His voice was almost a groan.

"She survived a heart attack last week, but I'm concerned that someone may arrange for her to have another one."

"My God," he said simply.

"How many survivors have been interviewed for your documentary?"

"Hundreds. People from all over the country, too, not just Los Angeles."

"I'd like copies of the bio sheets on all of them. I'll need names, telephone numbers, addresses so that I can contact them if necessary." If they were childless, widowed, living alone or in a retirement home.

"You think there may be others . . . ?" He bowed his head and cradled it with his hands.

She felt acutely sorry for him. "I hope not, but it's certainly possible. What do you know about Ernst Zimmer?"

Henry jerked his head up. "Why?"

Jessie didn't answer.

His eyes widened, like those of a startled deer caught in a car's headlights. "You can't think . . ." His voice faltered. "I don't know much," he said after a moment. "Just that he's trying to expedite the processing of claims handled by the foundation. I told you that."

"Has he seen the documentary?"

He seemed puzzled by the question. "Yes. I gave him a tape of the unedited footage. He's very interested in it. He told me he thinks it's a vital project."

Vital to his scheme, Jessie wanted to say. Zimmer had probably watched the documentary so that he could observe his prey and listen to their stories, learn the intimate details of their lives before he approached them. And use the knowledge to seduce them into trusting him.

Henry leaned forward. "You're *wrong* about him, Detective. Ernst is trying to *help* our people." His voice and eyes were filled with earnest pleading.

"Maybe." She reminded herself that she'd jumped to another conclusion just yesterday, that she'd been ready to accuse Gloria Pinkoff of murdering Anna Seligman and Mendel Blumenkrantz, and plotting to do away with Hilda. "I need Mr. Zimmer's address and phone number," she said.

Henry nodded. He stood uncertainly and walked to his office slowly, as if he were in a stupor. A moment later he returned and handed Jessie a green square Post-it on which he'd written some numbers.

"Here's his phone number. The card he gave me doesn't list an address, but I think he's staying at a small residential hotel."

She put the Post-it inside a flap of her memo pad. "Which hotel?"

"I don't know. We always met here, at the foundation. I can't believe what you're suggesting, Detective. Ernst has been working so hard. . . ." He ran his fingers through his hair again.

"What's the name of the group he belongs to?"

"Suisse General." Henry pronounced the name with a perfect European accent. "I've seen the group's official stationery. It's a legitimate organization," he said with a note of desperate stubbornness.

Jessie felt sorry for Henry—he was obviously in denial. And she couldn't blame him. If Zimmer were scamming, the ramifications for the foundation would be terrible.

"Anybody can print stationery," she said, writing down the name. Zimmer could be a black sheep of the organization, or the entire group could be involved in the scam. "Was Zimmer acting as liaison with one particular bank, or with several banks?"

"Several." Henry's voice sounded strangled.

"Do you have a phone number for the Swiss Bankers Association?"

Henry didn't try to hide his sigh. Leaning over Barbara's desk, he thumbed through her Rolodex. "Here it is. As I told you, Mr. Zimmer wasn't affiliated with them, and he kept an intentionally low profile. I doubt that they'd know his name." He dictated a series of numbers.

Jessie copied them down.

"I don't understand what any of this has to do with Mr. Pomerantz. He came to the foundation office only once, so obviously, he was never interviewed for the documentary."

"I'm afraid I can't comment at this point," she said with quiet authority and was gratified that Henry didn't challenge her.

She'd been asking herself the same question for hours, ever since she'd met with Joe Lifshutz. It was possible that there *was* no connection between Zimmer and Pomerantz's death, that she'd accidentally stumbled on a nefarious mercenary scheme that had ended in the murder of three elderly survivors. But she didn't believe it. Too much coincidence.

"If you speak to Mr. Zimmer or any of the other members of his organization," she said sternly, "don't mention our conversation. It might put you in serious danger."

"No, I . . . No, of course not." Henry looked ill. He walked around the desk and slumped down onto the receptionist's chair.

"One more thing," Jessie said, and saw him tense. "I'd like you to check a name against the Internet list of dormant Swiss accounts."

"All right," Henry said listlessly. "Let me get the on-line address." He flipped through the Ss in the receptionist's Rolodex, then swiveled to the computer. Seconds later he'd accessed the Internet list.

"What's the name?" he asked without looking up.

"Yerachmiel Shtuelberg. I'm not certain of the spelling. Maybe Yerachmiel is with a J," she added as Henry scrolled through to the Ss. Ezra, she'd noted, pronounced Jerusalem "Yerushalayim," and the prophet Jonah, "Yonah."

"There's no Shtuelberg," Henry said a minute later. "Are we done now?"

"Can you try some variations on the spelling?"

"I tried several. S-c-h instead of S-h. 'B-u-r-g' instead of 'b-e-r-g.'"

Jessie frowned. Pomerantz had said that his father and brother had deposited money and valuables in a Swiss bank. "Maybe he spelled the last name without an h," she suggested.

Henry returned to the beginning of the list, then scrolled downward slowly. He shook his head. "Nothing that resembles that name." He looked at Jessie expectantly.

"Thanks," she said. "I guess that's it."

She'd been so *sure*. . . .

31

AT HOME JESSIE phoned the number Henry had given her and told the receptionist who answered that she wanted to speak with Ernst Zimmer.

"He's no longer with us," the woman chirped in a sing-song voice. "He checked out several days ago."

Checked out, or flew the coop? Jessie felt stirrings of alarm. "Did he leave a forwarding number or address?"

"I'm afraid not."

Damn. "Did he indicate that he was planning to return at some point?"

"No, he didn't."

The woman's voice was grating on Jessie's nerves. She gritted her teeth. "I'm a Los Angeles police detective. It's vital that I contact Mr. Zimmer. How long had he been staying at your place?"

"A few months." The sing-song had been replaced with nervousness.

"Can you check your registry of the past few weeks for his home address and phone number?"

"I'm afraid I couldn't give you that information over the phone. I'd need to verify that you're who you say you are."

Why, Jessie wondered tiredly, did everyone have to be so damn cautious? "Where are you located?"

Zimmer had stayed at a residential hotel on Burton Way near Doheny. Pleasant, tasteful decor. Potted palms and a baby grand piano in the corner of a small, cozy lobby.

Miss Sing-song was blond and pert and not more than five feet tall. She studied Jessie's badge before returning it to her. "I'll be right back," she said.

"Right back" turned out to be more than ten minutes. The woman returned and handed Jessie a slip of paper.

"All we have is Mr. Zimmer's Zurich address and phone number," she told Jessie. "I don't know if that will help you."

Probably not—she assumed they were bogus. "How did Mr. Zimmer pay for his room?" Jessie asked as she pocketed the slip of paper.

"Traveler's checks. He used them for the security deposit, too."

Naturally—this way, he'd left no paper trail. "How did he guarantee his reservation?"

"He wired us the money."

A cautious guy, Ernst Zimmer. Smart, too. Jessie thanked the woman and was walking away from Reception when she realized why Zimmer had looked familiar.

She hadn't seen his photo in the *papers*. She'd seen him at the Golden Palms, the first time she'd talked with Hilda. He'd been leaving the reception area just as Jessie had been nearing it, and had been heading toward the residence rooms.

Going to pay Hilda a visit?

Jessie's heart was thumping as she left the hotel and walked to her car. Don't jump to conclusions, she warned herself as she drove to the convalescent home where Hilda was staying. But it was hard to stay calm.

Arnold Samber didn't think Hilda was up to having visitors. "Mrs. Rheinhart is still quite sleepy," he told Jessie reprovingly. "She's somewhat disoriented, too, I'm afraid. The medication, I think." He clucked.

Jessie nodded. "I'd like to see her anyway. I promise not

to tire her out." She ignored the manager's frown and walked down the hall.

Hilda's eyes fluttered open when Jessie entered the room. Jessie approached the bed and took the old woman's hand. "Hey," she said softly. "I told you you'd be back here soon." Hilda attempted a grunt. "Tired," she said.

"That's just temporary. You'll feel stronger every day." She smiled warmly, then pulled over a chair and sat down. "I talked to that friend of Anna Seligman's, just like I promised."

"Anna was my friend, but now she's dead," Hilda rasped. Tears formed in the corners of her eyes.

"Hilda, did Anna tell you she was going to try to get money from a Swiss bank account her parents opened before the war?"

"My father put money in a Swiss bank. I don't know how much."

"Did Anna tell you she was filing a claim?" Jessie asked again.

Hilda blinked rapidly. She stared at Jessie. "She *told* you about it? When?"

The manager had said that Hilda was a little disoriented. "She didn't tell me," Jessie said patiently. "What did she tell *you*?"

No response from Hilda. Because she didn't understand what Jessie wanted to know, or because she didn't want to answer?

"You asked me to find out what happened to Anna," Jessie said quietly. "You have to help me, Hilda."

The old woman's free hand was bunching up the blanket. Squeezing and releasing, squeezing and releasing. "I told her not to tell anyone," Hilda finally said. "She didn't listen, and now she's dead!"

"Told her not to tell anyone about what, Hilda?"

"The money. She got a lawyer who made sure they paid her what they owed. Well, not everything, but a lot of money. That's why they killed her," she whispered urgently. "I *begged* her not to tell anyone. 'If they know you're rich,' I told her, 'they'll go after you.' Why didn't she listen to me?" Clutching Jessie's hand, she drew herself up to a half-sitting position.

"You have to stay calm, Hilda," Jessie urged, anxious about the old woman's heart condition. She eased her back down against the bed and stroked her hand. "What did Anna tell you about this lawyer?" she asked when she was satisfied that Hilda was more relaxed.

"He took care of everything so Anna shouldn't have to worry. Anna told me he was very nice."

"Did she tell you his name?" Jessie held her breath.

"Maybe. But I don't remember."

Jessie bit her lip. "Was it Zimmer? Ernst Zimmer?"

Hilda frowned. "Ernst Zimmer," she repeated, then shook her head. "No. That's not it."

Jessie felt a wave of disappointment course through her. "You're sure?" She heard her voice—it was more insistent than she'd intended, almost strident—and was sorry even before she saw Hilda flush.

"You're angry at me that I don't remember. I'm sorry." Her lips trembled, and fresh tears coursed down her lined cheeks.

Jessie's face burned with shame. "I'm not angry, Hilda. Not at all." Leaning over, she took a tissue from the box on the nightstand and gently blotted the old woman's tears.

"If I remember, I'll tell you. I promise."

"Don't worry about it." She patted Hilda's hand. "You said your father put money in a Swiss bank. Did you file a claim to get it back?"

Again the woman didn't answer.

"Hilda?" Jessie prompted softly.

"He made me promise not to tell," she finally whispered.

Jessie's heart skipped a beat. "Who did?" she asked, forcing herself to sound casual.

"Mr. Leider. Herman Leider. He's helping me, because there are things I don't understand."

Jessie frowned. Who the hell was Herman Leider? "Was that the person who helped Anna?"

Hilda shook her head. "I told you—I don't remember his name." She sounded aggrieved.

"You're right. I'm sorry." Jessie smiled contritely. "Where did you meet this Mr. Leider?"

"He called me. He got my name from a friend of a friend—somebody I knew a long time ago when Leon and I were living in New York. He said he could help me get the money from the Swiss bank account, that I wouldn't have to wait years. Such a nice man." Hilda smiled for the first time today. "He was from Switzerland, you know. A real gentleman, and *very* cultured. He always brought me little gifts, and I don't know how, but he knew just what I liked." Another smile.

It was Zimmer, Jessie decided. He'd learned the name of Hilda and Leon's old-time friend by watching Hilda's documentary interview. He'd used an alias to protect himself, and because he didn't want the Steeles to find out what he was doing. For the same reason, he'd probably used yet another name when he'd approached Anna Seligman and Mendel Blumenkrantz.

"One time he gave me a pretty lace handkerchief—all the way from Switzerland, you know," Hilda said. "Another time he brought me packets of different flavored teas—I asked him how he knew I loved tea. He said he just knew. The last time he brought me a box of chocolates. I ate too many, but oh, were they good." She sighed again.

Beware of Swiss bearing gifts, Jessie thought grimly. "And you trusted him?"

"He showed me official papers from the bank," Hilda said simply. "He helped a lot of other people, too. I signed the papers last week—that was the same day that you came to talk to me. He came not long after you left."

Zimmer, Jessie thought again. It all fit.

"He was supposed to bring me a copy the next day, but then they took me here. I called Lilly and asked her to make sure to tell him where I am, but maybe she didn't give him the message. So he doesn't know where I am." Hilda sounded suddenly anxious.

He probably *did* know, since he'd probably engineered Hilda's becoming so agitated that she'd had to be transferred to the convalescent home. Had he laced her tea on that visit with something that would make her agitated? Doctored the chocolates?

"Do you have a number where you can reach him?" Jessie asked. Maybe Zimmer had given Hilda another, direct line.

She shook her head. "He always calls me, because he's so busy traveling all over the place, trying to help people like me."

Smart, Jessie thought. So damn smart. "Why did he ask you not to tell anyone about this?"

"He told me if too many people try to get quick settlements, the banks won't deal with him or anyone." She hesitated, then said, "I *did* tell Nachum—I was so excited, I had to tell someone, you know?" A frown darkened her face. "But I was sorry I did—he was so negative. He told me I shouldn't sign without having someone else check everything out. He wanted to meet with Mr. Leider, to ask a million questions. Just like my Leon. He would have asked questions, too." She sighed again.

"Did Mr. Pomerantz and Mr. Leider meet?" Jessie asked in a casual voice.

She nodded. "I thought Mr. Leider would be upset when he came to my room and saw Nachum, because I didn't tell him he'd be there, you see. I wanted to ask him first if it was all right, but Nachum said not to. But Mr. Leider wasn't upset at all. He answered all of Nachum's questions— Nachum didn't like *this* part, he didn't like *that* part. He wanted to know why Mr. Leider's name wasn't on the paper." She sounded impatient.

Jessie frowned. "You mean the paper that gave him power of attorney?"

"Right."

"Whose name *was* listed?"

"Mr. Leider's *partner,*" Hilda said, as if that were self-explanatory. "I don't remember his name. It was easier, because the partner was in Switzerland, so he could take care of things more quickly than Mr. Leider. Nachum didn't like that."

I'll bet he didn't, Jessie thought. Stanley Goldblum had said that Pomerantz was sharp. Had Anna Seligman signed over her power of attorney to this same "partner?"

"So Mr. Leider said he'd be happy to explain things again,

if Nachum wanted," Hilda continued. "And he said he would put Nachum in touch with the partner. But then Nachum died," Hilda said softly. Her eyes were bright again with tears. "I'm sure he liked Mr. Leider."

"I'm sure he did."

Had Pomerantz figured out Zimmer's scheme and become a liability? Even if he *hadn't* figured it out, if he'd seen the "partner's" name—Zimmer's real name, Jessie guessed—he could identify Zimmer.

"You told me Mr. Pomerantz went to meet someone at the Century Plaza the Saturday night before he died. Could he have been going to meet with Mr. Leider?"

Maybe he was mystery man number two—the one who, according to the waitress, Pomerantz hadn't been happy to see, at least initially. But then, who was the first man?

"Why at the Century Plaza? Why not meet here, with me, like the first time?" Hilda shook her head. "No, I don't think so."

The fact that Hilda didn't think so was hardly conclusive. Jessie wondered if Henry Steele had a photo of Zimmer. "Hilda, did you tell Mr. Leider you thought Anna Seligman was killed?"

She nodded. "He said he would look into it, but like I told you, he hasn't called." She brought trembling fingers to her lips. "Do you think something happened to him?"

"I'm sure he's fine." Too damn fine. "Would you like me to read to you a little? Unless you're too tired."

"You don't have a date with your boyfriend?"

Jessie smiled. "Not tonight. Anyway, I'm curious to find out what's going to happen next to Eleanor."

The romance novel was on Hilda's nightstand. Jessie opened the book to where she'd left off and began reading. Within a few minutes, Hilda was sound asleep, snoring lightly. Jessie shut the book and left the room.

Before she left the facility, she spoke to Samber and asked him to screen Hilda's calls and visitors.

The manager's eyes widened. "Are you saying she's in danger?" He sounded alarmed and excited at the same time.

A good question. Zimmer had checked out of his hotel

without a trace. No doubt he'd been frightened off by the investigation into Pomerantz's death—meeting Jessie at the foundation office had probably jolted him. He'd seen Jessie at the Golden Palms. He probably knew she'd spoken to Hilda. He was too smart to risk approaching Hilda right now, even though she'd already signed the papers giving him power of attorney. . . .

Then again, Hilda could identify him and expose him for the charlatan he was. And link him with Pomerantz. Who was dead.

"It's a strong possibility," Jessie said. "I want a list of everyone who calls. And I want Mrs. Rheinhart's visitors limited to staff and medical professionals. You can say she's too weak to have visitors."

Samber licked his lips and nodded.

"And if a Mr. Leider phones, try to get a number where he can be reached, and let me know immediately. And under no circumstances let him into Mrs. Rheinhart's room."

"What if he uses a different name?" the manager asked eagerly.

The man probably watched too much television. Jessie described the person she knew as Zimmer. "He's in his forties. Dark, graying hair. Glasses. He speaks with a Swiss accent."

The manager nodded. "I'll do my best."

And tomorrow Jessie would do her best to convince Espes to assign a guard to watch Hilda.

32

"IN JANUARY OF '45, the Russians were closing in. The Germans evacuated Auschwitz on January fifteen and sixteen, and Blechhammer—this was like a subcamp of Auschwitz—on the twenty-first. Maybe a hundred or so Jews refused to leave our camp. They were too sick to walk. They figured they would die anyway." Pomerantz swallowed. *"The Germans shot some of them. Others, they let live.*

"We left Blechhammer and joined with the Jews from Auschwitz. I searched everywhere for Moshe—he wasn't there. Then someone told me he was very sick with typhus and couldn't leave the camp.

"We marched two, three days. Then the Germans made us turn back—the Russians were coming from all sides. So we went back to Blechhammer. All the time I'm wondering, is Moshe still alive? Did the Germans shoot him? Should I say kaddish?

"A few days later, the whole camp was evacuated a second time. Again, some of the sick refused to leave—of the hundred, now there were only fifty to eighty. I learned later that the Russians came and liberated them. Auschwitz, also. Too late for Moshe." Pomerantz's eyes brimmed with tears.

"From Blechhammer they forced us to march by foot seven days

in the dead of winter. Those who couldn't continue or couldn't walk were shot on the spot and left on the road. A chazzan *I knew—a cantor—couldn't go farther. I and another person helped him along.*

"We walked through the snow and slept on the snow on a few blankets until we came to a barn filled with dirt and water. We slept there on the floor, and from that I got a terrible boil on my neck. We lay one on top of the other, tightly packed like sardines, someone's feet on my head and my feet on someone else's.

"From there we walked to Grossrosen. This was a concentration camp in Germany, where Jews came from all different camps. A terrible, terrible place." Pomerantz shook his head and took a deep breath. *"There were dead lying around, and a gas chamber, where I watched many of my friends, who were close to death, go. In Grossrosen we stayed in stalls. Then they liquidated the camp, and we were marched to Weimar, and packed onto a freight train that took us deep into Germany. Everyone was given a little sausage. Mine was stolen."*

Pomerantz paused. *"A lot of people died on the train,"* he said quietly.

Jessie had set her alarm to wake her at five o'clock Monday morning so that she could phone Suisse General's Zurich office—Henry had given her a photocopy of correspondence he'd received from Zimmer, typed on Suisse General letterhead.

She knew a smattering of high school French and no German, so she had an international operator place the call.

"That number is no longer in service," the operator reported a few minutes later.

Disappointing, but hardly surprising. "Can you find out when it was disconnected?"

"One moment, please."

The kitchen wasn't hot yet—maybe she ought to get up early more often, she thought, and found herself yawning in protest. She rubbed sleep from her eyes and scanned the front page headlines of the *Times,* which she'd brought in from the porch. Another deadly robbery at an ATM. More unrest in Russia. Yet another White House scandal.

Plus ça change, plus c'est la même chose. The French idiom popped into her head. Wouldn't her high school teacher be proud.

"Ma'am?" The operator was back on the line. "The Swiss operator says that number was disconnected as of Friday morning, Zurich time."

With a nine-hour time difference, that would have been late Thursday evening in Los Angeles. Thursday was when she'd met Zimmer at the foundation offices. "Can you please find out under whose name that phone number was listed?"

"I'd have to contact Swiss Directory Assistance," the operator told her. "That's a seven dollars and ninety-five cent charge. And I'm not sure they'd give us that information."

Probably not. Jessie would call from the station, and if necessary, have the Swiss operator call her back and verify that she was a police detective.

She tried going back to sleep—it was only five-fifteen, and she normally got up at six. But she was completely awake now, wired. She did thirty minutes of exercises, showered, and dressed. Ate a large breakfast—scrambled eggs and two slices of toast and a glass of orange juice, instead of an instant oatmeal packet. It was still dark out when she left for work.

Aside from some black-and-whites, the lot was practically empty when she arrived at the station. Another bonus of getting up early, she told herself as she parked the Honda.

It was a little eerie at first, being all alone in the large, partitioned detectives' room. Sitting at her desk, she dialed the long distance operator and asked to be connected with Directory Assistance for Zurich.

"Please stay on the line," Jessie added. "I may need your help."

A moment later the Swiss operator was on the line. Jessie asked the woman, who spoke fluent English with a thick accent, if there was a listing for an Ernst Zimmer.

There wasn't, Jessie learned.

No listing for a Herman Leider, either. And there was no new listing for Suisse General.

Three for three, Jessie thought. Her score could only get

better. "I have an old listing for Suisse General," she told the Swiss operator. "It's been disconnected, and I'd like to know under whose name the phone number was listed."

"I'm sorry, but we cannot give out that information."

"I'm a detective with the Los Angeles Police Department. That information is relevant to a homicide we're investigating. I understand that you'll need to verify my identity, so I'd like you to phone me here, at the police station. Will you do that?"

"*Ja.* All right." The woman sounded guarded.

Jessie gave her the station number and area code, then said goodbye and hung up the phone. She waited what seemed like half an hour but was only a few minutes until her phone rang.

She snatched the receiver from the cradle. "Detective Drake."

It was the Swiss operator. "What is the old listing you want me to check?" she asked Jessie.

Jessie read off the numbers from the Suisse General letterhead. More waiting. She drew a tic-tac-toe grid on her notepad and played.

Cat's game.

"Detective Drake?"

Jessie tensed. "Do you have that name for me?"

"*Ja.* Franz Koenig." The operator spelled the name slowly. "I checked to see if there is another listing under that name, but there is none. Is there anything else I can help you with?"

"No. Thank you very much."

She spent the next half hour talking to police in Zurich, explaining why she needed information about the whereabouts of Franz Koenig and/or Ernst Zimmer, and/or Herman Leider. "I think Zimmer and Leider are one and the same," she told the male detective. "I don't know about Koenig."

He promised he'd get back to her as soon as he had something to tell her.

Which could be never, she thought as she hung up the phone.

Espes arrived. He nodded in her direction and disappeared inside his office. Jessie gave him a few minutes before she knocked on his door.

"You're here early," he remarked as she entered.

"I've been up since five, calling Zurich."

He grimaced. "I hope you learned something for what it's costing the department. This has to do with the Pomerantz case?"

She nodded. She told him what she'd discovered about Anna and Mendel, explained her suspicions about Zimmer.

Espes had been tapping his pencil on his desk. "So he's conning them into giving him power of attorney so when the time comes, he can collect the big prize. But why does he have to kill them?"

"He's afraid they'll change their minds. They'll talk to their friends—the friends will tell them it's not a good deal. He probably rationalizes what he's doing—they're old, they're ill, they're lonely. They're going to die soon, anyway. He's doing them a favor, putting them out of their misery."

Espes grunted. "How does he kill them?"

"I don't know. Anna Seligman was diabetic. He could have doped her, then given her an insulin shot. Mendel Blumenkrantz died of congestive heart failure. I'm waiting to hear from his doctor, but I'd guess it's not too hard to simulate that."

More tapping of the pencil. Jessie wondered what Espes was thinking.

"How does this connect with Pomerantz?" he finally asked.

"Hilda Rheinhart told Pomerantz about her 'attorney.' She said Pomerantz met with him once, in her room. I think they met again—at the Century Plaza Hotel, the Saturday night that Pomerantz was killed."

Espes leaned back against his chair and rolled the pencil between his hands. "Why did Zimmer kill him?"

"Pomerantz could identify him. He saw Zimmer's real name—it was on the power-of-attorney form. Zimmer may also have worried that Pomerantz was onto his scam—Hilda said Pomerantz asked him a lot of questions. She also told Pomerantz she suspected that her friend Anna had been killed. I think Hilda's fear was based on paranoia. The irony is, she happened to be right."

"How did Zimmer choose his victims?"

"Anna Seligman, Mendel Blumenkrantz, and Hilda Rheinhart

were all interviewed for a documentary the Steele Foundation produced. Zimmer watched the documentary and used the information he learned about individual survivors to win their trust."

"Clever bastard," Espes said softly. "You said he paid them the 'settlement' money. Where'd he get it?"

She'd been giving this a great deal of thought. "Henry Steele told me Zimmer's an investment broker—he puts together financial deals. That may be another lie, but let's say it's true. He could dip into the capital his investors have put up for a certain project and use it to pay off these early settlements."

Espes tapped his pencil. "How does he cover his tracks?"

"He takes from Peter to pay Paul. He's betting on getting the real settlement soon—and he's killing the old people so there's no question about who will get the money."

"What happens with the money Zimmer *does* give them?"

"Anna planned to leave it to a charity, but I don't know if she wrote a will before she was killed. Zimmer chose victims who had no kids or close relatives, so I guess the state inherits."

"Could be a windfall for the state, depending on how many of these people Zimmer killed," Espes said dryly.

"I have the bios of all the survivors interviewed for the Steele Foundation documentary." Over three hundred bios. It would take her hours to sort through them. "I want to contact those who are widowed and childless and living in retirement homes or by themselves. Maybe Zimmer approached one or more of them." She hoped to God he hadn't claimed another victim.

"Good idea." Espes nodded. "You don't know where he is now?"

"He checked out of his hotel—he may have left the country by now. That's what I'd do if I were in his shoes. We don't even know his real name. I'm hoping I'll learn something from the Swiss police."

"Nice going, Drake." He smiled. "Looks like I was wrong about Pomerantz. I'll call Futaki and pass on what you told me."

Espes rarely complimented her. She flushed with pleasure. "Hilda Rheinhart is in danger, Lieutenant. She can identify Zimmer and link him to Pomerantz. I asked the manager of the convalescent home where she's staying to limit her visitors and keep a record of everyone who calls and asks to see her. But she needs police protection."

"You said yourself that Zimmer probably skipped the country."

"What if he didn't? What if he feels he has to eliminate Hilda first?"

"Why would he risk getting caught? He knows you're onto him." Espes was silent for a moment. "Let me think about it," he finally said.

As if she had a choice.

"What about Pomerantz's big secret?" Espes asked. "Where does that fit in?"

It didn't. That bothered her. And she couldn't understand why Yerachmiel Shtuelberg hadn't been listed among holders of dormant Swiss accounts. Not a big thing, but it bothered her, too.

"I thought you were the mortuary," Stanley Goldblum told Jessie. "I have to settle with them. The funeral was yesterday, by the way. The place was packed—Nachum knew a lot of people. And the rabbi spoke beautiful. Nachum would have liked it."

"I'm glad things went well." After watching the video so many times, Jessie felt as if she knew Pomerantz. She could picture him observing his own funeral, commenting wryly on the service.

"So. Now it's over." Goldblum's voice was thick. "I woke up this morning, I still couldn't believe Nachum's gone." He sighed, then cleared his throat. "You still don't know what happened to him?"

"We're making progress. Mr. Goldblum, in one of the interviews Mr. Pomerantz gave for a documentary, he said he was planning to try to obtain money and other assets his father deposited in a Swiss bank. Did he tell you about that?"

"Sure. Like I told you, Detective, from me he had no secrets."

Except for one, Jessie thought. "The thing is, I checked the Internet list of dormant accounts, but couldn't find his name."

"Because you used Pomerantz, right? His father's name was Shtuelberg."

"I know—Mr. Pomerantz explained that in the video. I tried Shtuelberg, but there was no listing for that, either."

"Can't be." Goldblum sounded indignant. "But they're still adding names to the list, no?"

"I think so. Did Mr. Pomerantz by any chance tell you the name of the bank?"

"A matter of fact, yes. He wrote it down for me on a paper. 'In case my memory goes,' he said. Wait a minute, I'll get the paper." A moment later Goldblum was back on the line. "You have a pencil?"

Jessie told him that she did. She took down the name of the bank, and the phone number.

"You'll let me know what you find out?" he asked.

"I'll let you know," she promised. She thanked Goldblum and hung up.

She looked at her watch. It was a little before eight; almost five in the afternoon in Zurich. She dialed for a long-distance operator, gave the woman the bank's phone number, and waited while she placed the call.

"I have your party on the line," the operator told Jessie a minute later.

"*Grüzi. Wie kann ich Ihnen behilslich sein?*" A male.

Whatever that meant. Jessie assumed it was a standard greeting. "I'm calling from America," she said. "Do you speak English? *Sprechen sie* English?"

"*Eine Minute, bitte.*"

A moment later another man came on the line. "Herr Mannheim speaking. Good day. How can I help you, please?"

"My name is Detective Jessica Drake," she said slowly, making sure to enunciate. "I need information about one of your dormant bank accounts. The account holder was Yerachmiel Shtuelberg. Or Jerachmiel. The first is probably spelled—"

"I can give you a toll-free number that you can call to obtain an application to file a claim. There is also an E-mail address. Which do you prefer?"

How was it, she wondered enviously, that Europeans seemed to master English while Americans were so inept with foreign languages? "I don't want to file a claim. I want to know if the account exists. I'm a detective with the Los Angeles Police Department."

"So this account does not belong to you or to your family?" He sounded cautious now.

"No."

"In that case, I am sorry, but I cannot discuss any details with you. We must protect the privacy of our clients."

Patience, she told herself. "I understand completely. But I'm not interested in details at this point. I simply want to know for certain that an account exists."

"You can check the Internet for that information."

"I did. I couldn't find the name. But I understand that the Internet lists aren't complete, and I have reason to believe that this account *does* exist. I simply want to verify that."

"One minute, please. I will have to check with my supervisor."

Five minutes later Mannheim still hadn't returned. Anchoring the receiver between her shoulder and ear, she played several games of tic-tac-toe while she waited.

"Detective Drake?" Yet another male voice. "Herr Guttman speaking. Herr Mannheim explained what it is that you require. Please give me your phone number, and I will call you back shortly."

She gave Guttman the station number and hung up just as Phil arrived. She waved hello.

"How was your weekend?" she asked.

He grimaced. "Hot. But Maureen and I took the kids to the beach. Yours?"

"Interesting, actually." She filled him in on what she'd learned about Zimmer. "So now I'm waiting for a call from the bank."

"Busy lady." He smiled.

The phone rang. She picked up the receiver. "Detective Drake."

"Detective, this is Herr Guttman. I'm sorry for the delay, but you can understand that we have an obligation to serve our clients with circumspection."

"What about the account? Does it exist?"

"No, it does not. But—"

"Did you check different spellings?" Jessie asked impatiently. Maybe Pomerantz had given Stanley the wrong information, she thought suddenly. So many years had passed since the account had been opened. Pomerantz could easily have forgotten the bank's name and chosen one that he thought sounded right.

"Allow me to explain. An account *was* opened in 1938 by Yerachmiel Shtuelberg."

What the hell was Guttman's problem? "So there *is* an account."

"No. It was closed."

"By the bank?" Jessie had read of cases where exorbitant cumulative fees were levied against accounts, eventually depleting all the assets.

"By the surviving son."

Jessie frowned. *Pomerantz* had closed the account?

"By the way, you are in luck, Detective Drake," Guttman said. "It would have taken me quite some time to get this information, but as it happens, someone else phoned three weeks ago about the same account. So this account is familiar to me."

"Was the person who phoned Norman Pomerantz?" But how had he settled the claim so quickly? As far as Jessie knew, no claims had been settled yet.

"Exactly." Guttman was obviously pleased. "I told Mr. Pomerantz the same thing I told you."

Jessie frowned. "I don't understand. *What* did you tell him?"

"That the account had been closed. Mr. Pomerantz was quite shocked to hear it, as I recall."

Her head was beginning to spin. "Are you saying that someone *other* than Mr. Pomerantz closed the account?"

"Well, of course. I thought I made that clear." He sounded like a teacher dealing with a thick-headed student. "The account was closed in 1946. I verified from our files that the son had the necessary documentation and the account number."

She sat, dumbfounded, holding the receiver. Pomerantz's brother had accompanied their father to Switzerland to open an account. . . . "Moshe knew the number to the account," Pomerantz had said. "I knew just the name of the bank."

"Moshe Shtuelberg?" she asked. She felt lightheaded.

"Moses Shtuelberg, yes. You know, Mr. Pomerantz was very upset when he phoned. He insisted that someone had stolen his family's money and belongings. But when I explained the circumstances, naturally, he was overjoyed. Imagine finding a lost brother after more than fifty years.

"Unbelievable, yes?"

33

LOST AND FOUND.

Jessie mouthed the words. Was that what Pomerantz had meant—that he'd found out his brother was alive?

"You all right, Jess?" Phil asked. "You look like you've seen a ghost."

She turned toward him. "I just spoke to the Swiss bank. They said Pomerantz's brother closed the father's account in 1946."

"No shit." Phil whistled, then frowned. "I didn't know there *was* a brother."

"Pomerantz said he had a younger brother who died just before the liberation. I guess he didn't die."

"Guess not. I've read about that—records getting screwed up, people finding out years later that they had relatives who survived."

Jessie nodded. "Ezra Nathanson told me about an L.A. man who traveled to his hometown in Czechoslovakia because he heard his brother was buried there. He goes to the cemetery, tells the caretaker his name, asks him to point out the brother's grave. The caretaker looks at him like he's crazy. 'Your brother's alive,' he tells him. 'He lives less than a mile from here.' "

"He must've been blown away."

Jessie nodded. "Ezra said they had to be careful how to tell the other brother—he had a heart condition, and they didn't want to shock him. Now they're both living here, in L.A."

"I like happy endings," Phil said. "Too bad we don't hear more of them."

"Too bad," she echoed.

"So does that mean Pomerantz's brother is still alive?" Phil asked. "And if he is, where is he? He closed the account in '46. Obviously, he thought his entire family, including Pomerantz, was dead. Where did he go?"

Her head hurt. She pressed her palms against her temples and, kneading her forehead, tried to put herself inside Moses Shtuelberg's head.

After the war was over, Moses had promised his older brother, he would find him and his sister, Liebe, and his parents and they would start over again, with the money and valuables their father had deposited in the Swiss account. Moses Shtuelberg had retrieved the money, and probably the valuables as well, but he hadn't found any of his family.

Where had he gone?

No parents, no wife, no brother or sisters. Nothing to draw him back to a town bereft of its inhabitants, nothing to keep him in a Europe that was devastated and was a constant reminder of the terrors he'd survived, that his family hadn't. . . .

"He came *here!*" Jessie exclaimed softly. "To L.A."

Phil snorted. "You have a Ouija board I don't see?"

"Work it backward, Phil. Pomerantz told his friend Stanley and the woman who interviewed him for the documentary that he had a secret that would change his life. He also told Stanley he might move to L.A."

"So?"

"So why would he leave New York, where he's lived ever since he moved to this country? He was eighty-four years old, Phil. Why would he leave his best friend and everything and everyone he's known and move to a new city where he doesn't know anyone?"

"For the smog?"

She punched him lightly in the arm. "Come on, Phil. Pomerantz's secret brought him to L.A. He found his brother. Lost and found—that's the message that he left for—" She stopped abruptly. "Shit!" she whispered.

"What?" Phil was looking at her strangely.

She could feel her heart beating in her throat. "Why did he go to the foundation, Phil? He wanted to see Maurice Steele, that's why—he told the receptionist he'd come all the way from New York for that purpose. And when she told him Maurice wasn't available, he wanted to see the sons. Why was that so important?"

Phil was frowning. "What are you saying, Jess? That Maurice Steele is Pomerantz's brother? The brother's name was Shtuelberg, not Steele."

" 'Maurice' could be 'Moshe' or 'Moses.' The brother probably changed his last name. Lots of immigrants did that when they came to this country—Americanized them, so they'd blend in."

"You're reaching," Phil said kindly.

"It fits," she insisted. "Ezra Nathanson told me Maurice Steele came to the States with a little money and parlayed it into a fortune. I think he got that money from the Swiss account his father opened." She paused. "Pomerantz came to reunite with his family. He left the 'lost and found' message because he assumed the brother would recognize Pomerantz's name and understand from the message that Pomerantz was alive."

"Why not just call up and say, 'Hey, bro, I'm alive, and so are you. Let's break out the bubbly.' "

Jessie shook her head. "That's not Pomerantz's style. He likes a little drama."

Phil raised his brows. "You're his best friend all of a sudden?"

"I watched the video about ten times, Phil. I know how he thinks. He wanted to surprise his brother by showing up. But Maurice wasn't there. So Pomerantz left the message. He figured his brother would understand it."

"And then what? Why didn't they have the grand reunion?"

"Because Maurice never got the message. The boys didn't give it to him. He was ill—a heart condition, I think. So why would they bother him with that? And then Zimmer killed Pomerantz."

Phil scowled. "Maurice's sons didn't recognize their uncle's name?"

"Maybe Maurice never mentioned that he and his brother had different last names. Why would he?"

Phil was silent for a moment, swiveling back and forth in his chair. "How did Pomerantz find out that Steele was his long-lost brother? The name isn't the same."

"He knew from the bank that his brother had survived the war. He must've learned something that made him think his brother was still alive."

"Like what?"

She sighed. "I wish to hell I knew."

She started scanning the bios of the survivors interviewed for the documentary, separating the ones of those who were widowed and childless and lived alone or in retirement homes. She'd looked through twenty or so when Lucinda Blake, the dead hooker's girlfriend, showed up at the station midmorning. Jessie recognized her immediately from the way she was twisting her fingers.

"Can I talk to you?" she asked Phil. Eyes lowered, voice timid.

"Sure. Have a seat."

He sounded casual, and he moved with slow-motion grace to pull over a chair from an adjoining desk. Jessie knew he was excited.

"I've been thinking about Cassie," the woman said when she was seated. "What she'd want me to do."

Phil said nothing. Laced his hands behind his head. Waited.

"I don't want to bring more pain to that family." Another pause, more wringing of fingers. "The thing is, I think her brother Duane did it." Lucinda looked up. "Killed her, I mean." She mumbled the words.

"Why do you think he did it, Lucinda?" Phil asked.

"He threatened he'd do it if she didn't get off the streets. It was killin' his parents, he said."

"Maybe he just wanted to scare her."

Lucinda nodded. "I thought that at first. But he's been calling me most every day since she was killed. 'How you doin', Lucinda?' 'What's happenin', Lucinda?' Wantin' to know did I hear anything from the police, do they have any leads on who killed Cassie. He never called me like that before."

"Why didn't you tell us about this before?" Jessie asked, careful to sound curious, not critical.

"I thought, what if I'm wrong? Duane's big and mean-lookin', you know? I don't want to mess with him. But then I told myself, 'Cassie's dead, girl, and if he did it, you got to tell the police.' So here I am." A proud thrust of her chin.

Phil asked more questions, got an address for Duane. Promised Lucinda he wouldn't tell Duane she'd sent them knocking on his door.

They drove in Phil's car. Duane was home. He blustered at first, but Phil pressed and pressed and then Duane started crying like a baby. "I didn't mean for her to die," he moaned.

He'd sent someone to scare his sister so she'd quit. "Cassie grabbed a knife when things were goin' a little rough. He tried getting it away from her, and things got out of hand."

"He stabbed her seven times," Phil said.

Duane looked green. "I'll kill him," he whispered.

"I think you have enough problems, Duane," Phil said. "What's this guy's name?"

An hour and a half later it was all over. Cassandra Jones's killer was sitting in a cell, waiting for a public defender. Duane was in a cell, too. The D.A. would decide whether or not to charge him as an accessory.

Espes was pleased—one down, two to go. Until the next homicide.

Jessie started typing up Duane's statement—Phil had offered to do it, knowing she'd insist on doing it herself. Halfway through, she phoned the school and caught Ezra just before he was about to start class.

"Thanks for the candlesticks," she said.

"You like them? I'm glad."

She could tell he was smiling. "I used them Friday night.

It was . . . special." She couldn't think of a better way to describe what she'd felt.

"I'm glad about that, too. By the way, do you know whether they had the funeral for Mr. Pomerantz?"

"It took place yesterday. Stanley Goldblum said it was a lovely service, lots of people. And the rabbi spoke 'beautiful,' to quote Stanley." She smiled.

"Stanley Goldblum sounds like a nice guy. And a good friend. I'd better go, Jessie. My class awaits. Speaking of which, will you be coming this week?"

"I'll try. Ezra, what does the name 'Shtuelberg' mean?"

"It's Yiddish. 'Berg' means 'hill.' 'Shtuel' means 'steel.' Does that help?"

"Maybe. Thanks." She hung up the phone and crossed the room to the water cooler, where Phil was standing.

"Shtuelberg means 'hill of steel,' " she told him.

Phil nodded.

34

"**WE WENT TO** a concentration camp in a town called Saal an der Donau. There was no food to eat, just dirty water. Even the SS went hungry." Pomerantz nodded with satisfaction. "Four of us—three butchers who were old friends, and I, the stranger—made a pact. One of us would watch out for the SS while another would get some dirty water, another would get some grass, and the last one would get pepper or salt. We would make soup.

"The soup saved us. But we had no strength, and we all swelled up to double our size. We couldn't walk at all and had to be carried. The Germans told us we were going to be taken to Dachau. While we waited for the wagons outside the camp, we continued to cook the soup until there was no more grass. When the wagons still didn't come, the Germans took us back inside the camp, where we found more grass. We stuffed it in our pants.

"Finally the wagons came. Along the way the Poles threw potatoes at the wagons. One of us caught a potato, and each of us took turns biting a small piece of it, until someone else grabbed it." Pomerantz paused. "From the four of us, only two survived. The strongest ones who had nothing to eat—they starved to death. One died in my arms. He lay there, dead, on top of me until we got to Dachau." Pomerantz stared at the camera without speaking.

"In Dachau they took us from the wagons. We could barely move. My partner traded some tobacco for beans. They were hard, but we chewed them anyway. Then the Germans made us undress completely—they said we needed showers and delousing." Pomerantz took a deep breath. *"We all thought, 'That's it—they're going to gas us.' But it was just a shower."* He sighed. *"We used the water to make soup. We ate it naked—they had taken away our clothes.*

"We were still naked when they marched us to a blockhouse and gave us cots. I couldn't go into an upper bunk—I could barely move, because the boil on my neck had gotten so large. So I lay on the dirt floor.

"There was a male Ukrainian nurse, but he wouldn't help us. 'Die already,' he told me in Russian. If the Americans hadn't come in a few days, I would have. They arrived with a chaplain and a soldier. I was on the floor, and my partner was near death. 'How many Jews are there?' the soldier asked. We told him three or four Jews were left. He looked at me. 'Why are you lying on the floor?' he asked. I showed him the boil and told him that the Ukrainian nurse refused to help me and the others because we were Jewish.

"The chaplain was crying. So was the American soldier. He ordered the Ukrainian to be taken out and shot immediately.

"Which he was."

Two people phoned the station with information about the dead baby.

Jessie took both calls. She wrote down their names and phone numbers, but after listening carefully to what they had to say, decided they had no real knowledge of the dead baby or his mother. Both callers had obviously heard of the ten-thousand-dollar police department reward. Jessie had heard it, too, last night on the eleven o'clock news, and this morning, on the radio.

Contacting the convalescent home was becoming a daily ritual, like watching Pomerantz's videos. Jessie spoke to the manager—Hilda was fine, he assured her. She'd spent a peaceful night. No, no one had called for her and no one had stopped by to visit. He would let Jessie know if someone did.

She hung up and resumed typing Duane's statement, but she was preoccupied with Pomerantz. Phil was right—how had the old man realized that Maurice Steele was Moshe Shtuelberg, his brother whom he'd presumed dead?

She retraced her steps to the beginning, from the time she'd first seen Pomerantz's body lying on the grass. Worked her way mentally through the next day, when they first learned his identity from Mason, the Golden Palms administrator.

There had been no personal items in his room, she recalled. No address book, no itinerary, no slips of paper with the names of people he'd planned to phone or visit. Jessie and Phil had both found that odd. There had been no photos, either. If she was right, and Pomerantz had come here to reunite with his brother, wouldn't he have brought along snapshots of himself and his late wife? Wouldn't he have brought the photos he'd mentioned in the video—family photos, taken before the war, that he'd been able save, photos like the one Frances had given Jessie?

Maybe he'd taken the photos with him when he'd gone to the Century Plaza to meet with Zimmer. But why would he do that, if the purpose of meeting with Zimmer was to question him on Hilda's behalf? The photos might be precious, but he had no reason to feel uneasy about leaving them in his room at the Golden Palms.

Had he met with one of the Steeles?

In her mind she scanned again the contents of his suite. Clothing, medications, luggage. Several issues of Jewish newspapers, she recalled—some in English, one in what she'd assumed was Yiddish. Was there something she should have read?

"I've been meaning to phone and ask what you wanted me to do with Mr. Pomerantz's belongings," Mason told Jessie. "But we've been terribly busy—one crisis after another."

She smiled sympathetically. "You still have everything?" Mentally crossed her fingers.

He nodded. "In storage."

They took the elevator to the basement, a large, dank area

cluttered with boxes, equipment, and a collection of mis-matched furniture—lamps, mattresses, tables, chairs.

"Here it is." Mason pushed aside an end table and pointed to an oversized box. Someone had written POMERANTZ in huge black capitals.

His clothing had been neatly packed and placed on top of his luggage. She found the newspapers, along with the *Art World* issue, inside the black nylon tote—she was grateful that whoever had cleaned Pomerantz's room hadn't discarded them.

She thanked Mason and, making a mental note to contact Goldblum for advice, told him she'd call him to let him know where to send Pomerantz's belongings.

In her car she scanned the copies of the *Forward*, the English-language Jewish newspaper. No mention of the foundation or Maurice, but someone—Pomerantz, she assumed—had underlined a small notice about a new collection that was currently on display at the Skirball Museum. She nodded. Randy, the Golden Palms driver, had mentioned chauffeuring Pomerantz there.

She picked up the Yiddish-language paper, and quickly set it aside. It was Greek to her. She'd ask Ezra to help her with it.

The *Art World* magazine looked well read. Curious that Pomerantz had brought it. Then again, he was an ardent art lover.

She thumbed through the pages, admiring the glossy reproductions. Halfway through she caught her breath.

On the right-hand page, underneath the caption, NOW AT THE SKIRBALL, were color photos of several art objects, all related to Jewish ritual. A silver menorah with a lion motif. A gold mezuzah case with an ornate design. A silver plate used to adorn a Torah scroll.

A large gold chalice.

"The Cup of Elijah, of unknown Italian artistry, circa 1745," read the italicized, fine-print description. "Encrusted with diamonds, rubies, emeralds, and sapphires. On loan, courtesy of the Steele collection."

Pomerantz had described the chalice his father and brother

had taken with them to Switzerland, and left for safekeeping in the bank where they'd deposited their money. It had sounded identical.

Moshe Shtuelberg had closed the account after the war. No doubt, he'd reclaimed his family's other valuables, too.

Pomerantz had obviously recognized the chalice. Before or after he'd discovered that his brother was alive? Jessie looked at the date on the front cover. June.

According to Herr Guttman, Pomerantz had contacted the bank three weeks ago. Which made it early July. *After* Pomerantz had seen the photo of the chalice.

Guttman had said that Pomerantz had been upset when he'd first called. He'd assumed, after seeing the chalice in the magazine, that someone had stolen it.

And then he'd learned the truth—that his brother was alive. And he must have realized that if his brother had reclaimed the chalice, and the chalice belonged to Maurice Steele, then Maurice must be his brother.

If A equals B, and B equals C, then A equals C.

"He couldn't be sure it was the same cup," Phil insisted. He'd listened quietly while Jessie had talked. "I'll bet there are hundreds of cups that look just like the one in the picture."

She shook her head. "Only five, according to Pomerantz. He said he'd recognize it anywhere." She'd stopped at her house on the way back to the station and watched the segment again. "Look at it, Phil. It's unique." She handed him the open magazine and pointed to the cup. "And his father's initials were etched into the underside of the base."

Phil peered at the photo, then looked at Jessie. "He couldn't tell that from this picture."

"That's why he went to the Skirball, Phil." She leaned forward. "Randy Taylor, the Golden Palms driver, told me he took Pomerantz there the first day. Not exactly the most significant tourist attraction L.A. has to offer, is it?"

"I guess not." Phil pulled at his mustache. "So Pomerantz verified that it was his family chalice?" he finally said.

"Exactly! You know I'm right—you just don't want to admit it." Jessie smiled. "Then he went to the foundation, because now he knew for a fact that Steele was his brother. And that explains why he didn't say anything to his good friend Stanley. He wanted to be *sure*—he didn't want to be embarrassed in case he was wrong. But if he was right, he planned to move here. It all fits, Phil." She knew she sounded schoolgirl-excited. She couldn't help it. Hell, she didn't care.

"So why didn't he tell the Steele boys he was their uncle?"

Jessie expelled an exasperated breath. "We went *over* this, Phil. He went to meet his brother but Maurice wasn't there. The sons wouldn't see him. So he left the 'lost and found' message."

Phil thought for a moment, then shook his head. "I don't buy it. He goes to the museum practically the minute he gets off the plane, just so he can confirm that Steele is his brother. Tuesday he goes to the foundation and leaves a message. Then he waits and does *nothing*? Till *Saturday*?"

"He may have tried calling again," Jessie said stubbornly.

"The receptionist would have told you. Come on, Jess. Something doesn't fit."

"Yes, it does. What's your problem?" She slapped the magazine onto her desk.

"What's yours?" he asked quietly.

Phil was right, damn it. She sighed and told him so.

"I think you're right about the cup," he said. "We could check out the base."

"I don't know if it's still at the Skirball."

"Easy to find out."

Pulling the art magazine toward him, he dialed the phone number listed at the bottom of the page. He spoke to a receptionist, then to an assistant curator.

"The show ended last Saturday," he told Jessie as he hung up the phone. "The pieces on loan from the Steele collection have been moved to a Pasadena museum, in preparation for a September exhibit."

"I met the curator of that museum when I was at Maurice Steele's house, talking to his sons," Jessie said. "His name is Larkins. He's excited about hosting the exhibit. Plus I think he's hoping Maurice will bequeath a sizable part of his collection to the museum." She had a thought. "Pomerantz mentioned that his father took a number of valuables to Switzerland. Maybe there's more than the chalice."

"Possibly." Phil nodded. "Maybe it's lucky for this curator that Pomerantz is dead."

Jessie frowned. "What do you mean?"

"What if Pomerantz had decided to claim the chalice and the other family art for himself? Larkins would have had to say goodbye to a major art donation to his museum from the Steele family."

"You don't know that Pomerantz would have done any such thing. He was an art lover. So was his father. So is his brother."

"Come to think of it, what if Pomerantz decided to claim his share of the dad's money? He's the older brother, right? He's making do on a shoestring budget, while Maurice is a millionaire."

She stared at him. "*Now* you're being ridiculous. You think the Steeles are involved with Pomerantz's death?"

Phil laced his hands behind his head. "Hey, they don't call it 'blood money' for nothing."

35

DONALD LARKINS WAS beaming as he moved from behind his desk and pumped Jessie's hand.

"Detective Drake! What a *pleasant* surprise! When my secretary said a Ms. Drake was here, I *thought* I recognized the name."

The curator's smile was broad but stiff. In fairness, Jessie couldn't blame him for being nervous. He was probably wondering what she was doing here.

"I was in the neighborhood, investigating a case," she said casually. "I thought I'd stop by and visit your museum." She saw Larkins relax and knew she'd been right to come without Phil. She'd wanted to make her visit low-key. "You whetted my interest the other day about the Steele exhibit, and I've been curious ever since to see it."

Larkins touched his hand to his chest. "Oh, dear. I thought you understood that we've only just begun to prepare the exhibit. It won't be ready for viewing until September."

He seemed anxious again. Jessie recalled vividly how startled he'd been at the Steele house when she'd told him she was a homicide detective. She'd thought nothing of his reaction. Then. Damn Phil for putting ideas in her head. . . .

"But you *do* have some of the Steele collection here, don't you? I read somewhere that several of the pieces recently on show at the Skirball were transferred here. I'd *love* to see them." She watched him carefully now.

"The Judaica, you mean?" Larkins nodded. "They're here, under lock and key, of course. But they're not on display. I haven't even had a chance to catalog them."

She flashed her best smile. "Can I take a peek?"

The curator wasn't impressed. "You could, but you wouldn't be seeing them at their best," he said seriously. "I haven't quite decided exactly where each piece of that particular grouping will be featured. Placement is so important, you know." He sounded a little prissy.

"Oh, I *know*." She nodded. "Well, what a shame." She sighed with disappointment.

A beat of hesitation. "I suppose I *could* show them to you. But you must promise to come back in September and see the full exhibit," he said with a burst of gaiety.

She couldn't figure him out.

Larkins led the way from his office to a large room lined with floor-to-ceiling dark wood cabinets. Unlocking the cabinet in the center of the room, he opened its tall doors.

"This isn't really doing them justice," he said as she stepped aside.

She moved closer and sighed involuntarily. Beautiful, she thought reverently as she took in the works of art on the shelves. She recognized the menorah, Torah plate, and mezuzah case she'd noticed in Pomerantz's art magazine. There was a prayer book with an intricately embossed silver cover. Next to it were a silver Passover plate and a gold crown.

"That's a crown for the Torah scroll," Larkins said. "We also have some beautifully illuminated *ketubot*—Jewish marriage contracts—but they're too large to store here. I think you'll be impressed when you see them displayed."

Jessie's eyes had already moved and were scanning the remaining shelves and the objects lying on them.

No chalice.

Repressing a frown, she turned toward the curator. "I seem to remember that there was a chalice in the Steele collection shown at the Skirball." It was a struggle, but she managed to sound curious, not suspicious.

"A breathtaking piece, if I do say so." Larkins nodded. "Mr. Steele—that's Henry Steele—was here not long after the pieces were transferred from the Skirball, to discuss the exhibit. He happened to notice that one of the stones was loose and sent the chalice out to be repaired."

Did he? Her heart thumped. She'd come here to verify that the chalice had belonged to Yerachmiel Shtuelberg. Now she'd learned something even more interesting. "Lucky the stone didn't fall out en route."

"Oh, yes." More vigorous nodding. "That would have been a terrible loss. The gems are quite valuable. I'm confident that the chalice will be back in our hands in time for the exhibit."

In your *greedy* little hands? "Thank you so much for this sneak preview, Mr. Larkins." She waited until he locked the cabinets and followed him out of the room.

Suddenly she stopped and turned toward him. "By the way, did you say Mr. *Henry* Steele? I thought Charles Steele was working on the exhibit with you."

"Charles was attending to some family business, so Henry came. They're both art lovers, you know." Larkins smiled. "As long as you're here, Detective, can I show you around the museum? At present we have an exhibit of local artists that you might enjoy."

Jessie checked her watch. "Wish I could. My partner's waiting for me."

"This is like an effing fortress," Phil remarked as the electronic gates swung open. He followed Jessie up the walkway to Maurice Steele's front door and looked around. "What do you think a house like this goes for? Six, seven million?"

"At least." The Rolls was in the semicircular driveway. So were the other cars.

A moment later Charles answered the door himself. "I see you've brought reinforcements," he said. Smiling tightly, he waved Jessie and Phil inside with a grandiose, mocking gesture.

Ignoring the comment and the gesture, Jessie introduced

the men to each other. She noted the fresh floral arrangement sitting on the center table. Purples and whites this time.

"Henry is waiting eagerly for us in the library," Charles said. "I hope this won't take long. I'm going to try to get home for dinner tonight—I've barely seen my wife in the last week and a half. She's probably forgotten what I look like."

"Is your brother married?" Jessie asked as she and Phil followed Charles. She was trying not to stare at him, but she wanted to see if she could find a resemblance to Pomerantz.

"Yes. To the long-suffering Lydia." He opened the door to the library and with another majestic sweep, waved them into the room.

Henry was standing with his arms folded, facing the far wall. He turned when Jessie and Phil entered. She introduced Phil, and they all sat at the round table. Fresh flowers here, too. Jessie wondered who took care of all the details. The mother? Sarah Miller? One of the maids?

"When you called, you said it was important," Henry said, addressing Jessie.

No offer of refreshments today, Jessie noted. "That's right. Mr. Steele—"

"I've filled Charles in about the documentary, and those people who died. I pray to God you're not here to tell us another one of the foundation interviewees has died."

" 'Murdered' is the correct term," Charles said. "That's what Detective Drake suspects. Isn't that right, Detective?"

"That's correct." She turned to Henry. "In answer to your question, I've started going through the biographies you gave me, but I haven't contacted any of the interviewees yet. Have you heard from Mr. Zimmer?"

He shook his head. "I still think you're wrong about him."

"I have to agree with my brother." No sarcasm from Charles now. "Zimmer's been working tirelessly to expedite these abominable claims processes."

"The Zurich phone number for his organization has been disconnected," Jessie said and watched the brothers exchange glances. She saw surprise. Feigned or real? "There's no new listing."

"Ernst explained that he and his colleagues aren't popular."

Henry leaned forward. "What he didn't tell you is that he's received death threats from those who oppose what he's doing. The group may have shut down the office and moved to a new, undisclosed location and obtained an unlisted phone number."

"Hard to help people if they can't find you." Phil smiled.

"Obviously they give out their new phone number and address to parties they can trust."

"That's another hard thing," Phil said. "Deciding who you can trust. People try to fool you all the time."

"How sad, Detective, that your occupation has made you so cynical." Charles shook his head. "I remain optimistic about the human race. I look for beauty, not ugliness. That's why I love art."

"By the way," Jessie said, happy to take advantage of this perfect opening, "I visited Mr Larkins's museum today, and he was kind enough to show me part of your father's collection that will be on exhibit in September." Was it her imagination, or had Henry tensed?

"Beautiful pieces, aren't they? I get the feeling Larkins thinks they're already his." Charles smiled. "He's counting on having at least some of them permanently housed in his museum, along with some of the other art my father has collected over the years. I don't blame him—they would certainly enhance his museum's status, and Larkins's as well."

Phil nudged Jessie under the table with his knee.

"Has your father decided what to do with his collection?" she asked.

"More or less. Some of the collection will stay in the family. Some pieces will go to local museums—the Getty, the Skirball, LACMA," Charles said, referring to the Los Angeles County Museum of Art. "And Larkins's dream will come true. My dad likes him, and so do I. He can be annoyingly fawning sometimes—a little nosy, too." Another quick smile. "But he knows his art, and he has a real passion for it. Which pieces did you see?"

"Primarily the Judaica. I was disappointed to learn that the chalice photographed for *Art World* wasn't there." Jessie turned to Henry. "I understand that you took it to have one of the stones reset."

"You didn't tell me," Charles said, his tone just short of accusation.

"One of the stones was loose," Henry told him. "Don't worry. The chalice will be returned in time for the exhibit." He faced Jessie again. "But you didn't come here to discuss art."

"No," she agreed. "There's been an interesting development in the investigation surrounding Mr. Pomerantz's murder."

The brothers looked at her expectantly.

She addressed Henry. "Yesterday at the foundation office, I asked you to check a name for me against the Internet list of dormant accounts."

Henry nodded. "It wasn't there."

"Right. That's because the account was closed over fifty years ago. I learned that today, from the Swiss bank."

"Well, that explains it, then," Henry said.

"The name I asked you to check was Yerachmiel Shtuelberg," she said, conscious of the fact, hardly important at this moment, that for once she'd produced the guttural phoneme effectively. "Mr. Shtuelberg was Mr. Pomerantz's father. Mr. Pomerantz was given his mother's maiden name because at the time of his birth, his parents weren't officially married, at least not according to Polish law."

Charles frowned. "This is all very interesting, I'm sure, Detective," he said in a voice that indicated otherwise. "But how does this concern us?"

Henry's eyes, she saw, were riveted on her face. "Actually, I think you'll find this a very touching story. Nachum Pomerantz had a younger brother, Moshe Shtuelberg." No reaction from either brother. "He believed that Moshe had died over fifty years ago, in Auschwitz. Three weeks ago he discovered, to his shock, that someone had closed their father's Swiss account fifty years ago. And then he learned that this someone was his brother, Moshe. He'd survived the war! And Nachum realized that he was still alive. And guess where he was living?" Jessie smiled. "Right here." She tapped the table and looked at Henry. She paused, then added, "In Los Angeles."

Charles cocked his head. "It's a *very* touching story, Detective, but I still don't see—"

" 'Shtuelberg' means 'hill of steel," Jessie said. "I found that out yesterday. I wonder what your family name was originally, when you first came to this country."

"As far as I can remember, it was always 'Steele.' " He glanced at his brother. "Henry?"

" 'Steele' is the only name I ever knew. I don't understand what you're getting at, Detective."

Jessie smiled. "I think you do."

Charles raised his brows. "Henry, I believe that Detective Drake has just called you a liar."

"Shut up, Charles," Henry said wearily.

"I couldn't see your face when I asked you to check Yerachmiel Shtuelberg's name yesterday," Jessie said. "But I can imagine the surprise you must have felt, hearing your family name."

Henry shook his head. "I have absolutely *no* idea what you're talking about. You asked me to check a name—I checked it."

"Your father's first name is Maurice. In Hebrew, that would be Moshe, wouldn't it?"

"It could be a lot of things."

"What name do they use when they call him up to the Torah in your synagogue?" She looked at Charles. She had his interest now, she could see.

Henry cleared his throat. "You're suggesting that our father is this Moshe Shtuelberg, that he and Pomerantz were brothers. I'm sorry to tell you, Detective Drake, but none of my father's family survived the war. They were killed—his parents, his sisters. Everyone."

"Did he have a brother?" Jessie asked.

Henry nodded. "There *was* a brother. He didn't survive."

"I've heard of a number of cases where Holocaust survivors have discovered after many years that a relative, believed to have died in the war, is really alive."

"Believe me, we all wish that were true. My father checked.

He searched and searched, but no one was left." Henry sighed. "So you see, you've jumped to the wrong conclusion. And in the process, I might add, you've caused us not a little pain. If that's it?" he said, half rising. "I'd like to check on my father."

"The story's not over yet," Phil drawled.

"When Moshe Shtuelberg closed the account," Jessie said, "he took with him not only the money his father had deposited, but also the valuables his father had left there for safekeeping, including some works of art."

Henry sighed and resumed his seat.

"Nachum Pomerantz recognized one of those works of art—he saw it in an art magazine," Jessie continued. "That's how he knew his brother was alive, living in L.A.—the magazine identified the owner of the art. It was a chalice—the cup of Elijah—embedded with precious gems. Mr. Pomerantz described it exactly in a documentary interview that he gave."

"From what my father told us, there were several chalices produced by the same Italian artist," Charles said. He was staring at his brother now.

"Yerachmiel Shtuelberg etched his initials on the underside of the base," Jessie said.

Charles nodded. "Well, that's easily cleared up, then. I don't recall ever seeing any initials on my father's chalice."

"We'd like to take a look at the cup," Phil said. "What's the name of the shop that's doing the repairs?"

"Actually," Henry said, "the chalice is here, in the house. I haven't had a chance to drop it off yet."

"Well, fetch it, dear Henry, dear Henry, dear Henry," Charles sang. "Let's get this over with."

Henry shot him a hateful look and left the room.

Charles drummed his fingers on the table.

A moment later Henry returned, the chalice in his hand.

It was magnificent—the photo hadn't done it justice. The diamond winked at her as Henry handed her the chalice. She turned the cup over.

The underside of the base was smooth.

No initials.

Charles was peering over her shoulder. "Well, that's that."

He sighed. "If you're right, this poor old man came all the way here to L.A., and it wasn't even his father's chalice. And then he was killed."

Jessie looked at Phil. His face was bland. She turned to Henry and handed him the chalice. "Which is the loose stone?"

He blinked. "What?"

"You told Mr. Larkins you were taking the chalice to have a loose stone reset. Which stone is loose?"

"I believe it was this sapphire." He pointed to a brilliant blue stone.

"May I?" Jessie took the chalice back and touched the sapphire lightly. "It seems solid to me." Slowly turning the cup, she checked all the other gems. "They're all fine." She injected a note of puzzled surprise into her voice.

"Perhaps I was mistaken." He ran a hand through his hair. "I tend to be overly cautious, and this *is* a precious object. It's a unique piece."

Jessie placed the chalice back on the table. "Obviously, you had the initials removed to prevent identification. What were you afraid of?"

"That's ridiculous!" Henry's voice shook with indignation. His face was ashen.

"I don't think it'll be hard to locate the person who removed the initials for you and resilvered the base."

"Couple of phone calls should do it," Phil said. "This isn't an item someone would forget."

"You're making a terrible mistake." Beads of perspiration dotted Henry's upper lip.

Jessie said, "Do you want to tell us what happened, Mr. Steele? Your uncle came to the foundation but wasn't able to see your father, or you or your brother. So he left a message— 'lost and found.' You told me you called the retirement home where he was staying, but never spoke to him. But you did, didn't you?" she asked gently.

"If my brother says he didn't speak to Mr. Pomerantz, then he didn't," Charles said.

"You knew when I asked you to check Yerachmiel Shtuelberg's name exactly who he was," Jessie said. "Your grandfather. The father of Nachum Pomerantz, your uncle, the man you said you never met."

"What happened, Henry?" Phil leaned forward. "Did he threaten to sue for half of your father's money? I can understand how you would have felt angry. Is that why you killed him?"

"All right. This interview is over!" Charles moved to his brother's side.

Henry's eyes had widened with fear. "I didn't kill him!" he whispered hoarsely. "My God! How could you *think* that?"

"I know this is hard for you, Henry," Jessie said kindly. "You might find it easier if you talked to us alone."

"I'm not leaving my brother so that you can trick him into admitting something he didn't do. I know what you people do." Charles smiled grimly.

Phil said, "The phone company is checking all the calls made to the Golden Palms from the day Pomerantz visited the foundation until the Saturday night he was killed. I'm willing to bet there were quite a few calls from the foundation, or from your own homes, or from here. We'll know soon."

Phil was a convincing liar. The phone company wasn't doing any such thing—yet. They'd need a search warrant first. But the Steele sons didn't know that.

Henry had slumped down into a chair and was cradling his head in his hands. "I didn't kill him! You have to believe me!"

"When did you meet with him?" Jessie asked quietly.

Charles clutched his brother's shoulder. "Henry, don't say one damn word!"

Henry looked up at him, anger in his eyes. "I can't do this anymore! They're going to find out anyway." He faced Jessie. "We both talked to him. First I did, then Charles."

36

"YOU ARE SUCH an idiot!" Charles hissed. He sat down and glared at his brother.

Henry ignored him. "He came to the foundation on Tuesday, but we were too busy to see him. Barbara left each of us a copy of his message and a phone number where he could be reached."

"What did the message say, exactly?" Out of the corner of her eye, Jessie could see Charles. He was stone-faced.

" 'Something's lost, and someone's found.' Charles got the same message—we had no idea what it meant, and we didn't want to bother Dad with it. He wasn't feeling well." Henry cleared his throat. "I phoned Pomerantz that night at the retirement home, but he wasn't in. I didn't leave my name." Henry cleared his throat again, then stood abruptly. "I need some water. Would you like anything?"

Jessie shook her head. So did Phil.

"Be sure to note in your report that my brother is the perfect host, even when being interrogated by the police," Charles said as Henry crossed the room to the bar.

A moment later Henry returned, carrying a cut-glass tumbler filled with a clear liquid. Water, Jessie wondered, or liquor? He looked as if he desperately needed a drink. So did Charles.

"Sorry." Henry resumed his seat and set the glass on a cork coaster. "Mr. Pomerantz phoned Wednesday afternoon—Barbara was at lunch, so I took the call. He told me he was surprised I hadn't phoned him. I explained that I'd called but hadn't left a message. I asked him what he'd meant by 'lost and found.' That's when he told me he was my uncle." Henry took a sip of water. His hand was shaking.

"Henry didn't believe him at first," Charles said. "He thought Mr. Pomerantz was pulling a scam."

"You have to understand, Detective. My father is an extremely wealthy man. I can't tell you how many times over the years people have approached him, pretending they're relatives, hoping to benefit from his largesse. And then Mr. Pomerantz told me about the chalice, how he'd seen it in the magazine and recognized it. How he'd contacted the Swiss bank and—well, everything that you've discovered."

"So you knew he was telling the truth."

Henry nodded. "I was stunned, excited, bewildered. So many emotions. . . ." He shook his head. "He wanted to see my father right away and meet the family. I told him that Dad had a weak heart, and that I was afraid if we told Dad straight off that his brother was alive, the shock might kill him. I said I'd call him the next day. He said he understood. He didn't want to endanger my father's life."

Jessie tried to imagine the depth of Pomerantz's disappointment—he'd traveled thousands of miles to be reunited with the brother he hadn't seen in over fifty years, a brother he'd just discovered was alive. The idea of waiting one more day must have seemed like an eternity.

Henry took another sip of water. "I told Charles. We agreed we'd talk to Mom first, and then the three of us would prepare Dad for the truth. But we never told her, because that night Dad became ill. Charles called Mr. Pomerantz on Thursday and told him we'd have to wait until Dad's condition improved."

So *that* had been the second call to the Golden Palms. "So you didn't arrange a specific date?"

"We planned on his coming here on Tuesday or Wednesday, if Dad was okay. I really felt bad about leaving things somewhat up in the air, but Mr. Pomerantz was so understanding, so sweet. He said—" Henry shut his eyes and sighed. "He said he'd waited this long, another few days wouldn't kill him."

"Why didn't you or your brother meet with him?"

"Looking back, we should have. We were just so frantic about our father. Anyway, Mr. Pomerantz was supposed to call me here Monday morning to confirm. When I didn't hear from him, I figured maybe he'd gone sight-seeing and wasn't near a phone. But when he still hadn't called by the end of the day, I started to worry. He'd been so eager to see Dad, to meet all of us. I called the retirement home—they told me he was dead. I couldn't believe it. I just couldn't believe it." Henry removed his bifocals and rubbed his eyes.

"You never told your mother?" Phil asked.

Henry shook his head and put his glasses back on. "She's been so preoccupied with my father's health, and she's not that well herself. We figured we'd tell her Monday night, if things were still a go, then figure out a way to break it to Dad."

"Why did you lie when I was here last week?" Jessie asked. "Why didn't you tell me Mr. Pomerantz was your long-lost uncle?"

Charles grunted. "I should think you would have figured that out for yourself, Detective. If we'd told you the truth, my father would have found out. And he would have been hounded by the media. Given his heart condition, we couldn't risk that."

Phil frowned. "So your father still doesn't know?"

"What would be the point of telling him one minute that his brother survived the war, and in the next, telling him that he'd been murdered?"

Jessie couldn't argue with that. "Why did you tamper with the chalice?" she asked Henry.

He glanced quickly at his brother, then faced Jessie again. "That was stupid, I admit. I panicked. I wasn't sure whom Mr. Pomerantz had told about the chalice. I didn't want him traced to my father. Again, I was trying to protect him." He paused. "I'm hoping you won't have to tell him now. What purpose would it serve? He doesn't know anything about his brother's death."

"If it's not necessary, we won't question him," Jessie said. Which wasn't really a promise. "Aside from the two of you, who knows that Mr. Pomerantz was your uncle?"

"I didn't volunteer the information to anyone," Charles said. "You can be sure of that. I'm sure my brother didn't, either." He glanced at Henry.

Henry shifted on his seat. "Actually, Ernst Zimmer knows. He was in my office at the foundation when I took Mr. Pomerantz's call. Ernst excused himself, of course. When I was done, and I called him back into the office, he asked me why I looked so upset." He faced Charles. "I didn't see a reason not to tell him—I was so excited, and you weren't there at the time."

Good old Ernst—he must have been shocked to learn that Hilda Rheinhart's friend was Maurice Steele's brother. Had he worried that Pomerantz would repeat his suspicions about Zimmer's "legal services" to one of the Steele sons? Coming from an uncle, Pomerantz's assertions would have taken on enhanced credibility. Zimmer would have been exposed as a thief—and possibly linked to murder.

"No one else?" Jessie asked.

Henry shook his head. He drained the glass of its contents. Jessie looked at Phil. He lifted his shoulders almost imperceptibly. *That's it for now.*

"We may have to ask you more questions," she said, standing. "If you think of—"

"Donald Larkins," Charles said. He was frowning. "He's been at the house so often lately, selecting art for his exhibit, that I don't even notice him. He was here that Thursday when I called Mr. Pomerantz—he was floating in and out of rooms. He may have overheard my end of the conversation, and my discussion with Henry about what we should do." He turned to his brother. "Remember?"

"You're right." Henry nodded slowly. "In fact, now that you mention it, I recall seeing Larkins in the family room. He was on the phone, and hung up as soon as he saw me. He apologized—said he hoped I didn't mind, he'd had to make a quick call." Henry paused. "Looking back, he seemed jumpy, but then, he always strikes me as being a little nervous. I didn't think anything of it at the time."

Charles's frown had deepened into a scowl. "You think he was listening in on my conversation with Pomerantz?"

"Maybe. That would explain why he hung up so quickly and looked nervous. Or maybe he was just embarrassed because he was using our phone without having asked."

"Right." Charles sounded uncertain.

"But even if Larkins *was* eavesdropping, Charles, so what? Why would Larkins care whether or not Dad had a brother?"

Jessie didn't have to look at Phil to know that he was smiling with satisfaction.

"I know what you're thinking," Jessie said when she and Phil were back in his car. "Larkins has been counting on getting the Steele collection for his museum. Now he's worried that Pomerantz will claim the stuff belongs to him, too. But that's hardly a motive for murder." She adjusted her seat belt.

"No?" Phil glanced at her, then turned on the ignition. "Without the collection, Larkins has no prestige. He's just a two-bit curator at a two-bit museum."

"That's a motive?" She flipped the air-conditioning to HIGH and settled back against the seat.

"I can see him getting angry, thinking about what he could've had, what he's going to lose because some lost relative—an old guy who probably won't live long anyway—is going to queer everything. You heard what Charles said— Larkins acts like the stuff already belongs to him."

It was still hot in the car. She put her hand to one of the vents. Warm air fanned her fingers. "You need freon."

"Tough to get since the EPA banned it. But I know a guy. Think cool thoughts." Phil pulled away from the curb.

She grunted. "So how did Larkins connect with Pomerantz?" she asked a moment later.

"Let's assume Larkins *was* eavesdropping on Charles's conversation with Pomerantz. He learns Pomerantz isn't going to meet with his brother until Tuesday at the earliest. He also learns where Pomerantz is staying."

"Lots of assumptions," Jessie said. "So how does he get together with Pomerantz?"

Phil was silent for a while. Jessie watched him frown in concentration.

"He calls Pomerantz," Phil finally said. "Says he's a friend of the Steeles'. They're a little busy right now, taking care of the sick father, but they feel bad that Pomerantz is on his own, and they asked Larkins to show him a good time."

Jessie laughed. "Gee, Phil. You're wasting your talents as a cop. You could make millions writing spec scripts. I heard Quentin Tarantino is looking for a partner."

"It works," he said doggedly. "He tells Pomerantz to meet him at the Century Plaza. He dopes his drink, then slips him the digitalis. No more Pomerantz, and Larkins can play with his toys."

"Then who's mystery man number two? He's the person who left with Pomerantz, remember."

"Right." Phil looked unhappy. "Okay," he said a moment later. "Larkins phones Pomerantz, same spiel. Pomerantz tells him he's meeting someone at the Century. Larkins 'happens' to come by. He's number two."

"And number one?"

Phil shrugged his massive shoulders. "Some acquaintance of Pomerantz's we don't know about. Maybe he met someone out here."

Jessie thought that over. "So now you *believe* the brothers Steele? Earlier today you thought they killed their uncle because they didn't want to lose any of Daddy's money."

"Earlier today you said that was ridiculous." He flashed her a smile, then returned his attention to the road. "Maybe one of the brothers is mystery man number one. Larkins overheard him planning to meet Pomerantz at the Century and showed up. That works, doesn't it?"

Jessie didn't answer.

"What, you changed *your* mind? You like *them* for the murder?"

She shook her head. "I'm not sure they're telling the complete truth, but I still don't see why they'd kill Pomerantz. The family's loaded, Phil. They're major philanthropists. If they give millions away to organizations and strangers, why wouldn't they want to share the wealth with a close blood relative?"

Phil shrugged. "No publicity in it for them?"

"Ezra told me they *hate* publicity, especially the dad." She twisted her hair and pulled it off her neck. Better. "I like Zimmer for the murder. When Henry told him about Pomerantz, Zimmer probably panicked. He realized it was only a matter of time before Pomerantz checked out Anna Seligman's death, and put two and two together and figured out that Zimmer was the one who'd conned Anna, and killed her. And was conning Hilda."

Phil nodded. "When is that Swiss detective getting back to you?"

"Not before tomorrow morning. It's the middle of the night there now. And he may have nothing to tell me."

"You think Zimmer left the country?"

"Depends on how much of a danger he thinks Hilda is."

"You check on her lately?"

"Just before we left to see the Steeles. She's weak, but fine. She had a few calls—friends from the Golden Palms. And one visitor—Lilly Gorcheck, the Golden Palms manager. A nice lady, Lilly." Jessie had been pleased, for Hilda's sake, to learn that people were showing concern.

"What about the physical therapist? Gladys?"

"Gloria. I told you—she wasn't Mendel Blumenkrantz's therapist."

"Still," Phil said.

"You're right. I'll tell the manager to let me know if Gloria calls."

They drove a while in silence. Jessie closed her eyes and imagined she was on a beach. With Gary. They were going out tonight to see a movie. Anyplace that's air-conditioned, she'd told him.

"Why do you think the Steeles aren't telling the complete truth?" Phil asked out of the blue.

She opened her eyes and looked at him. "For one, I can't

imagine that they wouldn't meet with the uncle. I was sure at least one of them was mystery man number one at the Century Plaza."

"They said they were too upset about Papa's condition."

"Maybe they're afraid to tell us the truth. They don't want to be linked to Pomerantz's murder. They don't want the notoriety."

"So you answered your own question."

"I guess."

"Something else?"

"I'm not sure. I can't put my finger on it."

"Something one of them said?"

"I don't know." She shut her eyes again. "It'll come to me."

37

"THEY TELL AN interesting story about the old Bobover Rebbe," Pomerantz said. "You never heard of him? He was a major Hasidic rabbi in Poland, and now in Brooklyn the son is the leader of a big Bobover community. Before the war my father took me and my brother a few times to Tchebin, where the Bobover Rebbe had moved with his whole family and his talmidim—his students. They had to leave Bobov, because of the Germans. But that's a different story." Pomerantz smiled.

"Anyway. This story that I'm going to tell you was written up in the Warsaw Jewish newspaper, De Moment. There was a murder in Kamionka—a town near Chrzanow, in Galicia. They found the dead body of a poer—mmn, how do you say this in English?" Pomerantz rubbed his chin and squinted. "A peasant." He nodded. "This peasant's name was Bellievsky. Suspicion for the murder fell on a Jewish bar owner, Bellaire, who lived in Kamionka, because two days before, the peasant had a fight with the bar owner and slapped him, twice. Bellievsky's friends claimed that the bar owner had murdered the dead man, and even though Bellaire insisted he was innocent, and there was no evidence, he was arrested.

"One of Bellaire's sons traveled to the Bobover Rebbe and told him what had happened. His father was innocent, he explained, and he, the son, had learned that there were three peasants who had been planning to kill Bellievsky for some time. But how could he prove it?

"The Rebbe told the son to go home immediately, before the dead man was buried, and convince the judge to bring Bellaire and the three peasants to the funeral home, where the dead body was lying. After the funeral all four men should be ordered to grab the dead man's hand. Whoever wouldn't be able to let go of the dead man's hand," Pomerantz said in a sing-song crescendo, raising his finger high—"that would be a sign that he was the killer." Pomerantz dropped his hand.

"You think it's silly, right? I can see it on your face." He smiled. "It's okay. I don't blame you. The judge thought the Bobover Rebbe's advice was silly, too. He laughed, even. But out of respect for the Rebbe, and because the Rebbe was so popular with his followers in the area, the judge agreed to the plan."

Pomerantz leaned forward. "Now listen what happened. At the funeral home Bellaire pressed the dead man's hand and moved away." He mimed shaking an imaginary hand. "So did one of the peasants. Yosef Polnick, the second peasant, was next. He stepped forward. Suddenly he pulled back—" Pomerantz pressed back against his chair and widened his eyes dramatically. "He started screaming and crying that he was afraid to take Bellievsky's hand, because the dead man would take revenge on him.

"The judge and all the people who were there witnessed what happened. And Polnick confessed in front of everyone that he had murdered Bellievsky—they had quarreled long ago about a piece of real estate. So Polnick was arrested, and all of Galicia spoke about the Bobover Rebbe, how clever he was and how he had saved a Jew from a terrible misfortune. A good story, no?" Pomerantz smiled.

"The Rebbe was very wise. Too bad the police don't have someone like him to give them advice, right? I hear almost every day on the radio that this one was murdered, that one was murdered." Pomerantz sighed and shook his head. "So many murders. The police try hard to catch the murderers, but sometimes the murderers are too smart.

"Not like that poer, Polnick."

The Zurich police detective had found nothing on Ernst Zimmer, he told Jessie at eight-thirty Tuesday morning. Or Herman Leider. Chances were that both names were aliases.

Jessie had been expecting as much. "What about Suisse General?"

"The address you gave me is an apartment that was rented to Franz Koenig, the person under whose name the phone number for Suisse General was listed."

Jessie's interest quickened. "So Koenig *does* exist."

"*Ja,* but the apartment is vacant. Koenig no longer lives there, and the management company that owns the building has no knowledge as to where he is now. His rent is all paid up—that's all they care about. He always paid with a bank check, by the way. He did the same with the phone company and the utilities."

Were Koenig and Zimmer/Leider the same person? If so, had Zimmer returned to Zurich to clean out his apartment and effect his disappearance? Or was Koenig Zimmer's accomplice? "Did you check his driver's license?"

"*Ja.* There is no license for a Franz Koenig. Though he may have paid someone to fake one for him. So this name, too, must be an alias."

"So you have no idea who this man really is?" How could Jessie find him, if the Zurich police couldn't?

"Maybe yes. We found a business letter in the trash bin outside the apartment building, together with some other things that one of the neighbors identified as having belonged to Koenig. It was addressed to a Franz Klagsvald. We believe Koenig and Klagsvald may be one and the same."

Lucky for the police that Klagsvald had been a little sloppy. Then again, he hadn't anticipated having to rush home and obliterate traces of his existence. "Were you able to find out anything about him?" She was almost afraid to ask.

"*Ja.* We have his driver's license number, his current address and phone number. We know that Klagsvald is an attorney, and that he no longer practices."

That fit with Zimmer. Klagsvald sounded like their man. She felt a rush of excitement. "What does he do now?"

"From the letter we found, it seems that he finds investors who will put up capital for different projects—this is what you told me this Zimmer did, *ja*?"

"Ja," Jessie said without thinking, and hoped the detective didn't think she was mocking him.

"I contacted the letter writer—one of Klagsvald's investors, as it turns out. He invested a large sum of money in a real estate deal. Lately, he was impatient with Klagsvald, because he hadn't been returning his calls. He made inquiries and discovered that Klagsvald had taken out a loan secured by the property that he and his fellow investors were developing."

Jessie nodded, even though the Swiss detective couldn't see her. "Klagsvald used the money to pay off the settlements of Mrs. Seligman and Mr. Blumenkrantz."

And possibly some other lone survivors. Yesterday, after returning to the station, she'd started contacting childless retirement-home residents who'd been interviewed for the documentary. Out of the seven widows and three widowers she'd spoken to so far, one woman had been contacted two months ago by a Swiss attorney who had offered, over the phone, to obtain an early, but reduced, cash settlement of her claim against the Swiss bank. The woman had been interested, but had told the attorney that she'd want her own lawyer to review all the documents before she signed anything. The Swiss attorney had agreed, but had never phoned again. She didn't remember his name. "Lucky I didn't sign anything," she told Jessie. Jessie didn't tell her just how lucky she was.

"We learned something else that might interest you," the Swiss detective said. "Klagsvald hinted to this investor that he's upset with the Swiss banks for agreeing to open the dormant accounts and pay out the assets to the surviving heirs. There *are* Swiss who feel this way," the detective added, in a tone that said he wasn't one of them. He sounded uncomfortable. "Klagsvald said he feared that this action could endanger Switzerland's financial security. Which is ridiculous."

Just the opposite of what he'd told Jessie. Hardly surprising, since everything about him was a lie, including his name. "Are you going to pick him up for questioning?"

"That would be difficult, Detective Drake. Herr Klagsvald took a flight Monday morning to New York. From there, he could certainly have taken a flight to Los Angeles. He'd have to show photo ID, of course, but my guess is that he has some

forged identification. The question is, under what identity is
he traveling?"

And why would he return to the States, and in particular,
to Los Angeles? Unless he had some unfinished business to
take care of.

Like Hilda Rheinhart. As far as Jessie knew, Hilda was the
only one who could identify "Leider" as Zimmer, aka Klagsvald. And link him to murder.

Fifteen minutes later Jessie had a facsimile of Klagsvald's
driver's license, with his photo. She'd had no doubts that he
was Zimmer, but she felt a little thrill of satisfaction when she
saw the face of the man she'd met at the foundation. *Almost*
the same face—he looked a little different. A mustache, no
glasses. And the fax was grainy as hell.

She showed it to Phil.

"That's him, huh?" He studied the photo. "What now?
You fax this to all the airlines that have flights to L.A., see if
anyone recognized him?"

"I can do that. But my guess is that if he arrived in New
York on Monday, he's probably here by now."

Phil nodded. "Under what name?"

She thought for a moment. "Koenig. He set up his Zurich
apartment under that name. He probably has fake ID to go
along with it."

"So he'll register in an L.A. hotel under that name, too?"

She shook her head. "He knows we can trace him if he
does."

"He doesn't know we're onto him."

"He's a cautious guy, Phil. He set things up very carefully—
using different names with Anna Seligman and the others.
The minute I showed up at the foundation, he probably
started to worry that eventually we'd be onto him. That's why
he went back to Zurich and cleaned out his apartment."

"So what if you were at the foundation? He didn't know
why."

"Henry Steele told us he confided in Zimmer about Pomerantz's arrival—it would be only natural for Henry to mention
that I was investigating Pomerantz's death. Zimmer has to

assume we're trying to find him, and that we may know all about Franz Koenig."

Phil thought for a moment, pulling at his mustache. "Okay," he finally said. "So what name is he using?"

"He can use any name he wants—he used traveler's checks to pay for his room at the hotel where he stayed here before. He's probably doing the same thing now. I'm going to leave a copy of this photo with the convalescent home where Hilda is staying."

"How's the old lady doing?"

"I haven't checked yet today." She picked up her receiver and dialed the facility's number—she knew it by heart—and was connected with Samber.

"I was just about to phone you, Detective," he told her.

Jessie inhaled sharply. "Is Mrs. Rheinhart all right?"

"She's fine. I'm sorry if I alarmed you. You asked me to let you know if Mrs. Rheinhart received any visitors. Well, Mr. Leider just came by to see her."

Jessie gripped the receiver. "You didn't let him into her room, did you?"

"Of course not. I told him Mrs. Rheinhart was too weak to receive visitors. He was very disappointed—he told me Mrs. Rheinhart would *want* to see him, if only for a few minutes. But I didn't let him."

She could hear the pride in the manager's voice. "You did very well, Mr. Samber. Did this man leave a phone number?"

"No. He said to please let Mrs. Rheinhart know that he'd been here, and that he would come by again this afternoon. He brought flowers, by the way—he asked me to give them to Mrs. Rheinhart. Should I?"

She supposed there was no harm in the flowers, but told Samber that she wanted to check them out first. Not that she thought Zimmer had hidden a tarantula or some other dangerous insect among the blooms. "Did he leave anything else?" Another box of chocolates—doctored like the last ones?

"No. He seemed genuinely concerned about Mrs. Rheinhart."

I'll bet, Jessie thought.

28

THE LATEX WAS itching her. Jessie peered into the mirror and sighed. "God, I look old." Her eyes had shrunk and disappeared behind folds of plastic skin.

The makeup artist smiled. "Not old enough. But we're getting there. Hold still, dear."

His name was Walter, and he free-lanced for several studios. Jessie had been sitting in Walter's apartment for over an hour, watching herself being transformed into an eighty-year-old woman. She didn't know how actors handled daily makeup sessions. No glamour there—just tedium.

With deft fingers, Walter applied more "wrinkles" to her face, concentrating on the area around her eyes, which she thought looked pretty damn old already. He spent half an hour on her throat and upper chest, stepping back numerous times to get a perspective on his work.

He did her arms, past her elbows. Then her hands. She watched, fascinated and appalled, as they shriveled in front of her eyes. He dipped a thin brush into some pots of color; ten minutes later a pale blue concentration-camp number was "tattooed" on her left forearm. It gave her an eerie feeling.

The wig was last. A latex, pink-skin-tone cap with tufts of

white hair. He secured it in place, then brushed the curls over her forehead and ears to camouflage the hairline.

Walter swiveled her chair around.

"So what do you think?" she asked Gary.

"You look sexy as hell, for an eighty-year-old broad." He grinned. "How about a little action, honey?"

"Not tonight, I have arthritis." She rose from the chair. She wondered what her mother and Helen would say if they saw her now. They'd probably faint.

"Be careful when you put anything over your head," Walter warned. "A nightgown that buttons down the front would be best."

"I'll be careful. Thanks, Walter." She winked at him, then rolled her tongue lasciviously.

"Watch the lips!" Walter moaned.

Gary drove her to Cedars.

"I hope you know what the hell you're doing," he said as he parked the car. "I'd feel safer if Phil were in the hospital room with you, under the bed."

"Phil wouldn't fit under the bed."

"He could wait in the bathroom. Zimmer wouldn't see him."

"Zimmer might check the bathroom before he tried anything. Look, I'm in no danger. Phil will be at the nurses' station, dressed in a nurse's uniform. The minute Zimmer comes near me, I'll tackle him and press the CALL button. Phil will be right there. In fact, he should be arriving soon."

They'd worked out all the details at the station.

When "Leider" stopped by the convalescent home in the afternoon, the new "assistant manager"—Marty Simms— would inform him that Hilda was unable to have visitors. Simms would hesitate, then reveal that Hilda was agitated after talking with police detectives, so upset that she'd been of no help to the sketch artist they'd brought along. Hilda was insisting on being taken to Cedars this evening for an overnight observation. If she received a clean bill of health— which Simms thought was likely—she'd be returning to her board-and-care facility. Simms would also tell "Leider" that the detectives had asked him what time tomorrow they could come back with the sketch artist.

"Vultures," Simms would say.

That was the script. They'd rehearsed it a few times in the station, then at the convalescent home. Jessie had felt sorry for Arnold Samber—she thought the real manager would be upset about losing his role. But Samber had been relieved—he'd admitted to Jessie that he'd been "nervous as a pig" when he'd had to tell "Leider" he couldn't see Hilda. He didn't think he could pull this off naturally.

Simms could. He'd played it just right at the last rehearsal.

And if everything went well tonight, and Simms was convincing, Zimmer would feel the pressure to act quickly before Hilda met with the police sketch artist—obviously, she'd be helping create a composite drawing of "Herman Leider."

And before she returned to the Golden Palms, where a death necessitated a call to 911.

Hilda, of course, would remain in the convalescent home while Jessie impersonated her. The move to the hospital and the controlled timing were essential to the plan: Jessie needed the aid of night—she was afraid that in daylight, Zimmer would detect immediately that she wasn't Hilda. And in a hospital, unlike a convalescent home, the comings and goings of visitors and staff were hardly noticed, even at night. Zimmer would feel safe.

Jessie walked with Gary to the South Tower, careful to slow her gait to that of an elderly woman. She thought she looked conspicuous, but no one paid her any attention. The guard opened the lobby door for her and smiled. So did the people on the elevator.

"We're almost there, Grandma." Gary patted her arm tenderly.

She kicked him.

They got off on the fifth floor and walked down the long hall toward her room. At the nurses' station Jessie stopped. There was Phil, sitting on a stool. She felt safer just seeing him. He looked straight at her and didn't blink. Then he noticed Gary and looked at Jessie again. He did a double take.

She stopped a smile by biting on the inside of her cheek—
she didn't want to crack her face.

In her room she placed the small suitcase on the bed and
began unpacking. A short-sleeved, floral-print cotton nightgown. Hilda's. A deck of cards and two romance novels, their
pages dog-eared. Also Hilda's. Small brown vials of Hilda's
medications. Hilda's comb, her pink Max Factor lipstick. Jessie put Hilda's slippers on the floor, next to the bed. She hung
one of her dresses in the narrow closet and placed a pair of
sensible shoes on the floor of the closet. Best for last: She set
the photo of Leon on the small nightstand—Hilda had
clutched the picture to her chest before reluctantly handing it
to Jessie.

She'd been stunned when Jessie had told her about
"Leider." "It can't be!" she'd cried, over and over. "He's
such a nice man!" Jessie hadn't wanted to tell her, but she'd
needed Hilda's props. She knew Zimmer was cautious. She
had to assume he'd check the room out before he approached
the sleeping figure in the bed. He knew Hilda well—he'd seen
her interview.

Jessie didn't know how he was planning to kill Hilda. She
still didn't know how he'd killed Anna Seligman and Mendel,
either. Had he slipped something into a cup of tea to dope
them up, make them sleep? Had he followed that with a more
lethal medication? A digitalis cocktail for Blumenkrantz? A
high-dose injection of insulin for Anna?

She checked her watch—*Hilda's* watch. It was five to seven.
She phoned Simms—no call yet from Leider. All day she'd
worried that Leider would show up too early, that he'd be
suspicious when he couldn't see Hilda right away, suspicious
about the fact that there was a new manager. Now Jessie worried that he wouldn't show up at all. She didn't know if she
could convince Espes to let her repeat this another day. He
hadn't been keen about the idea to begin with, even though
Simms and Boyd had been supportive.

She looked at Gary. He was playing with the control box
looped around the bed rail, using the buttons to raise and
lower the top and bottom of the bed.

"You're such a little boy," she said. "Having fun?"

"I always wanted one of these."

She could tell from his voice that he was nervous.

They watched the seven o'clock news, then *Jeopardy*. They played three rounds of "Spit." She was down to one card when her cell phone rang.

It was Simms. "Leider" had just left.

"I'm sure he bought it," Simms said. "Looked a little startled when I mentioned the sketch artist. He asked what room she was in, and I told him I didn't know."

Jessie's idea—she didn't want Zimmer to think things were too pat. Let him phone the hospital and talk to the main switchboard—the operator would tell him what room "Hilda Rheinhart" was in. Jessie called the switchboard now to make sure Hilda Rheinhart's name was in the system. It was. And she was in the right room, too. Not always a given with hospitals.

"You'd better go," she told Gary. "I'll call you the minute this is over."

"No matter what time, all right?"

"No, matter what time."

He held her close, careful not to disturb her makeup or hair. "I love you, Jess. Be careful."

She hesitated. "I love you, too." She pecked his lips gingerly.

She watched him leave, then pressed the CALL button and asked for Nurse Okum. A moment later Phil was in her room.

"He just left the convalescent home," she told him.

He was staring at her. "I can't believe it's you."

She smiled. "I'm not getting older, I'm getting better."

"Nervous, huh?"

"A little." Now that Gary had left, she could admit it. She'd been in too many situations where the "perfect" setup somehow hadn't turned out that way.

"I'm right down the hall, Jess. I know what he looks like— I memorized his face from that fax. When I see him, I'll announce 'Code Six.' You'll know he's on the way."

"He doesn't have the mustache any more, remember. And he may look different. Maybe that's why Patsy Williams didn't recognize him." Or maybe it hadn't been Zimmer at all.

Jessie and Phil had driven to the hotel and showed the fax of Zimmer's photo to the waitress.

"He doesn't have a mustache," Jessie had told her. "And it's only a fax. Is this one of the two men you saw?"

Patsy had stared at the likeness for a long time and finally shaken her head.

"It's him, but it's *not* him, you know?"

Jessie *didn't* know. What she *did* know was that *somebody* had met Pomerantz at the Century Plaza that Saturday night. *Two* somebodies. She wondered suddenly whether Phil had been right—maybe Larkins *had* lured Pomerantz to meet him. According to Hilda, Pomerantz had been excited about going to the Century Plaza. Why would he have been excited to see *Zimmer?*

If Larkins was mystery man number one, who was number two? And why had Pomerantz stayed with him?

Had one or both of the Steele sons gone to meet with their uncle? They'd denied meeting him at all, but maybe that was because they feared that if they were linked with their uncle's murder, the resulting publicity would violate the privacy their father so cherished.

Or maybe they'd really killed him. Blood money, Phil had said.

But why would they kill their uncle?

Wheels within wheels within wheels.

She wanted it over already.

She changed into the nightgown, careful not to smudge her face, then realized she couldn't leave her own clothes around—too youthful. She found a yellow plastic bag in the closet and stuffed her clothes and shoes inside. She put the bag in a bin labeled SOILED LINENS.

She climbed into the bed and turned off the overhead light, leaving on only a fluorescent tube at the head of the bed. She placed the control box under the light blanket, near her right hand.

Ready or not, here I come. . . .

39

SHE HADN'T CONSIDERED how difficult it would be to lie in bed in an almost-dark room and pretend to be asleep when her heart was racing and her hands were clammy, and she was afraid to move too much on the pillow because her face might come off.

She lay on her side, eyes open. She'd forgotten how noisy a hospital could be. It was two years since she'd been a patient here, when she'd had her miscarriage. She'd been on the third floor—the South Tower, where she was now, not the North. The north was for OB deliveries. The south was for gynecology. She didn't know why she was thinking about that now.

She heard a creak and froze. Then realized it was her bed. Anyway, Phil would have alerted her. "Code Six."

She checked her watch—ten-fifteen. She wondered what Gary was doing—probably sitting by the phone, waiting for her call. He was so sweet, so dear. She *did* love him, but she still wasn't sure about marrying him. Fear of failure.

Another hour passed. She was feeling sleepy, which wasn't a good thing. The adrenaline rush that came with anticipation had worn off long ago. She was too comfortable in the bed, but she couldn't sit up. She had only seconds from the time Phil signaled her, not enough time to rearrange herself, to pretend she was asleep.

Her eyelids felt heavy and itchy from the makeup. She was tempted to shut them but was afraid she'd fall asleep. She forced them open and started singing show tunes, the way she and Helen used to do on rainy days. Helen knew all the words to so many. *My Fair Lady, Les Miserables, Phantom.* Jessie had known them, too, but there were sections she couldn't remember now. She repeated the parts she *did* know. Phil was lucky, she thought suddenly—at least he had people to talk to, coffee to keep him awake.

"Code Six."

The words blared in her ear. Forcing herself to take shallow, even breaths, she reached under the blanket and wrapped her fingers around the control box. Thank God the CALL button was illuminated—she could imagine what would happen if she turned on the television instead, or activated the mechanism that raised and lowered the bed.

The door opened, bathing the room with yellow light from the hallway. Her heart was pounding.

Footsteps approached her bed.

"False alarm, Jess," Phil whispered. "I spotted someone who looked like our guy heading in this direction. Sorry."

She hadn't realized she'd been holding her breath until she let it out. Opening her eyes, she turned toward him and smiled. "It's okay. Good practice." Her pulse was racing.

"I don't think he's going to show," Phil said. "He probably got scared off."

"It's eleven-thirty. He may still come."

"You okay? Not getting sleepy?"

"I'm fine," she lied. Pride, determination to finish this. "What about you?"

"I'm pretty wired. I have enough coffee in me to open a Starbucks. Call if you think you're falling asleep."

She promised she would.

She wondered how Hilda was doing. Probably fast asleep, Jessie thought with a touch of envy. She'd played a quick game of gin with Hilda to calm her down after she'd told her about "Leider." Hilda had insisted on shuffling the cards and dealing. It had been painful watching the old woman coerce her arthritic fingers into submission. The sleeves of her nightgown had fallen back when she'd arranged her cards, exposing the blue numbers on her left forearm. She'd caught Jessie staring.

"You're looking at my numbers," she'd said quietly. "They bother you?"

Jessie had blushed. "I'm sorry."

"Don't be sorry. They don't bother *me*. After all these years, I'd feel funny if I didn't see them. Like I was someone else."

Jessie had frowned—something had nagged at her, like a picture just a little bit crooked.

"You don't believe me?" Hilda had said, misunderstanding the frown. "I could have had someone remove them, but I didn't want to. Nachum told me he had them removed—then he was sorry."

That's what Pomerantz had said in the video. Something about that bothered her, something he'd said about his brother. . . . She tried playing the video in her head. It was right there, she almost had it, but she was too damn tired.

She sang Beatles songs, then Simon and Garfunkel. She and Phil had done that once on a stakeout to pass the time. She had finished humming "Celia" when she decided it would be all right to close her eyes, just for a minute. She wouldn't fall asleep—she was very alert. The slightest sound would wake her. She'd certainly hear his "Code Six."

She considered contacting Phil, but he would call it all off, insist on taking her home. She kept her eyes open and sang "Killing Me Softly." She loved Roberta Flack.

At two o'clock she knew Zimmer wasn't going to come. Not tonight. Which was just as well, because her eyes were really impossibly heavy now, and keeping them open was a struggle.

She shut her eyes. Wonderful, she thought, this is wonderful. A short while later—maybe a minute, she thought, it couldn't have been more than a minute—the room seemed darker. She could feel the air from her nostrils, warm against her face, and then she couldn't feel the air at all, couldn't breathe, because something was blocking her air passage.

She knew it was just a nightmare—she'd had these as a child, had talked about them with her therapist. "You feel you're being smothered," he'd told her, and that's exactly how she'd felt, exactly how she *did* feel, right now, smothered, as if a pillow were being pressed against her nose and mouth, that was why she couldn't breathe.

Her eyes flew open, bulged.

He was here!

"So sorry, Hilda," he whispered. "Goodbye."

She hadn't even heard him come in.

No "Code Six"!

Her hand dove under the blanket and knocked the control box off the bed. It clanked against the metal railing of the bed. No air, no time. She stretched out both hands and grabbed one of his wrists.

Jerked hard and sudden, then twisted.

A crack.

A scream of pain.

She was wide awake now, her adrenaline pumping. She slid down the bed, wheezing, as he lunged toward her. She bent her leg and kicked him in the face. He staggered backward. She jumped off the bed and wrestled him to the ground.

Flipped him over like a flounder, heard the satisfying thunk of his face hitting the linoleum floor.

Twisting his arm behind him, she pressed her knee into the small of his back as her fingers swept the floor in widening circles for the control box.

She found it and pushed the CALL button.

Within seconds Phil was in the room. He switched on the light and bounded to her side, then handed her the handcuffs.

"Your collar," he said.

She yanked Zimmer's left arm behind him and cuffed both wrists together.

Zimmer moaned.

"I think I broke his wrist," Jessie said. "Maybe his nose, too."

"Poor baby."

They helped him to his feet. Jessie took Zimmer's wallet and flipped it open while Phil frisked him.

"Franz Koenig," she read from his driver's license.

"He's clean," Phil said. "Only in a figurative sense." He shoved Zimmer down onto a chair.

Zimmer's nose was bleeding and had started to swell. He was staring at Jessie, openmouthed.

Phil said, "They don't make grannies the way they used to, do they, Franz? You look pretty sharp, by the way."

He was dressed like a surgeon. Green scrubs, a cap on his head, a mask dangling casually around his neck. Below that, a stethoscope.

And he had a beard.

"No wonder you didn't recognize him," Jessie said.

"I should have." Phil sounded embarrassed now. His face was flushed. "Son of a bitch just looked so right—walked down the hall, waved at the nurses."

She decided not to tell him she'd been half asleep when Zimmer had accosted her. Maybe later.

"I need a doctor," Zimmer said. "I'm in a great deal of pain."

"Physician, heal thyself." Phil's smile was mean.

"I've heard about American police brutality, but I thought it was fiction," Zimmer said in a lofty tone. "I'm going to report this to your superior."

"Gee, Franz, I'm shaking in my boots. You want to tell us what happened?"

"Not particularly."

"We know you killed Anna Seligman and Mendel Blumenkrantz, and why."

Zimmer frowned. "Those names aren't familiar. Should they be?"

"We know why you tried to kill Hilda," Jessie said. "She's the only living person who knew your real name—Franz Klagsvald." She paused. "Pomerantz knew it, too. He was in Hilda's room one time when you visited her. He saw your real name on the power-of-attorney form."

No response from Zimmer.

"That's why you had to kill him, isn't it? Because he suspected what you were doing? Asked too many questions? You must have panicked," she added in a sympathetic tone. "I can understand that." She paused. "You'd make it a lot easier on yourself if you just told us what happened. You'd probably feel relieved. Did you kill Norman Pomerantz?" she asked softly.

"Why don't you ask Charles Steele."

"Why would Steele kill his uncle, Franz?" Phil asked.

Zimmer smiled.

And suddenly, Jessie knew.

40

"SOMETIMES I THINK about what we went through, and I can't believe it happened," Pomerantz said. "I talk to my friends—they feel the same way.

"Do we talk about it a lot?" Pomerantz laughed. "All the time. About this one and that one. There were good people and bad. Strong people died, weak ones lived. You didn't think about next week. You thought, let me get through today.

"In the end, you know, you did what you could to survive."

"I was hoping we'd answered all your questions," Henry said as he entered the library. He looked and sounded exhausted. "What can I do for you?"

"Actually, we need to talk to your father," Jessie said. She wondered where Charles was.

"That's impossible." Henry's tone was reproving. "He's taken a turn for the worse, and the doctor said no visitors."

"I'm afraid we have to insist," Jessie said with quiet authority.

Henry looked at her, then at Phil, then back at Jessie. "You don't understand," he began just as Charles appeared in the doorway.

He stepped into the room. "What's going on?" he asked Henry.

"They insist on talking to Dad."

"No way." Charles folded his arms across his chest and faced Jessie. "If you tell my father his brother was alive all this time, and came here and was murdered, it'll kill him."

"I don't think so."

"What the hell does that mean?" Charles glared at her. "If you don't believe me, I can put you in touch with my father's doctor. He'll verify that he has a serious heart condition."

"I don't doubt that, Mr. Steele. But I don't think the news about Mr. Pomerantz will shock your father. I'm sure he's aware of everything that's been going on."

Both brothers were staring at her.

Henry said, "I don't know how you reached that ridiculous conclusion. Charles and I have taken every precaution to keep all this from our father. Why on earth would we tell him?"

"I think *he* told *you*," Jessie said.

"Detective—"

"Henry." Charles put a hand on his brother's arm, then faced Jessie. "Detective, we've told you everything we know. No doubt you're frustrated because Mr. Zimmer has slipped through your hands. I'm sorry about that—if what you say is true, he's a vile, despicable person and I hope you'll apprehend him. But you seem intent on involving us in Mr. Pomerantz's death, and I feel it's in our best interests not to answer any more questions."

"I noticed that your father's eyes are a deep brown." Jessie pointed to the family portrait hanging on the wall. "Like yours. That's odd, because Mr. Pomerantz said his brother's eyes were blue. Sea blue, to be exact." She wondered how she'd missed that—she'd watched the video so many times. She'd zoomed through it again just before coming here, and that's when she'd picked up on the discrepancy.

Charles frowned. "What are you saying? That my father *wasn't* Mr. Pomerantz's long-lost brother? That Mr. Pomerantz was mistaken?" He narrowed his eyes. "Or did he *pretend* to be our uncle because he was after our money?"

Charles was good, Jessie thought. He'd been very convincing yesterday, too. "You know very well that Mr. Pomerantz wasn't pretending. The chalice belonged to Moshe Shtuelberg. Mr. Pomerantz recognized it. That's why he came here to L.A., to the foundation. To meet his brother."

"Then maybe Mr. Pomerantz was wrong about his brother's eye color," Henry said. "So many years have passed since he saw him. Maybe he's confused."

"Maybe. When Moshe Shtuelberg was in Auschwitz, he had identification numbers tattooed on his left forearm. When I came here on Sunday, I met your father. He was wearing a short-sleeved robe, and I would have noticed those numbers. But I didn't see any." *My brother Moshe wouldn't have had them removed,* Pomerantz had said. That's what Jessie had finally remembered.

Silence from the brothers. They seemed frozen in place.

Then Charles said, "Maybe my father had the numbers removed."

"Maybe." Jessie nodded. "Mr. Pomerantz had his numbers removed. Still, there's a scar. That's why I'd like to see your father. One look will tell us. And if I'm wrong, you have my deepest apologies."

She *wasn't* wrong. The Steeles hadn't rushed to meet their "uncle" not because they'd been busy with their ill father, but because they hadn't known how to deal with the man who *wasn't* their uncle.

"That's very big of you." Charles smiled grimly. "But in the meantime, you'll have upset my father and put his health in danger. No apology will undo that, will it?" He shook his head. "I'm sorry. I can't allow you to bother him."

"Then I'm afraid we'll have to take him in for—"

"What the hell do you want from him?" Henry whispered. "Can't you leave him alone? He doesn't know *anything,* I tell you!"

Jessie gazed at him steadily. "Mr. Pomerantz showed up at the foundation office on Tuesday and left a message. Your father *did* get the message—I think that's what caused his heart attack that Wednesday night."

Henry shook his head. "That's not what happened."

"That's when he must have told both of you the truth—

that he'd been masquerading as Moshe Shtuelberg all these years. When Moshe Shtuelberg died in Auschwitz, your father took on his identity. Obviously, he also learned about the Swiss bank account and the valuables—and somehow he got hold of the numbers to the account. Maybe Moshe shared them with him in exchange for an offer of help."

"Another fascinating story?" Charles sighed. "I'm going to have to ask you to leave, Detective."

"Enough!"

The raspy, shaking voice came from the doorway. Jessie turned and saw Maurice Steele.

41

"**YOU SHOULDN'T BE** out of bed." Henry hurried to his father's side and put his hand on his shoulder.

Déjà vu, Jessie thought. She could feel her heart pumping.

Maurice Steele shook off his son's hand. Leaning on his cane, he walked slowly to the table and sat down. He looked at Jessie. "What do you want to know?"

"Dad, don't do this," Charles implored.

"Enough, I said! They know." The father fixed him with a stern glance and faced Jessie again. "Sit down," he said, pointing to the chair opposite him. "You, too," he added, pointing to Phil.

More of a command than a request, Jessie thought as she sat down. Steele was obviously used to being in authority.

"Moshe Shtuelberg died from typhus two days before we were liberated," Maurice Steele said. "He would have died sooner, only I nursed him. I did everything I could to save his life— 'Don't die,' I begged him. 'Hold on. Just a few more days and we'll be free.' He didn't have the strength. The funny thing is, we wouldn't have met at all before they made everyone evacuate the camp. Jews were in one part of Auschwitz, gentiles in another."

Jessie tried not to stare. "You aren't Jewish?" she asked in a casual tone. She glanced at the sons—no reaction.

"You didn't know?" Steele lifted his brows. "I thought you knew everything, you're such a smart detective. I was Polish, a gentile." He grunted. "Why should I say 'was'? I never converted. Too afraid the truth would come out."

"Dad, you don't have to do this," Henry said softly.

Steele ignored him. "I was an orphan. Before the war I worked as a handyman for a Jewish family. Very decent people—kind, generous. I envied the way they lived—they were all so close, their house was so warm, loving. I liked their holidays, their rituals. I used to wish I'd been born Jewish, but then the Germans came, and I was happy I wasn't Jewish." He smiled wryly.

"How did you end up in Auschwitz?" she asked.

"When the Germans were rounding up all the Jews in our town, I hid my employer and his family in an empty barn I knew about. The Germans found out. They sent me to a labor camp, and later, to Auschwitz. I was a political prisoner—they made me wear a red cloth triangle. Better than green. Green was for murderers and other violent criminals." Another ironic smile.

"You didn't get an identification number?" Phil asked.

Steele shook his head. "I came to Auschwitz toward the end. They weren't bothering with numbers then. During the evacuation, some of us decided to stay. Moshe couldn't move—he was too sick. I wasn't sick, but I knew I'd die if I had to march for days in the bitter cold. Some of the inmates who refused to leave the camp, the Germans shot. I don't know why they didn't shoot me." Steele shrugged. "Not my time, I guess."

Jessie glanced at Henry and Charles. They stood like statues—stone-faced, not moving. She wondered what they were thinking now, what they'd thought when they'd first heard their father's story.

"After the Germans left, I moved into the Jewish block. That's when I met Moshe. Right away we liked each other." Steele's smile was wistful now, almost tender. "I did what I could to help him—I found food and fed him like a baby, one teaspoon at a time. I sponged him and tried to keep his fever down. But he was near death already. He knew it, too. He told me about the Swiss account—he had the number on a slip of paper that he kept in his shoe. He knew that his parents were dead. His sisters, too. He made me promise to try to find his brother, Nachum, and give him the account number. 'Nachum will share with you,' he told me."

"Did you try to find him?" Jessie asked.

Steele bowed his head. "No," he finally said in a barely audible voice. "I was afraid he would accuse me of killing his brother after making him give me the account number. This wasn't true—I did *everything* I could to save Moshe." Steele looked up. His face was flushed, but he met Jessie's eyes. "But why would the brother believe me, a Pole?" He had a coughing spasm and shut his eyes.

Henry took a step closer. "Dad—"

Steele held up his hand. "I'm okay." He coughed again, then cleared his throat. "After the war I went to the bank. I got the money and some valuable art pieces. Beautiful things—more beautiful even than Moshe had described them." He sighed again.

"Why did you take Moshe Shtuelberg's name?"

The number one question—Phil, she knew, was waiting intently for the answer. It didn't make sense, he'd argued when she'd told him her suspicions about Steele: Why hadn't Steele taken Shtuelberg's money and valuables and disappeared? Why risk exposure? I don't know why, she'd told Phil. But she'd known in her gut that Maurice Steele wasn't Moshe Shtuelberg.

"Who *should* I be, if not Moshe Shtuelberg?" Steele said softly. "Where would I go with the money, with the art—back to my hometown in Poland? There was nothing for me in Poland. And if I *did* go back, the police would wonder where I got the money and the other things. They'd put me in jail." He paused. "Before the war, I wanted to be Jewish. Now I decided I *would* be Jewish. I would be Moshe—I had his money, his possessions. I couldn't save him, but I could make sure his name would continue. And I swore to myself that I would live a life that would honor him."

An expiation of sins, Jessie thought. "Weren't you nervous that people would find out you weren't Jewish?" She reminded herself that she was here to investigate a murder, not to hear Steele's life story. But it *was* fascinating.

"It wasn't hard to pretend. My history was Moshe's history. I knew a lot from working for my Jewish employers, and I learned from watching others. Also, I wasn't observant, so I didn't have to worry so much about making mistakes. A lot of people after the war weren't observant anymore, so no one questioned me." He shrugged.

Like her own mother, Jessie thought. There was a definite irony here—Frances had abandoned Judaism after the war. Maurice Steele—whoever he really was—had embraced it. "How did you communicate with everyone? You didn't know Yiddish."

"I understood Yiddish, but I couldn't speak it. My accent was terrible." A half laugh. "So I told everyone that I didn't like Yiddish—it was the language of the ghetto, a language I wanted to forget. Again, nobody thought it was strange."

"Did you check to see if Nachum was alive?" Phil asked.

"No. I was afraid if I did, and he *was* alive, he'd find out who was asking about him. Officially, Moshe Shtuelberg died in Auschwitz just before the liberation—there were eyewitnesses. But I didn't feel safe. When I came to America, I changed my name to Maurice Steele—if Nachum *was* alive, or if there were some distant family members, no one would connect this name with Moshe Shtuelberg's.

"I got on with my life. I rented an apartment. I started a small textile business. I had myself circumcised, too." He grimaced. "A lot of pain, but I knew I had to do it. And I married a wonderful woman, also from Poland. I never told her I wasn't Jewish. I was afraid she wouldn't marry me."

"Your wife still doesn't know?" Phil sounded skeptical.

Steele shook his head. "I have to tell her, I know that. It's not going to be easy." He looked at his sons, then back at Jessie.

"Why did you move to Los Angeles?" she asked.

"I thought I would feel safe after changing my name, but always I was looking over my shoulder, waiting. I figured that if Nachum was alive, he'd probably live in New York. That's where most of the Jews from Europe ended up. So I convinced my wife we should move here. I was very lucky in business. God blessed me, so I helped others. I knew that's what Moshe would have done."

Steele had built his wealth using Shtuelberg's money. Maybe he'd felt the need to help others because he wanted to compensate for having stolen it, for not having attempted to find Nachum and give him what was rightfully his. "But you didn't want publicity, because you were afraid that Nachum would find you?"

"*If* he was alive. Yes." Steele nodded.

"But your sons were more in the public eye. They established the foundation."

"I tried to talk them out of it." Steele cast a quick, angry glance at his sons. "They're grown men, they knew better. And I couldn't explain."

Hardly. "So when Nachum left the message, you knew who he was. And you couldn't let him meet you, because he'd know right away that you weren't Moshe."

"*I* didn't get the message—Henry did. On Wednesday I heard him talking on the phone. I heard him talking to a 'Pomerantz.' I knew. Right away, I knew. Henry was so excited to meet his uncle. So was Charles. Then I told them the truth. What choice did I have?"

"You didn't really have a heart attack," Jessie said.

Steele shook his head. "We needed time to figure out what to do. We decided to tell Nachum that I had a heart attack. Believe me, it wasn't far from the truth."

Charles's idea, probably. He seemed to be the most in control. "You must have felt desperate," Jessie said. "Your whole life—everything you'd worked so hard to build—was going to be ruined."

"You think I killed him?" He snorted. "I can't even walk on my own." He pointed to the cane at his side.

"Pomerantz would have exposed you as a thief and a liar, a self-made philanthropist who stole a dead man's identity and money and valuables—the very things that the Steele Foundation is trying to return to their rightful owners."

Steele had flinched.

"That's enough." Charles's hands were clenched. His face was mottled with anger. "My father doesn't have to be subjected to this."

Steele turned to his sons. "I'm tired of hiding," he whispered. "All my life I've been hiding." He faced Jessie again. "Maybe I did wrong by not looking for Nachum. But over the years I did a lot of good for a lot of people. No one can take that away." He looked at her defiantly—chin up, eyes on hers. "I told my sons I had to face Nachum—no more hiding. I needed time to tell my wife—not just about Nachum, but about me. And then we heard that Nachum was dead. Killed. I couldn't believe it."

"You thought one of your sons had killed him." She watched him carefully.

Steele shook his head. "My sons aren't killers. I raised them right—the way Moshe Shtuelberg would have raised his sons."

Fine words, but the old man was avoiding her eyes. Whom had he suspected—Charles or Henry? Or did he think both sons had colluded to get rid of the man who would ruin their lives?

"I'm sure this must have been very painful for you, going over your past," Jessie said. "We really appreciate your candor. If we have any more questions, we'll let you know."

"We're done?" He sounded surprised and relieved at the same time.

Ditto for the sons—Jessie could see their faces from the corner of her eye. She nodded. "We're done."

"So that's it, then. You know the whole story."

He pushed himself up and grabbed his cane. Henry stepped forward and took his father's arm.

"I'm all right," Steele said. "I can manage on my own."

Jessie felt a twinge of pity as she watched the old man slowly cross the room. Henry followed a few steps behind. He shut the door after his father had left and returned to his position, near Charles. *United we stand.* . . .

Phil stood. "Henry, why don't you stay here with Detective

Drake. She needs to ask you some more questions. Charles, where can you and I go to talk?"

This was how they'd planned it on the way here: Phil would talk to Charles; Jessie would take Henry. He was the more vulnerable link, and he might open up more to a woman.

The brothers exchanged glances.

Henry frowned. "I thought we were done," he told Jessie.

"Just a few details we want to clear up." They'd decided to conduct the questioning here as opposed to the station—less intimidating environment for the Steele brothers, less chance that they'd demand to see a lawyer. At least, Jessie hoped so.

"Are we under arrest?" he asked in a shaky voice.

"Absolutely not. We just want to get some information." Tell a suspect that he or she was under arrest, and more often than not, he yelled for an attorney. End of questioning.

"I don't understand why you have to talk to us separately," Charles said.

"No big mystery." Phil smiled. "Why does that make you nervous?"

He scowled. "I didn't say it made me nervous."

"Well, that's fine, then. Where do you want to talk?"

Charles was silent, clearly mulling over the situation. "I think I should get an attorney before I say anything," he finally said.

Jessie tensed. At least he hadn't said he *wanted* an attorney. That would have ended the questioning, or made any information gleaned afterwards inadmissible. "Charles, you can call your attorney, if you want," she said pleasantly. "But it's really not necessary. You're not under arrest. You're not even a suspect." This was a lie, but it was a permissible lie.

"If you haven't done anything wrong—"

"I haven't," he snapped. "Neither has Henry."

Phil smiled. "Well, then, no one has anything to be afraid of, right? This is just a friendly conversation."

More silence. If either brother, or both brothers, refused to talk, there was nothing she or Phil could do about it, unless they arrested them. Assuming they had probable cause.

But which one would they arrest? Henry? Charles? Both?

She glanced at Phil. She couldn't tell from his face, but she assumed he was as anxious as she was.

"We can talk in the family room," Charles told Phil. He turned to Henry. "Don't answer anything you don't want to, okay?"

All right, Jessie thought.

42

"WE DIDN'T KILL him, Detective. I didn't, and neither did Charles. Ernst Zimmer did."

Henry was sitting across the table from Jessie, in the chair his father had occupied just minutes ago. His hands were folded—probably to keep them from shaking, Jessie thought.

"Let's go back a little bit, Henry." She made certain that she sounded calm, unhurried. "Tell me about your first phone conversation with Mr. Pomerantz."

"It happened just like I told you. On Tuesday night I returned Mr. Pomerantz's message—he wasn't in, and I didn't leave a name or phone number. He called the next day, Wednesday, and told me who he was."

"How did you feel, Henry?"

"Shocked, excited. I knew my father had had a brother and two sisters—but we all thought he'd died in the war. I told Pomerantz I'd get back to him later that day and give him a time for the reunion. I *was* concerned about springing this on my father—he does have a heart condition."

Jessie nodded to show that she understood, that she believed him.

"Zimmer was in my office when I took the call. He excused

himself, and when I called him back in, I told him what had happened. I didn't see why not—it was wonderful news," he said defensively.

Poor Henry—he'd obviously gotten flack from Charles and Maurice about having confided in Zimmer. "You couldn't have known," Jessie said. "Then what happened?"

"I was telling Zimmer the details when my father and Charles walked in. My father heard me say the name 'Pomerantz'—he cried out and almost fainted. Zimmer ran to get him water, and when he returned, my father was sobbing—he was a fraud, everybody would know it. Stuff like that."

"You must have been terribly concerned," Jessie said. She knew how important it was to show sympathy.

"You can't imagine." He wiped the sweat off his mouth. "I thought he was in shock from hearing that his brother was alive, or maybe he felt guilty because he hadn't done enough to find him all these years. And then he said Pomerantz would know he wasn't Moshe Shtuelberg, that he'd been living a lie." Henry expelled a heavy breath.

"And Zimmer was in the office when this happened?"

Henry nodded. "My father wasn't aware that he was there, of course. Charles was frantic—he was petrified that this would get out. I told him I'd talk to Zimmer, which I did. He promised he wouldn't say a thing, and I believed him. I believed he was an honorable man."

So are they all, all honorable men. The line from Mark Antony's eulogy for Caesar popped into her head. "So did you call Mr. Pomerantz back?"

"Yes. Later that afternoon. I told him my father's heart condition had deteriorated. I said I'd get in touch with him the next day. Thursday I called him again—I told him we'd have to wait a few days, until the doctor okayed telling my father the news."

"I don't blame you for stalling," Jessie said. "You were in a tough spot—you wanted to protect your father."

"That's right," Henry said eagerly. "Charles and I were worried about him, how he'd handle all this. How he'd tell our mother. I don't know how he's going to do that." He sighed.

"Mr. Pomerantz didn't find it odd that neither you nor your brother met with him?"

"I'm sure he did—he sounded hurt. I told him that we had to be with our father, that we were tied up with business. I didn't know what else to do. And then, over the weekend, my father told us that he wanted to tell Pomerantz the truth."

"You must have been surprised."

"A little," he admitted. "But Charles and I supported Dad's decision. We were proud of him for wanting to do the right thing."

Jessie frowned. "I don't know, Henry. If this had happened to me—if my whole life was going to be turned upside down, my family dragged through the media, our reputation ruined, all because of one person . . ." She shook her head. "I'll bet Charles didn't think it was a good idea. Am I right?" She knew she was—she could see it on Henry's face.

"We were both concerned about what would happen, about the ramifications to us, to the foundation. But we knew Dad couldn't go on like this—it was tearing him apart."

Still united. "Charles must have been worried about the art collection, too, right?" Another flicker on his face. She could see that she'd scored again. "He's so passionate on the subject of art stolen from the Jews—and here he has some stolen pieces in his very home."

Henry didn't answer.

She leaned forward. "You thought he did it, didn't you, Henry?" she said softly.

"No."

"There's nothing wrong if you *did* think so—that's not betraying your brother."

"Charles isn't a killer." He pursed his lips.

"People don't always set out to kill, Henry. We know that, and we take it into account. Charles wanted to protect your father—no one can blame him for that. He wanted to protect your mother, too. My God, I can't imagine how she'll deal with this, finding out that her whole life has basically been a lie." Jessie paused. "People panic. They don't think clearly. It doesn't mean they're bad."

"Charles didn't kill Pomerantz."

She waited a moment. "When you heard that Mr. Pomerantz had been found dead in the park, how did you feel?"

Henry licked his lips. "Scared. Shocked."

"A little relieved?"

He stared at her. "No. Of course not."

"Yes, you did, Henry. Anyone in your situation would have felt relieved. I would have." She waited again.

"I felt a *little* relieved," he admitted after a moment. His face was slightly flushed.

"Of course you did. You didn't even know Pomerantz. He was just a name to you. But then you started worrying, right? Who killed Pomerantz? Isn't that so?"

"I don't remember what I thought. My main concern was my father."

She cocked her head. "Who did you think killed him, Henry?" As if they were just having a theoretical conversation.

"I didn't know. I had absolutely no idea."

"Come on, Henry," she chided gently. "You can't expect me to believe that. Pomerantz arrives, your father's going to be exposed. Suddenly Pomerantz is dead, and everyone's off the hook. You knew it couldn't have been a coincidence. You didn't want to think it was Charles, but deep down, you *knew* it was."

"It was Zimmer," Henry said stubbornly. "I *know* it's Zimmer."

"But at the time, Henry, what did you think? That very first minute when you heard that Pomerantz was dead?"

Henry turned his head aside.

There was a knock, then the door opened, and Phil stepped inside. "See you a minute?" he said to Jessie.

She got up and walked over to him. She kept her back to Henry, who she knew must be watching them.

Phil leaned close. "Nothing doing with Chuck. He won't break. I can't tell whether he did it or thinks Henry did. You?"

"I think Henry suspects Charles, but he won't admit it. Part two?"

"Part two." He left the room and pulled the door shut behind him.

Jessie returned to the table and sat down. She sighed deeply. "I don't know how to tell you this, Henry."

"What's wrong?" He sat up straighter, tented his hands again.

"Apparently, your brother doesn't have the same sense of loyalty that you do." She paused to let that sink in. "He told Detective Okum that you did it."

Henry's knuckles were white. "That's a lie."

"Charles said you arranged to meet with Pomerantz on Saturday night at the Century Plaza." She saw Henry's startled look. Bingo. "You were going to offer him some money to go away—a big settlement in exchange for his promise of secrecy. He refused—so you had no choice. You killed him."

Henry had been staring at her, open-mouthed. Now he shook his head. "Charles would never have said that. You're lying."

"He said you did, Henry. He's in there right now with Detective Okum, giving his statement. He doesn't want to take the rap for this murder."

Henry placed his palms on the table and leaned forward, resting his weight on his hands. "I know what you're doing—you want to get me to say Charles did it. Well, Charles didn't kill Pomerantz. *I* didn't kill Pomerantz. Zimmer did!" He was yelling now.

"If you wait to tell me the truth, Henry, it'll be too late," she said quietly. "Charles is cutting a deal right now. Don't you want to tell me what happened?"

"You can talk and talk and talk, Detective. That's not going to change the truth. Zimmer killed him." Weary, now.

"Why would Zimmer kill Pomerantz?"

"You *know* why," he said impatiently. "Something to do with the documentary and those survivors he cheated. I guess Pomerantz found out about it."

"A little chronology problem, Henry," Jessie said gently. "A week ago you didn't know there *was* a connection between Pomerantz and Zimmer and the documentary. You only knew about it when I told you. Two days ago."

Charles buried his head in his hands.

"Tell me what happened, Henry," she said softly. "You

don't want to sit in prison for the rest of your life for something you didn't do. You know Charles did it. Talk to me, Henry."

After what seemed like an eternity, he looked up at her. "It's Zimmer," he said. "I knew it all along."

"Henry, Henry." She shook her head.

"On Thursday, the day after we learned the truth about Pomerantz and my father, I was talking to Zimmer. He was so sympathetic. He asked me what we were planning to do about the situation—'Such a disaster for your family,' he said. I said something like, 'It would be wonderful if Pomerantz would just disappear.' And Zimmer said, 'What would it be worth to you if he did? One million? Two? You wouldn't even miss it.'"

He had her attention now. She was looking at him intently. "Go on," she said. She had a tingly sensation in her fingers.

"We both laughed—I was certain he was joking, but I was just a little uneasy, you know? It had a . . . *nasty* tone. I told Charles—he said of *course*, Zimmer was joking. So I put it out of my mind. On Saturday my father decided he would meet with Pomerantz. The truth would come out. What would happen, would happen. I was very nervous—we all were. But we were also relieved we'd reached a decision." Henry wiped his brow.

Just listen, Jessie told herself. Just listen.

"We decided one of us should meet with Pomerantz that night—not to tell him the truth. Just to talk. Charles thought I would be calmer. I couldn't really argue with that. So I phoned Pomerantz and asked him to take a cab to the Century Plaza—I reimbursed him, of course."

"Of course," Jessie said. As if that mattered now. "Why didn't you pick him up from the retirement home?"

"I thought this would be easier. Pomerantz didn't mind."

Or maybe you didn't want to be seen, Jessie thought. "Go on."

"We had coffee and dessert. I wasn't really hungry—I was too nervous. And Pomerantz was too excited—he kept staring at me, asking me who Charles looked like. He showed me photos he had from before the war. I felt—" Henry took a deep breath, and expelled it. "I felt worse than I have in my entire life." He paused. "He was telling me stories about my father—about Moshe Shtuelberg—from before the war when Zimmer showed up."

The third man. Jessie kept her face impassive. "How did he know you were there?"

"He didn't—he'd just finished meeting with a client in the hotel, and had come to the restaurant to get a bite to eat. He was surprised to see me." Henry's eyes were on Jessie, watching to see her reaction. "Apparently, Pomerantz knew Zimmer—Zimmer had been helping a friend of Pomerantz, who was a resident at the retirement home where he was staying." Henry frowned. "He was a little confused—he thought Zimmer's name was Leider." He shrugged.

Pretty risky of Zimmer to show up under another name. Then again, Henry had probably attributed the mistake to an eighty-four-year-old man's imperfect memory. That was assuming that Henry was telling the truth now. A major assumption. . . .

"I wasn't comfortable talking with Zimmer there. I told Pomerantz I'd take him home, but Zimmer said *he* would. Pomerantz had wanted to discuss some things with him—why not do it now, when Zimmer had the time? Pomerantz agreed. So I left."

"You weren't nervous about leaving Pomerantz with a man who had offered to get rid of him for you?"

He looked at her earnestly. "I *told* you—I was certain that he was joking." He took another deep breath. "On Sunday I phoned the retirement home. The receptionist told me she hadn't seen Pomerantz since Friday. I was a little nervous. Sunday evening Zimmer phoned me at my house. He'd heard on the news that an old man had been found dead in the park. 'Maybe it's Pomerantz,' he said. 'Your problems would be over.' I didn't know how to respond, so I said nothing. I had a terrible feeling, and I talked to Charles about it. He told me I was looking for trouble.

"On Monday I called the retirement home again and learned that Pomerantz was dead. I *knew* Zimmer was responsible. Tuesday he came to my father's house and met with

Charles and me. He wanted a loan. He was having business difficulties, because he was devoting so much of his time to expediting the bank claims. I asked him how much. He said four hundred thousand would do it. I asked him if he would be requiring more financial help. He said he didn't think it was likely. 'At present,' he added. We all knew what was going on."

"What did you do?" Jessie asked.

"We had no choice. We gave him the money—in cash."

"That's what he wanted?" No surprise—he didn't want the money traced.

Henry nodded. "So did Charles. He didn't want to make a traceable payment to Zimmer—he said that if Zimmer was cornered, he could always say we'd hired him to kill Pomerantz."

A smart guy, Charles. "You could have gone to the police."

Henry laughed bitterly. "They would have suspected *us*, not him. *You* do. As you pointed out, Detective Drake, we had everything to lose if Pomerantz lived. Why do you think I didn't want to tell you all this?"

He sounded credible. Then again, he'd sounded credible yesterday. Jessie reminded herself that Charles was a good actor, and so was Maurice—he'd been acting a role for over fifty years. Maybe Henry was a good actor, too. It probably ran in the family.

"You told me Zimmer was remarkable. You denied that he was involved with bilking the elderly. You seemed genuinely shocked when I told you what I suspected."

"I *was* shocked! I had no idea Zimmer was using our documentary to find victims for his scam. I couldn't believe it when you said two of them were dead, that you suspected murder. But I couldn't let on that I believed Zimmer might be responsible. I was afraid that if confronted, he'd reveal what he knew about Pomerantz."

"And his murder would have been for nothing, huh? Your family would have been exposed."

"No." He looked at her steadily. "I wasn't concerned about our reputation. I was afraid that my brother and I would be charged with Pomerantz's murder."

Knowledge is power. "You're a convincing liar, Henry." Jessie shook her head.

"I'm telling you the truth."

"How many truths are there, Henry?"

Henry's face was flushed again. "Everything I told you about Zimmer is true. Ask Charles—go on. Ask him right now. He'll corroborate everything I've told you."

"So what, Henry? You guys seem to have everything rehearsed each time before we meet. Act One—you pretend you don't know who the hell Pomerantz is. Act Two—you hang tough for a while, then admit he called you and told you he's your uncle. Act Three: your dad admits he's not Moshe Shtuelberg. Now we're in Act Four, Henry, and to be honest, the play's been going on for too long."

She paused. "I don't believe you, Henry. I think you're trying to pin this on Zimmer because you know I suspected him of the other crimes. Want to hear my ending to the play, Henry? You meet with Pomerantz at the Century, but you arrange for Zimmer to join you. Pomerantz doesn't much like Zimmer, but his nephew seems to think he's okay, so he agrees to stay and talk with him a while and accepts a ride back to the retirement home."

Henry shook his head. "That didn't happen."

"See, it doesn't much matter who did the actual killing, Henry. You paid Zimmer to do it—it's the same as if you did it yourself."

"I didn't pay him! I had no idea he was going to be there!"

"Come on, Henry. Zimmer just *happens* to show up when you're meeting with Pomerantz?" She raised her brows to show her disbelief. "Charles knew you were going to be at the Century. So did your dad. One of them must have told Zimmer."

"My father has no idea about any of this. He's not involved."

Maybe yes, maybe no. Maurice Steele wasn't the weak man his sons had led her to expect. Even in a robe, he'd exuded authority. "Charles, then."

"No."

"Charles wasn't happy that your dad was going to come

clean to Pomerantz." If in fact the dad was going to do it—
Jessie had her doubts.

"He wasn't worried—there's plenty of money to go
around."

"But what about the family reputation? What about the
provenance of the Steele collection? What about the foundation, Henry?" She leaned forward. "Did you ask yourself why
Charles sent you to the Century, Henry?"

"I told you. He thought I could handle it better."

"He did it because he didn't want to be identified. Whose
idea was it for you to go to the museum to pick up the chalice?
His, right?"

"He had an appointment," Henry said, but he was staring
straight ahead. Thinking hard.

"He set you up, Henry. And he's in there right now with
Detective Okum, sealing your fate."

"Zimmer did it, on his own." Henry tightened his lips. "I
don't know how he knew I'd be at the Century Plaza, but he
found out—and not from any of us. He's devious, and very
clever. He checked out of his hotel the same day we gave
him the money. I called Suisse General—the phone has been
disconnected, and there's no new listing. I have no idea where
he is."

Join the club. "Actually, Henry, Zimmer is in Los Angeles."

Henry gaped at her. "Here?"

She nodded. "We have him in custody. We haven't had a
chance to interrogate him yet, but we will. What do you think
he'll say, Henry?"

43

"SO THAT'S MY story," Pomerantz said. "After I was liberated, I found some friends in Germany. We shared an apartment, we started a business. I didn't think I'd want to get married again. I lost my wife and two daughters, I couldn't go through something like that again.

"But then I was introduced to Lola." He smiled. "Right away I knew she was for me. Smart, beautiful. The funny thing is, she knew Estusha. She said to me, 'Don't think I'm like your Estusha—nobody was like her. She was special, one of a kind.' But Lola was wrong, you know." Pomerantz's eyes filled with tears. "Lola was special, too. Lola was one of a kind."

"Lola is gone five years now. I miss her something terrible. I miss Estusha, too, and the girls. And my parents and sisters and Moshe. Oh, what good times we had when we were children!" He sighed.

"Am I bitter? No, not anymore." He shook his head. "True, I went through terrible things. We all did. But I survived, I lived a good life. I'm still living a good life. I have my health, knock on wood." Pomerantz rapped his knuckles on the arm of the chair. "I have a few pennies saved. I have friends. Money comes, money goes. You have people who love you, you're rich.

"Who could ask for more?"

*   *   *

"Patsy Williams picked Zimmer out of a lineup," Jessie told Espes on Thursday. It was the mustache, and the poor fax quality, that had thrown the waitress. "She also identified Henry." No surprise, since Henry admitted he'd been there.

"What's the bad news, Drake? I can see it on your face."

"She doesn't know if Pomerantz left with Zimmer or Steele."

"Great." The lieutenant snorted. "Does she know who arrived first?"

Jessie shook her head. "She feels terrible about it, too."

"Send her a Hallmark card."

"We don't really need her identification. We have a match of one of Zimmer's prints with a partial that the lab found on the vial of digitalis."

Which Zimmer had said he'd gotten from Charles Steele, compliments of Maurice's medicine cabinet. Charles had denied giving Zimmer the digitalis. He'd denied everything.

Espes tapped his pencil on his desk. "So basically, we have Zimmer for attempted murder of Hilda Rheinhart, and we can probably nail him on Pomerantz. We have nothing on Henry Steele that the D.A. can make a case with. Nothing on Charles Steele, either."

"If Zimmer knows he's going down, he may take the Steeles with him. He'll say they paid him to kill Pomerantz."

"And they'll say he blackmailed them." Espes shook his head. "Who's going to believe Zimmer?"

"What about Anna Seligman and Mendel Blumenkrantz?" Jessie asked. "Hilda picked Zimmer out of a six-pack of photos. And we have the power-of-attorney forms, signed by Franz Klagsvald." The Zurich police had faxed Jessie the copies they'd found at Klagsvald's apartment.

"For Seligman and Blumenkrantz—and they're not in a position to identify Zimmer. We don't have Hilda's power-of-attorney form—he never returned it to her."

Jessie frowned. "So the D.A. isn't going to charge him with killing Seligman and Blumenkrantz?"

"Without exhuming the bodies, the M.E. can't determine whether they were murdered or died of natural causes. And even if they do exhume, and he finds evidence of murder, we'd need witnesses to connect Zimmer with Seligman and Blumenkrantz and show that he had opportunity to kill them."

"Somebody at the convalescent homes must have seen Zimmer. And Hilda can testify to what he was doing."

"He'll say she's confused, that he doesn't know who this Leider is. That he offered her a legitimate business deal. As for finding a witness at the convalescent homes—it's a long shot. Even if we find someone who saw him, are they going to remember what day he was there?"

"So that's it?" She couldn't believe it.

"We settle for what we have, Drake. You did good." He smiled.

"Thanks." She didn't feel like celebrating. She felt she'd let Anna and Mendel down. And maybe others she didn't even know about. She had more names to contact, childless, widowed survivors in retirement homes whom Zimmer may have approached. She hoped she didn't find out that he'd killed anyone else.

"You're welcome. Don't forget to hand in that questionnaire. It's due tomorrow. And don't look so glum, Drake. Life's not always tidy," he said kindly.

She knew that.

If life were tidy, she thought as she left Espes's office, there would be no unsolved murders. They'd find the mother who'd killed her infant son. People were still calling in response to the reward offer, but the murder was a month old. Jessie sensed they'd never find her, and she'd never be able to ask her why. Why did you do it?

If life were tidy, Jessie would have all the answers to Pomerantz's murder.

Not who killed him—she believed with total certainty that Zimmer had done the actual deed.

But had Zimmer done it on his own?

Had one or both of the Steele brothers paid him to do it? Their suggestion or his?

She recalled the story Pomerantz had narrated about the murdered Polish peasant. Whose hand would flinch from touching Pomerantz's dead body? Zimmer's, of course. Henry's? Charles's?

All three? And what about Maurice?

If the Steeles *hadn't* hired Zimmer, had they condoned the deed?

Jessie thought again about the killing of the heifer, the rite whose function had been to absolve the people of responsibility for the murder of someone found outside their city.

Charles couldn't absolve himself of responsibility for Pomerantz's murder. Neither could Henry.

Even if Henry was telling the complete truth, how could he have left Pomerantz in the hands of a man who had joked about eliminating him? And what had made Zimmer believe that the brothers wouldn't be averse to his "help"?

By their silence, they'd encouraged him.

Charles had finally "admitted" that he'd inadvertently told Zimmer that Henry was meeting Pomerantz that night at the Century. Maybe he'd suspected that Zimmer would show up and take care of Pomerantz. Maybe he'd hoped he would.

Or maybe he'd engineered the meeting, knowing what the outcome would be. That's what Jessie believed.

Even if the police could never prove that the Steele brothers were legally accessories to Pomerantz's murder, they were moral accessories. The heifer wouldn't have purged them of their guilt in trying to hold onto what had never really been theirs, what had never been their father's.

Sins of the father. . . .

Jessie didn't know whether Maurice had told his wife the truth. If not, he'd better do so soon to prepare her, because everything would come out at Zimmer's trial. The media would have a field day with all the angles. She wondered what would happen to the foundation, to all the institutions and people and causes that the Steeles supported.

And poor Donald Larkins and his much-anticipated art exhibit. Questions about the provenance of some of the items in the Steele collection would probably stigmatize the entire collection. Maybe the entire exhibit.

She could just see the headlines.

Gary was dying to scoop the other papers—he'd told her

so. But he'd promised her that he wouldn't say anything until she said he could. "You can trust me," he'd said.

She did. That was a step in the right direction. She looked forward to spending a relaxing evening with him tonight.

The previous night had been far from relaxing. She'd had difficulty falling asleep after watching Pomerantz's videotaped interviews. She wasn't even sure why she'd watched them, now that the case was over. She'd listened to Pomerantz's voice and cried a little. She'd tried to imagine what he'd felt when he'd learned that his "brother" was alive, tried to imagine what Henry had felt for those few minutes when he'd believed he'd been reunited with an uncle presumed dead.

What would I feel? she wondered, not for the first time. Frances was certain that none of her family had survived. She'd checked. But Pomerantz had been given wrong information, and there were stories, like the one Ezra had told her, of relatives being miraculously reunited after decades.

Ezra's story had been a terrible tease. So had Pomerantz's. . . .

After the trial was over, she would have no reason to hold onto the tapes anymore. She'd send them to Stanley Goldblum. It would be hard to say goodbye, and she supposed her mother was right—in some way she'd substituted Pomerantz for her grandfather.

She wasn't sorry.

Phil and Ed Boyd had already left for the day. Simms was at his desk, picking on his lip as he worked on his questionnaire.

"Caught me," he said when he saw her. "You look so young, Jessie. Using a new skin cream?"

She smiled good-naturedly. "Preparation H."

She'd taken a lot of ribbing from almost everyone in the division about her old-lady makeup. The station had been almost empty when she and Phil had brought in Zimmer at 2:00 A.M. on Wednesday, but word had spread. This morning she'd found dentures on her desk, a packet of laxative suppositories, reading glasses. She'd found it funny. So had Gary.

Helen hadn't. "It's tasteless," she'd told Jessie when Jessie had phoned to tell her.

"Lighten up, Helen. These are my friends. They're just

having fun." All in all, she decided, West L.A. was a pretty
good place. Not perfect, but pretty damn good. She'd write
that in her questionnaire.

"Mom wouldn't agree."

"You're right. And I have no intention of telling her. I'm
getting smart in my old age. No pun intended."

"By the way, Mom said she spoke to you last night. Did
you ask her about the Swiss account?"

You had to give Helen credit—she was nothing if not persis-
tent. "She brought it up herself. She's undecided. But she's
not as definitely against the idea of filing a claim as she was
before." Maybe it wasn't fair to Matthew, Frances had said,
or to the baby.

Even if Frances *did* file, the entire matter might turn out to
be moot. The Swiss banks were promising cooperation, but
that was because of world pressure. In the end, would they
really repay the huge sums they owed? Or would they try to
negotiate a settlement, drag things out until many of the
claimants were no longer alive?

Time would tell. Even if the banks repaid every cent, the
Swiss had their own moral accounting to do. No heifer would
purge them, either. . . .

Frances and Arthur were coming to L.A. for the weekend.
Jessie had invited them for Friday night dinner, and she and
her mother had made plans to have lunch and go to a museum
on Sunday.

Another step in the right direction.

She wondered suddenly what her mother would say when
she saw Jessie light the Sabbath candles. Would Frances be
touched? Upset? Uncomfortable?

It's your hair.

It's your home.

It's your life. . . .

Hilda was comfortably ensconced on the chair in her old
room. A multicolored computer-printed WELCOME HOME!
banner was taped to the wall above her bed. The framed
photo of Leon was back on her dresser.

"How beautiful," she said shyly when she saw the lace mantilla Jessie had given her. She looked up. "You didn't spend too much?"

Jessie laughed. "I didn't spend too much."

Leaning forward, the old woman placed her thin hands on Jessie's face and gazed at her. She kissed her forehead. "You're a dear girl," she murmured.

Jessie flushed with pleasure.

Hilda fingered the lace, then folded the scarf carefully into the gift box. "You want to play gin, Jessie James? Two out of three games?"

"You're going to beat me, aren't you?"

"I'm not *so* good." Hilda smiled coyly and shuffled the cards.